SACRED WRATH

BOOKS BY KRISTIE COOK

SACRED WRATH

FROM BESTSELLING AUTHOR
KRISTIE COOK

Published by
Ang'dora Productions, LLC
Mailing Address:
24123 Peachland Blvd
Port Charlotte, FL 33954

Ang'dora Productions and associated logos are trademarks and/or registered trademarks of
Ang'dora Productions, LLC

Cover design by Regina Wamba at MaelDesign.com
Interior by Nadège Richards at Inkstain Interior Book Designing

ISBN 978-1-939859-26-6 (Print)
ISBN 978-1-939859-02-0 (ePub)

First Edition August 2013
Updated November 2015

For Kristie's Crew, Kristie's Warriors,
& Team #KnightRiders

SACRED WRATH

1

HE WAS GONE. Really gone.

My little boy, my baby, the light of my life. Gone.

No matter how hard I tried, how far I pushed the boundaries of my mind to feel across the sea of mind signatures, I couldn't find his. Of course I couldn't. But I knew where I could.

My fingers curled into Sasha's white and gray striped fur, trying to soothe her, though I had no soothing vibes within me. I sat on my knees in the bedroom part of the safe house suite where I had left Dorian, where I thought he'd be safe when I couldn't be there to protect him myself. Barely bigger than my hand, the lykora lay on her side in her natural form, her silver blood staining the blue-and-cream Oriental rug under her. More coagulated on her back where one of her wings had been severed. Who could be so cruel? Stupid question. I knew that answer, too. He'd left my dagger under her to ensure I knew.

Heavy arms hung over my shoulders, arms that usually gave me comfort but now trembled with sobs.

"Can you heal her?" I asked, my voice sounding rough and distant. When I received no answer, I asked again, each word discrete and deliberate. "Tristan. Can you heal her?"

He lifted his head from my shoulder, but Blossom answered first.

"She's an Angelic being," she said from behind me. "She'll heal on her own."

"Good," I said. I picked up my dagger, wiped her blood off of it and onto my leather pants, put it back where it belonged on my hip, and flashed.

Tampa. Gainesville. Tallahassee. Rural Alabama and Mississippi. From here, I followed the path Vanessa and I had taken only two days before, barely seeing the landscape of each place before flashing to the next one. Tristan finally caught up to me outside of Kansas City, where the March air was significantly cooler than at home.

He wrapped his arms around me and held me tight against his chest, preventing me from flashing again.

"Where are you going?" he asked, his lovely voice distorted with the two primary emotions roiling within me—anger and grief. Mostly anger. The kind that didn't dissipate but built with each passing moment.

"To Hades," I answered flatly.

"Alone?"

"Unless you're coming with me, yes."

"Alexis, we can't just waltz into Hades—"

"Not waltz. Storm." Like the raging storm building inside me.

"Still. We can't—"

"I guess that's your answer then." I pushed a spark of electricity into him and used the moment of surprise to flip my way out of his hold. Then I flashed.

Again and again.

But my power was waning. After flashing halfway across the world once already in the last two days, fighting my way out of Hades, and escaping Lucas, the sperm donor, I hadn't been able to truly regenerate. I had to pause longer between each flash, but each time I did, I envisioned what I would do when I arrived in Hades. The throats I would slash. The Demons I would fry to a crisp. Lucas's life I would take, but only after slicing the smirk off his face, and carving his eyeballs out with my silver dagger and stuffing them into his lipless mouth.

The thoughts should have terrified me, but they only pushed me on.

Until Tristan stopped me once again in Wyoming.

"Alexis, you can't—"

I ignored him and flashed.

"Take them on by yourself," he finished in Idaho.

"Watch me." I flashed again.

"But we can't—" he started again in Washington.

"Damn it, Tristan. I don't want to hear 'can't'!" I yelled, and I flashed again.

And slammed into a wall.

At least, that's what it felt like. An invisible wall that blocked my flash, causing me to materialize in an empty field somewhere near the Canadian border. I tried again and appeared by a stream, the lights of Seattle not far off. I screamed with frustration.

"The border's been shielded," Tristan said from behind me. "And not a normal shield, either, but more like an invisible fence we can't flash through. No one can pass through at all, not even Normans, except at guarded border crossings."

I didn't reply before I flashed again, farther inland. No mage could have possibly shielded the entire border between the United States and Canada. I would find a way through. Focusing on the nearest state highway, I flashed to about two hundred yards outside a border crossing.

Several armed soldiers guarded a barbed-wire-topped steel gate that stretched across the two-lane highway, blocking anyone from simply crossing. Lines of cars waited from both directions. More guards surrounded the first car, pulling the driver and passengers out and training their flashlights on their eyes and hands. Others were searching the car and its contents. I absorbed all of this in a few seconds and knew that gate provided my way into Canada, and then I could resume flashing to Siberia. A steel gate and a few soldiers weren't about to stop me.

I sprinted for the crossing, planning to blur past them all, hurdle it, and be on my way without anyone noticing. But someone did. Perhaps those soldiers weren't all Norman. Gunfire tore through the night. Bullets flew at me. *You've got to be kidding me.* I flicked my fingers, and the bullets fell to the ground. As I ran, I lifted my left hand, a blue current already sparking. More gunfire erupted. I shot electricity, not aiming for any particular guard, but simply shooting bolts wildly as a warning. People screamed. More soldiers shot at me, but I was almost there. Almost to the gate.

And nobody—not even a dozen men with automatic assault rifles—could stop me from getting to my son.

Just as I was about to make the leap, though, something hard slammed into my side. The breath whooshed out of my lungs. My vision went dark.

Only for a moment. Like a blink. And when I could see again, I was lying on the ground, face up, sucking in a breath of air. Tristan blocked my view of the night sky, hovering over me with his hands on each side of my head and his knees on each side of my legs. He'd flashed me away from the gate. I guess there *was* someone who could stop me.

Using only my mind, I pushed him away and sprang to my feet.

"What the hell did you do that for?" I yelled.

"What the hell do you think you're doing?" he yelled back as he suddenly appeared right in front of me, towering over me. "Innocent people, Lex? What's the matter with you?"

"I was almost through!"

"And how many would you have killed in the process?"

"As many as it took."

He grabbed my shoulders and shook me. "You need to calm down. This isn't you."

No, it wasn't. But at the moment, I didn't care. "I just need to get there."

I flashed again. Hit another wall. Landed on my ass in a foot of snow.

"You can't get through," Tristan repeated, grabbing my hands and pulling me to my feet. "I've already checked the border from the coast to Minnesota. The Daemoni knew we'd come and must have sent their mages out."

I yanked my hands out of his grip. "Isn't this what they want, though? Don't they want to lure us right back there?"

"They probably want more of a head start. I don't know. But that's exactly why we can't go there."

"I don't care if it's a trap," I seethed.

"Alexis—"

"That was *my* house, Tristan. My safe house to guard and protect! My people! And they somehow found their way in, killed our mages, made a mockery of us. Of me. And they TOOK. OUR. SON!"

A rush of blood thundered in my ears as rage consumed me, the pressure in my head forcing my eyes to squeeze shut. My chest felt like iron crushing every last molecule of air out of my lungs.

"I will find him," I said, quietly because I had no air to force the words out with the vehemence that made my body quake.

"I know."

"And I will kill every single asshole who tries to stop me."

"And I will help you."

I opened my eyes with this declaration and finally looked at Tristan. He still stood right in front of me, his feet shoulder-width apart and his arms crossed over his chest, his muscles bulging with tension. I looked up at his beautiful face hardened into stone with the same fury I felt. His hazel eyes were like marbles, the gold in them sparks of fire.

His vow was what I needed. To know he stood by my side, that he would do whatever it took to get Dorian back and to make the Daemoni pay. I'd been afraid this had broken him. Or that he'd given in because everyone said losing Dorian was inevitable; we just didn't know when or how. Now we did. But I'd never give up.

I refused to allow this to happen. It wasn't Dorian's time. We were supposed to have years still to figure out how to break the curse that sent all Amadis sons to the Daemoni. I would fight for every one of those years, for every day, for every hour I could have with him in the meantime. And I needed to know Tristan would, too.

This knowledge allowed me to finally suck in the breath my body desperately needed.

"And they will be very slow and painful deaths," Tristan added.

"Damn right," I said. "So how do we get there?"

"We do it the right way."

"Which is?"

"Not alone. We need an army, Alexis."

"We don't have time for that!" I began shaking as the rage threatened to overwhelm me. "Every hour counts. Every minute. We don't have time to gather even a small team, let alone an army."

"You're thinking in human terms."

"He *is* human, Tristan! At least, in a lot of ways. He's growing and changing all the time. A day feels like forever to him. And I don't want to think about what they could be doing to him." I ended my rant with possibly the longest string of profanity to ever leave my lips.

Tristan clutched each side of my face, making me stop and look up. "Dorian is valuable to them. They won't hurt him. They'll treat him like a prince. Try to win him over."

"Even more reason to hurry. I can't stand the thought of Dorian being exposed to their lies and deceit. To their *evil*. He's only a little boy. And, my God, what about Heather? She's an innocent Norman who shouldn't be involved. What will they do to *her*?"

Tristan grimaced, having no answer. At least, not one I'd want to hear.

The feral energy within me couldn't be suppressed. I strode back and forth alongside the invisible wall, and pressed my hand to different parts of the shield, looking for a weak spot. Although I couldn't see the barrier except for a waver in the air here and there, the wall felt like stone under my palm. Maybe we could have broken through if Owen were here where he belonged, helping us instead of Kali, the damn traitor. Well, that line of thinking only pissed me off more. If Owen had to go down with the rest of them, then so be it.

I stopped in my tracks with that thought and looked toward Tristan, but without seeing him, lost in my own mind. He must have discerned something in my expression, because he rushed to me and gathered me into his arms.

"I'm no better than them," I choked out around the lump in my throat. "All I can think about, see with my eyes and in my head, feel with an intense and sickening delight is . . . murder."

I trembled in his arms, his touch still not comforting me as it usually did.

"I know, *ma lykita*. I know." He tightened his hold on me, to the point where it should have hurt but I was too numb to feel it. I would have welcomed the pain. "I felt it, too. But I know from experience it will subside. The irrational rage will eventually dissolve."

"But I don't want it to," I admitted. I wanted Psycho Alexis, with all of her rage. The fury. The irrationality of it. The overwhelming hate.

That feeling drove me to do what needed to be done.

"You can't let your emotions control you," Tristan reminded me. One of my weaknesses. One of many.

But I couldn't afford to be calm right now. To be rational. To think things through and respond rather than react. Dorian couldn't afford it.

"Otherwise, you'll go flying into situations you can't handle," he continued. "Situations that will get innocents killed. Get you and me killed. And then we'll be no good to anyone, including Dorian and Heather."

More anger bubbled within me. Anger that he was right. Charging into Hades, the Daemoni's underground city headquarters where the Ancient Demons themselves lived, would definitely get us killed. I would gladly sacrifice my life for my son, but the end goal was to release him from their clutches. I would die trying to do so, but I'd sure rather my last breath be drawn knowing he was free.

Shit. Rationality was already setting in.

I pulled away from Tristan and threw my hands into the air. "So what do we do now?"

"We build an army, gather intelligence, and create a plan. We arm ourselves in every possible way. Then we act. We take every one of them down and get our son. Or at least die trying."

"So, what? Go to Amadis Island?"

He shook his head. "We need to go back to the safe house first. That *is* your house. Our house. We need to take care of it and not leave Blossom to clean up the mess by herself."

The scene of the crime. I didn't think I could face it.

But then, seeing it all again would keep the feelings fresh. The rage I needed to hold on to. Just picturing the scene in my mind—the mages' blood smeared on the walls, Sasha's feathers strewn about the room—shot more fury through my veins.

"Fine," I said, still mad, but calming. I peered up at him. "You really checked the border that far already?"

"I'm not running on my last bit of energy like you are," he said. "And I'm much more experienced. Why do you think it took me a while to catch up with you?"

"So you wanted through, too. You were trying to get to Hades just like I was."

"At first, yes. But I'm also more experienced at gaining control of my rage than you are." He grimaced. "I have to be or innocent people would have been dead by now."

He was too dangerous to be running around like a loose cannon. I obviously was, too. Who knew how far I would have taken it if Tristan hadn't stopped me? I hadn't been thinking clearly. I could have killed anyone, including innocent Normans, and not cared. And then I really would have been no better than the Daemoni.

I did need time to simmer down.

We flashed back to Florida, slower than we'd come because I was so drained. The fatigue left, though, when we arrived in the safe house, and as I'd hoped, the ire returned, though more quietly.

We appeared in the foyer, where Blossom paced, her cell phone at her ear. She halted both her steps and her words when she saw us.

"I'll call you back," she said into the phone before hitting the END button. "I'm sorry, Alexis. I didn't start cleaning up yet. I had to call my Aunt Sylvie and make sure she and the coven were okay."

I swallowed and nodded. "Are they?"

"Yeah, they're fine. This seems to be an isolated incident."

With another nod, I turned toward the common room. I stared at the blood and the mages' decimated bodies with my hands balled into fists at my sides and my eyes burning.

"They deserve a proper Amadis send-off," I said through a clenched jaw.

"A fire outside will draw attention," Tristan said from beside me. "But we can take them out on the water."

I gave a cursory nod. "Then that's what we'll do."

I glanced around one more time, capturing the scene clearly in my memory so I could share it with Mom and Rina and anyone else who needed the details, as gruesome as they were.

"*Alexis,*" Blossom mentally called out, triggering my telepathy. I reached out with my mind to where she still stood behind me, in the doorway between the foyer and the common room. "*They're scared.*"

Not understanding—the mages were dead, how could they be scared?—I turned toward her. Behind her stood several of the local Amadis.

"*But they want to help,*" she added.

Somehow, through the anger and the need to have my son back in my arms, I found focus and managed to give orders. A were-shark from Captiva owned a boat we could use, so he, Tristan, and I took the mages' bodies several miles out on the Gulf and gave them the best Amadis send-off we could. By the time we arrived back at the mansion that afternoon, Blossom and the other remaining mages had the blood magically cleaned.

All of the local Amadis had gathered in the so-called safe house, either seeking direction or camaraderie. I wasn't sure which.

Why are they here? I asked Tristan. *It's not safe anymore.*

"*They're here for you. For us. And it's safer in numbers.*"

Damn. All I wanted to do was formulate a plan for rescuing my son and then execute it—sooner rather than later.

I can't deal with this right now.

Tristan nodded, then spoke aloud so everyone could hear, "There's plenty of room for everyone, and we're safe as long as we each take shifts."

"Are the Daemoni coming back?" someone asked.

"Not likely," Tristan answered. *They have what they want.* He hadn't said the rest, but I knew that was what he meant. "But we'll take no chances. We need any mages who can help to put up a shield and volunteers to take shifts."

A section of the small crowd parted, and a big tiger waltzed out. Sheree, volunteering. She, two vampires, and a were-panther each took a wing to prowl for the first shift while the mages worked together to put up as powerful of a shield as the witches and wizards could muster. A warlock would have helped to strengthen it, but there weren't any in the colony. Not since Owen had left.

The sun began to set again by the time Tristan, Blossom, and I could gather in my office to start planning a search and rescue. I dropped into my chair, crossed my arms over my desk, and lay my head down on top of them.

"You look exhausted," Blossom said.

"You need to regenerate," Tristan added.

"I'm fine," I muttered.

"Yeah, right. You're about to pass out whether you like it or not," Blossom said.

I let out a dark chuckle. "Even if I wanted to, I can't possibly sleep with my son and Heather out there."

"You may not be 'only human,' but you can't last forever," Tristan said. "You'll be of no use if you don't have all of your energy."

"How long has it been, anyway?" Blossom asked. "Three days now since you slept? Four?"

I lifted my head and glared at them. "Why are you ganging up on me? I seriously can't sleep right now. My mind won't shut off, even if I tried. But I don't *want* to try. I want to find Dorian."

Tristan and Blossom exchanged some kind of look, then Blossom flicked her wrist, and a faint purple light flew at me. My mind suddenly became hazy and my body floppy. *Did she put a sleeping spell on me, that . . . witch!* Through the fog that began to settle in, I felt Tristan carrying me. Down the hall, to the left wing, to the suite where we'd left Dorian. The smell of blood no longer lingered, and Sasha's baby-powder scent hung heavily in the air instead. The lykora lay on the bed, a few small, white feathers sprouting from her back where her wing had once been.

Tristan set me in the middle of the bed, next to Sasha, and he lay behind me. I didn't want to sleep, but a small part of me knew Tristan and Blossom were right. I needed to regenerate if I was going to have the energy to save Dorian. *Just a few hours*, I told myself, *then we start.*

"*Ma lykita*, you've been strong all this time," Tristan said quietly from behind me as he laid his arm over my waist and pressed his hand against my stomach. "You can cry now. Let it out. I'm here, my love."

But I didn't want to cry. For once in my life, tears evaded me. I refused to grieve this loss, because it wasn't a loss in my eyes, in my heart. It was a call for war, yes. But not a loss. I wouldn't allow it.

Besides, I was too mad to cry, even in my exhaustion, and enmity would carry me through to do what needed to be done.

As I curled my body around Sasha's, though, I realized the outrage within me had changed. I no longer felt irrational and blinding fury that dulled all other emotions. But that was okay. I really didn't want to be Psycho Alexis. This, what I now felt in every cell of my body down to the core, was better. My anger had condensed and solidified into a cold, hard stone settling within me. Something I could control and hold on to for the long term to keep me going and focused on the goal.

Wrath.

That's what I felt. And there was nothing worse than the wrath of a pissed-off mother.

2

I WOKE UP thinking it had all been one long, terrible dream—going to Hades, meeting Lucas, running for my life to escape his wolf pack, and then coming home to my worst nightmare. When I opened my eyes to find a tiny Sasha cuddling next to me, her new wing half-grown, the turmoil of emotions slammed into me again. My first thought went to Dorian.

Judging by the lack of daylight seeping under the heavy curtains, the complete regeneration my body felt, and Tristan sleeping by my side, I figured I'd awoken in the wee hours of morning, which meant Dorian had already been gone for twenty-four hours. Where was he? What was he doing? Who had him? Were they treating him like a prince, as Tristan expected? Did they have him in a cave in Hades, feeding him lies on a silver platter? What thoughts ran through his mind? Was he scared? Dorian wasn't afraid of anything, but he had to be terrified now. He had to know that whoever took him hadn't been sent by Tristan or me. He had to know he'd been kidnapped by the bad guys we'd warned him about.

And was Heather with him? She hadn't been here at the safe house, but she'd also disappeared at the same time. That's what Blossom had figured, anyway, when Heather's mom had called, looking for her daughter. Sonya, Heather's older sister and a vampire who was supposedly trying to convert, had killed our mages here and left at the same time, too, so it was a good possibility she'd taken Heather. Why she would do such a thing, I couldn't fathom, but I also had no idea why she'd done *any* of this to us, especially after everything we'd done for her. Maybe if Heather was with Dorian, they could at least help each other through this, but trying to imagine what they could both be going through broke my heart.

Why hadn't we prepared more for this? We'd let Dorian practice his flying ability, but not enough. We never tested what other powers he might have possessed, knowing the more they developed, the more the Daemoni would be attracted to him. He knew Aikido, but Lucas knew a lot worse. Dorian would never be a match for him or his cronies; Heather didn't have a chance. And if Dorian did manage to escape, he wouldn't know the way home or to Amadis Island. He didn't know there were safe houses he could go to around the world. I hadn't even let him have a cell phone yet. I didn't see the point of it since he was never supposed to be alone, and I didn't want to spoil him. How stupid of me!

His only hope would be Heather. If they were together. If she was even alive.

My second train of thought went to Vanessa. Was she really my half-sister? The reality of that shock still hadn't completely sunk in, making it difficult to believe it was true. What had happened to her last night anyway? She had run for the water when we first arrived at the horrible scene, staying far away from all of the blood, and I hadn't seen her since. Where had she gone?

My mind searched the mansion for her signature, but didn't find it. I expanded the search over Captiva Island, but it wasn't until I reached the opposite side of Sanibel, the adjoining island, when I found her. She wasn't alone, either. A Daemoni accompanied her, and a familiar one at that.

Oh, hell no. I bolted upright in bed.

"Tristan," I hissed, shaking his leg. "Wake up!"

Sasha sprang to her feet and, sensing my anxiety, began to grow. I took her head into my hand and scratched behind her ears, trying to be gentle through my impatience.

"No, girl, it's okay," I said. "You're not ready yet. I'll be okay."

Her dark eyes stared into mine, and she whimpered, then her body began to shrink into its natural toy-dog size. She curled up on the pillow, and I scrambled out of bed and began dressing in my leathers. I didn't remember Tristan taking them off of me, and someone had already cleaned them.

"What's going on?" Tristan asked as he moved out of bed, too slowly for my liking.

"Hurry up and find me." I didn't have time to wait for him in case they took off, so I gave him a mental picture of where I was going, grabbed my dagger by its hilt, and flashed.

Vanessa and Victor both jumped when I appeared right next to them at the top of the Sanibel lighthouse, on a landing below the light itself. The vamps weren't used to being snuck up on.

"How the hell . . . ?" Victor wondered.

"I warned you," Vanessa sneered, but I didn't care who she warned or what about. I'd deal with her later.

I lunged for Victor, knocking him against the metal railing that kept us both from plunging nine stories to the ground below. His back bowed over the railing as the tip of my silver dagger pushed into his chest above his heart. Amadis power flowed through the weapon while electricity charged from my other hand. I kept both powers at moderate levels only because I needed information before I killed him.

"Where's my son?" I demanded, practically spitting each word in his face.

His mouth contorted, stretching scars that marked his normally smooth and pale skin.

"I don't know," he hissed as his ice-blue eyes darted around nervously.

"*Liar*." I dug the point of the dagger further into his flesh. He let out a small yelp. "But if you really don't know, I have no reason to keep you alive."

"Give me that fucking dog of yours and maybe I'll tell ya," Victor said, throwing me off guard a little. He must have seen the flicker of confusion in my eyes. "Look what she did to me!"

His arms twitched at his side, drawing the moon's glow to more scars on his hands and forearms.

"You *were* in the safe house," I said, and hatred rushed forth again as his vision of him fighting Sasha filled my mind. I increased the current through my hand, electricity crackling between us accompanied by the sound and smell of singeing skin. "TELL ME WHERE HE IS!"

Victor began to tremble, and I pushed the dagger in deeper. The electric power charged through his body and into the railing. Vanessa jumped back with a small whimper—she must have been touching the metal that now carried the current.

"Alexis," Vanessa said quietly from behind me, "he's our brother."

"Shut the hell up," I yelled at her.

I didn't want to hear it. I couldn't erase from my mind the image he'd given me of his fight with Sasha. I couldn't ignore the fact he'd been there when Dorian was taken. He had probably taken him himself. The desire to plunge the dagger all the way in, twist it around, and grind at his heart until the organ was nothing but pulp became too strong to resist.

But the Amadis in me was even stronger. As the trembles of Victor's body became quakes and his eyes rolled into the back of his head so only whites showed, the guilt of what I was doing to him jolted through me.

As did the reminder that Vanessa was here, secretly meeting with him.

I pushed myself off of Victor and flew at her.

"You did this!" I screamed as my body plowed into hers.

We skidded across the concrete landing before coming to a stop at the edge with Vanessa on her back and me straddling her, my hands at her throat.

"You set us up, didn't you, you bitch? Got us far away from here so Victor could take Dorian?"

"No—" she tried to choke out.

"Lies! That's all either of you know how to speak! This whole thing has been a ruse, hasn't it? Lies and deceit everywhere. You didn't care about me getting out of Hades except to come back and see this, did you? Are you even my sister, or was that a lie, too?" Holding one hand on her throat, I held my dagger to her heart, ready to give her a taste of the pain I felt.

But someone yanked me off of her. I swung and kicked at Tristan as he held me from behind. The vampire bitch scrambled to her feet.

"Where *is* he?" I yelled as my gaze bounced wildly between the vampire twins. "What did you do with my son?"

Vanessa's blond hair swished as she shook her head. "I don't know. I honestly don't know."

"Bullshit. Tell me, or I *will* kill you!" I fought harder against Tristan, but his grip remained iron-tight.

"Calm down," he murmured against my ear.

"I swear I had nothing to do with this," Vanessa said, her blue eyes sparking as she jerked her head toward her brother. Our brother. Supposedly. "Ask *him*."

"Lies," I said again.

"Why would she be here?" Tristan asked, his voice still low in my ear. "Why would she hang around if the worst they can do is already done?"

"I don't know. Why *are* you still here?" I spewed at Vanessa.

She threw her hands in the air. "I have nowhere else to go. I'm Amadis, Alexis."

I stopped thrashing against Tristan, mostly because I knew he had a point. If everything had been a setup, why had she even bothered to come back here with us? Why was she *still* here?

"And, like it or not, I *am* your sister," she added. "Your half-sister. By blood, anyway."

I glared at her, not trying to break free from Tristan's hold because I didn't quite trust myself if he let go, but I did sheathe my dagger.

"If you're Amadis, then what are you doing here with *him*? What happened to you since we got home?"

She narrowed her icy eyes at me, except they weren't really icy now. More like cool water. "I'm Amadis in my heart, but that doesn't mean I feel like a part of everything yet. I didn't know what to do or where to go. Half your crowd is scared and crying, and I don't do the weepy thing. The other half is ready to fight—which I *will* do—but they want nothing to do with me. So sue me for not jumping right the fuck in." She tossed her hand toward Victor. "I sensed him nearby— a twin thing we have—and it was the only idea I had that might help."

"We've already had this discussion," Sheree said as she laid a long-fingered hand on my arm. Where had she come from? She towered over me, so she had to duck her head to catch my eyes with her brown ones. She was stark-naked, which meant she'd been in her tiger form, probably why I hadn't noticed her mind signature before. Or maybe because I'd been so focused on the lies before me. Which wasn't a good thing, not being alert of my surroundings. "I had to give up my watch shift to protect Vanessa from everyone else. We talked for a while. But then she left, and I changed and followed her here. I stayed down in those shadows—" her eyes flitted to a wild growth of trees and brush on the ground "—watching as she jumped all over Victor right before you got here, trying to get the truth out of him."

My gaze slid back to Vanessa. Her eyes pled her innocence.

If I ever discover you're lying to me, I said in her head, *you'll be the first one I kill. Then Victor. And when I'm done, there won't be any pieces of either of you to put back together.*

She nodded. "*I'm on your side, though. I want to help you. I never got to meet Dorian—*"

Don't you say his name! Don't you even think it!

She pressed her lips together and nodded.

I wrangled myself free of Tristan's hold and turned back to Victor, who was just now recovering after my attack.

"Where's my son?" I demanded again.

He stood to his full height—barely shorter than Tristan—and spit a wad of blood at my feet. "I told you I don't know."

"And I told you I don't believe you. Tell me, or I won't hold back next time."

"Why don't you ask that warlock of yours?" he snarled. "Oh, yeah, because he's not *yours* anymore is he? He's Kali's. And *they* know where your fucking little brat is."

Tristan blurred past me and heaved Victor's body into the lighthouse wall, his forearm pressed into the vamp's throat. I became suddenly curious what would happen if Tristan crushed his trachea, since Victor didn't technically need it to breathe. He did, however, need to be able to swallow.

"Watch it, asshole," Tristan breathed in Victor's face. "That's my wife. And you better answer the fucking question."

"I did," Victor choked out.

I dove into his mind, but he showed me what he wanted me to see: Owen tossing my dagger next to Sasha's limp body on the floor and taking Dorian into his arms.

"Lucas wants nothing to do with your son," Victor added. "Not yet, anyway. This is all Kali."

"Now see, we *know* that's a lie," I said as I tried to hold myself back from attacking again. Tristan handled the vamp perfectly fine, evidenced by the wheezing sound escaping Victor's throat.

"Find the bitch and . . . you'll know," the bloodsucker stammered. "And kill her . . . if you want. But you'll . . . be doing Lucas . . . a favor if you do."

I nearly screamed in frustration at his lies and his taunts. Tristan shoved his weight further into Victor's body.

"You've already admitted to being at the safe house," Vanessa reminded her twin, with her body, like mine, angled threateningly toward him.

"Not . . . for the boy," Victor wheezed, and his eyes rolled into the back of his head again.

"Then for what?" I asked, but Victor didn't answer.

"He's incapable of telling the truth," Tristan said.

"He's incapable of saying anything now," Vanessa mused.

Victor had slumped under Tristan's weight, unable to bear whatever power my husband had given him beyond brute strength, especially now that the sun had risen over the horizon. Tristan stepped back, and the vampire fell to the ground. Although he appeared to be completely out of it, I gave him a hard kick to the ribs to be sure. The vampire didn't move, but my foot felt as though my steel-toed boots had slammed into a concrete wall.

Frustration brought a growl out of me. As much as a part of me wanted to kill him—to destroy *something* to release the pressure of my anger—I wouldn't. I couldn't. I was, admittedly, all bark with little bite. At least until it mattered. When I learned for certain who took Dorian, God help those souls. Because I didn't think I'd be able to.

With a grunt of annoyance, I flashed back to the beach by the safe house, and Tristan, Vanessa, and Sheree appeared behind me. Without a word to them, I strode across the street, up the marble stairs, and into the mansion. I snaked my way through the crowd that had gathered in the foyer and pretty much everywhere else where they could find a space. As I headed for my office, I mentally called out for Tristan, Blossom, and Sheree to join me, glad to find Blossom already awake. Vanessa still followed me, too, but I shut the door in her face.

"Rude much?" she muttered from the other side.

I smirked, but then I immediately felt bad—my feelings about her were all kinds of conflicted—but I wasn't sure what to do with her yet. Trusting her as a confidante wasn't quite at the top of my list, though, and we had private matters to discuss.

"We've wasted enough time," I said to those I did want behind my closed door. Victor and his ridiculous lies had definitely been a total waste, and now a new day had begun, and we still didn't have a plan, let alone an army. I went behind my desk, but didn't sit down. Instead, I placed my hands on my desk and leaned forward. "We need to make a plan to find and rescue Dorian and Heather. We need a team. An elite team. Our very best."

"You need to talk to Sophia first," Tristan said.

"She called a few times last night and once already this morning," Blossom added. "She knew everything that happened before we even told her."

Of course she did. Mom could sense the truth. I hadn't told her about Vanessa's and my trip to Hades before we left, because I knew she'd try to talk me out of it. Forbid it, actually. If she didn't suspect something being wrong, she wouldn't have reached out for the truth of the situation. But all kinds of things went wrong, and we had to contact her for help to get home. We hadn't had the luxury of a lengthy explanation or lecture at the time, and now . . . I couldn't imagine how pissed off she was at me. Hopefully, her love for Dorian would eclipse her anger. And hopefully, she knew the truth of where to find him.

"She understood you needed to rest and regenerate," Blossom continued, "but she demanded that you call her the moment you woke up."

I sighed. "Fine. I'll call you guys back in here when I'm done."

Blossom and Sheree left my office, but Tristan stayed.

"There are some things you should know before you call her," he said when we were alone. "So that she doesn't catch you off guard."

Not liking the warning in his voice, I closed my eyes as I sank into my chair. "Like what?"

"Well, to start with, the Normans seem to be on the verge of war. Almost everywhere."

My eyes popped open. "*What?*"

"The Daemoni are escalating things. There have been two assassinations and four 'accidental' bomb detonations just in the last twenty-four hours. The whole world has gone on edge."

Damn it. Does it ever end? "Having their fun with the Normans? As if messing with us isn't enough?"

"Norman wars are the best way for them to build their army."

"Because they know taking Dorian has started our own war."

"We've always been at war, but yes, they're taking it to the next level. But not only with us, Alexis. With the Normans, too."

I rolled my head around on my neck. "Vanessa said they were planning it. Preparing to make their move to take over."

"Well, their move has been made."

I nodded and reached for my phone. "Okay. Good to know."

Tristan placed his hand over mine, preventing me from dialing. "Just be prepared that Sophia might not give you the answers you're hoping for."

I looked up at him. "All I want is to know if she has an idea of where Dorian is and an army to go get him."

"Exactly."

He held my gaze as I stared at him with incredulity. "Dorian's her grandson! She loves him. She would do anything for him, just like us."

He tightened his hand on mine. "I'm not saying I agree with them, but Sophia's taking orders from Rina, who must look out for the Amadis as a whole and all of humanity. Nobody's going to understand putting resources into a search and rescue of one kid who will eventually serve the Daemoni anyway. Not when the rest of the world is at risk."

My blood pressure shot up again, and I opened my mouth to protest, but he held his free hand up before I went off.

"I'm only saying what others will. Whether we agree with them or not, there are other valid perspectives."

His tone drove home his meaning. Mom and Rina had picked the Amadis over my family and me in the past. They were obligated to serve the greater good. Our role as the Amadis family was to protect our society and all of humanity, regardless of what it meant for us personally. I needed another angle, because our love for Dorian wouldn't be enough to convince the matriarch, her second-in-command, and the rest of the Amadis that he was worth fighting for.

If I only knew why the Angels had sent him on his own, without a twin sister. There had to be a reason.

"Do you want me to leave?" Tristan asked.

My brows pushed together, and the corners of my mouth turned down. "Of course not." I rose from my chair and rounded the desk, then pushed him back until he sat on the edge. I wrapped my arms around his neck and pressed my forehead against his. "You belong right here."

"We're in this together," he agreed before brushing my lips with his. He snagged my phone from the desk and handed it to me. I turned around and leaned back against him, and he wrapped his arms around my waist while I dialed Mom's number.

"I'm so sorry, honey," Mom said as soon as she answered. "I wish I could be there for you. The timing couldn't be any worse."

In other words, Dorian's kidnapping was inconvenient. My teeth immediately set on edge. Tristan moved his hands to my shoulders and squeezed, trying to massage the tension out, but it only built.

"I know you and Rina have a lot to deal with," I said, trying to show my understanding. "I know you can't completely drop everything."

"I would if I could. That boy . . ." She choked on her words. "I love him so much, Alexis. We knew this was coming, but you can never be adequately prepared."

Her tears almost got to me, but I refused to break. Not now. I needed to be strong. "No, you can't, especially not like this. They've overstepped their boundaries, and they know it. So do you. You feel that truth, right? He didn't feel drawn to the Daemoni like all the other sons did. He didn't choose to go. They didn't even give him that choice. So tell me this isn't wrong."

"No, honey, you're not wrong." She blew a sigh into the phone. "But it doesn't matter. Regardless of timing or methods, they have him. It was inevitable, and we know it."

Renewed anger clawed at my chest. "No. Not yet. *This* wasn't supposed to happen. Not like this. Not this soon."

"Everything happens for a reason."

"Yeah, well, maybe the reason is so we'll finally do what needs to be done—eliminate Lucas and the rest of the Daemoni. Destroy them once and for all. We need to gather our forces."

"Yes, we do," she agreed. "I need you and Tristan to help build our army, and eventually, train them."

"Right," I said, glad we were on the same page. "And we'll go in, get our son, and decimate Hades."

"No, Alexis."

"What do you mean 'no'? How else are we going to get Dorian back?"

"First of all, I don't feel the truth that Dorian is in Hades. I don't know where he is, exactly—there must be a powerful cloak on him— but I don't sense that Lucas has him."

"But he surely knows where he is. He did take Dorian, after all."

"I don't feel that truth, either."

"I know he did! He all but warned me that he was going to when I was there only hours before, and he left my dagger that he'd taken from me as his calling card."

"This isn't really something Lucas would do himself," Tristan said. "He would have sent someone, like Victor."

"Technicalities," I muttered. "Victor doesn't have Dorian, so he obviously took him *somewhere* during the night. And Lucas knows exactly where."

"Nonetheless," Mom said, "we can't and we won't raid Hades. We're not powerful enough."

"So we get that way. Build our army, like you said. We have strong fighters. We'll take our best. Tristan and I can—"

"Slow down and listen to me for a minute, please." Mom's voice had grown unusually impatient, causing me to pause. "We're on the defensive. And we're not in the position to take the offense. We have to put all of our resources—our best people, all of our time and money—into protecting the Amadis and the Normans. The Daemoni have already acted. They control some of the world powers, and now they're moving in on the United Nations. There are secret meetings all over the world as we speak. Lucas's men occupy many of those war rooms, and if we don't do our job, humanity will go up in a forest of mushroom clouds."

"So why aren't we in those secret meetings? We're the damn Amadis. Why don't we have people in there stopping them?"

Mom's heavy sigh sounded almost like a groan. "We do, honey. But too many politicians are power-hungry and corrupt. They feed off the lies the Daemoni give them and don't want to listen to us. Even those who want to do right will do what's necessary to protect their own. If another country or faction—or *species*—attacks their people, they're not going to stand around and do nothing. They're going to retaliate."

"And that's exactly what the Daemoni want." I pulled away from Tristan and started pacing.

"Yes, it is. They'll turn the dying into theirs until they have an army big enough to take over humanity. Normans will become their slaves. If they have to wipe out half of the human race with a nuclear war to achieve this goal, they will. Which is why we need to counteract their every move and convert as many as we can."

"Which will build our army. Then we can go into Hades before it's too late."

"Hopefully, yes. While our best diplomats are with the politicians, we need to be working on our primary mission of building our army. I need you and Tristan to focus on this."

"Okay," I agreed. "But we're not losing focus on rescuing Dorian, Mom. As soon as we have the people we need, that's *our* primary mission."

"I want Dorian back as much as you do," she said, "but he can't be our primary mission. Not yours. Not anyone's. The Amadis and the Normans need us. These are your people, Alexis. They look up to you. They need to see that you can lead. That you will do what needs to be done for them and all we stand for. A waver like this from our primary creed will create a lot of distrust that you may never be able to rebuild."

"And abandoning my son won't? How can they trust me to stay true to them if I can't do so for my own child?"

"You know how they feel about Dorian. About any Amadis son. And choosing one soul over all others—especially one we know has no hope in the end—"

My temper flared. "There is *always* hope! And I won't give up on him, Mom. I can't believe you and Rina gave up on Noah so easily. He was her *son*. Your twin. How *could* you?"

My accusation must have hit Mom unexpectedly because she sucked in an audible breath and didn't answer for a moment. When she did, her voice came out much softer than it had been. "He was already deeply entrenched in the Daemoni before Mother knew he was still alive."

"Well, Dorian's not. And the sooner I find him and rescue him, the less likely he will be. As for the Amadis—they don't know the future. They don't know what Dorian could mean for them. Right now he is one of us, and we won't give up on anyone, no matter who he is. At least *I* won't. Tell that to anyone who questions my loyalty."

Mom fell silent again, apparently having no rebuttal for my excellent point. But her silence was also a response, and not the one I wanted.

Because this was how it was going to be. What Tristan had been warning me about. The council didn't give two shits about Dorian, and Mom and Rina hadn't come up with a strong enough argument to change their minds. If they'd even tried. From what Mom had said so far, it didn't sound like they had. Not even they believed he was important enough. They'd already determined this years ago, the day he was born.

"So I'm supposed to give up on him? That's what you're asking me to do?" The question barely made it out as my throat constricted around the words. *How could she ask that of me, one mother to another? How could she be so cold and heartless?*

"Honey . . ." She paused again, and I could picture her pinching the top of her nose with her thumb and forefinger. When she finally continued, grief tainted her voice. "Dorian is where he belongs now."

I shook my head in protest.

"No." I wanted to yell, but I could only manage a whisper.

My whole body trembled with such outrage at those words that the phone nearly fell from my hand. Visions of the rampage I so badly wanted to go off on occupied all my thoughts until a buzz filled my head, drowning out whatever else she had to say.

"Heather," I finally said, interrupting whatever she'd been telling me. "What about Heather?"

Mom fell silent again, apparently surprised by my question. Heather must have had nothing to do with her one-sided conversation.

"The Norman girl's safety and well-being *is* a concern," she said. Finally, some reasoning. "We have a team searching for her now, but . . . Alexis, it may be too late for her."

My heart skipped a beat. "*What?*"

"She knows too much, and the Daemoni know that."

And now my heart took off in a panicked gallop. "Let us go search for them, Mom. *Please.* She and Dorian are probably together."

"If we find the girl close to you, we'll send you out. It's the best I can do right now."

"You can do better!"

"No, I can't. I'm sorry. It's not up to me."

My jaw popped, I clenched it so hard. I wanted to throw the phone, but knew that would do no good. I closed my eyes and forced a breath through my nose as I reeled my anger in once more, forming it into that tight little ball that sat in the pit of my stomach.

"I will not give up on them," I said through gritted teeth. "On either of them. I will not abandon my son."

"You will not abandon your people or your duties," she said just as firmly.

"So give us our best and let Tristan and me take care of this immediately. Then we can focus on whatever you want us to."

"I can't afford to give you our best. I need them where they are."

"*We can make our own team,*" Tristan said in my head. "*We can build her an army and do this at the same time.*"

"Then I'll make my own team," I said to Mom. "Tristan's already coming up with a plan."

"Alexis—"

"Don't worry, Mom. It's all about building the Amadis army."

"Good. That's where your energy needs to go. Thank God and the Angels for Tristan's level head."

I rolled my eyes.

"Don't lose focus," she warned.

"Don't worry," I said again, although my focus was a little wider than hers.

"Don't abandon your people, Alexis," she repeated.

"Don't worry about that, either. Unlike you, Mother, I won't abandon *anyone.*"

3

"SO YOU HAVE a plan?" I asked Tristan after hanging up with Mom.

"The beginnings of one," he said, "but the only way you were going to satisfy Sophia was to convince her we'd build an army. Which we'll do. If you want to do things your way, Alexis, you have to learn how to make her and Rina trust you. Make your goals and theirs one and the same."

I stood in front of him and jutted a hip out while dropping my hands to my waist. "But they don't want to try to find Dorian. How am I supposed to agree with that?"

"I'm not saying you have to agree on everything. Only the big things. Build an army and fight the Daemoni. That's what you're agreeing to. You don't have a problem with it, do you?"

"Of course not. As long as we can rescue Dorian in the process."

"Exactly. Serve their goals, *ma lykita*. Build and train our army. If Sophia's right about Dorian not being in Hades, we won't need to wait on a full army to get to him. We can put together a special ops team for a search-and-rescue mission. All part of the training program."

For the first time in days, maybe even weeks, a smile tugged at my lips. I threw my arms around him.

"You're brilliant!" I said.

He shrugged under my embrace. "That is how they made me, isn't it?"

"And we're going to use all that brilliance and everything else they gave you against them. We're going to destroy them. Once and for all."

He shifted under my hold. I pulled back to study his sublime face. The gold in his eyes shone darkly.

"What?" I asked with trepidation.

"As much as I'd like to decimate them all, we might have to settle for restoring balance."

I narrowed my eyes.

"That's how the world works, my love. That part is beyond our control. If the Angels and the Heavens only want balance restored, that's what we'll achieve. We can do everything in our power, but in the end, it's not up to us."

I huffed out a breath of resignation, knowing he spoke the truth. "Fine. As long as I get to kill Lucas."

He nodded. "Without Lucas's direction, the Daemoni will be lost for a long while. He holds them together, keeps them from killing each other. That could restore balance."

"And Kali," I added. "And we know that's okay because the Otherworld wants her soul."

"Right, but Hades is a no-go. For now, anyway. No use wasting our time and losing lives if Dorian isn't there."

"Agreed. But what *is* the plan?"

He began ticking items off his long fingers. "First, we need to figure out what to do with all the people here. If Sophia still wants it as a safe house, we need to take measures to make sure it's actually safe, since we won't be here. And we need a task force. A team of trackers and converters. And a protector."

He paused and looked up at me, knowing just the word would feel like a stab in my gut.

I pressed my lips together to block out the emotional pain of Owen's betrayal and shrugged. "I'm sure Mom will give us our best. Hopefully that's one she'll give to our cause. *The* best is no longer ours, but his mother is."

Tristan nodded. "If they really want us to build an army, Rina and Sophia will send Char to us."

As if on cue, the warlock's mind signature entered the safe house, along with a few others belonging to Amadis. The others hung back in the foyer, but Charlotte made a beeline for my office. I waved my hand to open the door for her, and she strode in and up to me and wrapped her arms around me in a bear-hug.

"I'm so sorry, Alexis," she said. "I feel for you. I really do."

She knew what it was like to lose her son to the Daemoni. Only, hers had chosen to go. Damn traitor.

She stepped back and assumed a soldier's stance with her feet spread apart, her spine ramrod straight with her leather-clad chest out, and her hands clasped behind her back. Her straw-colored hair, which she'd cut boy-short after Kali announced that the previous seventy or so years of her life had been a scam, had grown out enough to be pulled back into a tight ponytail. Her sapphire blue eyes fell on me.

"At your service," she said. "What's the plan?"

"We're still formulating one," Tristan said from his perch on the edge of my desk. "We need a team, and we need to secure the safe house before we set out."

"I brought people for the safe house on Sophia's orders." Charlotte's posture softened, and she rocked on her feet. "They'll take care of security for the whole colony so we have room here for any new converts we can make in the area."

"Good. That's checked off the list," I said. "Now, what about our own team? We have the three of us. Who else?"

"We don't want to be too numerous to be noticeable, but we need enough to protect ourselves," Tristan said.

"Right," Charlotte agreed. "You two are an excellent start, but we should have at least one Were, though two would be better. And a vampire or two."

Tristan shifted his weight back and leaned against his hands on my desk. "I'm sure Sheree will volunteer."

My stomach knotted with the idea of taking sweet Sheree on such a dangerous mission. "Shouldn't she stay here for faith healing?"

"Do you really think she'll stay?" Tristan asked with a brow raised. Probably not. She felt so indebted to us, and she also loved Dorian, which meant she'd be on our side when it came time to break away from the army.

"She could use the field experience," Charlotte added. "And a big cat is always nice to have around."

"Okay," I relented. "So who else? Do you think Trevor, the werewolf, would come?"

"I'm sure he would for you," Tristan said, "but he needs to stay for his pack. They'll be dealing with enough, and he needs to be there to lead them."

"Too bad Jax is so far away," I muttered, missing the were-croc who'd helped us in Australia.

"Hmph," Tristan grunted. "I'm sure he'd do anything for you, too. He's already come this far for you once."

"I don't know if it's fair to ask, though. He'd be completely out of his element. He's stayed in the Outback for a reason."

"We're at war," Charlotte said. "Every Amadis knows what that means. If they can fight, they will."

"I don't want anyone to feel obligated. Our team should want to be on it." I began to pace again. "Let's move on. Who else? What vamps?"

"Vanessa is an obvious one," Tristan offered.

Charlotte chuckled. "*That* is one hell of a story. Rumor has it she's your sister. Lucas's other daughter."

"Rumor spreads fast." I rolled my eyes. "But it's true. At least, according to Lucas and Vanessa, but I don't know if I trust her."

"She's here. She's Amadis," Tristan said. "She'll be better with us than left behind. What better way to let her prove her loyalty?"

"And if she is loyal, she'll be able to share insider secrets," Charlotte pointed out.

I grimaced.

"You know she's an excellent fighter," Tristan pressed.

"Fine," I huffed. "Vanessa. Who else?"

"I'm sure there's another vamp or two out there who will accompany us," Char said.

"You don't think Rina would give up Solomon, would she?" I asked with a small trace of hope.

Charlotte snorted. "Not likely. He's at the United Nations right now."

Of course. I could see Solomon being a good diplomat.

"She might give us Julia, though," Char said.

I cringed at the thought of the raven-haired vamp. She may have apologized for her actions, but she'd still been part of the accusers who almost banished Tristan from the Amadis. Julia wasn't exactly my favorite vampire in the world.

"She probably won't leave Rina's side." I hoped.

"If Rina asked her to, she would," Tristan said.

I scowled at this truth. Julia would do anything for Rina, even lie down and die for her. But she remained far from my top choice as a travel companion, especially since our secret mission was to rescue Dorian. She'd try to stop us, probably sabotage any attempt we made. Maybe even accuse us of treason again. Char followed Mom's orders, but I hoped when the time came, she'd understand my need to go after Dorian. Maybe she wouldn't go with us, but I didn't think she'd try to stop us. Having a son herself, she'd understand. Unlike Julia. Plus, if Heather was with him, Charlotte would definitely do what it took to rescue the Norman girl. Again, unlike Julia. The vamp gave me the impression she was loyal to the Amadis, but not necessarily to humanity.

I paused in my tracks to tally up our roster. "We have the three of us, Sheree, if she wants to, and Vanessa. Do we really *need* anyone else? I don't know who I would trust."

"We need another mage," Charlotte said. "I can't do it all on my own. Not this kind of job, when I'll be spending a lot of energy on converting, too."

"What other warlocks do we have available?" I asked.

"None," Charlotte answered.

I gaped at her. "None?"

"They're all on assignment already. Some are protecting colonies and villages around the world. Others are guarding conversion teams."

"Surely Rina and Mom will give us one."

"They have." Char smiled as she cocked her head to the side.

Oh. Right. I supposed if we only got one warlock, at least we had her.

"What other mage would you recommend?" I asked her as I resumed my pacing.

She tapped her fingers against her lips as she thought. "I don't know who would be available. This mission is important, but the

Amadis is already stretched thin, either protecting or doing the same thing we'll be doing around the rest of the world. And covens are like packs—they stick close to each other. If we ask for one witch or wizard, they'll all want to come."

"So we need someone who's not tied to a specific coven," Tristan said.

Charlotte joined me in my pacing as she tried to think of a mage who could complement our team. Tristan moved around to the back of my desk, probably to get out of our way.

"Ahem." The clearing of a throat sounded from the corridor. *Damn.* I should have had Charlotte muffle the room.

The warlock opened the door, and I lifted my head to see Blossom step into the office. "I'm sorry, but I couldn't help but overhear."

I stopped pacing and put my hands on my hips. "No way."

Her face crumpled.

"Blossom, I love you dearly." I walked over to her and took her hands into mine. "I really do. You're my best friend. Which is why there's absolutely no way I will ask you to do this."

She flipped her blond hair back and squared her shoulders. "You don't have to ask me. I'm volunteering."

"It's too dangerous."

"Everything is dangerous now. I'm up for the challenge."

I shook my head. "No. I'm not taking you out there."

"I'm stronger than you think I am. My magic is more powerful than anyone wants to admit."

"You're not a warlock, though. You're not built to fight."

She put her fists on her hips, and her big hazel eyes narrowed with determination. "I can help you, Alexis."

I leaned back on my heels and crossed my arms over my chest. When she focused, Blossom's magic wasn't as weak or sporadic as everyone seemed to think it was. But I couldn't fathom the idea of sweet Blossom taking on the mages we'd be facing. The Daemoni would have their most powerful warlocks out there, perhaps sorcerers and sorceresses, too. There was a good chance we'd come up against Kali . . . which meant Owen. Which meant even Char could become a problem, if it came to that. *Crap.* I'd started to feel confident in my team, and now I didn't know how we were ever going to accomplish all of these objectives.

"Please, Alexis," Blossom implored. "Let me be on your team."

"No. It's too dangerous. And we need you here."

"Let me make that choice! Let me take the risk. I want to be there for you. Do you really think I can watch you walk out of here without me? Do you really think I'm any good here when I'm worried about you and Tristan? And Dorian? And Heather?" Tears filled her plea. "Those two are like my own. The kids I didn't have to raise. You're all *family* to me. Don't make me stay behind."

Unable to look her in the eye, I resumed pacing in front of my desk as Tristan watched me from the seat he'd taken in my chair. With a long exhale, I pushed my hands through my hair.

"Passion and love go a long way," Charlotte murmured.

I turned sharply and eyed Blossom. "But is it enough to *kill* for? Because that's what it might come down to."

The witch's eyes widened, then her gaze traveled around the room and to the floor.

"That's what I thought," I said. "You don't have it in you."

After a moment, Blossom straightened her spine, squared her shoulders again, and lifted her chin. "To protect you or myself, yes. I would."

"But you shouldn't have to," I snapped. The memory of my one and only true kill in the caves of Hades flooded through me, taking my breath and nearly knocking me to my knees. My hands grasped the edge of my desk to keep me from falling to the floor.

He was an evil werewolf trying to kill me, but the way his wolf's body shrunk into human form . . . his blood spurting from the artery I'd sliced with my dagger . . . I'd never be able to cleanse that from my mind. I shouldn't have been able to. I. Killed. A. Person. Someone whose soul I might have been able to help. I *should* have to live with the hellish memory and the sickening feeling in my gut and heart the rest of my life.

"*You okay?*" Tristan silently asked.

I closed my eyes and nodded.

I should have to live with those images, those feelings, and, sadly, I *could* live with them. Maybe because I had Daemoni blood flowing in my veins, or maybe because what they'd done to me already had left a dark stain on my soul. But Blossom never should have to live with it. Her heart was too big and too warm. Her soul remained clean. Taking a life would destroy her, and I didn't want to know the person she'd become. I loved the person she was now too much.

Charlotte cleared her throat. "Tristan, Vanessa, and Sheree—"

"You'll bring Sheree but not me?" Blossom demanded.

I pushed the memory of my kill back into the dark corner of my heart where it would forever live.

"She's a *tiger*, Blossom," I said, turning back to her. "With big muscles and huge teeth and sharp claws. And she's a Were, which means she stands a good chance against a vampire. *And* she's killed before."

Blossom pursed her lips.

"As I was saying," Charlotte said, eyeing me, "with those three, and especially if we get another Were and vamp, it's likely Blossom won't have to fight, even if you and I are in the middle of a conversion." She turned toward the witch. "I could train you in conversions, too. So if one of us does need to fight, you can take over."

Blossom shifted her weight to one leg, threw her hip to the side, and crossed her arms over her ample chest. "See. I can be useful in all kinds of ways. And don't you deny it, Alexis, because you were the first to raise the idea of me doing conversions."

With a sigh, I looked across my desk at Tristan, who leaned back in my chair, his hands folded across his stomach.

"I don't like it either," he said. *"If something happens to her . . ."*

Exactly. I'd never forgive myself.

"But if anyone would support our personal mission, she would."

I made a face at his point. This argument wasted valuable time, and apparently I was in the minority.

"So what else will you be able to do?" I asked her. "Convince me that you're an asset."

Blossom blinked at me. "Well, uh . . . you know I've been working on my magic, prepping for a disaster, although I hadn't imagined it would get this bad so soon. But you haven't seen what I can do now. New spells. And potions—all kinds of new potions that would help."

I cocked my head with a thought. If she was really determined to help me and would go to any lengths, I had a way for her to prove it.

"Tristan, can you please talk to Sheree and Vanessa?" I requested. *"Ask* them if they want to be a part of this—I don't want to force anyone. We don't need anyone on the team who doesn't want to be on it. Charlotte, please help your people get settled and take care of the colony. I want to move out as soon as possible."

"On it," she said, already on her way out of the office.

"Blossom, come with me." I headed for the door.

Tristan's brow wrinkled.

"Sheree and Vanessa," I reminded him.

He nodded. I could tell he knew I was up to something, but if I told him what, he would probably try to stop me. Besides, I really didn't want him to know the thoughts in my mind. They weren't exactly the normal Amadis way.

I led Blossom through the crowd, into the corridor, and down to the suite I'd slept in last night. The one where Dorian had last been seen. My heart squeezed painfully at the sight of his video games and other toys abandoned by the TV. Sasha hadn't moved—still curled in a ball on the pillow—but her new wing had grown to nearly full size. She lifted her head when we walked in, rose, and stretched, then padded across the bed. I gave her a scratch before turning back to Blossom.

"First, show me how strong your shield is."

She wrung her hands and made a face. "I'm still working on that. If it were strong enough . . ."

I pressed my lips together. She didn't need to finish the sentence. If her shield were strong enough, we wouldn't be in this situation. My mages wouldn't be dead. My son wouldn't be gone. But that wasn't her fault.

I swallowed the lump in my throat. "I need to know its strength."

With a sigh, she closed her eyes, lifted her arms above her head, and twirled her hands. Then she opened her eyes, dropped her hands, and looked at me.

"No wand?" I asked since most witches and wizards needed a wand.

She gave a small smile. "I don't need one anymore. Wands enhance the magic, and I've learned how to do that with my hands."

"Nice." I nodded. "Did you muffle the room, too?"

She thrust her hands out in front of her. "It is now."

"CHARLOTTE," I yelled, making Blossom flinch. Charlotte flew into the suite. I looked at Blossom. "Not strong enough."

"What's not strong enough?" Char's gaze scanned the room. "What's wrong?"

"Sorry," I said. "I didn't mean to alarm you. We were testing her shield."

Char's eyes came back to me, filled with understanding. She gave me a small smile. "Not too many witches can shield *me* out. That's not a good test. Besides, she'll only have to maintain my shields. I can put them up."

"Unless you're incapacitated," I muttered.

"Alexis—" Char began.

I waved her off. "I know. It's not the biggest of my worries. I was only curious."

Char studied my face for a moment, then nodded and left.

We'll have to talk like this, I said to Blossom's mind. *I don't want to be overheard, and with all of the powerful hearing around here . . .*

Blossom nodded.

You know we're not going out only to convert people who the Daemoni have turned, right?

"*I know you, Alexis. You won't let Heather suffer or Dorian go so easily.*"

It's not really official Amadis business, though. At least not Dorian, and I don't know about Heather yet. For now, only converting and training our army is the official order. But Tristan and I are going to be searching for Dorian and Heather, doing the conversions along the way.

"*I want to help the Amadis any way I can,*" Blossom said, "*but honestly, I insist on going because of Dorian and Heather. I love them. And I was in charge of the safe house when all of this went down, and I can't help but blame myself—*"

I held my hands up. *Stop. We could go on and on about who's to blame, but it's definitely not you, and we don't have time to argue.*

She nodded. "*So what do you want me to do? How can I prove that I can help so we can get going sooner rather than later?*"

I sat on the bed next to Sasha and stroked the soft fur on her back for a few moments before peering up at Blossom.

How far are you really willing to go to save Dorian? I asked.

She tilted her head. "*I'll do anything. I swear I will. When I said I'd kill if I had to, I meant it.*"

How many? I asked.

Not understanding—or not having a good answer—she squinted her eyes.

I made my question more direct. *Is it possible to wipe out a whole mage coven or vampire nest at once? Is there a spell for that?*

Blossom reeled back, her already large eyes wider than normal. "*What?*"

Is there a spell for that? I repeated.

"*Um . . . yeah. I'm sure there is.*"

Are you powerful enough to do it?

She visibly gulped, and her hand went to her throat. "*Maybe. I don't know. But that's a lot of souls. Surely some can be saved.*"

I twisted on my butt to face her more directly. *Here's how I see it. If we can wipe out an entire nest of vampires, how many human souls would be saved instead of turned by them? If we do it enough times, the Daemoni will—*

"*Come after us and kill us!*"

I shrugged. *Maybe not if we give them an ultimatum. Return their hostages and we stop. Easy as that. Then we can focus on the business of building our army as they return to theirs.*

Blossom stared at me as if I'd lost my mind. "*But Alexis—*"

Can you do it or not? Would you do it? That's all I'm asking.

She shook her head. "*I don't know. I haven't ever considered it.*"

So consider it. There's a huge nest in Fort Myers still. Can you do it from here, or do we need to do a quick flash-trip?

She gasped loudly, and her hand moved from her throat to her mouth. "*You're talking dark magic! I . . . I can't—*"

You said you'd do anything, I reminded her.

"*But that's . . .*" She shook her head again. "*I'm Amadis. I don't have that kind of dark power.*"

I rose to my feet, leaned toward her, and looked her directly in the eye. "That's exactly why you can't go. We're all Amadis, but there's darkness in us, too. Enough to do what needs to be done. You haven't gone there yet, and I won't be the one to take you."

I turned my back on her and headed for the door.

"Wait!"

4

I PAUSED BUT didn't turn back to the witch. To my friend.

"I can't stay here," she said. "I can't be here. Please let me go with you. Please let me choose. It's all on me, okay? Not on you at all. Everything I do will be my choice, and I'll do *anything*."

"Anything?" I asked.

"Yes. I'll try, anyway. I don't know if I can, but I'll give it my best. I just can't stay here where everything went bad. I can't go into the common room without seeing the blood. Standing in this suite where Sasha and Dorian were . . . even walking by the door . . . please, Alexis. I have to *do* something!"

I turned back to her.

"So you'd try it?"

She bit her lip and nodded. "Yeah, I will. I need to do a little research first, though. I've never studied dark magic before, but I'm sure there's some kind of spell that will—"

The front door to the suite opened with a crash, and Tristan tore into the room. Not stopping, he grabbed me by the shoulders and pinned me to the wall.

"Blossom, leave," he ordered, sparks in his eyes as he glared down at me. Blood rushed in my ears, so I didn't hear her go, but she must have. "What the hell do you think you're doing?"

I glared back at him in shock. "What do you mean?"

"Don't you think I already thought of that solution?" he asked. Of course he had. He must have heard Blossom's mention of dark magic and known my request. "You can't ask that of her, Alexis. It's dark magic. Do you have any idea what that means?"

I blinked at him. No, not really, but I didn't say so.

"Do you know what that would do to her?"

"No, but she does, and she made the choice."

"Alexis!" he nearly yelled. He glared at me while inhaling through flared nostrils, then blew the breath out. When he spoke again, his voice came low, barely controlled. "She is sworn to the Amadis way. Dark magic breaks that vow, putting her soul at risk. It could kill her. And if not, it could destroy her soul. In most dark magic, that's exactly what must be sacrificed. Her soul, and others' as well."

I gasped. "I . . . I had no idea."

Two years in this world, and there was still so much to learn.

"Which is why you don't go around asking people to do such things," Tristan replied. "You and I will do anything for Dorian. I would sacrifice my life. My soul, too, if it would save his, even after everything I've been through. But we can't ask that of anyone else. He's *our* son. Not theirs. People, especially Blossom, will do what you want them to, Alexis. You're their future leader. You have to be careful what you ask."

Ouch. I placed my hands on his chest and pushed him off of me. "Chill out. It was just a test. I wasn't actually going to have her do it. Even if it is the fastest way to get Dorian. With probably the fewest fatalities, especially *human* fatalities."

"It's not the Amadis way."

"Well, obviously, in this case. But when it comes to other things, maybe the Amadis need to change their ways if we have any hope of winning this war."

"But we can't ask anyone to risk their souls," he said, his voice softer now.

I sighed as I gathered my hair behind my head and twisted it. "I know. I'm sorry. I get it. It's just . . . that conversation with Mom really pissed me off. I know we have a plan, and my head knows it's the right thing to do, but all my heart wants is to focus on Dorian, no matter what it takes."

"I know, my love." He pulled me into his arms. "Trust me, I know."

I wrapped my arms around his waist and stood in his embrace, letting our love mix and cocoon us in its warmth for just a moment before facing the cold world again. As I rested my head against his chest, I inhaled deeply, his scent and touch calming me and giving me strength at the same time.

I'd sensed Blossom in the other room—she hadn't left the suite entirely—and called out to her as I turned in Tristan's arms. "Blossom, I'm so sorry for testing you like that. It was inappropriate. Please forgive me."

She stepped into the bedroom, and I reached my arm out for her. When she moved close enough, I pulled her into a one-armed hug.

"I really am sorry. I just—"

"You're just a mom who's worried about her son."

I nodded. "Still. It was inexcusable."

She gave me a squeeze and pulled back. "It's not your fault. I said I'd do anything. It's my choice."

"I know, and I'm sure you will. I shouldn't have even needed to test that," I said as I reluctantly pulled away from Tristan's comforting arms. "But when I do ask you to do something, you have to tell me what exactly is at risk. I'm still pretty ignorant when it comes to the ins-and-outs of mages and your magic."

"Well, there *is* something I can do that's not risky at all. I can't guarantee anything, especially if he's really far away or if there's a strong shield around him, which there might be, but maybe we'll get lucky, so I can always try—"

"Blossom," Tristan interrupted. She stopped her rambling and looked up at him. "What is it?"

"I can do a tracking spell," she said.

My mouth dropped open and hope lifted my spirits. "Why didn't you say so sooner?"

"You were . . . well . . ." She scrunched her lips, trying not to say what I'd so horribly done to her—the position I'd put her in. "Anyway, um, like I said, I can't guarantee anything. I've already tried a few times with no luck, but I want to keep pushing myself further. And maybe between the two of us—with you searching for his mind at the same time—maybe we can find Dorian."

Tristan and I exchanged a look of cautious optimism.

"What do you need?" I asked.

"Well . . . before we cleaned up the blood in here, I took a sample to see if any of it was his—" She paused, her eyes wide at my reaction as the blood rushed out of my head, and then she hurried on. "No, no, it wasn't. I'm sorry. I didn't mean to scare you, but none of it belonged to him from what I could determine."

I exhaled sharply. "It must have been Victor's. Or maybe even Lucas's." I wasn't entirely convinced he hadn't taken Dorian himself. "If so, I hope Sasha got him good."

She nodded. "Yeah, probably, but anyway, it would have been helpful for the spell, but hopefully that means Dorian wasn't hurt. I needed something of his, though, and the closer the better, but Sasha doesn't work, which I don't know if it's because she's a living being or what, so I tried one of his game controllers, but it's still not enough."

Tristan held his hand up, again making her stop to take a breath. "What *will* help?"

"Maybe if I'm in his room? I didn't want to leave on my own, with everything going on, but maybe sitting in his room, surrounded by all of his things . . ."

"Let's go," I said, preparing to flash.

"I don't like you going alone," Tristan said. "Not after what happened."

"I've been keeping my mind open, but there aren't any Daemoni signatures for miles. Victor's long gone."

"You never know when they'll pop in, though."

"Then come with us and keep watch." I didn't understand the problem. "Have you talked to Sheree and Vanessa?"

"I was sort of interrupted," he said with a pointed look.

Guilt tightened my shoulder muscles. "Fine. I'll call them."

A minute later, Sheree and Vanessa entered the suite, and through mind-talk, I told them about our plan. All of it. They both volunteered immediately. Problem solved.

"Charlotte's working on securing the safe house and the colony," I told them. "As soon as it's ready, we're leaving. So be prepared."

They nodded and took off to help.

"Now we can go." I flashed to our home, more determined than ever to try anything that would lead us to my son.

Going into his bedroom proved to be a lot harder than I expected, though. As soon as I crossed the threshold, my lungs seized up. Tears filled my eyes as they took in the mess—his typical mess showing that he'd been here recently, having fun, being himself. His natural scent of oranges and grass, mixed with a hint of Sasha's baby-powder fragrance, lingered on the air. I strode over to his bed, sat down at the head of it, and pulled his pillow to my chest. I buried my face in it and inhaled. *We're coming, baby. Mom and Dad are coming for you.*

A weight settled on the bed with me, and I opened my eyes to find Blossom crossing her legs and fisting her hands into Dorian's blankets.

"His presence is so strong here," she said. "Open your mind with me, and let's search."

She closed her eyes and began chanting something under her breath. I closed my eyes, too, and opened my mind to her as well as to the area around us, scanning the mind signatures. I broadened the area in my mind, going east to the mainland, as I'd already done before, and still no signature belonging to Dorian. Blossom's chant became more urgent, and I pushed harder, reaching out as far as I could go.

Something suddenly nudged my mind north. Pushed it farther than I'd been able to go on my own. I continued scanning the tens of thousands of mind signatures, looking for the only one that mattered right now, until my head felt as though it were imploding. Another nudge north, but my mind couldn't follow. Ignoring the pressure, I tried with all of my ability anyway, pushing, pushing, pushing—

But I was jerked out of it.

Panting, I opened my eyes to find Blossom staring at me with a frown.

"North," I mumbled. I tried to stand up, to get moving, but my head pounded a strong protest, keeping me seated. "We need to go north, right?"

Blossom nodded, but her frown remained. "Are you going to answer that?"

Her eyes glanced at my hip. I didn't realize my phone had been buzzing in my pocket. The annoying sound stopped before I could answer it, but my screen showed Mom had called. Apparently a couple of times. Blossom and I must have been too out of it to notice.

"We might have been able to go farther, if you want to try again," Blossom said.

I lay back on Dorian's pillow and rubbed my temple. "I don't think I can. I guess *I'm* the one not strong enough."

"Rest a moment and maybe—"

My phone rang again. Mom wasn't letting up. But I wasn't in a good state of mind to talk to her, especially since she probably knew what we were doing and had a few choice words for me. So my fingers fumbled until they found the ignore button.

"I've never been able to go so far before," I said. "Not even close. I can work on it, but I don't want to sit here forever trying. At least we have a direction to head."

I sat up when Tristan entered the room with an obvious purpose to his stride, but when he looked around, he stopped in his tracks. His chest rose as he drew in a deep breath. He picked up a picture of the three of us on Dorian's dresser, and his Adam's apple bobbed as he worked to swallow. He put it down and looked at me, and his hazel eyes focused, as though he finally remembered why he came in.

"North's going to be a problem," he said, his voice thick. He cleared his throat. "Charlotte won't buy into it."

"Why not? We're about as far south as we can be, so going north means more souls to help." I thought it made perfect sense.

"Not when there are three Daemoni clusters in our backyard. Fort Myers Beach, South Beach, and Key West are all minor now, but they can easily become one large Major Cluster. She'll want to go there first."

Blossom's shoulders sank. "He's right."

"Well, then we need to think of something to make her want to go north," I said. "And we need to leave soon."

"Alexis," Tristan said, "that's a lot of souls to abandon down there."

"We have to find our son," I insisted.

"I know, *ma lykita*, but—"

"We can still look for him." Blossom reached over and put her hand over mine. "If we're converting close to home, we can come back here and keep trying. It might be better than hitting the road for a physical search when we're not sure exactly how far north we need to go."

"It'll take forever to get through those clusters, though." I pressed my palm against my forehead and thought for a moment. "Maybe we don't take Char. She can go south with a team, and we'll take our own team north."

"We need her. She's the only warlock we have," Tristan reminded me.

I pushed to my feet with a sudden need to punch something. My phone buzzed again, and I whipped it out of my pocket.

"What?" I barked, having no patience for Mom's lectures but tired of her insistent calls.

"Alexis?" came a girl's voice, sounding small and scared.

My breath caught in my lungs.

"*Heather?*" I practically shrieked into the phone. Both Tristan's and Blossom's heads snapped toward me. "Oh my God, are you okay? Where are you? Is Dorian with you? Tell me where you are, and we'll come get you. You're okay, right?"

"I'm . . . uh, yeah, I'm fine." Her voice sounded a little better than I'd thought at first. I let out a breath of relief.

"And Dorian? Please say he's with you. Please say he's fine, too. Please tell me you two got away." The pitch of my voice raised a couple of octaves as I spoke.

"I'm . . . I'm with friends. I'm fine. I had to check in with my mom, let her know I was okay, and she said you guys were probably worried about me because she'd called Blossom—"

"Is Dorian with you?" I practically screamed, unable to listen to her nervous babbling a moment longer.

"No," she whispered. "He never was. Is he . . . he's *gone*?"

I closed my eyes and swallowed, my throat tight.

"Oh my God. I should have known something was wrong," she continued, though her words were distant in my mind as I tried to recover myself. How had I let my hopes soar so high so quickly? "Sonya warned me to get far away. She called me the other night and said to run as far and as fast as I could. To hide. So I . . . I came to some friends up at FSU in Tallahassee. I thought Dorian was at the safe house. I thought he'd be okay."

"He was," I managed to say through clenched teeth. I couldn't bring myself to tell her exactly what Sonya had done. Heather had tried so hard to make sure her sister never hurt anyone again, and how did Sonya repay her? Us? She turned on all of us and massacred my mages. Allowed my son to be taken. "Something happened, though. We're still figuring it out, but I need you to stay away from Sonya, okay? Hopefully, she'll stay away from you, too, but . . . I don't know. I just need to know that you're safe, and it's not safe with her. You're with your friends now?"

"Um, yeah. I'm going to hang out here for a while, probably all of my spring break." She paused for a long moment. "We're watching movies. You know, the ones with the hot werewolf and the vampire that looks like a drug addict."

"Good," I breathed. But relief only lasted a moment as realization set in.

"I'm so sorry, Alexis," she said, her voice small again and full of sorrow.

"Stay safe, okay?" *We'll be there soon,* I didn't tell her.

"Please don't worry about me. Just . . . find Dorian."

Yeah, right. I felt nothing but worry about her as I pressed END on my phone's screen.

"Sonya has her," I told Tristan and Blossom. Heather's sister had used the exact same words to describe a movie once. Heather had been giving me a message.

"We need to go!" Blossom jumped to her feet.

Tristan and I agreed without hesitation, and I called Charlotte to let her know where we'd be going. I wouldn't call Mom back, though. I didn't have time to argue with her.

"I don't like it," Char said.

"Sonya's a baby vamp, and it's daytime. Tristan and I can handle it."

A pop outside had me peeking through the curtains to see Vanessa. She blurred into the house. "I'm going."

I cocked my head.

"She's a vampire," Vanessa explained. "I can help. And it's better than hanging out here where no one wants anything to do with me."

"Vanessa's going, too," I told Charlotte.

"And me," Blossom said. "That's my girl we're saving."

Of course she'd want to go.

"Sheree wants to go," Char said through the phone.

"I was close to Sonya," Sheree said from the other end of the line, though her voice came from farther away than Char's. She knew I'd hear her, though. "Maybe I can talk her down."

With the image I had in my head of what I wanted to do to Sonya, I didn't think it would be good for Sheree to be there.

"No," I said to Char. "Sheree can't go. She needs to stay and help you at the safe house."

"From the look on her face, she doesn't agree."

"Too bad. Keep her there. We'll be back later with Heather."

Not waiting for further argument, I disconnected the call. Tristan, Blossom, Vanessa, and I took each other's hands, and Tristan led us for the flash to Tallahassee. We had to flash around the city a few times before I finally latched on to Heather's mind signature near the Florida State University campus, as she had said.

"She's definitely with Sonya." I focused harder, and then frowned. Some *friends* Heather had. But it made sense for them to be near the campus—college kids were probably prime targets for food and turnings. "And a whole nest of vampires."

"Is—" Blossom's throat moved as she gulped. "Is she . . . ?"

"Turned?" I shook my head. "No. Her mind signature is still human."

The witch let out a loud breath of relief. "We need to go get her."

With a nod, we set out on foot, and I led the others toward Heather's mind signature until we came to a row of townhouses. Five mind signatures were within the homes, all vampires. Heather and Sonya, however, were behind the row of houses, in a park-like area clustered with maples, palms, and huge oaks draped with Spanish moss. Two other vampires were with them. I listened in as we approached.

"For the hundredth time, you have to turn her, Sonya," a female vamp's voice said. "It's for her own good, and you know it."

"For the hundredth time, no," Sonya's familiar voice answered. "I won't make her live this horrible existence."

"Oh, it's not so bad," came a third female, menace underlying her taunting words. "Besides, your only other choice is that we eat her."

"No!" Sonya's voice came sharper. "Leave her alone, Lesley."

Tristan and I looked at each other and nodded, then we both blurred to the edge of a small clearing. Vanessa and Blossom showed up at the same time, Vanessa's fist swinging toward me. I ducked, then heard a body hit the ground behind me. I spun to find a fourth vamp at my feet—someone inside must have sensed our arrival.

"Thanks," I murmured to Vanessa.

"That's what I'm here for," she whispered, then added, "Sis."

"There are more of us around," warned one of the two females threatening Sonya—the one who wanted to eat Heather. With a short blond bob, she stood in front of Sonya with her back to us, wearing a tank top and shorts with cowboy boots.

Her companion, another blonde, though she wore her hair long, nearly to her butt, leaned less threateningly against a nearby tree, her arms crossed over her chest. The two dark-haired sisters faced us, Sonya standing protectively in front of Heather, who was backed up against the trunk of an oak.

"Let them come," Tristan said as we stepped closer.

"Tristan," Heather squeaked. "Alexis!"

The two blondes sucked in air noisily as they turned to face us. Sonya's blue eyes popped open wide, and her jaw trembled. She took a step back, smashing Heather against the tree.

"Give us the Norman," Tristan said. "That's all we want."

"Unless any of you want to convert," I added, because I was supposed to—and because the Daemoni often thought of that as a threat. I didn't really expect either of them to want to.

The shorter vamp, the one with the bobbed hair, hissed. It was an odd sound coming from someone with her slight stature and sweet face. Her light blue eyes sparked with a wicked gleam.

"Fools," she screeched, plenty loud enough to alert the rest of their small nest. Then she disappeared, only to reappear on Vanessa's back, her fangs long and poised over my half-sister's neck.

Vanessa hissed and spun in a blur, and the two vampires bounced around the park, ramming each other into trees and rolling on the ground. Thank God nobody else was around. Watching them, I couldn't help but think about the fight Vanessa and I had had in the woods in Washington when we were on our way to Hades. This must have been what we looked like.

"Lesley, stop!" the vamp with the long blond hair said. She must have realized none of the other vampires from the houses were coming to their rescue. "You know we're outnumbered and out-powered."

I didn't know if it was the warning or the distraction that did it, but suddenly Vanessa and the other vamp came to a standstill. Vanessa's arms were wrapped tightly around Lesley, pinning the Daemoni's arms to her sides. Vanessa's fangs were fully extended, ready to bite if necessary.

"Heather, come here," I ordered, seizing the opportunity. She ran into my arms. I gave her a quick hug, and then handed her over to Blossom, who swallowed the girl into a bear hug. "Sonya."

It wasn't a kind greeting, and she knew it. Her eyes focused on me, still wide and mixed with fear and confusion. The vamp let out a little whimper. My heart had been pounding hard in my chest this whole time, wondering what we would come upon. Wondering if I could bring myself to kill this young vampire since it was her attack that caused the mages to drop their shield over the safe house, thereby allowing Lucas and/or Victor inside to steal Dorian. I expected her to be vicious, knowing how pissed off we'd all be, especially Tristan and me. But strangely, though smartly, fear waved off of her.

I couldn't let her faked innocence get to me. I had to remember what she'd done—the blood smeared on the walls, the mages' mutilated bodies on the floor. She was a cold-blooded beast, not someone to feel sorry for. I took a step forward. She tried to step away, but she'd backed herself into the tree.

My voice came out low, my abhorrence for her weaved into each distinct word. "Give me one good reason not to kill you."

"Please don't hurt me," she begged, her voice barely more than a whisper.

"What's *wrong* with you?" Lesley demanded as she squirmed in Vanessa's arms. Vanessa growled in her ear and lowered her mouth so her fangs scratched the other vamp's skin. "We can take on these pansy-asses!"

The other vamp, the one with the long hair, rolled her eyes. "Don't you know who they are? We can't kill them."

"Sure we can, Alys!" Lesley said, and then she gasped as Vanessa's fangs gave a quick pierce into her skin.

"Shut up, or we'll call in the Weres," Vanessa warned. "We have a tiger who might not seem so bad, though I wouldn't underestimate her. And we happen to know a few others, too. They're not far, and they're just waiting to chomp on a pretty little bitch like you."

Though we knew Vanessa was bluffing, Lesley obviously didn't because she finally fell still.

"I . . . I'm sorry, Alexis," Sonya said, turning her attention back to me. "I really am. Please . . . please let me explain. I . . . I can help you find Dorian."

I flew at her, and my hand wrapped around her throat as I lifted her up against the tree.

"You have no right to say his name! It's your fault he's gone!"

"I know," she choked out. "I'm sorry. But please listen. I can lead you to him. But I . . . I need your help first."

"Please don't hurt her," Heather whispered from behind me, and I forced myself to let go of Sonya and take several steps back for Heather's sake. She didn't need to see what I had planned for her sister, and that could wait until Heather was long gone. "She really didn't mean to do any of it."

"Honey," Blossom said, also from behind me, "you're safe now. You don't need to protect her."

"No, really," Heather said, her voice pleading, "Sonya couldn't help it. Let her tell you."

I strode closer to Sonya again. Alys, the other vamp, wisely stepped farther away. I didn't know what was up with her—her thoughts were a hot mess of confusion between attacking us or running away, though running felt stronger. So I didn't know why she stayed. She had to know we didn't give a rat's ass about her right now. So I stopped for a second and turned to her. She stood quite a bit taller than me so I had to crane my neck nearly as much as I did to look at Tristan.

"Do you want to convert?" I asked her.

She stared at me with big blue eyes, not answering.

"If not, then get the hell out of here. We have what we want."

The vamp took a step backwards.

"Alys," Sonya said. "You don't—"

"Hush!" I barked. "You have no right to say anything."

The two Daemoni vamps exchanged a look, and then Alys disappeared. I nodded at Vanessa, who loosened her grip on Lesley. The shorter blonde crouched as though she planned to attack, but Tristan's hand flew up.

"Leave. Now," he commanded.

Her eyes swept over all of us, and she let out a growl, but then she blurred off across the park and eventually disappeared.

"So what is it you have to say?" I demanded of Sonya. "Why do you think I'd want to help you with anything, except your death?"

Heather broke free of Blossom's hold, rushed to her sister's side, and took her hand. I immediately regretted the harshness of my words. The vamp had kidnapped the girl, but Heather still stood by her sister's side faithfully—trusting her.

"Tell them," Heather said.

Sonya nodded. She inhaled a deep breath, though she didn't really need it, then blew it out, buying herself time. I tapped into her mind to find her thoughts in a jumbled mess she was trying to straighten into sense. She pushed her dark hair out of her face before beginning.

"The Daemoni set you up. Me up. You thought it was Vanessa who was trying to trick you, but it was me all along," the vamp admitted. I bit back an insult. Her words began to come faster as she practically vomited an explanation. "I didn't mean to, though. You have to believe me. I didn't know what I'd gotten myself into. They put this stone into me a long time ago, and I didn't really know what it was, but then the other night . . . I—I lost all control over my own body." She hiccupped as though suppressing a sob, and Heather squeezed her hand. Tears filled her voice as she continued. "It was all Lucas. He . . . he took *control* over me, Alexis. He made me fly through the safe house, into the commons room, and before I even knew what was happening, I'd . . . I'd killed them all. The mages. I killed them and then left them in a bloody heap."

Heather put her arm around her sister as the vamp cried against the younger one's shoulder.

"I'm so sorry," she sobbed. "I wish . . . I wish I'd never done this. I wish I could go back to being a Norman. I screwed up when I chose this life and keep screwing up since then, and now I've done the worst thing imaginable. I never thought . . . I'm . . ." She pulled back and looked at me with blue eyes so dark, you could drown in their sorrow. "I'm not a writer like you. I don't have the words to express how truly sorry I am."

Her apologies seemed sincere enough, but her story didn't make any sense and had a lot of holes. But there was only one thing I cared about.

"What happened after you killed the mages?" I managed to say though my throat was dry and constricted with the mental images she'd shared with me. "Did *you* take Dorian?"

She shook her head violently. "No. No, of course not! It was all Kali. Kali and—"

"*What?*" I interrupted, my patience running thin. "What does *Kali* have to do with anything?"

"Kali has to do with everything. She has Dorian."

"Lucas or Victor took Dorian."

"No."

"You're saying Kali took Dorian?" Tristan asked from right beside me.

"No, but she has him." She looked to Tristan, then back at me, and her tongue darted over her lips. "Um . . . Owen took Dorian."

5

MY STOMACH SQUEEZED as though I'd been punched. I took several steps back, shaking my head in denial. I knew Owen had betrayed us, of course. He'd turned on me—and Vanessa—right in our faces and joined Kali's side. But this? He'd go so far as to take my *son*? The one vulnerability he knew both Tristan and I had? Did he really become so ingrained with the Daemoni that he would willingly hurt us like this?

If so, that meant when he came back with Vanessa's body parts, he'd already been a part of the Daemoni. A servant to Kali. Because only hours had passed between the time he deserted us in Hades and when Dorian had been taken. So either he'd switched his allegiances that quickly, or he had long before then and had deceived us while he was at the safe house.

Tristan and I looked at each other, and his expression reflected my own feelings—surprise mixed with a heavy dose of doubt. What Sonya said . . . I couldn't fathom Owen going so far. And I couldn't believe Victor had told the truth.

"You can read my thoughts," Sonya said. "I know you can. Check my—"

Sonya's face contorted, cutting her off mid-sentence. A scream rose from deep in her chest, and her mouth opened wide to let it out. Then her eyes, no longer blue but a glowing red, glazed over as she cocked her head at me.

The next thing I knew, the vampire lunged at me. Her hands reached out and scraped at my throat. At my necklace.

Help me, Sonya's voice came in my mind. *Get . . . the stone.*

A strange growl ripped through Sonya's chest this time as her body jerked side to side.

"*She's all mine, Alexis, and I'll kill her. Don't think I won't.*" Kali's voice. In my head. From Sonya.

"Kali's controlling her," I said, though it almost sounded like a question. "Like she has a faerie stone in her."

Sonya's head barely twitched in a nod. Her body jerked and twisted as she tried to hold on to even a little control. While one hand still reached for my pendant, her other one clutched at her own chest. Her fingers closed in on my necklace and ripped it off my neck. She stumbled away from me, but didn't get far. Tristan paralyzed her, one of her hands still digging into her chest as she fell to the ground.

But still her body convulsed. Pinkish foam started bubbling from her mouth, followed by liquid blood.

"Kali's killing her!" I gasped.

"Help her," Heather screamed as Blossom held the girl to keep her from running to her sister.

"Blossom, muffle us," Tristan ordered, then he said to me, "Your dagger. If she really has a faerie stone in her, it's the only way."

Seeing this, I had no doubt she did. And if by chance she didn't . . . well, she deserved this anyway for what she'd done to us all. I pulled my dagger out, fell to my knees, and plunged the blade into Sonya's chest, not for the first time. The vampire's scream matched her sister's. I dug the blade around until the tip hit something hard, and with a twist of the knife and a sickening slurping sound, a small stone flew out of the hole I'd carved into her chest. I caught it in my free hand as I withdrew my dagger. Sonya's skin immediately began to heal, and her body fell still. Tristan released his power from her, but she didn't move.

We waited, all of us silent and our breaths held, for seconds that turned into minutes. Heather whimpered her sister's name. The vampire stirred, and her eyes finally opened. They were clear and blue again as they found my face. She held her hand up, my necklace dangling between her fingers.

"How long have you had that stone?" I asked as I snatched my necklace out of her hand.

"Convert me," she whispered. "For real this time. I want to be converted, and when I tell you everything, you'll know I'm telling the truth."

I pressed my lips together as Tristan's hand squeezed my shoulder, then I stuffed my necklace and the other stone into my pocket before leaning back and crossing my arms as I studied her. I hadn't left her mind, so I knew Kali was gone, and now I focused in on Sonya's intentions. My hand reached out and wrapped around her forearm, and I pushed Amadis power into her. She didn't even flinch.

"It's all in my mind and my soul still," Sonya said to me. "Everything you and Sheree gave me, everything you taught me. Only my heart was blocked before. Now it's open to you."

I narrowed my eyes as I pushed the power harder. She seemed to grab a hold of it, gulping it in almost as hungrily as she'd drink blood. When I felt satisfied with her response, I gave Tristan a nod. He took Sonya in his arms, I took Heather, and we all flashed back to the safe house.

Heather sucked in a deep breath when we appeared. "Wow. That was . . ."

"Weird?" I finished for her as I set her on the ground.

"Very."

As soon as we were in the safe house, the new team Charlotte had brought took over Sonya's conversion. Although having a Norman here made some of the Amadis uncomfortable—Heather wasn't supposed to know about them—I wasn't about to send her home where she'd be vulnerable. Everyone would have to get over it because she would be staying at the safe house, too.

We told Charlotte what had happened—the little bit we knew so far—and we all shared theories about the holes in Sonya's story. We wouldn't really be able to fill those gaps, though, until the vampire had fully converted. I agreed with her: she needed to be converted, for real this time, before I'd believe anything that came out of her mouth.

Tristan and I returned to our home for the night, but sleep eluded us. Although Dorian was just one little boy, his presence made the house a home, and I didn't like being here without him. We lay in bed, holding each other in meaningful silence, sharing our love and our pain wordlessly until we both succeeded in drifting off for a couple of hours.

The sun had barely risen before Tristan, Charlotte, and I had settled into my office to regroup when a conversion team member knocked on the heavy wooden door.

"Sonya wants to talk to you," the gray-haired witch said after I'd opened it for her. "All of you."

"She's done already?" I asked with disbelief.

She nodded and pushed her glasses up her nose. "There's no trace of Daemoni in her. We'll need to spend more time with her, of course, and it'll probably be a few months before she can be left to her own decisions, but all of her energy is Amadis."

Wow. Had Sonya actually been telling the truth about wanting to convert but not being able to? I pulled the stone out of my pocket and scratched the dry blood off with my thumbnail. While mine was ruby-colored, this one that came from Sonya was a dark emerald green. And while mine tended to warm when I touched it, this one grew cold. Charlotte peered over my shoulder.

"Definitely looks like a faerie stone," she said. "I can sense magic on it, but not mage magic. That's power from the Otherworld."

"Huh. If we'd only known . . . " Without finishing my sentence, I rushed to the vampire's room and held the stone on display between my index finger and thumb. "Why didn't you tell us about this?"

Sonya's dark eyes glanced at the stone, up at me, then at something on the blanket covering her as she sat in her bed. The same bed where she'd spent months, *pretending* to convert.

"I was scared," she finally said, and after a pause, she began babbling again. "I was scared you would throw me out for trying to fool you, and I thought I was stronger than the damn thing, and then the conversion seemed to be working. Sheree kept saying I was doing so well, that it always takes time, so I really thought I was overcoming the stone, and once I did, then I planned to tell you."

"Whoa," I said, my brows pushed together. "You're not making any sense. What does it have to do with your conversion?"

"Start from the beginning," Tristan suggested. "Where did you get it?"

"Right. Back to when I was still with the Daemoni." Sonya grimaced on the word and then nodded. "So one night, a few days before you guys and Heather came to Fort Myers Beach to see me, my nest leader said Lucas had an important mission for me, and he took me to meet Kali. She told me to go to you and say I wanted to convert, but she said I would only be pretending. She had a plan so the conversion wouldn't work, she'd told me, but they wanted me to gather valuable information for them. That's what she said anyway, but apparently they were scamming me, too. Anyway, I really did want to convert, which was why I was okay with the whole thing. I'd hoped her stupid plan would fail. When I agreed to do it, she pressed some kind of rock into my chest, over my heart. It sunk down, beneath the skin."

"The faerie stone," Tristan said.

"Yeah, I guess," Sonya said. "They called it a loyalty stone, but obviously it was more than that. I . . . I didn't know how bad it would be. If I had any idea this could have happened, I would have never done it. I *swear* to you. I had no control that night. I couldn't help it."

I studied her face as I searched her mind, but I couldn't find anything to contradict her words. I didn't know if I could ever fully trust her again, but I, too, could only feel Amadis in her. She had to have been telling the truth about this.

"So tell us everything that happened the other night," I said. "The whole story."

Sonya's eyes came up to my face again, then her gaze traveled behind me to the doorway. I sensed the whole gang waiting there— everyone who would probably be on my team. We all moved farther into the room.

The vamp swallowed, then began. "Kali stopped me from sharing my memories, so now you'll know if she's really gone. She didn't want you to believe me."

"Believe what?" Charlotte asked.

"What *really* happened here."

Sonya's memories of the night of the attack—only three nights ago, though it already felt like years—played in her mind, and I watched and shared them with the others while Sonya told the story aloud.

"Lucas took control of me first. He made me kill the mages, but that's all he wanted from me. After the shield fell, I was compelled to go out to the beach. But that was *Kali* controlling me, just like she'd done yesterday. She'd taken over control from Lucas, and she stood out there, waiting." Sonya's eyes flitted over to the curtained window, as though she could see through it and out to the beach. Her voice came out quieter. "Then Owen showed up, too. He was kind of bloody, and he had Dorian in his arms. Kali let out a funny noise—almost like a squeal of happiness. Then those two disappeared with Dorian, leaving me alone on the beach. I was so scared. Scared of Kali. Scared of you guys. I got as far away as I could before I did anything worse."

"But you kidnapped your sister," Blossom said. "Your mom was freaking out!"

Sonya nodded. "I had to. Kali became so engrossed with Owen and Dorian, she forgot about me. Lucas seemed to, as well, but I didn't take anything for granted. I was scared of what they'd do to Heather, so I had to get her away to keep her protected."

"Yet there you were with her and several Daemoni vamps," Tristan said.

"Vamps who wanted to *turn* her," Blossom pointed out.

Sonya shook her head. "They're not like most Daemoni. Lesley's a little more evil than the others, but none are really bad. They wanted to turn Heather for her own good. Her own safety, so she'd be strong like the rest of us. That's all. In fact, I'm pretty sure Alys wants to convert, but she was probably too scared to say so."

"Who the hell cares," I muttered under my breath, but everyone must have heard me because the room fell silent, and all eyes turned toward me.

My mind remained focused on what she'd said about Owen and Kali—what she'd *shown* to us—and hurt and anger had bloomed. Again. Biting my tongue before I unleashed on anyone what was truly meant for Owen, I flashed to my office.

"Alexis?" Tristan had appeared right next to me. "That was—"

"Rude? Yeah, I know." I blew out a breath. "But trust me, it was better for me to disappear and get away than to explode like I wanted to. Heather is here and safe. We need to find Dorian, but to do so, we need to figure out who we're really looking for, not talking about a bunch of Daemoni vamps we don't even know."

He stepped in front of me, placed a hand on each side of my face, and tilted my head upward to look at him. His touch had its normal calming effect on me, and his eyes held mine until I relaxed.

"You don't believe Sonya?" he finally asked as his hands slid to my shoulders.

"I don't know what to believe," I admitted. "She seemed sincere. Her memories seem real. Do you believe her?"

"It is hard to swallow."

"It doesn't make any sense. Lucas had my dagger last, and then here it was, where Dorian should have been. Where Sasha was left to *bleed out*."

"Lucas could have given it to Kali to test it for magical powers."

"And Owen would have brought it back to you," Vanessa said, her voice small as she stood in the doorway with Blossom, Sheree, and Charlotte behind her.

I turned on her. "You're *still* taking his side?"

Whether Sonya spoke the truth or not, Owen had definitely betrayed us. She shouldn't have been defending him, as far as I was concerned. Vanessa came into the office, leaned her butt against the wall, lifted one foot against it to brace herself, and scowled at the floor. Sheree, and Blossom filed in, too, followed by Char, who waved her hands to muffle the room so we could have some privacy.

"Even if Owen had some good reason to take Dorian, I can't imagine him doing that to Sasha," Sheree said quietly. I couldn't imagine it either, but then I couldn't help it, and the vision sickened me.

"Maybe he didn't," Vanessa said, and before I could fly at her, she held her hand up. "Victor pretty much admitted to being there, too, remember?"

"And you believe *him*?"

"He had the fresh scars."

"They could have been fake." I knew how far-fetched the idea sounded. Victor was a vampire, after all. There weren't too many things— or creatures—who could leave scars on him. Although, Weres could, so my theory wasn't entirely impossible, if he'd had a friend nearby.

"Why would he fake it?" Sheree asked. "What's the point?"

I didn't have an answer. "I don't pretend to know how the Daemoni think, but I do know they like to deceive and play games, no reason needed. Besides, Sonya said Owen's arms were bleeding, too."

"Maybe they weren't bleeding, but were smeared with someone else's blood," Blossom suggested. She made a face. "There was plenty of it around."

"And Lucas could have given Victor the dagger before he sent him here and took control of Sonya," Tristan said.

I peered up at him. "You just said Lucas could have given *Kali* the dagger. So which one is it?"

His gaze slid out of focus for a moment and then came back on me. "They're both strong possibilities. I don't have enough information to determine a best answer."

"You sound like a freaking robot," I muttered as my hand rubbed over the back of my head. "So what are we going to do? Was it Victor or Owen? Kali or Lucas?"

"Could have been both," Charlotte said, and she grimaced. Pain flickered in her eyes, her feeling of betrayal having to be a hundred times worse than mine. "They could have been working together, all of them sent by Lucas."

That answer seemed to make the most sense based on what both Victor and Sonya had told us, but something about the whole thing bothered me. More than the fact that neither of our sources was very trustworthy. Even if we *could* trust them, there were too many unanswered questions. Like, why make Sonya create such a bloodbath when Kali and Owen together were powerful enough to break our weaker mages' shield? Were they trying to make some kind of statement? Possibly. But I couldn't help but wonder if there was more to it. If we were missing something important.

"Do you think Kali could have put one of those faerie stones in Owen?" Sheree asked, her words floating on hope that seemed to suddenly fill the room. All of us wanted to believe in Owen. Including me.

"That would explain a lot," Blossom said. "But he's a pretty powerful warlock."

"He's *too* powerful." Charlotte sighed, as though she wanted to believe the possibility, but couldn't bring herself to allow our hopes to live on. "She wouldn't be able to force a stone in him. He'd have to *want* it."

"And he'd never want it," Vanessa added, her voice glum, full of defeat. "He'd never allow anyone to control him like that. Not after what Kali did to Martin. Whatever he's doing, he's doing it on his own volition."

Charlotte's narrowed eyes studied the vampire closely. I didn't have to hear her thoughts to see her suspicion of how Vanessa would know this about Owen. Char didn't know the two had had some kind of weird relationship going on before all of this went down.

"I have to agree," Char finally said. "Owen's too stubborn and thick-headed to allow it."

"So you think he willingly did this to us?" I asked, my voice thick, my chest tight and heavy. "And worked with Victor?"

Vanessa blew out a sharp breath. "I don't know about Victor. I haven't been able to stop thinking about what he said and what he didn't. On the one hand, he flat-out said he was there, and he made a point of you seeing the scars Sasha would have left."

"But he also made a point of showing Owen dropping the dagger next to Sasha and taking Dorian," I reminded her.

"Right. But on the other hand, if he'd had anything to do with taking your son—the big *trophy* besides you and Tristan—he'd have been bragging all over hell and back about it. We'd have never heard the end of it." She wrinkled her nose with disgust. "Then again, Victor's not as stupid as I've always made him sound. He's a pain in the ass and a spoiled brat who always gets to do whatever he wants, which usually consists of parties and girls. Lucas trusts him for a reason, though, and now that things are getting serious, he probably is, too. Victor said all kinds of things, but there was a lot he *didn't* say, and any of it could be lies anyway. He could be covering something much bigger, for all we know."

"That's comforting," Blossom muttered.

"Bottom line," Tristan determined, "both said Kali has Dorian, and Owen is probably with them."

"We need to find him," I said. "Them. *All* of them. Dorian, Owen, and Kali. I owe the faeries anyway."

I snorted. How ironic. I supposedly owed them because I asked them to help Owen. And now he was on my shit list, too.

"It's time to head out," I said.

"Are we still going north?" Blossom asked.

I glanced at the clock on the wall. A full day had passed since we'd done the spell. "We should try again. The direction might have changed by now."

Charlotte's brows lifted as she cocked her head.

"Blossom worked a tracking spell yesterday," I explained to all of them. "We didn't get a lock on Dorian, but we did feel a push that he's north of here."

"Did Sophia or Ms. Katerina have anything to say about it?" Charlotte asked.

I frowned as I debated what to tell her, unsure of how she'd react to our plan. Surely she'd want to pursue her son and the sorceress who destroyed her family, but would she defy Mom and Rina's orders? I knew it wouldn't be the first time she ignored the council—there was a reason she and Mom were such good friends—but our orders weren't only from the council.

Tristan must have decided the best solution was to tell her because he opened his mouth before I did.

"They haven't given us a specific direction or area, but our primary mission is to do conversions and build our army. We're not officially authorized to find Dorian," he finished, and everyone in the room frowned, including Charlotte.

"That could possibly change if they know Kali has him," Char suggested.

"Possibly," Tristan said, "but bringing it to their attention could just as easily cause them to give us more specific orders. Orders that won't help us and could actually hinder us. I think it's best that we stick with the plan Alexis and I have already started."

"Which is?" Sheree asked.

I recited what I'd basically told Mom. "We agree to uphold our purpose of protecting the Normans and converting those who have been infected, allowing us to build an army that we know will be needed." I paused as everyone nodded, though their mouths twisted in a grimace or a scowl. "But at the same time, we'll be searching for Dorian. Unless Blossom and I find something different when we're done here, that means going north, even if it doesn't make sense for our mission of conversions."

"And it looks as though we'll be searching for Kali if we're to find Dorian," Tristan said.

"We aren't certain she has him," Vanessa said and then added, "though it seems pretty likely."

"She probably does." I sighed. "All evidence seems to be pointing that way."

Blossom and Sheree agreed. We all looked to Charlotte.

"As much as it pisses me off because it means my son was involved, I have to agree," she said. "I'm not sure of her motive, but based on what she did to all of us with the Tristan fiasco, I'd say it has something to do with gaining power among the Daemoni. She's capable of anything."

"She's extremely powerful," Vanessa agreed.

"And dangerous," Tristan added. "So if you don't feel comfortable with our covert mission or going up against Kali, now's your chance to speak up."

Everybody stared at us. Nobody spoke up.

"So everyone agrees?" I asked, specifically looking at Charlotte. "We do our conversions while we seek out Dorian, regardless of where that takes us. And even if it means taking on Kali . . . and maybe Owen, too."

"Agreed," Blossom and Sheree said at the same time.

Vanessa made a face, but she nodded. "I'm with you, little sister."

We all looked at Charlotte again, and her sapphire eyes skimmed over everybody's faces before ending at mine. She gave me a single nod.

"I'll kill that sorceress bitch," she said. "For everything she's done to my family. And to yours."

"Not if I get to her first," I replied, and my mouth tugged up with a small smile of relief that we had a real team and a plan.

6

CHARLOTTE, SHEREE, AND Vanessa returned to their preparations for our departure, and Blossom said she was going to run home to look up something in her books before meeting Tristan and me at our house. Tristan and I flashed to our home to wait for her. While Tristan said he was going to do a weapon check, I went straight to Dorian's room and paused in the doorway. I couldn't believe three days had gone by, and we were still here and not out there looking for him.

Needing something to do, I began cleaning his room, picking up toys and placing them on the shelves, and throwing dirty socks in the hamper—he seemed capable of getting everything else into the hamper but gross, stinky socks. I sat down at his desk to straighten his books and found his notebook full of notes for the story about dragons that we'd been writing together. My heart clenched. Would we ever get to finish it? I ran my fingers over the words he'd handwritten in blue ink and had to blink away tears so I could read them. There were several lines of scribbles and restarts, and then three straight lines crossed out with heavy, deep gouges of the pen. An arrow pointed here with a note, "Mom's part. She'll know how to fix it."

With a force that rattled the desk and knocked the chair over, I pushed myself away. *I won't cry. I won't cry.* The pain was so great, though. Just as bad as when Tristan had left me. Worse, I thought, because I not only felt my own agony, but I could feel Tristan's, too. I felt his torture through his mind signature, which was heavier than usual, and through the stone in my chest that gave us an unearthly connection. Doubled like this, the heartache was nearly unbearable. But I wouldn't cry. I shook my head hard and inhaled ragged breaths until the threat of tears slipped away.

And then I saw his stuffed shark on the floor, sticking out from under his bed.

My chest tightened as I bent over and picked it up. I stared into its black, glassy eyes, and then clutched it to myself as though it were a piece of my son. What was it doing here? He usually slept with it, but apparently hadn't taken it to the safe house with him that night. In fact, now that I thought about it, I couldn't remember the last time he'd slept with it. Was there a reason the shark had been lying under the bed? Did my baby feel like he was too old to sleep with a stuffed animal? Probably. Because he wasn't my baby anymore, was he? Even if we found him tonight, this little act of the Daemoni's—of Owen's—had surely pushed him far beyond his innocent years.

I screamed and threw the shark at the wall. The urge to throw all of his toys, to shove everything off his desk and shelves, to tear apart his dresser and closet nearly overwhelmed me. But I couldn't do that to his belongings because it felt like I'd be doing the same to him. So I stood in the middle of the room, balling my fists, and reigning in that anger, letting it swirl in my gut until it tightened once again.

I will not cry.

But I would not let go of the quiet rage. I would hold on to the wrath for as long as I needed to, as though it were my lifeline. As though it were sacred.

I closed my eyes and took slow, deep breaths until my heart settled, until my soul hardened again with resolve. We planned to leave in a few short hours. We'd finally be on our way to finding my son.

"Ready?" Blossom asked a few minutes later as she strode into Dorian's room. She frowned when she looked at me. "Are you okay?"

I opened my eyes and nodded. "Beyond ready."

Just as we were about to start, though, my phone rang. I sighed when I looked at the screen, but I couldn't ignore the call. I'd been waiting for it.

"Do I need to remind you of your priorities?" Mom asked, her voice curt.

"We already have one convert," I answered, and I told her about Sonya. Mom gasped at the story about the faerie stone they'd used in the vampire and said she'd warn the council about this happening again. She didn't react to the part about Owen's involvement, though.

"What's next?" she asked brusquely.

"We're putting our team together and getting the colony settled. We'll be taking off tonight, I hope."

"And where do you plan on going?"

I closed my eyes and inhaled deeply. "We were just about to figure that out but . . . maybe north?"

I purposefully made it a question, hoping she'd give us her blessing to move completely out of the area. No such luck.

"Why would you do that?" Her tone told me she already knew the answer. She'd obviously been keeping her sense of truth focused on my actions. But how could she really expect me to forsake my son? What kind of person did they all think I was? Apparently, emotionless and coldhearted like them. "Alexis, there are thousands of people's lives on the line. Their *souls* are at risk if you don't do what you're meant to do."

"How could I forget?" I threw a hand into the air. "Nobody will let me. But I won't abandon Dorian. I won't let this go."

"I understand. I lived with the same fear throughout your childhood. I wish I could tell you something different, that this news about Kali would change everyone's minds. She hurt the Amadis, including many council members, but vengeance isn't the Amadis way. We need to focus our efforts on what's important. On our duty. Including you."

"You had converters out there before me," I reminded her.

"Everyone else who can convert *is* already out there, except you. And now Char."

Guilt poked me in the side, softening my tone to more of a plea. "And we're heading out there now. Just let us go north, though. Blossom's been working a spell, and together we felt Dorian north— at least north of us. We can keep trying until we find exactly where he is. We'll convert souls along the way, I promise, but please let me do this. And if we can end Kali at the same time, we're all better off."

More silence, but then she said, "I'm sorry. It's not my place— hold on."

She paused again, and I assumed someone on her end was speaking to her, although I didn't hear anyone. Perhaps Rina spoke to her telepathically.

"Honey," she said when she came back on the line, "Rina wants you to come here to the island. Immediately."

Oh, shit. Shit, shit, shit. I must have pushed too far. "Is that really necessary?"

"She wants to speak with you in person."

I rubbed my forehead, wishing my flash range reached a lot farther than a hundred miles at a time. But it didn't, and going overseas to Amadis Island meant traveling by plane. I didn't have time to fly all the way to Greece. And who knew how much farther away from Dorian the trip would take me?

"Tell her I get it. My purpose and all that. I don't think we should waste any more time, with everything going on." Hopefully I showed enough agreement to placate them both.

"Alexis, you don't deny Rina," Mom said, her voice full of warning. "When the matriarch calls for your audience, you come."

I frowned, thankful Mom couldn't see me. "Is that what she's doing? Because I don't need to hear her tell me everything you already have. Like I said, I get it. You two—and the rest of the Amadis—aren't budging."

"Come to the island, Alexis," Mom said more firmly. "You and your team. Rina wants a personal meeting with all of you, and she's already sent the jet."

"*All* of us?"

Mom paused again, and I assumed she spoke with Rina.

"Yes, all of you," she confirmed when she returned. "When you're done here, you'll be starting on your mission. So you and Char ensure the safe house and the colony are settled and will be able to operate without you. I don't know how long you'll be gone."

What? I didn't understand them. A minute ago she told me to stay nearby to save those souls in our own backyard, and now they wanted us to fly halfway around the world and didn't know when we'd be back? *All* of us tied up in this unnecessary trip?

"But—"

"Matriarch's orders, Alexis. Don't delay."

Great. Freakin' great. I hung up the phone, and once again, I wanted to hurl it across the room. Instead, I flopped backward onto Dorian's bed and covered my face with my hands. How could Rina and Mom do this to me? To Dorian? How could they claim to love someone so much but then desert him in his time of need? How did I know they wouldn't do the same to me or Tristan or anyone else? I thought I'd made a valid point the other day—if your own loved ones couldn't rely on you, how could anyone else? But apparently, the Amadis didn't believe the same way. Or, at least, the matriarch didn't foster that kind of culture. When I became matriarch, that would certainly change.

Every soul mattered.

"We'd better get going," Tristan said. "We don't want to leave the matriarch waiting, and she's given us the jet, which could probably be used elsewhere."

I pulled my hands away from my face to give him a dirty look. Was he as bad as them?

"The sooner we get this done and over with, the sooner we can get on track to find Dorian," he added.

"We can keep trying the spell while we're gone." Blossom glanced around Dorian's room. "His presence here really helped. I need to take something . . ."

I sat up and lifted the blanket bunched in my hands. "How about this?" I pushed my face into it once again and inhaled. "It smells so much like him. He's all over it."

"A whole blanket is kind of awkward to carry around," she said. "And I can't flash with it if we need to."

Oh, right. I glanced at the shark in the corner, but that would probably be too bulky, too. So, I pulled out my dagger and cut away two squares from the blanket that could be folded and stuffed into a small bag or pocket—one for her and one for me. Then I stood and blew out a heavy breath.

"He has a room at Rina's, too, so maybe we can try again there." I handed her the piece of fabric. I stuck mine in the back pocket of my leathers until I could move it to my backpack and returned my dagger to its sheath. "I guess we go get this done with. Another stupid lecture. You ever been to Amadis Island, Blossom?"

Her face paled, and she shook her head. "Oh, no. Never. I don't even know what to do."

"Well, we're going. All of us. Matriarch's orders." I let out a hollow chuckle. "This should be especially fun with Vanessa."

Tristan and I gathered a couple of things we could take with us and stuffed them into my leather backpack where the faerie's jar for Kali's soul still hid. Then we secured our home as best as possible before flashing to the safe house. With Vanessa and Sheree's assistance, Charlotte had everything taken care of. The people she'd brought to the mansion with her were experienced converters, and since Sonya proved to be an easy patient, they were already discussing their first target in Fort Myers Beach.

"Don't worry about a thing here," Char said to me when my impatience and worry began to show. "They're a good team. Everything's taken care of."

"It's not that," I said. "I'm glad they're here. I just wish we were rushing off for other reasons than for a trip to the damn island. And it's my fault Rina's being a pain."

Charlotte's brow shot up. "I'm sure she has her reasons for needing to see us. Remember to never underestimate her."

Right. A lesson we learned with the Martin/Kali debacle. When we all thought Rina had lost her mind completely to the sorceress, she'd actually been setting up Kali's downfall and Tristan's acquittal.

Before we left, Tristan and I took a few minutes to be alone in the suite we'd been using.

"I hate this," I told him as he pulled me into his arms. "I feel like we're putting more miles between us and Dorian rather than fewer."

"I do, too, *ma lykita*, but who knows where they've taken him? There's a chance he could be in Europe or Asia, just as much as here. He could be anywhere by now."

I let out a sigh. "You're not making me feel any better."

He leaned down and brushed a kiss across my lips. "Does that help?"

One corner of my mouth tugged slightly. "Maybe a little."

He pressed his lips to mine again for a deeper kiss, but he pulled away too soon.

"I'd offer more, but we'd better get going," he said, regret in his voice. "The last thing we need to do right now is anger the matriarch."

I nodded. "Right. We'll do what we need to do to make them happy so we can get to work on our own plans."

"While we're there, do me a favor. In fact, as we move forward, do this for me, please."

I eyed him with hesitation.

"Don't do anything stupid," he warned, not for the first time. I had a bad habit of doing stupid things like jumping into situations that were over my head. "You're no good to anyone, especially Dorian, if you're dead."

I pressed my lips together and nodded again. "I promise I won't be stupid."

He pulled me tighter against him, and I leaned up on my toes for a long kiss that didn't last long enough.

"We need to go," he murmured, and I frowned. He caught my protruding lower lip between his teeth before delivering another kiss. "Let's get this over with."

He scooped up Sasha, whose wing had completely grown back, from the bed and deposited her into my arms before we left the suite. We found the rest of the team waiting for us in my office.

"Are we ready?" Charlotte asked. Blossom, Sheree, and Vanessa all nodded.

"Wait," came an urgent voice from the foyer. Bree the faerie flew into my office and came to a halt, her golden eyes glancing around at everyone. "I need a minute with Alexis, please."

"The jet's waiting," Charlotte said.

"I only need a moment," the faerie insisted. "Tristan, you can stay, too."

The others filed out, and Bree closed the door behind them.

"Take off your necklace," she demanded. I lifted a brow. "Sorry to be blunt, but the jet *is* waiting. For me, too. Ms. Katerina has summoned me as well. But first, just in case, I want to take care of something."

"What do you need the necklace for?" Tristan asked as he took Sasha from my arms so I could unclasp the chain. He'd fixed it for me last night after Sonya/Kali had ripped it from my neck.

Bree ran a hand through her golden hair. "When I took you through the veil to go to Hades, Tristan, I wasn't allowed to remain in the Otherworld, but they did allow me to stay temporarily. The Angels—"

"Did they tell you where Dorian is?" I broke in with excitement.

"No." She frowned. "I'm sorry. It must not be my place to know. But they did say I'll be meeting them again soon, so maybe . . ." Her voice trailed off as she gave a noncommittal shrug, leaving me with little confidence they would help. "For now, though, they ordered me to take care of that stone of yours once and for all so we don't have any more issues with it."

I reached my hands behind my neck, but paused. "What does that mean? Take care of it?"

She held out her hand and wiggled her fingers. "I'm going to make sure you can't lose it again so easily—or that it can't be taken from you. I'm going to make it permanently in your possession."

Tristan and I exchanged a look, but he gave me a nod. With a little trepidation, I dropped the pendant into Bree's hand.

"Sorry about the artwork, Tristan," she said as she twisted the red triangular stone out of the pendant he'd designed, then dropped the silver into his hand. "But this is a better way for Alexis to keep the stone."

She then moved my leather jacket to the side and pulled the bustier down to expose the Amadis mark on the rise of my left breast. Tristan and I traded another look as Bree cupped her hand over the mark and pressed the rock against my skin.

"Is this okay?" she asked.

Understanding now, I gave her my consent, then gasped as a warm tingle fluttered into my flesh, followed by the stone. After several heartbeats, Bree pulled her hand away and nodded her approval. The Angel stone hadn't sunken down and hidden in my heart, as it had with Tristan when he was a little boy. Rather, it had embedded itself into my skin, a ruby-colored embellishment to my Amadis mark. In fact, the stone had settled into the hilt of the sword in the design, similar in appearance to the amethyst in the hilt of my dagger.

"Will my skin grow around it?" I asked, perplexed.

"No," Bree said. "You want it exposed to do what it needs to do for Tristan. But now your connection will remain strong and steady, and no one can take it away ever again."

Well. I would take this bit of goodness after all the bad in the past seven days that felt like seven lifetimes. If only we had time to try out the stone's fertility qualities. But Tristan was right—the sooner we met Rina's demands, the sooner we could begin the search for our son. And right now, Dorian was more important than the daughter we may never have. At least, in my eyes he was.

With that bit of business finished, we could finally set off. The Amadis jet *had* been waiting on us, and within two hours of hanging up with Mom, we were ready for takeoff.

"Ms. Alexis," the pilot said before closing the cockpit door, "I suggest all of you find a seat for the duration and buckle your belts. We've been ordered to travel at warlock speed."

"Warlock speed?" I asked.

"Yes. My copilot will be giving us a magical boost so we can cut the travel time in half."

"Oh," I said with mild surprise. I knew the Amadis jet kept a warlock on crew for safety reasons, but didn't realize he could serve another purpose. At least Rina agreed we didn't have time to waste. Which meant she really did have a good reason to see us in person— maybe more than to give my team and me a scolding about following orders and doing our duties? I could always hope.

Sheree and Blossom fidgeted in their seats for the entire trip, both of them nervous to go to Amadis Island and possibly meet Rina. Although Mom hadn't specifically said Rina wanted to talk to all of us, why else would she call my whole team? Probably to lecture them about keeping me on task. Making sure they understood what lay on the line if they followed my errant lead. And that dilemma caused most of their high-strung nerves—they wanted to go after Dorian as badly as I did, but hated the idea of defying the matriarch's orders. In other words, they didn't want to have to choose between Rina and me. Charlotte sat with them on the cream-colored leather sofa grouping, trying to calm them, but I couldn't blame them for being a little edgy.

And Vanessa . . . the vamp wasn't just nervous. Sitting in a row of seats by herself, she was downright frightened, wringing her hands and staring out the window with wide, glazed-over eyes. She trembled so hard, I was surprised she didn't throw the whole jet off course or into a spin. Her fear was somewhat understandable—she'd done a lot of horrific things to the Amadis in the past—but she had to know by now that forgiveness had already been granted. Clemency was part of becoming Amadis.

So why was she so scared? Was I right to be suspicious? Had the last several days, or even months, been nothing but an act on her part? Were we taking our enemy right into the heart of the Amadis? With all of the betrayal lately, I couldn't help but wonder. Especially after everything she'd put us through before and during her conversion.

Charlotte came over to the group of chairs where Tristan and I sat and slid into a seat across from us. She tapped her temple, and I tuned into her mind while burying my fingers into Sasha's fur as the lykora slept on my lap.

"*You should go talk to Vanessa,*" she said. "*She's a wreck, and a jumpy vampire isn't an asset. I'd do it, but she's wary of me and seems to trust you.*"

I chuckled to myself at the irony. *Well, I don't trust her. I don't know if I ever can completely.*

"*Then what's she doing here? Trust is necessary for us to succeed.*"
We don't have anywhere else to put her.

"*Maybe you should leave her on Amadis Island, then. Let the Island—*"
Absolutely not. I wouldn't dare.

Char let out a sigh. "*I feel the Amadis in her and not a trace of Daemoni.*"

I looked out the window at the dark ocean below us. *Yeah, well, nobody sensed Daemoni on Martin, either, did they?*

She didn't respond, and I knew that was a low blow, but it made my point.

"*She's not Martin, and definitely not Kali,*" she eventually said.

I shrugged. *I still don't trust her.*

"*Alexis.*" Charlotte paused until I returned my gaze to her. "*You need to talk to her as much for yourself as for her.*"

I glanced over at Vanessa, somewhat content to see the normally cocky vamp looking frightened. We'd been through so much together, and her hatred of Lucas and the Daemoni had felt very real, especially while we were struggling to escape Hades. We'd worked well as a team, and I *had* trusted her. Until we came home to a nightmare. Tristan and I had thought her desire to convert had been a trick, but we'd let Owen convince us otherwise. But now I couldn't trust Owen. So maybe Tristan and I had been right in the beginning. I didn't say this to Char, though.

I don't think a little fear is a bad thing for her, I said instead. *If anything, it's humbling her, which she needs before she sees Rina. And I'll feel a lot better after Rina assesses her.*

Charlotte pursed her lips, but nodded. "*I'll be ready to throw a shield, but I think if Vanessa does anything, it'll be more out of nerves than malice. As surprised as I am, I personally can't deny what I feel from her.*"

I wondered if she'd feel the same if she knew Vanessa's amorous feelings for Owen . . . and that Owen had possibly felt the same about the vamp. But it wasn't my place to tell her. Besides, I didn't need to add any more drama to my already battered team. Even if Rina declared Vanessa clean of all evil, we had enough problems. No need to create more.

I closed my eyes, done with the subject of Vanessa and wanting to focus on my son instead. My heart ached with the pain of missing Dorian, but the ire swelled again, which was good. I needed that fire to remain fed, because if it died, my heart would go cold and die with it, leaving only ashes of memories to blow away in the wind.

Mom met us at the runway although it was nearly midnight here, and swallowed me in a hug as soon as I stepped off the plane and onto Amadis Island. The island itself gave me a burst of positive energy I desperately needed, along with Mom's love. I clung to her small body, happy to see her even under the circumstances. Even with her coldhearted demands of me. After all, I hadn't seen her for nearly a year.

"We have a very short time and much to accomplish," Mom said when she pulled away from me and eyed the rest of my team in the darkness. I didn't know why Rina had insisted on us leaving so quickly when we'd arrive here in the middle of the night. "The matriarch has been anxiously waiting for your arrival. Come with me."

7

WE FOLLOWED MOM'S flash to the other end of Amadis Island and into the matriarch's mansion, where fires in the hearths and torches in the wall sconces threw an eerie dance of light and shadow onto the walls and everyone's faces. Vanessa's eyes bounced around wildly, her body tense as a tightly coiled spring ready to burst free. But if she'd truly had anything to worry about, she wouldn't have come off the plane. Actually, she wouldn't have stepped foot on the jet in the first place, because both the plane and the island were shielded, meaning she had no escape. So either she was letting her guilt get the best of her—or she'd signed up for a suicide mission, knowing she'd die here if she attempted anything.

We stood in the grand foyer where the staircase swept upwards to the second and third floors, and Mom turned to look at us. Her focus fell on Vanessa.

"The matriarch wants to see you first," she said to the vampire before looking at the rest of us. "You may wait in the sitting room. I'll be back in a moment."

Vanessa's gaze found me, her eyes wide. "*Is she going to do that mind-spying thing you can both do?*"

I shrugged. *Probably, but if you have nothing to hide, there's nothing to worry about. Right?*

Her eyes tightened, and her lips pursed. "*It's like letting her peer into my soul.*"

If you're truly converted like everyone believes, including yourself, then your soul is wiped clean.

She rolled her eyes. "*You know what I mean. My memories are still there.*"

Mom had already crossed the foyer and stopped at the doorway to the corridor that led to Rina's office. She looked over her shoulder at Vanessa.

"The matriarch is waiting," she said.

Vanessa still hesitated, and unable to help myself, I reached over and patted her arm. "You'll be fine. Go on."

I didn't point out that she should probably worry more about being alone with Mom than with Rina. After all, Vanessa had been taught to hate the matriarch, but she'd chosen to be a total bitch to Mom all on her own. Of course, if Vanessa was fooling all of us, this could be her opportunity to take Mom out. I ran a check for mind signatures and found Julia's in the same hallway Mom and Vanessa headed down. So neither would be left alone with the other. Which was probably a good thing.

Tristan and I led Charlotte, Blossom, Sheree, and Bree through the doorway from the main foyer and into the sitting room. The room looked the same as it always had—a fire burning in the large stone hearth, two brown leather couches sitting perpendicular to the fire with a table between them, and tapestries hanging on the walls. Including the one that covered an entire wall by itself and depicted the Ames family vine, with silvery-green leaves for the daughters and brown ones for the sons.

My eyes zeroed in on Dorian's leaf, which had not yet separated from the vine like the other sons' leaves had. I didn't know if that meant there was still hope for him, or if the tapestry simply hadn't been updated yet. Obviously, I chose to believe in hope. In fact, if the leaf were to fall off the vine in front of my eyes this very moment, I wouldn't believe it. I'd yank the thing down, wad it up, and throw it in the fire before I took that to mean anything.

None of us seemed to be able to relax enough to sit in the sitting room. Charlotte and Bree stood by the fire warming themselves, Sheree and Blossom inspected the images in the tapestries, I paced, and Tristan watched me, though his mind didn't really see me. It focused on the same thoughts mine did—all about Dorian. Where was he? Who was he with? What were they doing to him?

Mom returned in a few moments, sans Vanessa. "Bree, Blossom, and Sheree, we have guest suites available for you. Charlotte, I assume you'll be staying in your own place?"

"What do you mean, staying?" I interrupted. "We don't need rooms or beds or anything. We can sleep on the plane on the way back."

"Alexis, you're not going straight back. Maybe tomorrow night or the next day. Rina has plans for you all, but for now, you may as well rest."

What are they up to now? Another distraction? I stared at my mother for a long moment, into her deep brown eyes.

"She needs to assess Vanessa and wants to spend time with her," Mom explained. "She wants to spend time with each of you. Please be patient."

Patient? When my son was out there? Yeah, right.

"*Alexis, darling,*" Rina said in my head, "*relax. I promise you will not regret your time here.*"

My nostrils flared, but I bit my tongue. I regretted every single minute I wasn't searching for Dorian, but I kept my promise to Tristan that we would do as they asked.

"I'll stay at my place, of course." Charlotte finally answered Mom's question when she realized we had little choice in the matter.

Mom nodded. "Very good. Can you stay here for a minute, though? I'd like these three to get settled, but I have something to ask of you."

Char cocked her head, questioning Mom, but no explanation came. Instead, Mom led Bree, Blossom, and Sheree out of the sitting room and up the stairs to the second floor guest suites.

"Dorian's room is on the third floor, right?" Blossom asked, her voice carrying down the stone stairs.

"Yes," Mom answered.

"I can feel his presence," Blossom said.

Mom didn't say anything right away, but then replied, "I think you'll make an excellent converter. You're very intuitive."

"I'd never thought about it until Alexis mentioned something before..." Blossom's voice trailed off, but I knew "before" what. Before shit hit the fan. Before our safe house fell. Before Dorian was taken.

Mom murmured something to Blossom, but she'd dropped her voice low and they'd moved too far away for even me to make out the words. I didn't bother eavesdropping on their thoughts. If Mom—or Rina, the council, or anyone else—blamed Blossom at all, I'd hear about it soon enough and clarify everything. Otherwise, Mom would be telling her what I already had: it hadn't been her fault. The blame fell squarely on me, and I'd paid the ultimate price for it. The piece of my heart that walked in this world outside of my body had been taken from me.

Char remained by the fire, I paced again, and Tristan waited patiently for Mom to return, which didn't take long. With just the three of us, she must have felt more herself, because her whole body sagged, as though she'd been keeping up a pretense of strength and leadership for everyone else's sake and could finally discard it. She and Charlotte exchanged a look and then fell into each other's arms for a long embrace. For the first time since I'd returned from Hades, I saw real emotion on Charlotte's face.

My heart, already in pieces, broke into smaller ones for her.

Her son was officially a traitor. How does a mother deal with that? Dorian hadn't chosen to leave us for the enemy, but Owen had. He'd deserted his primary job of protecting me right when I'd needed him most and had possibly done the exact opposite—hurt me worse than anyone could physically do. He'd basically told me and the rest of the Amadis, including his mother, to fuck off, because he'd rather serve Kali. The very soul that had hijacked his father's body. I knew how *I* felt about that, but couldn't imagine Charlotte's feelings. Actually, being a writer, I probably could imagine them, but didn't want to. I had enough bad feelings to deal with already regarding Owen and my own son.

"Well, we're not dead yet," Mom murmured as she still held her longtime friend.

"Then we must be getting stronger," Char said. She gave Mom a final squeeze before stepping away. They traded small, sad smiles. "Which we'll need to be."

"Yes, we will." Mom continued scrutinizing Char's face.

"I'll be okay, Sophia," the warlock said. "I have a lot of faith."

Mom studied her friend one last moment, then finally nodded. "Go get some rest. I'm sure you need it. Can you muffle the room for me first, though?"

"Sure." Char said her goodbyes to all of us, and then she headed for the door while moving her hands around and out. She gave Mom a final nod before disappearing to the place she kept on Amadis Island.

Mom rushed over to me and threw her arms around me again, just as she had when I'd first come off the jet. She held me tightly against her while one hand stroked down my hair and back.

"Honey, I am so, so sorry," she said, her voice a little choked. "I really am. I've been trying to be what everyone else needs me to be, but all I can think about is our boy. Our little boy out there, probably scared to death. I keep trying to think of how we can do something, but—"

I pulled away from her to see her face. "What do you mean?"

Since she couldn't hold me in her arms, she took my hands into hers. "You're right, Alexis, this wasn't supposed to happen. Not now. Not like this. Dorian was kidnapped, and if he were any other Amadis child, everyone, including Rina and the council, would be all over it. But ... unfortunately ..."

"They're not," Tristan finished for her.

She shook her head, her eyes filled with misery. "He's an Amadis son. It's his destiny. And nobody can argue with that fact, not when it's happened consistently for over two thousand years."

"But you don't agree with it?" I asked, hope fluttering within me. If I could convince Mom to back me up, maybe she'd persuade Rina to change her mind, and the council would have to accept her decision.

"It doesn't matter what I think. Or you, either of you," she said, looking to Tristan and then at me. She released my hands to push her own through her hair as she turned and paced a few strides before turning back. "That's what you need to understand. I want to go after Dorian as much as you do, honey. And Owen, too, the little . . ." She didn't finish, but I could imagine what she wanted to call him. "Believe me. But I meant what I said on the phone. We have a duty. Thousands of people—billions if you include all of humanity—need us."

Anger replaced the hope I'd felt only moments ago, and my muscles tensed. "I told you. I get it."

"I don't think you do," she said. "But you need to. Earlier today, when you and Blossom were about to work that spell—my sense focused on you. I knew what you were doing, and I secretly hoped it would work. But Alexis, I was also in a meeting with Rina and the council. She was too tired to be in the room physically, but she attended mentally, which meant her mind had been open to all of us. When I sensed the truth about you, she knew, and the whole council did, too. You can't be doing stuff like that."

"Maybe you should stop focusing your sense on me," I suggested not too kindly. "Especially when Rina's mind is connected to yours."

She let out a sigh. "Easier said than done. You're my daughter. He's my grandson. I can't stop worrying about you. It's not a conscious decision to focus my sense on you right now. I can't help it. It goes to you automatically."

Great. Tristan and I looked at each other, silently sharing the same thoughts. This would be a serious problem if we continued with our own plan to rescue Dorian. With everything else going on in the world, she could surely train her sense on those things, but saying so now would only tell her we were up to something—something she, Rina, and the council wouldn't sanction.

"I can't just let him go, Mom," I said quietly.

"I know." She drew me back into her arms, and if I wasn't so angry about the whole thing, I might have finally cried. It felt good to be held by my mom again. "Trust me, I know. But unless something changes, you're going to have to. At least make it look like you are. If I can find a way to persuade everyone that rescuing Dorian is in all of our best interests, I will. But so far, I haven't been able to. Even pursuing Kali or Owen can't be justified in their eyes. Not when all of humanity need us elsewhere."

I could tell by her voice, by the way she held me, by the exhaustion in her eyes she truly had tried. And she would keep trying in her own way.

"In the meantime," she said, "I have to keep you on track. There are too many lives at stake. Too many souls. So please don't hate me for it."

"I could never hate you, Mom. I love you."

"I love you, too, honey. And Tristan and Dorian. Very much. Maybe . . . maybe we'll find a way."

She left us with that bit of hope at the entrance to our wing on the third floor. But after the warmth of the heart-to-heart wore off, I realized there really wasn't much hope in what she'd said. I was glad to know she hadn't completely dismissed Dorian, that she loved him and wanted to keep him with us. But she didn't want it badly enough. Not as badly as Tristan and I did. We would risk it all to save our son. Thank goodness we had others who were willing to help.

I AWOKE IN our suite at the butt-crack of dawn, no longer able to sleep, although it had only been four hours since I'd laid my head down. The other side of the bed was empty—Tristan apparently couldn't sleep, either. I found his mind signature in the gym behind the mansion, and his thoughts were tightly focused on Lucas as his body beat the hell out of a punching bag. I let him be and felt out for other minds that were awake. Three so far—Mom, Vanessa, and Ophelia, the head of staff in the mansion.

After laying in bed until I couldn't lie there a second longer, I showered and dressed, then made my way to the kitchen to find Ophelia already pouring coffee for me in the dining room.

"Ms. Alexis," she said with a curtsy. "Chocolate croissants and strawberries?"

I didn't feel exceptionally hungry, but now that I thought about it, I couldn't remember the last time I ate. "Some bacon, too. Thank you."

Ophelia inclined her head, then disappeared, only to reappear a minute later with my breakfast. I'd barely begun eating when Mom joined me at the table, followed by Vanessa, who looked considerably calmer than she had the last time I saw her.

"*She spent almost the entire night with Rina,*" Mom said silently to me. I lifted a brow. "*You can talk to Rina about it later.*"

Vanessa only stayed long enough for Ophelia to bring her a glass of what might have looked like tomato or vegetable juice to a Norman—it even had a celery stalk and a parsley sprig for flourish— but I knew better. The vampire took her breakfast and disappeared. Mom shook her head after Vanessa left.

"It's still hard to believe, but can't be denied," she said quietly.

"Her conversion or that she's my sister? Because I'm not sure I totally believe either yet."

"Oh, I sensed the truth about her being Lucas's daughter decades ago, but he would never confirm it, even when we were together."

"*Seriously?*" I demanded. "You knew, and you didn't bother to say anything to me? To anyone?"

"I said I *sensed* it, but I didn't know for certain." Mom reached across the table and placed her hand over mine. "Until she decided to come to us, there were too many risks and no benefit in spreading possible rumors. *She* didn't know for certain until the other day, right? I feared what she might do to you if she knew, and also how it would affect you if I told you, especially if my sense happened to be wrong. She was Daemoni. Our enemy. Things might have been different if I'd known what she really wanted back when I took Tristan."

"She told you about that?" I asked, somewhat surprised Vanessa disclosed so much. "How she'd wanted to convert when he did?"

"She told us many things. She didn't think herself ready then, but I might have been able to help her." She sighed sadly, but then her voice lifted. "But it all happened the way it was supposed to, and she's here with us now. As I said, Rina will tell you more when you see her."

I finished chewing my bite of croissant as I watched Mom. "I know it's how we're supposed to be, but you sure did forgive easily. Vanessa hasn't exactly been your biggest fan for the last thirty years."

"That *is* how we are," Mom said with a shrug. "We forgive. But . . . we may not forget. I won't forget what she's done to you and me, to other Amadis, and to innocents, but it's all in the past. She's not the same person anymore."

"Hmm . . . " came my only response.

Mom pushed her chair away from the table and stood. "I need to get some work done before Rina wakes up."

"How's she doing, anyway?"

Mom grabbed the back of her seat to push it under the table, and the corners of her mouth twitched, but I didn't know if she was trying to force a smile or fight a frown. "Not well, to be honest. Not as well as I'd hoped she'd be by now."

I picked the stem off a strawberry leaf by leaf. "I thought maybe since she stayed up all night, she was doing better."

"She took a long nap yesterday afternoon to be ready for you and your guests."

"Oh." Not the news I'd wanted to hear.

"She did warn us that she'd never fully recover, but I'd hoped she'd been wrong. She tires easily. She has me doing a lot on her behalf for official business and Julia taking care of other tasks." Mom's eyes darted around the room as she inhaled an unsteady breath. "I honestly don't know how much longer we have with her, honey. Although . . . she can be quite stubborn, so who really knows?"

She gave me a quick smile and a hug before hurrying out of the room, as though trying to escape the subject. Mom and Rina had never been very close. Mom had resented Rina and the council after my birth because of the control they tried to exert over both of our lives, but I thought there were lots of hurt feelings between them that went back further. In fact, I suspected their relationship began to deteriorate when they were both Normans, before Rina had left Mom to go through her *Ang'dora*. Now, however, it seemed as though Mom wanted to make up for all of their history. Maybe she wanted to close the gap in their relationship because hers and mine wasn't as close anymore now that we had separate lives. Or maybe she simply knew time with her mother would be short, as she'd just said.

I pushed my plate away and stood, not wanting to be here alone. Not wanting to think about losing Rina.

I considered releasing some stress by working out with Tristan, but I had the feeling he wanted time alone, and I really didn't want to spend my energy on beating up a sandbag. I didn't want that kind of release. I wanted answers, direction, guidance. Since I was stuck here, I figured I might as well make the best use of my time. And I knew the place that might hold the secrets I needed to know. With the house so quiet, it was a perfect time to check out the Sacred Archives.

Apparently I wasn't the only one who thought so.

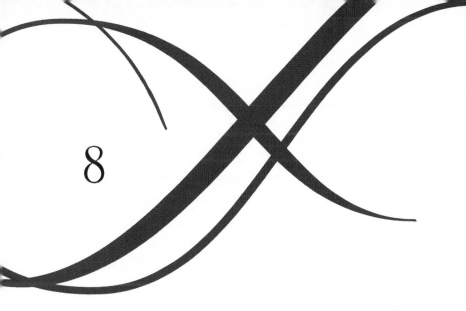

8

WHEN I ROUNDED the corner between Rina's office and the hallway to the Sacred Archives, I found the door ajar and my grandmother inside. The room glowed around her in that luminous way it does, and she looked as majestic as the day I first met her, wearing a pale pink ball gown, her chestnut-brown hair tumbling in curls down her back, her skin healthy and beautiful. Although she was over a hundred years older than me, she didn't look a day over twenty-eight. She, Mom, and I could practically pass for triplets. Until you looked into Rina's eyes and saw the wisdom of time, or into Mom's and saw the strength one could only gain from decades of living with heartache. Me—you still saw youth and inexperience. In fact, I did look a few years younger than them, more like early twenties or younger. I was practically an infant compared to them, and nowhere near ready to serve as matriarch. Good thing I had a long time. Even if Mom was right about Rina, hopefully we had a few decades or longer of Mom holding the seat of matriarch before anyone had to rely on me.

"Alexis?"

I came out of my thought-trance at the sound of Rina's voice. She stood outside the door of the Sacred Archives now, and something about her had changed. Without the Otherworldly glow of the room, I could now see the tightness in her brow, the tug downwards at the corners of her lips, the exhaustion in her eyes. Her skin and hair seemed less bright, the coloring in both more sallow. She held her arms out for me, and when I hugged her, her embrace didn't feel as strong as it had in the past. I couldn't help but think the Sacred Archives had given her Otherworldly strength, but the Earthly realm drained her of it.

"Shouldn't you be in bed?" I asked, the concern obvious in my voice. "Mom said you were up all night."

Rina tsked. "Your mother exaggerates. I had four hours of regeneration, much of it in the Sacred Archives. That is plenty, considering."

"Mom worries about you." Rightly so, it seemed.

Rina let go of me with one arm, holding her other around my waist as she began to walk toward her office. I kept an arm around her, too, and I'd say she pulled me with her, but it was more like I held her up, giving me no choice but to go with her because I was afraid she'd fall.

"A little too much," Rina said. "There is much else for us to worry about."

We paused for her to open the door, and although her breaths seemed to come evenly, I could feel the tightness of her muscles under my fingers as she struggled for air.

"Please stop," she said, her voice sounding firmer than I'd expected with her condition. "Do not worry about me. I am strong enough to do what needs to be done, which is all that matters. When it is my time, it is my time. Only God knows when it will be, and there is no use in wasting our energy worrying about what we cannot change. Your mother is strong, and she will be ready to be matriarch when the time comes. As will you, dear Alexis."

I stifled a snort, but she must have seen the doubt on my face as I helped her sit in the throne-like chair behind her huge mahogany desk. She smiled.

"I know you do not believe it now, but you *will* be ready when your time comes, darling. For now, however, you are our warrior."

I let out a small chuckle. Ten years ago I would have never thought such a thing. Actually, *three* years ago I wouldn't have believed it. But now I knew *warrior* was the right term for me.

"A warrior, like Tristan. And we need that right now." She motioned for me to sit down in one of the chairs across the desk from her. "Sophia is emotionally and spiritually strong, but not physically. Her blood is too diluted. She has her power of persuasion and can often sense the truth, and that makes her a powerful converter. She is just and fair. But physically, she does not compare. She is faster and stronger than Normans, but we do not fight Normans. She can channel water when a large body is nearby and fight for a while against the Daemoni. But, she is not a warrior. She is not you, Alexis."

I'd started to wonder where Rina was going with this inventory of Mom's strengths and weaknesses, but now she made her point: I may have looked like Mom and Rina, and we may have shared a few other similarities, but I was set apart from them. I was different. As always.

"Sophia and I are meant to lead from here." She lifted her hands and spread them to indicate her surroundings. "From this desk, this office. You, darling, will one day be here, too, but not now. As much as the council wants to fight me about it and keep you here on the island to ensure your safety and that of our next daughter, I know this is not where you need to be. Whether you believe you are ready to lead or not, your time has come—"

This time I couldn't hold back the snort.

"Your time has come," she repeated, "for the battlefield. That is where you belong."

"I think I would go crazy here on the island," I admitted. "Especially right now. Please don't let them—"

Rina cut me off. "I know, darling. I will not make you stay here, regardless of what the council thinks. At least, not until you become pregnant, at which time, we re-evaluate. However, we do need to discuss your current directives."

Here it comes. The lecture I'd been expecting since we left Florida was about to start.

"First, though, I have other business to address. Preparations to make before I send you and your team away." She glanced at an antique clock sitting on her desk. "Give me a few hours, then I will call for you and Tristan, yes?"

I understood the dismissal and nodded before I stood and headed for the door. After leaving Rina's office, I returned to the Sacred Archives. The door still stood open, as though waiting for me, and I basked for a moment in the change in the air, how it smelled and tasted like sunshine, how it felt thicker but somehow cleaner against my skin—the air of the Otherworld, I was sure. But once inside, I found nothing useful. I still couldn't decipher the swirly lines and images that covered the pages in the majority of the books—symbols I thought the Angels might have made. I called for the *Book of Prophecies & Curses*, and once again, it floated through the air to me. Although I could read the Latin now, nothing in its pages helped.

I studied the curse about the brothers more closely, but there was no new information to gain. No clear-cut answer on how to break it.

An Amadis person must sacrifice themselves to the Daemoni to benefit the greater good, but nothing stated who or when or how. Tristan apparently hadn't broken the curse when he'd gone to the Daemoni to protect all of us, so it couldn't be just anyone in the Amadis. It had to be someone specific. A daughter? A son? The matriarch? Or perhaps a certain situation. Lucas had said if he kept me against my will and Dorian tried to save me, the curse would be broken. But I didn't know if that meant Dorian could break it, or if the fact that he was saving an Amadis daughter would break it, or if Lucas had any clue at all what he was talking about. He could have been bullshitting me, and probably was. He probably planned to lead me down a rabbit hole with such a lie.

I studied the prophecies again, too, and found the one Vanessa had been told belonged to her. But I found no prediction that any of us would break Eris's curse. No foretelling of Dorian being kidnapped or anything indicating he would ever return to us. The Angels were not being very helpful.

Or maybe I wasn't ready to understand their messages.

The hours dragged by as I waited for our turn to speak with Rina. I felt as though she was putting all the pieces into place before talking to Tristan and me, and once we did receive her lecture, we could finally be on our way. Until then, I was like a horse in a starting gate, my competitors already halfway around the track while I still pawed at the ground waiting for release.

Blossom and I spent some time in Dorian's room, and her spell gave us a big push west, but my mind couldn't reach beyond the Aegean Sea to the mainland of Greece. If the strength of the shove to go west was any indication, Dorian remained much farther away than I could ever reach. Blossom, however, couldn't make the spell focus beyond that general direction, and Rina interrupted us to request

Blossom's audience. After a lengthy meeting with the matriarch and her second, the witch immediately went to the village on an errand she couldn't tell me about.

And still Tristan and I waited. Until, finally, Rina silently called out for us.

As we approached her office, I couldn't believe whom we found coming out of Rina's door, closing it behind him.

"*Jax?*" I asked, my eyes popping at the sight of the big, bald were-croc who should have been in the Outback of Australia.

"G'day, princess," he said with a grin.

"What the hell are you doing here?"

He pushed his hands into the pockets of his faded jeans and shrugged nonchalantly, but a frown tugged the scar over his brown eye, betraying his true feelings.

"Kuckaroo never got to be all right again," he said, and I knew he spoke of the Daemoni attack when we were there two years ago. "We lost too many mages. Now that hell's breakin' loose, those who can't fight came here for safety."

I tilted my head as I studied his face and considered this. Jax was mighty and powerful and not someone who'd hide instead of fight . . . unless he worried about being around Normans too much, which had been the whole reason he'd isolated himself to the wilderness.

"I'm here for a diffr'nt reason," he said. His eyes slid over to Rina's office door and back to me. "Ms. Katerina just gave me her blessin'."

"Speaking of," Tristan murmured next to me.

Right. Rina. I didn't need to delay any longer.

"I wish we had time to talk, but, well—"

"I know, princess. No worries. We'll have time to catch up later." He gave me a wink, then strode off toward the main entrance of the mansion. Nothing against Jax, but I hoped there wouldn't be a later—that we'd be in the air shortly after this meeting.

"*Come in, darling,*" Rina called out before I could knock.

As soon as I saw her form, sagging as though the weight of the world physically rested on her shoulders, worry crept into my heart.

"Do you need to rest?" I asked, feeling guilty as I secretly hoped she'd say no.

She gave me a soft smile from her seat in one of the wingback chairs by the fireplace. "I can regenerate anytime, but this is an urgent matter. I have someone I would like to join your team, and some things must be said by the matriarch. Your mother may be my second and doing much of my work, but people accept some messages more powerfully when delivered by me personally."

Tristan and I sat on the leather sofa next to her, and we both leaned forward on the edge of the seat. The hairs on the nape of my neck prickled with curiosity. Not about the new addition to my team. I knew she'd send Julia to watch over us and ensure we followed the Amadis rules and stuck to the mission. Charlotte had prepared me for this possibility during our flight over. I didn't like it—I didn't like Julia—but arguing about her would be futile, and we had more important things to discuss. Especially now that Rina had mentioned messages.

"Like what things? What kinds of messages?" From the Angels, maybe? Were they going to help us get Dorian?

Rina's mahogany brown eyes scanned my face with consideration. "You, for example, need to believe Vanessa is trustworthy."

My shoulders deflated, and I sunk back against the sofa. "Do you believe she is?"

"I have assessed her. We spent much time together. Yes, I believe she is." She flattened her hands against her thighs and tilted her head. "No, I do not only believe. I *know* she is."

"A message from the Angels?" Tristan asked. "Because they might be the only ones who will convince your granddaughter here."

Not the message I'd hoped for, but Tristan was right—their confirmation about Vanessa would have been comforting.

"No, not from the Angels. A message is not necessary. Vanessa is fully converted. You have done a very fine job, Alexis."

With all of my prior insecurities, Rina must have thought I doubted my own conversion abilities. She didn't know how complicated Vanessa's situation was, with her involvement with Owen, the traitor, and all.

"I know it all, dear, but I also know what is in her heart and in her soul. I feel it so completely, I have sent her into the village for enhancements—her own leather gear, enchanted weapons, and a supply of mage blood suited to her particular needs."

"And you think that's a good idea?" I asked, pretty skeptical myself. If Vanessa was pulling one over on us, the last thing I needed was her powered up with mage blood.

"I do. If she is to guard you, she will have every advantage we can possibly give her. I also have spent time with Blossom, and now she is with your mother and Charlotte, taking a—what do you call it? A crash course?—heavy training in conversions."

"That's great, but it's not Blossom I'm worried about," I muttered.

"You do not need to worry about Vanessa, either. Just as you accept Tristan for the man he is *now*, you must accept Vanessa for who she is now, not then."

Of course she was right, and I really wanted to. Life would be a bit easier if I knew Vanessa was definitely on our side. But there were still too many questions in my mind, regardless of what Rina said.

"Your family has grown again," Rina said. "Embrace it, darling. Family is very special."

I twisted in my seat to face her more fully and leaned toward her. "It *is* special. All family is. Including our sons."

Rina's mouth formed a scowl as she looked away from me and to the flames dancing in the hearth. Did she really think we could avoid the subject? Or maybe she'd only been waiting for me to bring it up. A moment passed before her gaze returned to me.

"The Amadis *is* our family, Alexis," she said. "We are called a matriarchal society because I—like my predecessors—am a mother to our people. They are all my children, and I love them as though they are. I must care for *all* of them. As will you some day."

So I'd been summoned here for a lecture after all. I'd hoped I might be able to convince her to let me look for Dorian while we built our army so we wouldn't have to be secretive about it, but she had nothing more to say than what Mom had already told me. I had a duty. There would be no changing her mind. I had to go with Tristan's scheme and say what needed to be said so we could be on our way.

I reached for Tristan's hand and squeezed it. I pulled on his strength, needing it to give me the composure I required.

"I know. I already do love them like family." Which wasn't a lie. I *did* love the Amadis people. "I will do what it takes to protect them."

"Including those who are not part of us yet. Those taken by the enemy."

"Yes," I agreed sincerely. After all, I did want to help the innocents. "And I'll build our army. My team and I will."

Rina nodded with approval. "Very good, darling. Doing so is as paramount to our survival as is your having a daughter."

"Tristan and I will work on that as well," I said automatically. *If we have the time* . . . Of course, we'd make time. We had to, not only for the Amadis, but also for our own relationship.

"Oh, I am sure you will," my grandmother said with a small smile.

"So, see? You had nothing to worry about." I bit my tongue about what a waste of time this trip had been. Although, Vanessa and Blossom were benefitting, so maybe it wasn't a complete waste.

"Alexis," she said, her voice quieter than before, "I do understand where your heart is. I understand the conflict you feel."

Now it was my turn to look away and study the flames. Did she understand? Did she really have any idea? At least when she lost Noah, she'd thought him dead. His soul safe. She didn't have to worry about what evil things were being done to her son, what kind of beast they were turning him into, because she had no idea the Daemoni even existed. She didn't have a clue what I was going through right now.

"I would have done anything for my son, Noah, if I had known he was still alive," she continued. "However, I had *not* known. I thought he had passed with his father in the bakery fire. I had already mourned his loss decades before I learned he still lived."

"And when you found out?" My eyes swung to her to study her face.

"Of course, I wanted to save him right away. As soon as I learned the truth about the Amadis and the Daemoni, about us, I thought he could be the first soul I saved." She let out a sigh pregnant with grief. "But I realized quickly the cause was already lost."

I gasped. "He's lost his soul? Given it over to the Daemoni?"

Rina's eyes moistened, and her gaze dropped to her hands as she folded them in her lap. "I do not know for sure. He has kept himself secluded for nearly a century now. But I know the Otherworld requires balance. I know now—and I knew then—my Noah was no longer my son. I had and still have Sophia. The Daemoni have Noah. And there is absolutely nothing we can do to change that."

I wanted to argue the point, and feeling me tense against him, Tristan squeezed my hand, warning me not to. But it took all of my control to hold back. Not only could we change things if we discovered how to break the curse, but more urgently, my son's situation was completely different. Besides the fact that he'd been stolen, not summoned, his being taken didn't do anything for balance, especially since we didn't have a daughter. And there was something we *could* do about Dorian. Maybe we couldn't rescue Noah or the other sons—not yet anyway—but there *was* still hope for our son.

Saying any of this remained pointless, though, and I had to keep my promise to Tristan. We'd obviously never convince her to allow us to search for Dorian. She probably brought up the subject of Noah as a way for me to see we had such a tragedy in common, and I needed to suck it up like my ancestors did and move on. If she and the council believed I'd actually give in so easily, though, they were sadly mistaken. Because my whole heart told me not to—not to give up on Dorian, not to let him go. Not yet. It wasn't his time. First with Tristan, second with me, and then with Dorian, change had come to the world of the Amadis and the Daemoni, and the Amadis needed to change with it. They should have learned this already with everything going on, but if I had to be the one to show them that things could be different, starting with Dorian, then I would.

"I had believed there was nothing we can do for all of these years," Rina continued. "But I believe it no longer. Something can be done. We have our duty, and we cannot stray from it, but I believe there is some way we can serve our sons. There is something happening to them. I do not know the specifics, but I believe we must act. And we start with Dorian."

My gaze shot to her eyes as my pulse sped with surprise. "Are you saying . . . ?"

I couldn't finish the thought, scared I'd misinterpreted her meaning. Trying not to let my hope soar too high that she was actually giving her blessing to our plan, I braced myself. Tristan's hand squeezed my thigh in anticipation as we both leaned forward, hanging on her every word.

Her lips danced, and the smile showed in her eyes, piercing through the cloud of sadness. "It would be a lovely miracle if you could save all the sons. Including my Noah."

9

WHOA. MY HAND flew to my mouth. I hadn't been expecting *that* kind of a blessing.

"Do you think we can break the curse?" I asked, my voice full of both confusion and disbelief.

Rina tilted her head. "I cannot tell you that. I cannot even confirm the curse exists. But I do believe we can help the Summoned in some way. My intelligence team has noticed they, as well as many of their offspring, have gone missing in the last several months. Some may have disappeared as long as a year ago or more."

"Wait. How many brothers are still alive?" I asked.

"Oh, darling, they live much longer than we do," Rina said. "I know of at least six brothers, but when Tristan first came to us, he said there are more who have been in hiding. Perhaps all of them, back to Andronika's son. Is that so, Tristan?"

"I'd heard rumors, but never confirmed it myself," he clarified. "I don't think Lucas even knows. When I was still with them, though, I knew of at least nine who were still alive."

My jaw dropped. "And they're *all* missing?"

"The ones we know about, yes," Rina said. "As well as some of their descendants."

Wow. I hadn't realized there were so many.

"What do you mean by missing?" Tristan asked as he settled against the back of the couch, his leathers squeaking against the leather cushion. "As in none of our people have seen them? Or as in they've disappeared from the face of the earth and not even the Daemoni know where they are?"

"Our people have not seen them anywhere in some time. They have tried to force Daemoni to talk, but have learned nothing, and our new converts also say they do not know anything. Including Vanessa."

"So either the Daemoni don't care, or Lucas is keeping it under wraps," Tristan said.

"Correct," Rina agreed.

"Do you think they're dead?" I asked. "Did they kill them?"

Rina shook her head. "No, I do not sense their deaths. My instinct tells me they are in trouble, however. And I believe we can help them. *You* can help them."

"And you think their taking Dorian has something to do with it?" Tristan asked.

"I do not know for certain, but I believe it may be related."

I tapped my fingers on my chin. "But we still don't know if it's Lucas or Kali who has Dorian. Could they have them all?"

Rina didn't answer me, but her head tilted the other way. A moment later, the door to her office opened, and Mom entered. Rina nodded at her, Mom closed and locked the door, and came over to join us. I asked my question again, thinking Rina had been mentally distracted by Mom, but it was Mom who answered.

"Our people are still trying to find out more information," Mom said, "but no, right now, we don't know if it's Lucas or Kali. My sense tells me it's both, but my sense isn't always reliable when it comes to Kali."

"Which may be why you can't sense Dorian, either," Tristan suggested. "If she has him."

"Or it may be because there's a powerful cloak on him, which could be done by any strong warlock," Mom said.

"Like Owen," I muttered.

"It's possible," Mom agreed as her gaze dropped to study something on the floor.

Rina's eyes drifted over to the fireplace again, but she seemed to be farther away, her voice distant. "Nothing breaks the heart more than the betrayal of those we trust most. But we cannot permit such pain to consume us. Others' actions and decisions cannot break us unless we allow it, which we must never do. We must forgive, and we must heal. We must learn to open our hearts and love again. Otherwise, our souls will become as dark as theirs."

Was she saying Owen had allowed himself to be broken? That his soul had become as dark as that of the sorceress he once despised? Such sadness filled Rina's voice, I didn't think she only spoke of Owen's heart, but of ours as well. And not only of his decisions, but of others before him. He hadn't been the first Amadis to abandon ship, and each time someone did, her heart must have truly broken.

"They are like my children, so each time is like losing Noah all over again," Rina said, apparently listening to my thoughts. She returned her focus to us and lifted her voice. "We must move on, however. There are many who need our love and attention. Sophia, please brief them. You understand and can explain the technology better than I, no?"

Mom nodded. "As I told you on the phone, the Normans are on edge and with good reason. The Daemoni are doing all they can to instigate war. They're hoping for World War III, if they can pull it off."

"And all of the Norman politicians are in Lucas's pocket?" Tristan asked. "He just has to tell them to move, I assume."

"No, not all," Mom answered. "Many yes, hoping to be protected by Lucas when all hell breaks loose. We have a few who actually take our advice as well. But most Normans are leery of the Daemoni *and* of us. They don't trust anyone who's not completely human, and they're working together to figure out how to eliminate all of us. Alexis, you and Vanessa already experienced the silver ammunition when they caught you in Alaska?"

"But silver's only good against the Daemoni," I said. "I mean, getting shot didn't exactly tickle, but it won't incapacitate us like it will the Daemoni."

"Except for the few in higher power positions and certain departments, the Normans don't know that," Mom said. "They're still testing, trying to figure things out. In fact, civilian Normans don't know we even exist—yet—and most of those in lower positions or smaller governments have only heard rumors."

"We need to try to keep those rumors unproven," Rina said. I looked at her with my brows pushed together, not sure I understood.

"We need to protect our secrecy as long as possible," Mom clarified. "The Daemoni have technically broken our treaty of secrecy by not only telling some of these power-hungry Normans about us, but Lucas has convinced them *we're* the dangerous ones. If such a rumor spreads to the masses, we could be in big trouble. For now, however, we still have our secrets, and we need to keep it that way."

"We also have our relationships to manage," Rina added. "We have worked hard over many years to build rapport with those authorities who are willing. We do not want to jeopardize losing those liaisons."

Tristan stretched his arm over the back of the couch as he studied Rina, then Mom. "We appreciate the information—" he looked over at me with a glint in his eye, knowing how I hated politics "—at least, I do—but why are you telling us this? Does it have something to do with Dorian and the Summoned brothers?"

"It's information we'll be sharing with all of the Amadis," Mom said, "but you and your team really need to understand the danger out there because you'll be traveling so much."

I cocked my head. "Where exactly are we going? Do you know something?"

"I sense Dorian, and maybe the others, in America. I believe on the East Coast, and if Blossom's spell is working right, north of Florida. Unfortunately, this is the best information we have at this time."

"So we start in Florida or Georgia and work our way north," Tristan said. "Hopefully Blossom's spell will keep us on a path."

"There's a problem, though. You probably shouldn't flash," Mom said.

"*What?*" I sputtered, thinking I heard her wrong. "Why not? What are we supposed to do?"

How could we do covert operations and free ourselves from danger if we couldn't make a fast escape?

"The Normans are testing new technology, and not only weapons, but things like force fields that can stop a flash. In fact, they've created invisible walls even they can't pass through, supposedly to protect their own people."

"Like the wall on the Canadian border?" Tristan asked.

"Yes," Mom said. "And there are others. Smaller contraptions with an electromagnetic field that interferes with the magic that allows us to flash. They're basically traps—making us appear out of nowhere right where they want us. A few of our own have been caught with these. Even some of the smallest counties and cities are trying these to find proof of the rumors. Others are putting up your standard checkpoints, but not for drunk drivers. They're looking for non-humans. These are becoming really popular in the United States right now."

"Wow. Checkpoints and traps in the *U.S.*? How far off are we from a military state?"

"Not as far as you think," Mom deadpanned although I'd meant it rhetorically.

The Daemoni were definitely taking things to a new level, and the Normans were feeding right out of their hands. I hoped Rina had plans for stepping us up, too, or we'd never win this war.

"And if you get caught, any of you," Mom continued, "you must be very careful in how you handle the situation."

She seemed to be directing this especially at me, but Tristan caught on to her meaning before I did.

"We have to keep our calm and work with them," he said.

"Correct," Mom replied. "We don't want to prove the Daemoni right that we're dangerous. We don't want to expose our secrets if we don't have to. We need to be cooperative."

"You must protect the relationships we have, as well," Rina added. "Please take all precautions to do so."

"In other words, we can't lose our cool," Tristan said as his hand landed on my knee and gave me a squeeze.

"Okay, I got it. You'd better tell the rest of our team, though," I said, thinking specifically about Vanessa.

"We have, darling. They all understand what is at risk."

I sat back against Tristan and crossed my legs. "So checkpoints and traps and no flashing."

"Flash if you must," Mom said, "but be prepared for problems if you do. I'd recommend good old Norman transportation as much as possible. It may be slower, but it's safer and helps you blend in."

"Understood. Anything else we need to know about?" I asked.

Mom and Rina exchanged a look, but Mom shook her head.

"That's all we know at this time," she said. "We do have people listening and watching, trying to gather more intel. But for now, all I can say is to be careful, honey. And remember your role—protect the Amadis and all of humanity, even when they're being difficult."

"Listen to their minds, Alexis," Rina said. "Find out who they serve. If your lives are in danger, do what you must. I know you will make the right decisions, whatever you may face. You are ready for this."

Mom stood and went over to Rina's desk, opened a drawer, and pulled out a bag of what looked like weed. At least, what I'd seen in pictures and on TV, since my own experience with the stuff was standing in a haze of smoke at a college frat party Tristan had taken me to when we first met.

"And don't forget," Mom said, "we still need another daughter. Blossom will ensure you drink the tea."

She tossed the bag into my lap, and I wrinkled my nose when I recognized the herbal leaves. "Blech. The nasty tea I spit out all over the floor?"

I tried not to gag at the memory of drinking the concoction that tasted like gasoline.

"It will prime your body for pregnancy," she said. "It worked for me, so hopefully it will work for you."

I nodded with resignation. I still wasn't sure we needed a needed a daughter—I still wanted to believe Dorian could lead the Amadis one day—but I would certainly try my damnedest to produce one. I felt as though a daughter would complete our family . . . although I struggled with the idea of bringing a baby into this world. She would bring a whole lot of hope to the Amadis, though, and hope was always a good thing.

"Anything else?" Tristan asked. "Or can we begin our mission?"

"The rest of your team is being prepped," Mom said, "but you should be able to leave tonight."

"We do have an addition to your team," Rina said, and I suppressed a groan, expecting Julia to walk in at any moment. But she didn't. Nobody did. "He is also being prepared."

My brow lifted. "*He?*"

"Jaxon, the were-crocodile from Australia." She smiled when my jaw dropped. "You must have made quite an impression on him, darling. We had not heard from him directly for decades, and not only has he traveled all the way here, but he has specifically requested to be assigned to your guard."

Tristan looked at me with a smirk as he shook his head. "Yeah, quite the impression," he murmured.

"Do not worry, Tristan," Rina said. "His intentions are noble. I made certain of it. However, Blossom, the dear, may have caught his eye."

"Really?" I asked.

"I believe so. They crossed paths only briefly in front of my office door, but his thoughts about her came quite clearly. And loudly."

"I can only imagine," I muttered.

This could become very interesting . . . or a problem. Blossom needed a distraction from her breakup with the vampire-barista on Captiva, and she deserved a good guy like Jax. But none of us needed either of them to be distracted from our missions with a budding romance—or worse, a disastrous one. Of course, Rina hadn't said anything about Blossom having similar thoughts, so there may have been nothing to worry about.

Besides, love was not something to worry about anyway. We had real problems to conquer.

Mom explained that Jax would make an excellent guard. "His species, the saltwater crocodile, is the biggest and most dangerous form of reptile in existence today. He's an ideal soldier against other were-animals and vampires. The power of his jaw could hold any creature captive without tearing it to pieces . . ."

"Unless that's the goal," Tristan said, but when he looked at me, the corner of his mouth lifted slightly. "He's no match for me, of course, but he'll hold his own with anyone else."

"He is a perfect addition to your team," Rina added before dismissing us. I could tell she'd already had a strenuous day and hoped she'd be able to catch a nap.

A few hours after the sun slid behind the horizon, she announced in all of our heads that the jet was ready and waiting for us.

I immediately jumped to my feet from the couch in Mom's office, dumping Sasha onto the floor. The lykora let out a snuff of annoyance as she glared at me. She'd been in my lap while I poured over a list of names of Normans who could help us if we needed it, while Mom studied reports at her desk, mumbling to herself about how first-graders would do a better job than the idiots in political office. Listening to her confirmed my thought—and Rina's opinion—that I didn't belong here, doing their kind of work. I belonged in the field, and it was finally time to go.

"I wonder if we should leave you here where it's safe," I said aloud to Sasha, and she cocked her dog-like head to the side.

Tristan, who'd been sitting with me, rose to his feet. "There's a reason I gave you the nickname I did. Like you, a lykora isn't meant to be tucked away in a safe place. She's meant to defend, to fight."

Mom came around from behind her desk to accompany us to the airstrip. "Let her serve her purpose, Alexis. She's stronger and more resilient than you can imagine, and she wants nothing more than to be at her master's side. She's probably aching to find Dorian as much as you are."

I scooped her up and gave her a pat on the head. "I guess that's settled then. You come with us."

Her blue tongue swiped over my hand in agreement.

Before flashing to the airstrip, we stopped by Rina's office to say goodbye. I wrapped my arms around her frail little body, hoping she was wrong about not getting any better. She'd once said she believed I'd gone through the *Ang'dora* at such a young age because the Amadis needed as many daughters as possible for this war. I held on to the belief that she would be with us for many years to come.

"Thank you," I murmured into her ear, "for letting us find our son. I promise if there's anything we can do for the others, we will."

"I know, darling. I know you will be the leader you are meant to be."

I pulled back slightly to look at her. "I love you, Rina."

Tears glistened in her eyes. "And I love you."

"We'll see you soon, right?"

She pulled me into a hug and whispered, "I hope so, dear. But that is in God's and the Angels' hands."

Sadness welled up in my chest and constricted my throat as we held each other for a moment longer.

"Go now, darling," she said as she pulled away from me. "Go find your son."

We flashed from Rina's office to the airstrip where my team began to gather.

"Don't forget your main objective," Mom reminded me as we strode over to the others.

"I know. Protect humanity. Convert everyone we can. Build our army."

She slipped her arm around me and pulled me closer to her. She whispered into my ear, "And have lots of sex."

"Mother!"

She chuckled. "What? We need a baby girl. At least one of your missions is fun."

I shook my head, then was suddenly saddened by Mom's still single status. "Have you met anyone on the island?"

"Hmph. Those who live on the island aren't exactly my type."

I understood. Most of the island residents were Amadis who weren't strong fighters for one reason or another. They lived here because it provided a place of refuge. They wouldn't know how to handle Mom, and she'd get frustrated, needing someone strong and adventurous.

"Don't worry about me, though," Mom said. "Time with my true love may have been short, but it was more powerful and full of more passion than most people get to experience in a lifetime. I have other things to worry about, as do you."

We reached the bottom of the steps to the jet, where the others congregated. Everyone who came to the island with us had arrived, as well as Jax, except Bree. I opened my mouth to ask if she was coming when she appeared in front of us, all golden and shining in the night.

"I wondered if you were coming with us," I said. "You're the last to arrive."

"Well, no, I'm not." Her mouth stretched into a grin that lit up her inhumanly beautiful face, and although I was disappointed she wouldn't be coming with us, her excitement for whatever she'd be doing was undeniable. "I'll still be helping you, though, but in other ways. I get to return to the Otherworld!"

"Oh! That's wonderful!" I threw myself at her in a hug.

"The Angels told Ms. Katerina I had served my duty here and performed it to their satisfaction. They're allowing me back with full faerie privileges."

I stepped away so Tristan could congratulate her and say his goodbyes. They didn't have anything resembling a normal mother-son relationship, not after what they'd been through, but they held mutual respect and adoration for each other. Bree loved Tristan unconditionally as parents do, and I thought Tristan had grown to return that love once he came to know her as the person she really was, not the evil witch the Daemoni had made her out to be.

I had my own mother to say goodbye to, and it was a lot harder to do so than I'd thought it would be when we first arrived last night. I'd thought her uncaring and hard-hearted at the time, and I should have known better, but had been too single-mindedly focused on finding Dorian.

"I wish you could come with us," I said as I held on to her in a tight hug. "Why don't you? You *are* a strong converter."

"I wish I could, too, to be honest," she said. "But I am needed here. Rina requires my assistance."

We hadn't even left yet, and my chest already tightened with longing. "I'll miss you. I already do."

"I miss you, too, honey. But you do what you need to do now. As soon as you get pregnant, you'll be back here, and we'll get sick of seeing each other so much."

"I doubt it. You were always my best friend." I gave her a tighter squeeze. "But for now, I must find Dorian."

"Yes, you must. Go get our little boy, Alexis, and bring him home. This is where he belongs, at least for a few more years."

A lump formed in my throat as we gave each other one last hug and said our "I love yous." Why did I always feel when I left my mom that things would only be worse the next time I saw her?

10

"YOU'RE SURE YOU'RE up for this?" I asked as my team flew across the Atlantic Ocean at warlock speed once again. Jax sat across from me on the Amadis jet, decked out in new fighting leathers. Part of me couldn't be happier about him being here, but I worried about him. "I know there's a reason you stayed away from people all those years. Please don't feel like you have to do this."

He stroked his chin as he looked out the window, though the only way to distinguish the sky from the ocean below was the smattering of stars that showed every now and then when the clouds allowed us a glimpse.

"At some point in his life, a bloke's gotta rock up and do what's right. The Amadis are the closest I got to rellies, and it's time for me to stop bein' a piker and take care of ya." He puffed up his chest as he gave me a smile. "I'm fit as a Mallee bull. No way could I hide in the bush when my mates need me. 'Specially you, princess. I'll do whatever I can to help you find your lad, even if it's just keepin' you and your team of pretty sheilas safe."

Tristan, who sat next to me, let out a low growl.

Jax gave him a mischievous grin. "Well, maybe you're no sheila, but you are a beaut, too."

Tristan growled louder. Jax threw his hands in the air in surrender.

"No worries, mate. I'll behave." Yet right after making that promise, his eyes slid over to Blossom who sat with Vanessa and Sheree.

Rina must have convinced everyone else of Vanessa's trustworthiness because the three of them sat with their heads close together, in deep conversation. My grandmother hadn't quite convinced me, though. With her assessment, I felt ninety-nine-point-nine percent sure Vanessa was good, and I hoped to strengthen our relationship. However, I would still keep hold of that sliver of doubt, just in case. That suspicion would keep me alert if I turned out to be right about her being in on Owen's plan for massive betrayal.

My anger bubbled up again at the thought of my former protector, creating an ache for the chance to zap him with a few billion volts of electricity. I looked out the window to see us zooming toward dark storm clouds and lightning, apropos for my mood. Sasha, who'd been sleeping on Tristan's lap, sensed my ire and nuzzled her snout against my hand. Tristan noticed, too, and the arm he held around me tightened.

I pulled on his love to calm me, closed my eyes, and told myself to sleep while I could, because as soon as we landed, we'd be heading out on our mission. We'd already lost too much time. Everyone else had settled down, and the cabin became quiet, though Jax let out a loud snore now and then. I was just about to doze off when the plane hit some turbulence.

"We're headed for some rough weather near the coast," the copilot's voice said over the speakers. "We're going to keep our speed, so hang on. It could get a little bumpy."

A "little bumpy" turned out to be the understatement of the day. The jet bounced, rose, and plummeted like a roller coaster, making my stomach dip. Everyone woke up instantly. Tristan dropped Sasha into my lap, then leaned over to jab a button on the console, turning on the information screen that hung on one wall so we could see how close we were to Florida and how long we'd be flying in this weather. The image of our plane nearing the coast of South Carolina and Georgia flashed on the screen, and then it went blank. The entire cabin fell dark.

Lightning lit the sky outside and flashed through the windows. A burst of thunder shook the plane. My seat came out from underneath me as the jet lost hundreds of feet of altitude, and then I slammed back into it. Blossom screamed.

"This isn't good," Tristan said.

What's going on? I asked the pilot.

"*Mayday! Mayday!*" came the only response as the pilot tried to call for help.

Another flash of light. The plane rocked sideways and downwards. My body banged against the seat and the wall, and Sasha fell off my lap. I grabbed for her and held on right before the plane rolled over and then upright again.

"*Ms. Alexis, the storm tore through my shield! The Normans have spotted us and are firing at the plane,*" the warlock copilot said to me.

What?

"*You must leave!*"

The jet shuddered again as something slammed into the side of it.

And then the metal and fiberglass tube began to spin like a top as we plunged toward the earth.

"*Flash! You all need to get out of here,*" the pilot yelled in my mind.

"*We've been hit!*" the copilot shouted. I hesitated for a fraction of a second, not believing what I heard. "*Hurry! We're going down!*"

"We have to flash out of here," I yelled over the thunder outside as I shoved Sasha into the front of my jacket. I threw on my backpack and lurched for the center of the cabin as the plane continued to rock side to side and back and forth.

Tristan's hand wrapped around my wrist, and he tugged me closer to him. He reached his other arm out to the others, and yelled, "Come to us, and I'll lead us for the flash."

Everyone's movements looked disjointed and awkward in the lightning that lit up the cabin in strobe-like fashion. Charlotte lunged for Tristan, and Vanessa grabbed my hand and stretched for Sheree and Blossom, who reached for Jax, but the jet tilted again, throwing us off balance. I fell to the side, catching myself on a seat with my arm to protect the lykora in my coat, and pushed myself upright.

I stumbled again for the center of the cabin, as did the others. Lightning flashed, imprinting my team's faces on my brain, their wide eyes filled with worry and their mouths set with determination. We had nearly formed our circle when the plane jerked once more with the sound of thunder cracking all around us. Wind suddenly whooshed through the cabin, knocking us off our feet. And that's when I realized the ear-shattering sound hadn't been thunder.

"The jet's breaking apart," Tristan yelled.

At the same time, I also realized we weren't surrounded by only Amadis mind signatures. Several Daemoni were nearby, probably the real cause of the impending crash.

Sasha shuddered inside my jacket with a growl, and she squirmed her way to the top of my zipper. As soon as she freed herself, her wings burst from her back, and her body began to grow.

"Is she in there?" a Daemoni yelled from outside the plane.

"Be careful if she is," said another, "she has a helluva bite!"

I didn't know who they spoke of—me? Vanessa? Sheree? I didn't wait to find out.

"Let's go!" I yelled, holding my arms out.

Vanessa grabbed my hand again as the jet split farther apart and another powerful gust of wind knocked us into a wall. Something sharp cut through my leather pants and jagged across my hip. I clenched my jaw against the sting before the cut healed. Charlotte and Sheree braced themselves on the other side of the break, and Charlotte busted the cockpit door open. Blossom and Jax were behind me, near the plane's tail.

And my husband blurred past me toward the chasm between the two parts of the jet. He dove downward. Out of sight.

"TRISTAN!" I screamed as I tried to follow, but the gap between the two parts closed.

"*Go*, ma lykita!" he said. "*Get them out of here. I can't hold this for long.*"

Something hit us again, pitching the jet sideways. Another hole burst into the side of the plane.

"*GO!*" Tristan yelled, his voice thundering in my head as he strained to hold the jet together.

The copilot swept past me in midair and flew out of the hole. Sasha followed right behind him.

"No!" I screamed as I dove after both of them.

Daemoni mages waited outside, hovering in the air, as the ocean below surged toward me and wind roared in my ears. Squinting against the rain and rushing air, I couldn't see Sasha, but the copilot was only feet below me. He instantly became my first concern, and I stretched my arms downward to try to catch his foot or leg. An orange light streaked through the rain and hit the warlock. His body jerked, then fell limp as he continued plunging toward the wall of black sea. I threw a bolt of electricity in the direction the spell had come from, then I tried to reach for our copilot again, but my hands only grabbed air. Another light streaked in my direction, yellow this time, but it missed. Someone screamed from a distance, but I didn't recognize the voice. A big, white body flew by—Sasha as big as a horse—and another scream ripped through the night, followed by a round of thunder.

A hand clamped onto my ankle. I tried to shake it off and twisted in the air to hit its owner with a jolt, but then my mind registered it belonged to an Amadis. I prayed it meant my team was close enough to follow my trail, and I flashed.

I envisioned as our target the beach at Hilton Head Island where Mom and I had taken Dorian once. That wasn't where we appeared.

Like the other night when I'd tried to cross the border into Canada, my body slammed into an invisible wall, and I fell to my ass into a muddy puddle. Another body thudded next to me—Vanessa. We both jumped to our feet, squinting through the pouring rain for the others. Lightning lit up the area, immediately followed by an ear-piercing crack of thunder.

Tristan! No response came. I mentally called out for the others.

"Where are they?" Vanessa shouted over nature's cacophony.

Still hearing nothing from them, I reached out for their mind signatures, but they weren't in my range. Unfortunately, others *were* nearby. Not Amadis or Daemoni. Only Normans, but they were heavily armed.

Grab my hand, and let's go! I mind-yelled at Vanessa while I shared the thoughts I heard with her. We had to get away before we were seen. But when we tried to flash, we couldn't.

"Hold it right there!" a male voice called out. "Hands up where we can see them."

"Shit," Vanessa muttered.

"Yep," I agreed. Shit was right. We hadn't even made it to ground before one of their damn traps had caught us. I sucked in a deep breath, trying to suck in a level of calm with it so I could be diplomatic, as Rina and Mom had requested. Well, ordered.

Five Norman police officers surrounded us, and it took every ounce of control Vanessa and I had to not fight them. Our self-preservation instincts bucked against us, but we cooperated as they handcuffed us and pushed us into a marked car. The whole time, I kept my mind open, but I could only find Norman mind signatures. Where were Tristan and everyone else? I tried not to think about what could have happened to them, especially to my husband. *He's Tristan. He's okay. He and Charlotte are probably taking care of everyone else.* I kept repeating this to myself until I believed it.

"We have our proof now," said a policeman as he ducked into the front passenger seat. "Whatever those Savannah folk did, it worked."

My eyes cut to Vanessa at the mention of Savannah, and she peered back at me with narrowed eyes as water slid off her hair and down her face.

I don't sense any Daemoni minds, I told her. She scowled, but didn't reply.

Another cop slid into the driver's side, and they both yanked their doors shut before more rain poured inside. "Yeah, but I don' trust 'em."

"You want to call Atlanta?" the passenger asked.

"Don' know yet. All I know is we ain't bringin' them nowhere. Whoever wants 'em can come see for theirselves that we got 'em, but they're ours 'til we know what's goin' on."

"Damn straight," the other said as the driver cranked the engine over.

They're acting on their own, I told Vanessa after listening to their thoughts as they drove us toward the lights of a small town. *Not with the Amadis or Daemoni. They don't know exactly why they have us except that we appeared out of nowhere, so there's obviously something wrong with us. They don't really know what to do. They know*

Savannah, Atlanta, and a few other nearby cities and clusters are looking for people like us, but they don't know who to trust.

"*Hopefully not the Daemoni,*" Vanessa said. "*I'll fight if they do. I won't be captured by them.*"

Just do as Rina said for now until we know for sure.

I hated being passive as much as Vanessa did. Probably more because not only did I worry about the risk of being captured by the Daemoni, but now the search for my son had been delayed even longer. An angry growl threatened to escape my lips, but I kept it suppressed. I didn't want to piss off Rina by ruining anything or exposing our secrets. I didn't need to give her or the council an excuse to change her mind about our mission.

"Do you have anything to say for yourself?" the cop who'd been on the passenger side of the car asked me a while later as we sat in a small room with no windows, a wooden table, and two folding chairs. A cliché interrogation room. He had greenish-gray eyes, which were about the only attractive feature on him. A reddish five-o'clock shadow covered his soft jaw, and his coarse orange-red hair was flattened around his crown with police-cap hat-head. His tobacco-stained fingers drummed the wooden table as he waited for my answer.

"Only that I've done nothing wrong," I said.

He let out a flat guffaw. "And what makes you think I'd believe that? Anyone who can do what we saw you do ain't no good. Not in no one's book."

"And what did you see us do?" I asked innocently.

He jabbed his yellowed finger at me. "You and your friend appeared out of nowhere."

I had to try to convince him he hadn't seen anything, and I suddenly wished for Mom's power of persuasion. "That's absurd. How would we be able to do such a thing?"

"You tell me."

"It's impossible, isn't it? Are you sure the lightning wasn't playing tricks on your eyes?"

"We've been watchin' that locale for days," he said, leaning toward me. "We'd heard through the grapevine of freaky stuff like this happenin'. Wanted to see for ourselves, and, finally, there y'all were. Right outta nowhere!"

I rolled my eyes. "We were simply out for a walk."

"In the weather? It's rainin' calves and hogs out there."

I shrugged. "Our car broke down."

"And where were y'all headed?"

I paused, trying to remember my Georgia and South Carolina geography from our time in Atlanta. I didn't remember much from that era—the *Ang'dora* had taken me back to when I was mentally strongest at nineteen, so most memories for those seven years had been dulled, pretty much forgotten. The only ones that really survived my transformation were special moments with Dorian. "Statesboro?"

His brow rose. "Lemme get this straight. Your car broke down while y'all were headed for Statesboro, and you decided to walk there?"

I widened my eyes and lifted my brows to portray innocence. "Exactly."

He sat back in his chair. "Statesboro, huh? Or do you mean Walterboro?"

"Um . . ." Was that near Hilton Head, too? I had no idea.

He shook his head. "It don't matter. Either one would be a hell of a long walk in the rain."

"We like the rain. Thunderstorms are beautiful."

"So y'all think you were gonna walk over forty miles in it?" He cocked his head as he studied my face. I couldn't come up with any more lies. Lying wasn't exactly my strong suit. "So, what are you, you and your friend? How do you do it? What else can you do?"

I didn't answer him. He might have believed what Vanessa was because she was a creature he likely knew from pop culture, but he wouldn't understand, nor believe, me, part Angel and part everything else. And what people didn't understand, they feared. I could have shown him some things I could do—like give him a shot of electricity—but showing off and instilling fear of us were exactly what Mom and Rina had warned me not to do. When he finally accepted that I wouldn't answer, the metal feet of his chair scraped against the linoleum as he pushed it back and stood up. His hands gripped the edge of the table, and he leaned over me.

"Well, then, I guess y'all get to spend the night with us," he said as though he'd delivered a horrible threat, "and we'll decide what to do with you and your friend in the mornin'."

Now that could have been horrible, if they decided to call the Daemoni, but I wasn't sure yet what they planned to do. *They* weren't sure yet, according to their thoughts.

Taking a risk, I went for a different angle.

"All you need to know is we're the good guys. If we wanted to hurt you, we would have already," I said, trying to keep my voice steady and nonthreatening. "Your facilities aren't built to contain us, though."

He leaned over closer to me, and his eyes became slits. "I'd like to see you try to break out. We have silver ammo."

So he did know *something*. But not enough. I smiled. "Then give us your best shot. The silver only works against the bad guys."

He pulled back and cocked his head again as he glared at me. Then without a word, he strode out of the room.

A few minutes later, I let another officer escort me to a small cellblock, where the fumes of human urine mixed with body odor hung heavily in the air. They separated Vanessa and me by one cell, as though it would keep us from conspiring against them. There were only three cells, though, so I supposed they had no choice.

"Do I get my phone call?" I asked the guard as he shook the barred door, making sure I was locked in. I suppressed the urge to roll my eyes. They thought these bars and walls could hold us, so they really didn't know much.

"Y'all ain't human. You don't get no human rights," he snapped, and I stared after him with my mouth hanging open as he walked through the door to the offices beyond. Things really had changed, even in the good ol' US of A.

"*We're flashing out of here, right?*" Vanessa asked me as I sat down on a wooden bench, the only furniture in the cell besides a small metal toilet in the corner.

Ugh. I dropped my head into my hands and massaged my temples while listening to the rhythm of her pacing. I could not believe I was actually in jail. I'd never been sent to the principal's office as a kid and never even had a speeding ticket. And I hadn't done anything wrong this time, either, yet here we were, locked up like criminals. I'd given up on wanting to be normal years ago, but I never imagined being imprisoned because I wasn't.

As much as I want to, we can't, I replied. *I promised Rina I'd cooperate, and I will . . . as long as my patience lasts, anyway.*

"*Where do you think the others are?*"

I chewed on my lip with worry about Blossom, Jax, Charlotte, and Sheree, and the pilot, too. I already knew the copilot hadn't survived, and I had to believe Tristan made it out fine, because if he hadn't . . . no, I wouldn't go there. Dorian's disappearance was bad enough. I would not think about anything happening to my husband. *He's okay. He's Tristan.* The stone in my chest would surely alert me if something were wrong with him.

But what about the others? Had they all survived? If so, where had they landed? I couldn't sense any of their mind signatures in my range, and I wondered if they'd been caught in a different trap. Were they being held prisoner somewhere else? My breath caught in my throat with a thought. What if the Daemoni had captured them? What if their captors took them straight to Savannah? Oh God. What if they appeared right in the middle of Savannah, a minor cluster for the Daemoni? We'd never see them again. Not alive, anyway.

Unless Tristan appeared with them. And Charlotte may have been powerful enough to get them out, too.

Not knowing about the others wore my patience thin. Vanessa and I had to get out of here, and I had to find out what happened to everyone else. I had to get a hold of Tristan. If only my telepathy could reach a few hundred miles farther. The only minds in my range were the couple of Normans in the police station and a couple thousand Normans in the sleepy town beyond. I studied the cops' minds to try to grasp onto something that could be helpful. Finally, a thought about the local pastor doing an exorcism skittered into the guard's mind. Mom had said many clergy would know to help us, and I had a whole list of them in my head that I'd memorized while waiting to leave the island.

I banged on the bars and yelled for the guard. After several minutes, he finally stepped through the door.

"What?" he growled, though his Norman growl sounded more like a whine compared to what I was used to.

"I'd like to see Reverend Stephens, please," I said sweetly.

"You know Rev. Stephens?" he asked with surprise.

"Yes," I lied straight through my teeth. Hopefully, *he* knew *me*. Or at least knew Rina.

The guard eyed me for a minute then disappeared again through the door. I paced the stupid little cell as I waited for Rev. Stephens.

And waited. And waited. Maybe the guard hadn't called for the good pastor after all, but a search of the guard's thoughts told me he had. The reverend didn't understand my urgency, apparently. He needed to hurry up. Promise or no promise to Rina, Vanessa and I would be getting out of here soon, whether we flashed or walked out. I understood public relations was important for the Amadis in this war, but I could only restrain myself for so long. The lives of my team and my son were at stake.

Besides, as long as we remained here, we were sitting ducks for the Daemoni.

Finally, a tall, lanky African-American man with dark, wrinkly skin and a head full of wiry gray hair walked through the door and down the corridor along the jail cells. He eyed Vanessa with curiosity as he passed her, and then came to a stop at my cell.

"Do you know the Amadis?" I asked him, getting straight to the point.

He squinted his eyes with confusion.

"Katerina Ames?" I asked with a trace of hope, but he shook his head. I started going through a list of the clergy names, monitoring his thoughts to make sure he told me the truth.

"Oh, yes," he finally said. "I do know McCorkle. Who doesn't now? He's well-known throughout the Southeast."

"I would like to see him," I said firmly.

His white brows jumped. "You know Pastor Richard McCorkle?"

"Yes, and I don't think he'll be very happy to see me in here." Of course, I'd never met the guy, but what did Rev. Stephens know?

His eyes squinted again as he seemed to consider me.

"Make sure you tell him Alexis Katerina Ames needs him," I said, hoping the name would be enough to bring this McCorkle guy to our rescue.

The older man finally nodded and strode back out to the police station. More hours passed, and although no windows broke up the smooth expanse of gray concrete wall surrounding the cellblock, I sensed we were well into the next day. Damn. It.

All right. We're not risking it any longer, I told Vanessa. Her mind perked up.

"*You're finally ready to get out of this godforsaken piss pot?*"

Any ideas on the best way out? If we flash, they could catch us again.

Before she could answer, the door swung open, and a forty-something guy with a smooth face and salt-and-pepper hair strode in, a new guard following after him.

"Ms. Alexis," he said, "I am so sorry about—"

He stopped in front of my cell, and his jaw literally fell open. I stared at him with a lifted brow.

"Um...pardon me. I just, uh..." He stammered as his eyes seemed to drink me in. "I, uh, never met any of y'all in person. You're, uh..."

His throat worked although no more words came out of his mouth, but I heard the rest of his thought: *real*. Again I wanted to roll my eyes, but gave him my sweetest smile instead. Seemingly speechless, he waved his hand at the guard, who unlocked my jail cell.

"Thank you," I said, holding my hand out for a handshake, assuming he was McCorkle. He gawked at it. "I'll, uh, make sure Rina knows about your helpfulness."

He grabbed my hand and pumped it nonstop. "Oh, thank you, yes, thank you very much, anything I can ever do for y'all, I'm at your service, just call, use my name like you did, whatever you need, I'm here to help..."

Before, he didn't know what to say, and now he apparently couldn't shut up.

The police had our few belongings ready for us, and Vanessa and I finally sauntered out of the jail, after wasting nine hours of precious time. I sure hoped it was worth it for Rina and the Amadis. As soon as we were out of earshot of the police station, I turned on my phone to call Tristan. I breathed a sigh of relief when I saw a text from him, which meant he was okay. *"Rendezvous at Rincon, GA."* He sent an address, but I barely saw the whole thing before the screen went blank. The battery was dead.

Crap. What the hell now? We were in the middle of BFE South Carolina with no idea where everyone was and no way to get a hold of them. A string of profanities raced through my mind, but then I had an idea. Probably a stupid one, but what did I have to lose? With a trace of hope, I let electricity rise into my hand, out of my palm, and into the cell phone. A small squeak of excitement popped out of my mouth when the screen flashed an icon, but then it darkened again. Feeling encouraged, I pushed a little more power into the device, and the screen lit up . . . then the next thing I knew, the phone hissed and crackled, and smoke rose from it, the acrid smell of burning electronics wafting in the air.

"Shit! Shit, shit, shit." I threw the phone on the ground and stomped on it until only a pile of broken plastic and glass remained. I turned to Vanessa with my hand out. She stared at me with a look of bewilderment. "I need to get a hold of Tristan. Can I use your phone?"

She gave me a pointed look. "I was locked up at the safe house for months, and we've been on all kinds of exciting adventures since the day I got out, but none of them have included a stop at the AT&T store. Remember?"

"So Rina gave you fighting leathers and weapons, but no phone?"

The vampire shrugged. "Smart phones don't seem to be at the top of her list of necessities."

She had a point. But what the hell were we supposed to do now?

11

I GLANCED OVER my shoulder at the police station.

"I'm not going back in there," Vanessa declared, and I couldn't blame her. Not quite what I wanted to do, either.

So we stood in the middle of the sidewalk in some tiny South Carolina town near the Georgia border and probably near the ocean, but other than that, I didn't know where exactly. I pushed my hand through my hair as I turned in a circle, hoping to find an answer. Also hoping to see Sasha patiently waiting for us. I didn't see the lykora, though, and the police station's sign gave me a county name, but it meant little since I wasn't exactly an expert on South Carolina's counties.

"Well, I guess we find our way to Rincon, Georgia," I said.

"Where?"

"Rincon? Tristan sent a text with an address where we're supposed to meet him."

"So everyone survived in one piece?"

I frowned. "I don't know. Tristan did, apparently, but I didn't catch the time or who we'd be meeting, so I don't know about the rest. We may have even missed them by now, since they don't know we couldn't exactly get there." I glanced around our surroundings again, still hoping to catch a glimpse of Sasha. I hated leaving the area without her, but I didn't sense her nearby. The last time I saw her, we were half a mile above the ocean. She could have been anywhere now, but since she wasn't here, I could only hope she was with Tristan and the others. "We need to find a map and get directions, then figure out how we're going to get there. We'll probably have to run."

"You shouldn't say such things too loudly," a warm male voice said from behind me. Pastor McCorkle had just stepped off the last stair to the police station. He seemed to have completely recovered from his earlier shyness. "Rincon's a good ways from here—not running distance for normal people. It's on my way to Atlanta, though, so I could give y'all a ride if you need it."

Vanessa and I exchanged a look.

"*Ditch the slimeball,*" she silently said, then she took off in a run, leaving me there with the pastor.

What the hell? Sure the dude was a little on the smarmy side—a little too much like a politician, and after what Rina and Mom had told us, the less contact we had with politicians, the better. But his thoughts seemed harmless enough, although as a pastor, he probably shouldn't have been thinking about Vanessa and me in *that* way, even if it was a private fantasy he didn't plan to act on. Besides, he'd bailed us out of jail *and* offered us a ride when probably everyone else in this town would have nothing to do with us. So why did she tell me to ditch him and then went and ditched me? I had half a mind to take the ride, ditching *her* ass because she didn't have the address. Although, Rincon probably wasn't too big for her to find us.

I opened my mouth to accept the ride, hoping it would piss Vanessa off because I didn't follow her, when she came around the corner on a motorcycle.

"Hop on, little sis," she said with a mischievous twinkle in her eye.

Relieved that I wouldn't have to be cooped up in a car with this guy, I gave the pastor the best smile I could conjure. "Looks like we have a ride, Pastor McCorkle."

"Rick," he corrected. "Please, call me Rick."

I didn't know if we'd ever see him again to call him anything, but I went along with it. "Right, Rick. If you could just tell us which road to take to Rincon, we'll be fine."

His brows pushed together as his gaze swept over Vanessa on the bike. "Where did you get that?"

"Oh, it's an Amadis thing," she said with a winning smile. "We keep transportation in odd places so none of us ever get stranded."

He stared at her for a moment longer and then seemed to buy the lie because he gladly gave us directions and went on his way. I couldn't help the urge to wipe my hand on my pants after shaking his.

"Do I want to know where you got this?" I asked as I climbed onto the back.

"Probably not. But if so, there's another one there if you want to ride your own. I wasn't sure if you knew how."

I did, but that was beside the point. If she'd stolen the motorcycle, which she must have, we certainly would not steal another one.

She revved the engine, and we took off, hopefully putting this place behind us forever.

I can't believe you picked me up on a stolen vehicle in front of a police station, I said, mind-talking instead of yelling over the rumble of the engine. *We're going to end up back in jail.*

"I didn't really steal it. I left a contact number on the other one."

A bogus number. You don't have a phone, remember?

"Tristan does. I left his number."

What? Now he'll end up in jail!

"Nah. Nobody will mess with him, especially when he offers up the cash to more than pay for the bike. And they'll get the bike, too. I mean, you guys are good for it, right?"

That's not the point. We'll be lucky to even get that far. The owner just has to send the cops out to look for us, and we'll be right back where we were.

"Give me a little credit. The bikes were under a tarp in the lot of an abandoned building. Nobody's going to miss it. We'll get to this place Tristan said to meet him at, and we'll pay someone to bring the bike back. No one'll ever know."

Sheesh. This reminded me of the plane we'd taken to get out of Australia. In fact, the situation wasn't really much different, so why did this feel so wrong when that hadn't? Probably because it was Vanessa doing the stealing rather than Tristan.

She raced along the roads Pastor Rick told us to use, and I prayed we wouldn't get caught. I also formulated a plan for how to return the motorcycle and remunerate the owner, enough so they wouldn't press charges, which was the last thing we needed. Rina certainly wouldn't be impressed, and that thought made me feel even worse. By the time we arrived in Rincon, guilt had almost overridden my primary emotion of anger.

We pulled into a gravel parking lot of what looked to be a biker bar, and I had to wonder if I'd remembered the address correctly. I climbed off the back of the "borrowed" bike, and my eyes scanned over the dozens of motorcycles outside the squat, concrete building. Was this really the place? It wouldn't have been too surprising, knowing Tristan. One of his "guys" probably owned the place. Still, not feeling too good about walking in blind, I opened my mind to those inside. The building was larger than it looked from the outside and was filled with . . . Were signatures. All Amadis and all wolves. But no Tristan. I reached my mind out to the surrounding area, and still no Tristan, Char, or Sheree, but I did find Blossom and Jax, about half a mile away.

Blossom, we're here, I said, and I could practically hear her squeal of joy.

"*On our way,*" she replied, relief heavy in her mental voice.

I turned to watch for them, feeling their mind signatures coming closer, and finally they came into sight. Jax sauntered toward us in his black leather pants and black t-shirt as he held his jacket over a shoulder. Although Blossom had the standard leather jacket and combat boots, for some reason they hadn't given her pants and a bustier like they had to the rest of us girls. Rather, she wore a black smock that reached a few inches above her knees and black tights. She broke into a sprint for us and threw her arms around my neck as she nearly knocked me over in a hug.

She immediately spouted off like a geyser. "I was so worried about you, but we didn't know what to do after everything Ms. Katerina had told us about being cooperative, so we hoped you'd get out, and everything would be okay, but Tristan said to come here, and we'd get you out if we had to, but it looks like you're fine, and I've probably driven Jax up the wall—"

"She's been yabberin' away like a macaw on speed," Jax said, but he didn't sound mad or even annoyed. In fact, I sensed a bit of awe and appreciation in his voice as he spoke of the witch. "We've all been worried as hell, princess."

"I've been worried as hell, too," I said, giving them each a hug, and then I glanced around. "Where are Tristan and the others?"

"They're not here yet," Blossom said, and I didn't see Sasha with them, either. I hoped to God that meant Tristan had her. Blossom opened her mouth to launch into another monologue, but I stopped her.

"Can I use your phone?"

She lifted her brows. "It fried in the swamp, where we appeared."

"Then how'd you talk to Tristan?"

"We didn't. Jax and I were just making our way out of the swamp, thank God he was with me, because he made himself a crocodile, and we clamored out of there without getting eaten by anything, and then Bree showed up out of nowhere right in front of us. She said she already talked to Tristan, and she told us all about you and Vanessa, and said Tristan, Charlotte, and Sheree—"

"They're all okay?" I asked, having to interrupt her so she'd take a breath before she passed out from talking too much.

"Yeah, they're all together."

"Do they have Sasha?"

She tilted her head. "I don't know. Bree didn't mention Sasha, but they all appeared way down by Jacksonville, and had the pilot with them, so they had to find transportation and get him to the airport. And I guess Tristan already talked to your mom and the matriarch and told them everything that happened, too. I mean, I don't know who knew what when, but Bree pretty much knew everything since she'd been watching us from the Otherworld, and she came to our realm to be our messenger because she saw we had no other way of communicating with each other, and we were all split up, and it was such a big mess. Anyway, the pilot's already off to get a new Amadis jet, and Tristan, Charlotte, and Sheree are headed up this way—"

Jax put a hand on Blossom's shoulder. "Stop a minute to breathe, woman."

The witch inhaled a deep breath and blew it out. "Sorry, but there's so much to tell, and I know Alexis has been scared to death, and you need to know what's going on. So anyway, they were on their way here, but they've been a little delayed."

My heart stuttered. "What's wrong?"

"They found a newborn vamp on the side of the road," she explained. "Charlotte couldn't just leave him there."

"Of course not," I said as my heart returned to its normal rhythm, but then I realized what it meant. Hours, maybe a day or more, before they could hit the road again.

"Tristan told Bree to tell us he'd call when he had further info," the witch added. "Or send her again, I don't know."

"Well, then, I guess we go in for a drink?" I asked, not knowing what else to do. Besides control my urge to punch something again. One thing after another. At least everyone was okay, but we were never going to find my son at this rate. *Blossom, do you think we could try your tracking spell while we're waiting?*

Her shoulders lifted in a shrug so small only I noticed the gesture. *"Maybe if there's some place quiet here. It's a Were den, though, so don't get your hopes up."*

As soon as we walked inside, the loud din of conversation fell to complete silence. Vanessa had entered first, followed by Blossom and Jax, with me trailing in behind. I could feel the animosity in the air as the Weres in the bar sniffed, sensing we were Amadis, but not wolves like them.

"Who the hell do you think you are, stealing my pack's bike?" bellowed a female voice as a figure rushed across the room. A tall, thin woman with raven hair, obsidian eyes, a flannel top tied into a knot between her breasts, and holey jeans that hung on her narrow hips stopped in front of Vanessa, her face dangerously close to the vampire's. She apparently didn't know who Vanessa was. Or maybe she didn't care. She didn't look like she'd be scared of too much in this world. "And don't deny it. I get a call that it's gone. I look out the window, and there it is. And here you walk into my bar. The only people who don't belong here."

My team parted as I pushed my way to the front of them, knowing I needed to take responsibility for this misfortune (and planning how I'd get Vanessa back for this). More dead silence passed, followed by a loud ruckus with the scrape of bar stools against a wooden floor as everyone dropped to their knees, their heads down. The woman, who only a moment ago had been yelling at Vanessa, saw me and also went down to one knee.

"What the fuck's goin' on here?" a familiar voice called out as he came from what I assumed to be the kitchen behind the bar. I had to suppress a chuckle at his seemingly standard entrance when I was around. The large man, wearing a vest that showed off his burly muscles, hurried around the bar and to my group, then also dropped to a knee. "Ms. Alexis. Surprised to see you in these parts."

"Trevor! What are you doing here?" I asked as soon as he rose and the others in the bar followed.

"Sundae," he said, addressing the woman next to him, "you better let me handle this."

Her dark eyes skated over each of us, and she let out a growl before striding back to the bar.

Trevor led us to a nearby table and shooed away the guys who had been sitting there. They quickly scattered and found a new table at one end of the building, near the dartboard, but their eyes never left us. Never left me, to be more specific. Booths lined the outside wall of the place, and at the other end was the only area with much light—a lamp hanging over a green felt-covered pool table. A couple of men leaned on their pool sticks as they watched us. Well, me, again. Sometimes, like with Rick, being Amadis royalty came in handy, but most of the time, I hated it.

"I banded my pack up with the Georgia one," Trevor said in answer to my question, "and opened up a second shop here. We all gotta do what we gotta do these days. So what brings you here?"

"Long story," I said as I sat on a stool at the bar-height table. "Tristan's on his way, but it could be a few hours."

Trevor's hard gaze traveled over the others, lingering on Vanessa as a low growl rumbled in his chest. He narrowed his brown eyes at Jax. "You were the Were in the Everglades last year. You met some of my boys."

Jax gave a curt nod. "That be me, mate."

Trevor turned back to me. "Did you really steal a ride from Sundae's pack?"

"We didn't know," I answered before Vanessa could open her mouth. "We had to get out of that town and—"

"I'll take care of it," he said with a nod. "But keep an eye on these guys or Sundae will kick them out on their asses."

"Excuse me?"

"Sundae, the leader of the Georgia pack. The woman you just met? My shop's out back, but this place is hers. She and her pack don' like outsiders, but since it's you and all . . ." He shrugged, and then lumbered toward the rear of the building, where he'd come from.

Sundae came over to our table.

"Glad to have you, Ms. Alexis," she said, her voice hard as she emphasized my name—delivering the message that the rest of my team wasn't quite as welcomed. Her sweet name sure didn't match the threat of the wolf simmering below her surface. "I apologize for my temper a moment ago."

She didn't sound at all remorseful.

"No, I'm sorry we took the bike."

"Oh, please. If I had known it was you, I wouldn't have acted like I had. My pack is always at your service."

I somehow didn't quite buy that.

"Don't worry. We're not planning to stay long," I said as warmly as I could manage.

"You're welcome as long as you need to," she said, the edge in her voice softening. A little maybe. Her gaze swept over my companions. "All y'all. We're not used to others, and everyone's a little on edge with all the shit going down in Savannah." Her eyes flicked to Vanessa. "And having a newly converted vamp around, especially *her*, makes us a little . . . prickly."

Vanessa sat back in her stool, crossed her arms, and rolled her eyes. I glared at her. *You can at least* try *to convince them, especially after stealing her bike.*

She sighed and then put on a syrupy smile as she leaned toward Sundae. "You really have nothing to worry about. I'm matriarch-certified and everything. The motorcycle was a simple misunderstanding."

Sundae's dark brown eyes fell on me.

"It's true," I said. "Rina, um, *Katerina* assessed her. We're all on the same side here." I hoped. "And we can repay whatever you need for the bike."

The werewolf snorted, dismissing my offer. "So, then, what can I get y'all to drink? Besides blood. We ain't that kind of dive."

Her newly adopted tone sounded kinder, but her words still bit—she trusted Vanessa less than I did. A tap into her mind showed me Sundae would be keeping a close eye on the vampire the entire time we were here. She made that thought loud and clear, but hid anything else she may have been thinking behind a wall of mundane mind-chatter.

That was the problem with telepathy, at least *my* ability. People's thoughts didn't come conveniently—I couldn't exactly pick out the precise thought I needed, but could only hear what ran through their minds at the moment—and often they didn't even come coherently. When they knew about my ability, like most of the Amadis and the Daemoni did, they carefully filtered their thoughts or found ways to obscure them. Some people had become quite good at doing so, effectively shutting me out.

Jax, Blossom, and I ate a lunch of fried bar food while Vanessa watched with her nose slightly crinkled. She didn't need blood yet, which was good. I hoped Charlotte knew where we could obtain more mage blood, since the supply Rina had given her was somewhere in the Atlantic Ocean or smattering the shores of the Outer Banks. *Gross.* I'd hate to be the Normans on the beach today.

"So you landed in a swamp?" I asked Jax and Blossom to make conversation as I eyed them. "You don't look or smell like it."

"Don't you love magic? These enchanted clothes are great! Of course, I had to clean up the rest of us." Blossom waved a French fry around her head, indicating her clean hair, and grinned. "But yeah, we did, right in the middle of a mucky old swamp. Jax gave me a ride to land. Thank God and the Angels he was there!"

"Thank God and the Angels you helped me flash," Jax said to Blossom. Something in the way they looked at each other gave me pause. Did Blossom feel the same attraction Jax had made loud and clear to Rina?

"And Bree helped you get here?" I asked, still trying to make sense of Blossom's earlier deluge of words.

"She gave us a message from Tristan," the witch said. "I guess the faeries in the Otherworld felt bad for us or something, since we had no way to contact each other. They allowed her to come to our world and help out."

"Hmm . . ." I wasn't sure what to think about that. Bree, a faerie, had done us a favor. Would we have to pay her back now, too? Or did we get a free ride with her, considering Tristan's her son? Thinking about faeries brought Lisa and Jessica to mind, and I pulled my backpack onto my lap and felt around it. The jar they'd given me for Kali's soul remained tucked away inside, seemingly intact. Good. Because Kali was going to pay for this. All of it.

We still hadn't heard from Tristan by the time we finished eating, so I asked Sundae if she had a quiet place Blossom and I could go to try her spell once again. We followed the Were through the kitchen and into a small office with a window that looked toward the side of the property. I thought there'd been a lot of bikes out front, but there were dozens more out here, perhaps over a hundred. Several mind signatures floated in the rear building, which apparently wasn't part of the bar, but not enough for all of those motorcycles.

The desk in the office overflowed with paperwork, but a small couch against the wall provided the space Blossom and I needed. She pulled out her scrap of Dorian's blanket, and I reached into the backpack and pulled out my own, just to smell it. To inhale his scent, which, admittedly, wasn't that of a little boy anymore and normally not the best smell in the world. But it brought me closer to him somehow.

"Let's begin," Blossom whispered, her voice thick with sadness. I chose to hold on to the wrath instead. If I didn't—if I let the grief take me—I'd break. And a Broken Alexis would be useless. Even Psycho Alexis was better.

I closed my eyes and opened my mind to Blossom's. Once we had a connection, I took my mind farther out as she chanted her spell under her breath. Nothing nudged us north or in any other direction. My mind expanded more, reaching out as far as I could go, skipping over the thousands of mind signatures in all directions. Blossom's chanting became more urgent as I pushed even farther. I thought I felt another slight nudge north, but I couldn't be sure, so I tried expanding my whole radius, stretching my mental boundaries as far as they would go. Blossom's voice fell quiet. I squeezed my eyes tight with concentration, and all sound, all senses—the whole world— ceased to exist around me as I reached as far as I possibly could.

And there.

A pull.

I strained for the distant mind signature. Forced myself to follow it. Almost touched it. And—

"*AAAAAAHHHHHH!*" A scream. A voice I couldn't distinguish as either male, female, or even human. Cold pain knifed into my head, like an ice pick stabbing into my brain.

All mind signatures disappeared. My mind went completely blank. And so did the world.

I came back to reality with my eyes still squeezed shut, my hands over my ears, and my body curled into a ball on the couch in Sundae's office. A soft moan came from my own throat, though I didn't realize it was me at first.

"Alexis." Blossom's voice, a soft whisper near my ear. I opened my eyes to find her on her knees on the floor in front of me, her hand on my shoulder. "Are you okay?"

Slowly I pulled my hands from my ears, only to find blood on them. Blossom reached for some tissues from a box on the desk and handed me a couple. I pressed them against my ears, and they came away with more blood. There must have been a small trickle from each one. Blossom used another tissue to dab at my lip—more blood, from my nose. My brain still felt like an ice pick was lodged into it.

"What happened?" the witch asked, her voice shaky and her eyes wide. I tried to sit up, but she held me down. "Take it easy. Something . . . wrong just went down, I think."

"Did you hear it?" I asked, my voice hoarse.

Blossom shook her head. "I couldn't get anything this time. I think my swim in the swamps may have washed too much of Dorian out of my blanket scrap."

"You didn't hear it through me?"

"I think you blocked me out somehow," she said quietly.

"I don't think it was me. I think . . ." I sat up, ignoring her insistence that I stay down. My nose and ears had stopped bleeding, though the pain in my head remained. "Someone felt me in their mind, and they didn't like it. They were really powerful and tried to push me out . . . or something. That's the only way I can explain it."

"Who? A guy? A woman?"

"I don't know. The mind signature felt so far away, I couldn't tell if it was a man or a woman or even if it was human."

Blossom's forehead creased as she studied my face, her eyes still filled with concern. "I don't like what it's done to you. Maybe doing this spell isn't a good idea."

I grabbed her wrist with my hand as near panic rose in me. "We *can't* give up, Blossom. This could be our only way to find Dorian."

She studied my face for a long moment as I silently pleaded with her.

"Okay, but if it happens again . . ."

"I'm sure it was nothing," I said a little too quickly. "I mean, my mind can only reach maybe eight or ten miles out, so it probably won't happen again once we're out of here. We'll be far away from them, whoever it was.

And really, it could have been my own mind doing it because I tried to push too hard. I'll be more careful. So don't worry, okay?"

I didn't tell her that with her spell, I was able to reach farther. Probably more like forty or fifty miles out. If she worried too much and thought she was making it worse, she might not try again, and we *had* to keep trying.

"Fine, but we don't do it again until we're far away from here," she said as she pulled her arm free from my grip.

"Deal," I agreed.

A knock on the door was followed by Sundae entering her own office.

"You have a phone call," she said to me, and she pointed at the phone on the desk. "You can take it right here."

Blossom discreetly took the bloody tissues from my hand and followed Sundae out of the office.

"What happened to your phone?" Tristan demanded as soon as I picked up. "It went straight to voicemail. I've been worried as hell about you."

12

HEARING TRISTAN'S LOVELY voice again sent a thrill through me, though the furious tone of it should have made me pee myself. It probably would have scared anyone else, but I knew the worry behind it. We'd been separated before. Our son was missing. We couldn't help but worry about losing each other again.

"Sorry. It, um, broke." I didn't have the heart to tell him I broke it myself during a minor temper-tantrum. "I'm glad you found me, though, and everyone's okay. I was worried, too, you know."

"I know, *ma lykita*," he said, his voice softer now. "You're right—we're all okay, and that's what matters. We'll see each other in a few hours—"

"You're still so *far*?" My heart sank. I didn't think they'd started that far away, and I'd hoped he'd been calling to say they were almost here. We seriously needed to talk. And I seriously needed to feel his arms around me.

"We're headed for the Atlanta safe house with this new convert. You'll have to meet us there."

"Okay," I said, trying to hide the disappointment I felt. "You have Sasha, right?"

"Erm, no. I thought she was with you."

My heart plummeted again and formed a pit in my stomach. "I haven't seen her since the midair fight with the Daemoni."

"She's tough, Lex. I'm sure she'll show up soon."

"How will she know to find us in Atlanta, though? Maybe we shouldn't go so far away."

"We don't know where she flew to. She could *be* in Atlanta. She'll sense the Amadis out wherever she is."

I blew out a sigh of resignation. I had a hard time picturing the sweet little dog we usually knew as being able to fend for herself for so long. To be able to travel so far. But, of course, she was more than the sweet little dog we usually knew, and I had to keep that in mind.

"So any ideas on how we get to Atlanta?"

I could have probably figured it out on my own, but when you have someone who could see the best solution, why take the time and brain power? Especially after what my poor brain had just been through.

"Trevor will set you up," he answered. "Just be careful, my love."

"Of course. I can take care of myself, but I have others here, too."

"I won't stop worrying about you until you're in my arms again."

"Well, that goes for both of us."

"See you soon."

Not soon enough, I thought as I hung up. A knock sounded on the door, and I waved my hand to open it.

"So, you need some transportation," Trevor said as he strode into the office, wiping his hands on a greasy rag. He chuckled at the look on my face. "I spoke with Tristan before we sent the call back here. How 'bout I give you something so you don't have to steal this time? Get your group and come 'round to the rear of the building."

I returned to the bar to retrieve everyone, and we went outside and out back, passing all of the motorcycles.

"Can you ride one yourself?" Trevor asked me. My eyes widened. This was what Tristan meant by the Were hooking us up?

"Don't you have a car or something?" I asked.

"Ha!" He laughed as though I'd made a hysterical joke, and then gave a shake of his head. "We're *bikers*. Cars are for pussies. Someone might have a truck or somethin' somewhere, but it could take a few hours to track one down."

"We don't have that kind of time," I muttered with a sigh. "Tristan's given me a few lessons, but I haven't really ridden by myself."

"The rest of y'all?" Trevor asked as his eyes scanned the others.

"No worries here, mate," Jax said.

"I'll, uh, ride with Jax," Blossom answered, taking a step closer to the were-croc. She looked up at him. "If that's okay with you?"

His face broke into a grin as he gave her a nod.

"I think you know my answer," Vanessa said.

Trevor's gaze came back to me. "Do you want to ride with her again or on your own?"

I cocked my head as I considered his question, grateful my headache had faded.

"On my own," I finally said with assurance. As Vanessa would say, I needed to pull on my big girl panties, and this was one of only a few ways I could be independent. I already relied on others for so much. "As long as Blossom can handle the extra shield?"

"You have to have your own shield anyway," she said. I opened my mouth to protest, but she stopped me. "Council's orders, direct from the matriarch."

Trevor gave me a refresher course, and then I made a few circles of the property as practice. Afterwards, the pack leader led us to a group of bikes at the far end of the parking lot.

"These are the ones I can spare. Take your pick."

He helped me choose the best one for me—a Harley Softail he'd customized into a bobber with flat black paint and purple trim. It couldn't have been more perfect.

"You were kind of my inspiration on this one, so it's fittin'," he admitted.

"You built all of these?" I asked, not sure what to make of his admission and not wanting to embarrass him.

"I mostly repair. The packs keep me pretty damn busy with all their fuck-ups, especially when they go Daemoni hunting, but I build when I can."

"Wait—*Daemoni* hunting?" I asked, my stomach knotting. The Amadis had rules, and hunting down the enemy as I imagined a wolf pack would do did not fall under those rules.

"Don't get your panties in a bunch," Trevor said. "We run the woods, and when we find them too close to Normans, we run them off, is all. Protect the innocents. It's the most fun we can have during the full moon."

I nodded as an idea occurred to me. "Instead of running them off, you think you can trap them somehow? Capture them without hurting them?"

He eyed me with bemusement. "Maybe the newly turned."

"Perfect." I gave him Tristan's and Charlotte's cell phone numbers so he could call us when his pack captured any young Daemoni—or others who wanted to be converted. "If we can get here, we will. Otherwise, we'll send someone else to take them to a safe house. You'll be helping us build our army."

I tried to make myself sound authoritative so my order came out that way—as an order. Because I knew Trevor and how he put his pack before all else.

"Anythin' for you and the Amadis," he said, although I didn't miss the reluctant grunt that followed.

Well, it was better than nothing. At least I felt like we'd accomplished something for our mission.

When we arrived at the Atlanta safe house after a maze of backcountry roads to avoid checkpoints and Daemoni hunters, I hadn't expected to see two more motorcycles there. After a long hello kiss and embrace, Tristan explained that he'd bought them in Jacksonville. They were the first vehicles they found for sale where they'd appeared.

"They *bought* them," I emphasized to Vanessa.

She shrugged. "I didn't see a wad of cash or a stack of credit cards in that backpack of yours." She lifted her chest and gave her breasts a shake. "Unless you're talking about using other 'currency'."

I rolled my eyes, but she was right—Tristan had had all of our cash on him when we'd had to bail off the plane.

I'd thought he'd been speaking to me while they were on the road, but I hadn't heard the loud Harley engines in the background. Charlotte explained she'd magically muffled the sounds.

"Wouldn't a car or van be easier?" I asked. "Especially now with all of us?"

Charlotte shrugged. "With Blossom's help to shield and cloak, the bikes aren't difficult. A lot easier to squeeze into tight spots when other drivers can't see you. Or to sneak past a checkpoint."

"Huh," I said with a nod of understanding. "We managed to avoid any checkpoints. Did you pass a lot?"

"Three, which are three too many, considering this is the United States of America." She shook her head slowly. "Not normal at all."

So apparently we'd be riding motorcycles for our mission, but for now we only rode from the safe house to my old home in Atlanta, which served as a secondary safe house and wasn't occupied at the moment. Although the Amadis had made it appear to have burnt down a couple of years ago, A.K. Emerson's "heirs" rebuilt it, making it look exactly like it had before. Because it *was* exactly like it had been before—the fire and resulting rubble had all been an illusion.

An odd mix of emotions slammed over me when we walked in through the back door by the garage and I flipped on the lights for the family room. Tristan had never lived here with us, and, at the time, I hadn't known the rest of the people here whom I called friends and even family now. Sheesh. I'd been nearly Norman then, nothing like the person I'd become. So having them all here felt a little weird, even if my own memories of the place were practically nonexistent. I did know that Mom, Dorian, and Owen had been the people in my life at the time, and one was gone by choice and the other against his will, and Mom was halfway around the world. My heart squeezed as I suddenly wished she were here, telling me everything I was doing wrong but loving and supporting me anyway. I bit my lip as I thought about how much I needed my mom.

Ridiculous. I had to hold on to the anger. I couldn't let this place get to me.

When Tristan and I passed Dorian's old bedroom on our way to my former suite, I nearly broke down. The Amadis had changed it, though, into more of a generic guest room rather than a little boy's room. *It's not his anymore,* I reminded myself. *It's just a place.*

Climbing into my old king bed in the master suite with Tristan on the other side felt weirder than any of the rest, though. But in a good way, because I hadn't forgotten the loneliness of my soul while I lived here. I snuggled into his arms, which he wrapped around me tightly. Finally, for the first time since several nights ago when Blossom had magicked me to sleep, I relaxed a bit. And I caught him up on all of my events and experiences, down to what happened in Sundae's office.

"You don't know who it was or where they were?" Tristan asked when I finished. His heart pounded into my ear as I lay on his chest and drew random shapes with my finger over the ridges of his hard stomach.

"I was pushing really hard and completely lost track. They could have been five miles from where we were or fifty. Maybe more. But I'm sure it's nothing. No one to worry about."

"Probably. Unless you think it could be Kali?"

My finger stopped by his belly button, and my brows pushed together. I hadn't considered that possibility. "I don't think so. I think I'd recognize her signature by now, even from that far away. On the other hand, whoever it was became enraged when I found them. I'd never felt anything like it before, not even when Vanessa used to push me out."

"Mad because you found them or because you were in their head?"

"You mean, like they're hiding something and knew who I was?"

"Maybe. They could even know Dorian's whereabouts."

"Huh." My finger returned to skating over his abs as I pondered this idea. "So maybe we *should* go back and try to find them again?"

"Let's see what you and Blossom can do from here first," he said as his hand rubbed circles over my lower spine. "You said the spell nudged you north again?"

"I think so, but I could have imagined it. You're right. We have to stay focused on Dorian. If it *was* Kali, then maybe he's not with her."

I tilted my head up to look at him, and my breath caught at his beauty. How he could still do that to me was beyond my understanding, but I wouldn't complain.

He curled down around me and kissed me on the forehead. "We also need to see what conversion missions Charlotte comes up with around the area so we can make the council happy."

Right. Our "official" mission.

Tristan's lips moved along my temple and down my jaw as he rearranged us so I lay on my back, and he leaned over me. His mouth traveled over my chin, along my neck and collarbone, and to the stone over my heart. As soon as his lips touched it, warmth zinged through me.

The feeling in my lower belly brought on a realization, and I groaned. "The tea mix. It's gone."

"We can't let that stop us from trying," he murmured against my chest. "We're still on a mission."

"At least this one is nice," I said in agreement.

His lips moved to my breast and made all kinds of promises of exactly how nice it would be. Unfortunately, with everyone in the house, I didn't quite get to enjoy it as much as I would've liked—I held back at the last minute so I wouldn't share my orgasm with my team.

THE NEXT MORNING, we all set to work right away. Charlotte, Sheree, and Jax went hunting for potential converts in downtown Atlanta, while Blossom and I sat in the middle of Dorian's old room, Tristan nearby to keep watch. Blossom began her chant, and we pushed and pushed until everything went black in my mind.

"That same thing again?" Blossom asked when I opened my eyes. I was surprised to find my head in Tristan's lap, my body curled in the fetal position next to him on the floor.

"No," I said as I pushed myself up. Dizziness waved over me, and I blinked against the gray trying to cloud my vision. My brows pushed together—I couldn't remember anything but stretching my mind as hard and as far as it would go. "I didn't hear anything this time. Why?"

"You're bleeding again," Blossom said.

Tristan's thumb wiped over the curve of my jaw and came away with a smear of red. I rubbed my finger over my upper lip, and it also showed blood.

"I'm fine," I muttered as I wiped my finger on my leathers. "It's not like yesterday."

Blossom looked at me with pursed lips.

"I *promise*."

Although it didn't feel as if an ice pick were lodged in my gray matter, my head did throb, but I refused to admit it. At least it didn't feel as bad as before, and this time nothing strange had happened. I began to wonder if I'd imagined that part yesterday.

"I think you're trying too hard," Tristan said. "Pushing your boundaries."

He reiterated what I'd told Blossom yesterday, and the idea may have been truer than I'd thought.

"What else am I supposed to do? Our son is out there somewhere. We *have* to find him. And unless you have a better solution, we have no other way."

He pulled me into his arms and soothed his hand down my back. "Pushing your boundaries isn't a bad thing. I'm not saying that. Just don't push too hard too soon. It's like a Norman weightlifter trying to exceed his max. If he goes too hard too fast, he gets injured. You injure this head of yours, you're no good to Dorian or the rest of us."

So we treated my ability—and Blossom's—as though we were training, pushing a little further each time but not to the point of my passing out. My ears did stop bleeding, but my patience wore thin. Nothing was working. Using my old house as a home base, we physically rode the streets of Atlanta, its suburbs, and beyond while I searched for Dorian's mind signature—and Kali's, Owen's, Victor's, and Lucas's, too. But we found no sign of Dorian or any of them. We questioned new converts, but they could only tell us that both Kali and Lucas seemed to have been up to something, but they didn't have the status to know what. Days grew longer as we moved into spring, and they turned into weeks with still no progress.

Dorian's birthday came, and Tristan and I spent the day like every other—searching for him, both physically and mentally. But in the end, all we could do was promise that we'd celebrate it with him as soon as we had him home. I refused to let myself cry even on that day. Worry and fear of what the Daemoni might have done to him tried to squeeze my heart, but I let the wrath smother them.

Sasha never showed, either.

"We have to do something else," I declared, thumping my fist on the table as my team stood around the kitchen one morning. "He's been gone a damn month already, and we're no closer."

"Where are we supposed to go, though?" Sheree asked. "What else can we do?"

I pushed myself off the table and threw my hands in the air. "I don't know. *Somewhere.* North, I guess, since that's the little bit of feeling we get."

Charlotte's phone rang, and she grunted when she saw the number.

"Alexis, we haven't really felt that for weeks," Blossom said as she watched Char leave the room to take the call.

"Maybe you haven't, but I have."

The witch cocked her head, her blond hair falling over her shoulder. "Really?"

No, not really. If I'd felt anything at all, it had been only the tiniest of nudges, which I couldn't know for sure meant anything. "Well, it's more than anything else we know."

"Come on, Alexis," Charlotte said, returning to the kitchen. "We have a job that will take your mind off things for a few days, then we can regroup on this."

"Char—" I started.

"Don't Char me." She stepped in front of me and crossed her arms over her chest as she pierced me with sapphire-blue eyes. Eyes like her son's. "Sheree and I have been handling almost all of these conversions, but it's time you get to work doing what you're supposed to be doing. And it sounds like this is too big of a group for me to handle on my own anyway."

I scowled.

"You need the distraction," she said.

I looked around the kitchen at all the pairs of eyes on me. I'd missed most of the conversion attempts Charlotte had made because I'd been focused on finding Dorian, but I *had* promised Rina I'd make this a priority, too. So far, though, our conversion opportunities had only been onesies and twosies, enough for Char to handle with Sheree's help. No big groups that would make a difference to the Daemoni.

"How big?" I asked, trying to let the idea excite me. Char was wrong—I'd never be distracted from my main goal of finding Dorian—but maybe going out on a conversion attempt, especially a big one like this, would give this one part of my mind a chance to rest. When I used to write and I'd have writer's block, doing something mindless or using a different part of my brain would help me unstick myself. The overtaxed part of my mind could wander freely without pressure, and lo and behold, my brain would often trip over the solution to my problem on its own. So maybe this could work. Besides, I really did need to show some effort in this area.

"There was a vamp party in Buckhead last night," Charlotte said. "Our guys saw at least twelve people turned, but they've been abandoned in an old apartment building."

"*Twelve?*" I asked, my eyes widening. "Shit. They're getting brazen, aren't they? Wait. How are we supposed to convert so many on our own?"

"See why I need you?" she asked before letting out a sigh. "We'll be lucky to get them all anyway, but we have to give it a shot."

I held my hands up. "All right. Fine. Let's do it."

We went over the plan, and then we moved out to a shoddy area near Buckhead. Charlotte and Blossom cloaked and shielded us when we came closer to a nest of Daemoni vamps. A coven of mages wasn't too far away, either. I tried to keep my mind open to everyone so we could hear our enemies' thoughts, but all the noise in their heads was too much for everyone to handle.

Rina had taught me that in battle, she'd monitor the enemies' thoughts and direct her people with her mind, allowing everyone else to focus on their fighting. I'd experienced this myself the day Tristan disappeared. Unlike her, though, I couldn't stay far away from the battle itself. Not this time anyway. Charlotte did need me. So when we went in, I'd have to keep part of my mind roaming the area surrounding us to listen for danger while keeping another part focused on our potential converts.

Two vans from the safe house waited for us in an underground garage near the target location with Amadis vampires as their drivers.

As soon as the bikes were parked and we dismounted, one of the vamps handed us some silver spikes.

"Once they state their desire to convert, and you get them near the vehicle, they'll need to be staked," Charlotte said, and the blood drained from my head. "It's the only way to get them safely back so we have more time to work with them."

My stomach clenched. I'd done this before. I'd plunged my dagger into Sonya's heart to keep her knocked out while Tristan drove us to the Captiva safe house the first time we tried to convert her. That had been way worse than cutting the stone out of her. Blood had spattered over my face and all over the backseat of Tristan's truck. But it had effectively kept her out cold for the rest of the drive and up until we removed the dagger from her heart once we were ready to begin the conversion. We'd have to do the same thing over and over again today. *Ugh.* Maybe this *would* be a real distraction.

"Tristan, you stay with Alexis, and Vanessa, you stay near me," Charlotte ordered. "Sheree and Jax, you two keep watch between here and there, and be ready to morph if necessary. A shield will attract that mage coven four blocks over, but if I do need to throw one up, Blossom, I need you ready to hold it. You come in with us so you can watch and learn. You might need to jump in. If so, just follow orders."

The witch nodded her understanding. Although Mom and Char had worked with her on Amadis Island, this had the potential to be her first real attempt. Nothing like trial by fire—that's how I had learned, first with Sheree and then with Sonya and Vanessa.

The two vamps from the safe house would stay by the vans, keeping watch on this end. My mind would be kept busy as I tried to stay connected to each of the guards while we did our thing.

A few minutes later, Tristan, Vanessa, Blossom, and I followed Charlotte around the corner and into an alley that ran through the middle of the block. We were surrounded by apartment buildings, most of them rundown and empty. Char shook two fingers in the air, signaling a second floor apartment in the first building to our right. I directed my mind up to it and found a dozen mind signatures. They all felt Norman . . . almost. They were still going through the transformation, and their signatures came faintly, almost dead, but with a hint of vampire lacing through them. If we accomplished this before dusk, not only would they be weak from the sun, but also from the transition. Once night fell, however, their transition would be basically complete, and they'd wake up all kinds of pissed off. And thirsty. Very thirsty.

Unfortunately, we couldn't simply sweep them away unconscious so they woke up at the safe house. They had to *want* to keep the goodness still inside them. So we crept upstairs and into the apartment, finding them all out cold, scattered on the living room floor. Charlotte and Vanessa grabbed a woman, Tristan and I grabbed a man, and we carried them outside before forcing them awake. These first two were easy—they were boyfriend and girlfriend and had been attacked without warning. They still had so much love for each other, making their decisions straightforward. After I checked with Sheree and Jax that the coast remained clear, we took them to the vans where they sat and waited. They didn't even have to be staked.

The next two weren't quite as simple, but not difficult, either. Charlotte and I had to talk to them for a while, Blossom listening closely, as we tried to explain what had happened to them and what their choices were. Eventually—*finally*—they agreed to come with us, but as we came closer to the vans, one started freaking out, which caused the other to flip out, too. Tristan plunged a stake into our vamp's heart, but Vanessa hesitated over hers. Before the newborn could get away and alert the Daemoni of our presence, Charlotte staked her with the silver.

"Sorry," Vanessa whispered. "I remembered what it felt like."

This excuse of hers tumbled around my mind as we rushed back to the apartment. Was that compassion she felt? Or remorse for herself? I tried not to worry about it as we pulled the next two out.

And then things went bad. In a hurry.

13

CHARLOTTE'S GUY STARTED screaming like a woman giving birth as soon as he roused from his slumber and saw us, which woke my guy up fully. Mine had a small build for a man, so he'd nearly completed the transformation. Which meant he was thirsty. He dove for my neck without hesitation.

"Stop!" I ordered as I pushed him off and he tried to fight me.

He didn't stop. His hands flew out in front of him and grasped onto my shoulders, and he yanked me towards his face, his fangs out. I kneed him in the stomach and shoved him off of me for the second time. He tried to dive for me again, but Tristan paralyzed him.

Char's newborn saw this and started screaming again. Then he sprang upwards. Whether he knew what would happen or not, we'd never know, but his new force flew him to the top of the building. He barely landed on the edge and tumbled off. Not knowing any better, he only screamed as he plummeted to the ground and landed on his back with a loud crack. When he discovered he hadn't died, he sprang to his feet and ran off yelling in a panic. Char and Vanessa ran after him.

"It . . . it worked?" the new vamp in front of me asked after witnessing the circus-like scene. His eyes widened and filled with malice as he answered his own question. "It really worked! We're vampires!"

"You wanted this?" I asked, my stomach sinking.

"Fuck yeah! Who wouldn't?" He tried to move against Tristan's power but was unable to. His eyes narrowed as he glared at my husband. "What the hell are you doing to me? I'm gonna fuck up your girl if you don't stop."

Tristan simply rolled his eyes.

"Shut up and listen to me," I said. "Did you really want this? Do you understand what it means?"

"I've been wanting something like this since I was a kid—a chance to get back at all those bullies. They'll never see it coming. I'm not exactly, well, him." His eyes flicked up toward Tristan's imposing figure. "But now it doesn't matter."

I tried to talk him out of it, tried to convince him that what he had to give up for his revenge wasn't worth the time he'd give those bullies, but the idiot refused to listen. We went round and round, but he'd made up his mind long ago, as soon as he thought vampires might truly exist. And he became more and more irate as the pain of the thirst filled his eyes.

"We can't force him," Charlotte said, appearing by my side. "Let's move on. We don't have much more time. That dumbass out there will be bringing their creators down on us any minute."

"Good! You all deserve to fucking die, keeping me like this, and I can't wait for it," the guy in front of me said. His tongue darted out and swiped over his lips. "I bet you taste good, sweetheart." His gaze slid down to my hips. "Can't wait to bite into that thigh—*oof.*"

The guy's head swung back, smacking against the brick building. Tristan's fist had darted out so fast, none of us had seen it coming.

"Guess we'll have to take care of you first," the newborn snarled as he glared at Tristan.

Tristan chuckled, and then he leaned over, his face only inches from the vampire's. His voice came out in a low growl. "You have no idea what you've gotten yourself into. Don't think for a minute that you're truly at the top of the food chain now."

Uncertainty flashed in the vamp's eyes, but only briefly before the orbs hardened into marbles. I scanned his mind to make sure he didn't want to come with us. He really didn't know anything about this world he'd become a part of, but he believed wholeheartedly the lies he'd been told. I shook my head at Charlotte.

Maybe eventually when he realizes the truth, I told her, *but not now.*

"Hold him here, Tristan," she said, "for as long as we can get."

"Glad to." Tristan lifted the side of his mouth in a smirk. The new vampire hissed, but could do nothing else.

After checking the area again and finding no new mind signatures, Char and I went in for another pair, but they woke up before we managed to drag them out of the room. They broke free and took off. The others began to wake, too, then suddenly more vampires were popping into the room. The whole Daemoni nest came for their newborns.

"*We need to get out of here,*" Charlotte said.

A female Daemoni squealed with glee when she realized who we were, and then she soared for me. Others followed suit, and Charlotte and I had no choice but to fight our way out of the apartment.

Tristan, we could use your help, I called out to him. He barged into the doorway and started blasting the vamps with his power. Charlotte and I tried to go for the remaining newborns, but the Daemoni protected them closely.

"*Let's just go,*" Char said.

With the mage coven so close and not knowing what kind of traps were around, we couldn't flash back to the vans, but could only run at top speed. Of course, the vampires were nearly as fast as us, and then other Daemoni blocked our way. A white crocodile clamped his jaw over one of them and shook it side to side. A tiger lunged into the alley and attacked another. Blossom shot spells as fast as she could while Tristan carried her since she was the slowest of us all. With his free hand, he blasted those he could reach with his power.

"We don't have any more," Charlotte called out to the safe house vamps by the vans when they came in sight. "Go! Just go, go, go!"

They jumped into the vans and peeled out, carrying off only four of the twelve newborns. Charlotte and Blossom shot spells at the vampires chasing us, and lightning jolted out of my hand as we ran for the bikes. Vanessa plowed into a Daemoni and ripped his arms off, slowing him down. As soon as we were on the bikes, Charlotte cloaked us, and Tristan blasted a wall of his power at them, knocking them several yards away, giving us the chance we needed. Not close enough to find us and cloaked from their vision, they scrambled after us blindly, and we were able to escape.

I didn't let out my breath of relief, though, until we were back at the safe house.

"I can't believe we only got four of them," I growled as we headed inside to begin the real work of the conversions. "I thought we were doing well."

"We were for a while," Charlotte said. "But this wasn't unexpected. It happens every time. Four's not bad. It's a third."

"Which means they gained twice as many as we did. We'll never build an army that can beat them at this rate."

"Have faith," Char said. "We don't need to be as big as them. Only better."

I didn't reply, because I didn't see how we could be better without changing our ways. The Daemoni would always have the upper hand because that's how the physical world worked—while the good guys stuck vehemently to their principles, the bad ones ignored everything but their end goal, regardless of the casualties and consequences to get there. They schemed, sneaked, squirmed, and stampeded their way to success. In contrast, we came across as meek and soft. Not that there was anything wrong with relying on our faith more than our brawn or adhering to our ideologies, but I thought there were some smaller changes we could make that might make a big difference in the coming war. But what did I know? I was still a baby in this world.

We went to work immediately, and the conversions of the vampires took another three days of focus from my team. With the converts who were already there, the safe house was at near capacity, which meant before long, they would need to use the house where we were staying. That reinforced my belief that we needed to move on and let the Atlanta team do their thing here. Of course, this meant a lot of new Daemoni wouldn't be converted simply because we didn't have room. Without a place to help the converts, we'd never be able to keep up. We needed to beat the Daemoni to the Normans and prevent them from being turned in the first place. That wouldn't help our numbers, but would at least protect the humans. But we were already at a disadvantage and couldn't protect them until we had a bigger army. We were in a Catch-22 situation.

There had to be something we could do differently. A way to draw out the Daemoni who could still be saved and demolish the rest. I couldn't see how their constant advantage and ability to grow maintained balance. It sure as hell seemed the world was tilting further and further off balance every day, and one day soon, we'd tip over into ruins. But again, what did I know? Whenever I brought up ideas such as this, I was immediately shut down, even by Tristan, who said it wasn't our place to question the Amadis way. Not yet, anyway.

"I guess we should head north now," Charlotte said the evening we'd finished with the vampires as she, Tristan, and I sat around the living room. Vanessa was watching a movie in the family room, Sheree had stayed at the safe house working, and Jax and Blossom were . . .

Where were they? They'd been spending a lot of alone time together lately, but Blossom hadn't said anything to me yet, which wasn't like her. Of course, Dorian and our missions consumed all of my waking thoughts—and most of my sleeping ones, too. I wasn't being a very good friend, and I'd have to find a way to make it up to her. Someday, when life and death, including my son's, didn't preoccupy me.

"Actually, we need to hit Savannah first," I replied to Char's suggestion. I'd been right about the distraction of the conversion allowing my mind to think more clearly about our problem. "We should have gone there a long time ago, really. Where else is there a better opportunity for answers?"

"Savannah's pretty dangerous," Tristan reminded me. "Is it a risk we want to take?"

"It doesn't matter. You know we need to. Mom still feels Dorian is here in the Southeast. Maybe Blossom and I aren't feeling any more nudges because we're so close as it is."

This argument had grown old. Tristan and I had already discussed it several times and knew we needed to go. Of course, we hadn't found signs of Dorian anywhere near there when Blossom and I had tried while sitting in Sundae's office, but time had passed. Maybe he'd been brought there now, since Savannah had such a heavy Daemoni presence. Probably not, but even so, people there might know things. People who might be thinking about him and his location.

"And the risk to our team?" Tristan asked again.

The question led to the whole reason why we hadn't yet mentioned going to Savannah to anyone else: Our group was too big to sneak in, but definitely not big enough to take on all of the Daemoni there.

"You know the answer," I said.

He rubbed his neck and nodded. Charlotte's eyes bounced between the two of us for a moment before the answer dawned on her.

"No way in hell," she said.

"If we're by ourselves, Tristan and I can get close enough for me to scan thoughts without being seen. And if we *are* seen, well ... we're the strongest of our group."

"And you're royalty! Sophia and Rina would have my ass if something happened to you," Charlotte said. "You can't simply flash out of there unless you want Pastor McCorkle bailing you out again. I'll go with you so we at least have a cloak."

"They'll sense your magic," Tristan said.

"Let them," Char replied. "Like you said—we're the strongest of our group."

Tristan and I exchanged a look. She was right—after him and me, she was our strongest. And the three of us, with her cloak, would be better than the two of us alone and visible. If Owen were here, we'd take him with us. Well, at one time we would have. Now the bastard would probably turn us in. Char was his replacement, which meant she'd be going with us on this mission.

"What about me?" Vanessa asked from the doorway. "You know I can help."

And here came the problem Tristan and I had anticipated: Everyone would *want* to go, regardless of the risk. They'd known of the danger they'd be in when they volunteered for the team, and they all wanted to help. Whether to actually find Dorian or to protect me, though, was still a little up in the air. Vanessa, however . . . I think she wanted to prove herself every chance she could get, and I appreciated her effort. In more ways than one. Except now.

"You didn't want to go near Savannah before," I reminded her. "A little too risky, remember?"

"That's when we were already captured. When I thought we'd be delivered straight into the bastards' hands. But I did go into Savannah before. To find out where your pendant was." She leaned against the decorative pillar at the entrance of the living room and crossed her arms over her chest. "I know exactly where to take you, where you'll be safe so you can scan all the brains you want."

Blossom appeared behind Vanessa, and I let out a sigh. *Here we go.*

"I'll stay back," she said. "Jax and I can hang out here."

Thank God. She'd been the one I'd worried about most. She wanted to do everything possible to help us, but I hated having her in the middle of fights, and things could get especially nasty in Savannah.

"I'll convince Sheree that she needs to stay at the safe house," Char said.

And so it was decided—the next morning before dawn, the four of us left for Savannah.

As we approached the small city, the evil energy of the Daemoni swirled around me like a dark mist, so heavy it hung palpably in the air. When Vanessa and I had been here barely over a month ago, the evil hadn't felt this thick. At that time, I'd been so worried Vanessa had set me up, only fear had coated my skin. A small part of me still thought she could be tricking us, but none of me felt fear now. The tight ball of anger that sat in my heart expanded and whirled in my chest, overtaking all other emotion. These assholes here shouldn't be allowed to live. Not when their leaders had my son. Once again, I considered the dark magic that could potentially annihilate all of them. If only it didn't come at such a great cost.

"*Alexis, if you don't gain control, I'm not taking you in there,*" Tristan said in my mind. "*If you're not focused, you're nothing but a liability.*"

I'd ridden on the back of his motorcycle this time instead of on my own, and he felt my rage escalating. I inhaled deeply, but the Daemoni energy gagged me, and I blew it out quickly. So I focused on the feel of my body against his, on the rumble of the bike underneath us. He shared with me a sexy image of the two of us together, which partially annoyed me—how could he think of that right now?—but succeeded in distracting me.

I'm fine, I said after a moment, and I was.

"*For the record, I can think of you naked anytime,*" he said. "*Especially in times like this when I need the distraction myself.*"

Thanks for the tip.

"*My pleasure.*" I could feel him smirking. "*Maybe when we get out of here, we can act on it.*"

Hmm . . . it would be nice to have some time alone.

"*That's what I'm talking about.*"

My lower belly warmed, making the distraction a complete success. My temper came back under control, and I wanted control now. Because I would wait to unleash this wrath I embraced so dearly onto those who truly deserved it: Lucas and Kali. We had no further information about which one took Dorian, but I didn't care. They'd both done enough to hurt the people I loved to deserve everything I could give them.

Vanessa directed us to a church on the outskirts of town, close enough for me to reach the central area of the Daemoni's keep—down by the river, home to the bar and tourist scene, as well as the port, where freightliners docked. We crept inside the church, but it had apparently been abandoned. Go figure, considering the state of the city. Charlotte put up a shield and cloak over the entire building, then I sat in one of the wooden pews, closed my eyes, and opened my mind.

I scanned the entire area first, reaching as far as I could possibly go, which proved to be much farther than I could a month ago. Our training had apparently been working. Holding on to a small thread of hope, I searched for Dorian's mind signature, but didn't find it. In fact, I found only a handful of child mind signatures in the whole city. What had the Daemoni done to all the children? A sick feeling crawled along my spine, making me shudder.

I searched for Lucas and Victor, and Kali and Owen, too, but none were here.

So then I began sweeping through the Daemoni minds, skimming over their putrid thoughts, stopping only when something sounded interesting. Very little did. My mind was open to Tristan, Charlotte, and Vanessa, so they could stop me if they heard something I didn't.

"Whoa, back up," Vanessa whispered at one point. We'd just heard the word *summoned* from a vamp by the docks and *Virginia* from another with him.

"*What the hell is this guy talking about? He's a fucking idiot,*" the first vamp thought.

"*I'm tellin' you, man. It's in Virginia,*" the second guy said aloud, but the first only snorted in response before moving the discussion on to the jewels in the crate at their feet.

I looked at Vanessa, and her eyes tightened for a moment. "I guess it was nothing."

"Are you sure? You look like you know something," I said, studying her face closely.

The corners of her mouth turned down. "I heard those two words—*summoned* and *Virginia*—and it sparked a memory of something I heard a long time ago. Something Lucas was spewing about one time, about the Summoned."

"As in the sons?" I asked, excitement lacing the question.

"I think so, but I'm not definitely sure. It's not like he told me anything when it came to shit like that."

"But he did have plans for them?" Tristan asked. "Did he mention Virginia?"

She shook her head, the tips of her blond ponytail swishing across her back. "Like I said, he hardly said anything. Nothing that made sense, anyway. It was just one of his typical blowups that he never mentioned again. I don't even know if this is relevant."

"But it *could* be," I persisted. "Dorian could be a Summoned. Rina said we needed to watch out for them, and Mom thinks they could all be together. Why are you just now mentioning this?"

"He's *not* a Summoned, though. Not yet. And what Lucas was saying— I didn't understand his rant, but he sounded angry with them. Whatever it was, if it had been anything at all, he wouldn't have lumped Dorian in with the rest of them. He values the boy's potential way too much."

"But something must have clicked in your mind," I said. "Something in Virginia?"

She threw her hands up. "I don't know what to tell you, Alexis. The two words caught my attention, so I said something, but apparently there's nothing to it. Now that we've listened to them, I can tell you I don't know those two, so if there's anything to this at all, I know for sure *they* wouldn't be in the loop. They don't have the status. But you said if anything caught my attention to let you know, so I did."

"They could have been talking about anything," Charlotte said. "Who the hell knows? Maybe his creator is in Virginia, and he's being summoned there. Vampire masters can do that, you know— summon their children. There's no telling what these guys were talking about."

I sat back in the pew, tapping my fingers against my lips, but nodded. Char was right. There could be nothing to the whole thing. Probably just mundane thoughts like everyone else's. Nobody knew anything here. *Except, perhaps, Vanessa.*

Still, I kept my mind focused on the docks for a little while longer, skipping back to those guys a couple of times. The word *summon* popped in again, but before I could grasp onto the full thought, something else caught my attention. Something very close. As in right outside the church.

"*Two newborns,*" Tristan said.

I focused my mind on their thoughts. *Seems like they're only a couple of days old. They're lost and confused.*

Tristan and Char nodded, then she crept over to a window. I snuck up behind her, and we peered outside. Two women who appeared to be in their mid-twenties huddled together near a tree barely outside the church's property line. They wore torn dresses, their hair looked like rat nests, and dirt smudged their newly porcelain skin. Their eyes were big and glassed-over as they darted around, unable to settle on anything. One woman's hand scratched at her throat, and on closer inspection, I noticed their eyes were sunken deeply into their cheeks with purple half-moons under them.

"They're starving," I whispered.

I sought out their thoughts and shared them with the others. The women seemed to have no idea what had happened to them. They knew they were thirsty and what they were thirsty for, but they hadn't found any humans since they'd awoken. In fact, they hadn't seen a single soul since their transformation. Damn irresponsible vampire parents. If there had been any humans nearby, these two would have massacred them without proper guidance. Especially as thirsty as they were now.

"They're prime," I said. "We need to go out there."

"Let Vanessa and me go first," Tristan said. "They get a whiff of you, and we'll have a bigger problem on our hands."

He motioned for Vanessa and Charlotte to head for the front of the church, and I followed him to the side door in the back. He and Vanessa went out first, and as soon as they had control of the two newborns, Charlotte and I came out and began our work. We'd barely said, "you're safe with us," when I felt the surge of mind signatures heading for us.

"It's a trap," I yelled.

We blurred for the motorcycles, but Daemoni already surrounded us.

"Thought we sensed Amadis around," a female vampire said as she sauntered closer to us, "and look who we found."

Tristan, Charlotte, and Vanessa all moved in on me, but I wasn't about to let them fight without me. I pushed myself between Tristan and Char, and we all stood in a square, shoulder-to-shoulder. I swiped my thumb over the dagger at my hip and extracted it from its sheath at the same time Char pulled hers from her cleavage. Brass knuckles, covered in silver, already covered Vanessa's fists.

Ten Daemoni, all vampires, closed in on us. Fools. The sun shone brightly over us, which had to have weakened them at least some, and there weren't nearly enough to overtake us.

Easy peasy, I thought just as they dove for us.

Not as easy as I expected, though. The sun barely affected these vamps, which meant they were older and, therefore, more experienced. They fought expertly, and it became apparent they'd been sent purposely to kill Amadis. Based on their thoughts, though, they hadn't expected Tristan or me, and were a little unsure of what to do with us. They knew they couldn't kill us, but they did their best to not let us get away.

I fought hard, slashing them with my dagger, elbowing them in the jaws, smashing their noses against my knee, and plowing my foot into temples and groins. The dagger did the most damage so I focused on using it, but they kept jumping out of my way. So I blasted lightning at them, then dove in, sending electricity through my dagger as I plunged it into a vamp's ribs, straight into the heart. He bucked and screamed, and I jumped off, pulling my dagger with me, right before he flashed away.

Another vamp came for me, but I blasted her with electricity followed by Amadis power. Her body seized and convulsed, and I took the opportunity to slash my dagger across her chest and stomach. She fell to her knees, and her hands clawed at my legs. I swiped out again, opening a gash through her cheek. She screamed and disappeared. Tristan's arm ensnared me, and he blurred us to his motorcycle while shooting his power at the vamps on Char and Vanessa, and I blasted more Amadis power at anyone I could hit. The Daemoni flew far enough away that Char and Vanessa could scramble for their bike. Vanessa took the driver's seat, and Char hopped on the back, throwing up shields and cloaks over us as we took off.

We sped down the country roads, leaving the newborns behind. Again. This whole conversion thing and building our army was proving to be harder than I expected. Charlotte had been so busy with conversions the last couple of years, I thought it would be easy enough.

One here and another two there had kept her and the safe houses busy and nicely full, but they weren't enough now. Not at the rate the Daemoni were turning Normans. Especially when they kept ambushing us.

We had been cloaked and shielded in the church. How did the Daemoni even know we were there? How did they know to set the trap at that particular location?

14

FOUL MOOD DIDN'T begin to describe how I felt by the time we arrived back at the familiar house in Atlanta. I had to reign in all of my self-control to keep from punching something.

"Aikido?" Tristan asked as I stomped into the kitchen with him right behind me.

I glanced around the room—at the natural gas stove I had rarely ever cooked on but now missed so much, the granite-topped island, the décor that was still in the neutral beiges and browns Mom favored. She'd decorated it, after all, since I hadn't cared much about what my home looked like at the time. And now here stood Tristan, the one piece that had been missing in those days. And even so, life remained incomplete. Probably always would be. Our lives would always be fu—

"It will help you relax," Tristan said when I hadn't replied.

I shrugged off my backpack and leather jacket and draped them over the back of a wooden chair at the kitchen table. "Yeah. Sounds good."

He followed me out the rear door to the backyard. We walked around the pool reflecting the twilight sky and into the grass under the tall oak trees. And I went on the attack.

Tristan took every punch and kick I threw at him, but didn't do much in the way of fighting back. I danced around him, and my gaze traveled over to the back fence, where two years ago I'd thought I'd seen him standing there watching me—where I *had* seen him but didn't believe it—during my last days at this house. Emotions other than anger tried to break through and take over my heart. So I swung harder at Tristan as I reminded myself of *why* I hadn't believed it was him at the time. *Why* he'd been gone so long. *Who* had held him captive. Who held our son now. Tristan deflected the punches easily. I threw all my force into a roundhouse kick, and he parried it.

"Fight back," I growled at him, and knowing what I needed, he did. Everything I did became fiercer than the move before it as the fury swelled again, and I embraced it. I took the beating he gave me, and I delivered it right back to him.

"Stop," he finally said as he grabbed me around the waist from behind, pinning my arms against my body. I squirmed against his hold.

"No."

"This is supposed to be relaxing, and you're not relaxing. If anything, you're getting more worked up."

"Good. That's what I need."

He held me tighter, his breaths lifting his chest against my shoulder blades. "Talk to me. Tell me what's going on in that head of yours."

I fell still. "What the hell do you think? I'm pissed at them for taking Dorian, but that's okay. I need to be. I *want* to be."

"It's more than that. You've been harboring anger for weeks." His cheek pressed against mine, his tangy-sweet scent wafting into my nose and mouth as his breath tickled my lips. "What else, *ma lykita*? What else is wrong?"

I huffed. "Oh, I don't know. Let's see. My protector—the guy who's like a brother to me—betrayed us. We haven't made any progress in finding Dorian, probably because they have a cloak on him, which means we'll never be able to locate him, let alone rescue him because we don't have a mage strong enough to break through. We've converted a whole four people in the last week, which is nothing compared to the number of humans the Daemoni have infected in the Atlanta area alone, but it doesn't matter because even if we converted three times as many, we still wouldn't compare, and we don't have a place to put them all anyway." I inhaled a deep breath before continuing. "Blossom and Jax seem to have something going on, but we don't get a chance to talk about such normal things, and what's the point when we're in the midst of what could become World War III, which will be unlike any war this world has seen? And you and I . . . shit, Tristan. The stone hasn't worked yet in giving us a daughter, but it's not like we've had much chance to let it work."

"Ah." His arms released me only for his hands to clamp on my shoulders and turn me around to face him, and then he pulled me in closer. "I understand."

I studied his face before falling into his stunning eyes, the gold sparkling beautifully at the moment. My brow furrowed. "You understand what?"

"Everything." The corners of his lips tipped up in a sexy smirk. "But mostly, I understand exactly what you need." His head dipped down, and his lips pressed against my neck. "You're sexually frustrated."

I snorted. "Possibly. Okay, very much probably. But I think it's the least of my problems."

"Maybe." His mouth opened slightly, and his tongue swept over the sensitive spot under my ear. "But it's one problem I can solve right this very minute."

I steadied my legs as my knees began to quiver. "Right this minute?"

"Well," he sucked on my ear lobe, and he may as well have sucked in a very different place, as it had the same effect, "over the next many minutes. Maybe hours, but I don't think you can last that long."

I chuckled, the sound husky as my body responded to his hands, which had drifted down my arms and fell to my waist, his long fingers sliding under the waistband of my leathers. He grasped my hips and pulled me up against him so my breasts pressed against his hard chest, and his erection pressed against my belly. He kissed his way along my jaw until his mouth finally reached mine.

"Unfortunately, under the circumstances, I don't think you can solve this problem," I said against his lips. He sucked my bottom one into his mouth, scraping his teeth over it before letting go.

"What circumstances?"

I let out a sigh. "My issues? Too many people here? The whole reason I'm frustrated in the first place?"

His tongue swept out, over my lips, into my mouth. I met it with my own, practically losing myself in the kiss. My mind opened wide.

"*What people?*" Tristan asked, feeling me inside his head.

I realized for the first time there were no mind signatures around. Not in or around the house, anyway. There were some down the block, in the other homes in the neighborhood, but they all belonged to Normans.

Where is everyone?

"*You were so mad, you didn't notice they stayed at the safe house.*"

We carried on the conversation even as he continued kissing me senseless. *Seriously? Why?*

"We have a couple of hours to ourselves. I may have made a special request."

For the first time in weeks—probably since Rina gave her approval to search for Dorian—my heart skipped with pleasure.

Have I told you lately how much I love you?

"Why don't you show me?"

In answer, I deepened the kiss while pressing my body tighter against his, eliminating any air between us. I raised my hands to his neck and dug my fingers into his hair, pulling his mouth closer to mine. One of his hands remained on my hip while the other slid down to my butt and lifted. I wrapped my legs around him, and we continued kissing as he carried me inside.

As soon as we reached the bedroom, I dropped my legs and extricated myself from his arms. I missed them already, missed the heat of his body against mine, but we had too many clothes on. Way too many clothes on. Tristan's shirt came off first, followed by my corset, then our boots and leather pants.

Our hands and mouths were all over each other, kissing and caressing and playing, enjoying such a rare occasion of time alone. We needed this, this time to bond, to feel our hearts beating as one again, to remind our souls we were in this together. We were together in everything. Forever. And together, we would conquer.

For now, we only had to conquer ourselves. Our lust. Our primal need for each other.

As Tristan's mouth returned to mine and his hands slid over my back, I pressed mine on his chest and gently pushed him, walking him backwards until his legs hit the bed. He sat down and pulled me between his thighs until my breasts were at his mouth level. His hands explored my back and butt and thighs as his tongue lingered over my nipple, licking and twirling and flicking before pulling it into his mouth. One hand moved to my other breast, caressing, massaging, and then grasping as the other hand slid between my legs. His teeth grazed the hard ball of my nipple at the same time he slipped a finger inside me.

I arched my back, sweeping my hands down my sides and to my front, where I found him big and hard. He groaned against my breast when I took him in my hands, and he sucked harder as I stroked him. The feeling of his finger inside, curling and stroking, combined with the pleasure I gave him made the fire in my belly burst.

"I want you," I panted. "I want all of you. Inside me."

He pulled back. Grabbed both of my wrists with one hand and tugged them off of him. Raised them over my head.

"Nuh-uh," he said as he stood, then turned us around. "This night is all about you."

He gently pushed my arms backwards until my body had to follow, and I lay on the bed, my butt on the edge, my feet barely touching the floor. He kneeled in front of me. I quivered in anticipation. He kissed my lower belly, made lazy circles with his tongue on the sensitive skin where my thigh met my pelvis. His hands slid under my thighs, pushed them up and out. And finally . . . oh God, finally . . . his tongue dipped down. And he lapped and twirled and sucked while his fingers filled me, pumping and stroking until I screamed his name with utter release as the first orgasm washed over me.

"Now." I panted. "*Please.*"

"Not yet."

He continued to tease and excite and arouse me as my muscles convulsed and another wave took me under. I called out his name, begging for him to fill me, screaming when he didn't relent. But then finally, slowly, he moved his way up, his mouth exploring every inch of my skin, and my body jerked and arched, waiting for him to finally slide inside. And then we were everywhere with each other. Our bodies moving with each other, against each other, bucking and riding, thrusting and rocking. We played our favorite games, used our powers to tease each other to the edge, hit roll after roll after roll of climax until we were completely shattered.

Then we lay naked in each other's arms for the first time in ages, our bodies spent but our souls full.

"Still frustrated?" Tristan whispered, his breath hot and tangy-sweet against my cheek.

"You did take care of that problem," I said with a smile. "For now anyway."

If only our other problems were so easily solvable.

MY MIND EXPANDED, sweeping over the neighborhood, the area, the city, stretching beyond its normal limits, while staying connected with Blossom's mind. Hundreds of thousands of little energy pricks wavered around us—mind signatures. We'd discovered the cover of night made this easier, when most Normans were sleeping. I could always pick out Dorian's signature, whether he was sleeping or awake, but it would be much simpler when not surrounded by the energy of so many others. We swept over Atlanta, tried to push out toward the coast. But . . .

There.

"*I felt it!*" Blossom's mental voice nearly squealed in my mind.

We both felt a nudge. A gentle bump. North again.

She picked up the chanting of her spell, concentrating harder as I tried to steer us farther north. We slid over the countryside, pushed until I thought we might even have moved beyond the state line. Another slight tug to keep going. But my head pounded. Blackness started to seep into the edges of my consciousness. I snapped our minds back before I passed out.

"Definitely north," Blossom said from her cross-legged seat in front of me. She released her tight grip on my hands.

I pressed my fingers to my head and rubbed circles into my temples.

"Yes, north," I agreed as I opened my eyes.

My thumb did a quick check under my nose and by my ears, and I was grateful to find no blood this time. I had been close to pushing my limits . . . but never had I been able to reach out so far. Way beyond what Rina had ever mentioned being capable of doing.

"We'll discuss it with the team tomorrow." First, I needed to talk to Tristan about it.

Before I could, however, a call came in from Trevor and Sundae. They'd cornered five newly infected were-panthers during their first full moon. Panthers weren't indigenous to the area, and Trevor thought them dumped by their creator. We made the trip once again to the Georgia countryside near the coast and returned with five new converts.

Maybe things were beginning to look up.

"Tristan?" Charlotte asked a few mornings after our little success as she leaned over the kitchen island, her elbows on the counter. Her hands fisted together, and she rested her chin on them as she looked up at us.

He and I stood on the other side of the island, and the rest of the team was gathered in the kitchen, as well. Tristan took my hand between his, closed his eyes, and focused for a long moment while the rest of us waited silently.

"Alexis and I discussed it, and nothing has changed," he said. "We go north."

So the next day we packed up our few belongings on the bikes and prepared to depart. Right as we were about to leave Georgia for good, a white fur ball bounded up the driveway.

"Sasha!" I squealed as I scooped her up and snuggled my face into her little neck. "Where have you been? We almost left you!"

She licked my face as if to say she knew. I wondered what she'd been up to on her own for these past few weeks and wished I could read her thoughts. Animals were like faeries, though—I could sense their mind signatures, but drew a big blank when I tried to dig deeper.

When we headed out, we looked like a small biker gang: seven of us dressed in leathers and black on five Harley-Davidsons. Sheree rode my bike while I rode with Tristan. Sasha stood on the gas tank in front of him, wearing the goggles and leather coat I hadn't been able to resist buying at Trevor's shop, hoping she'd turn up again. Charlotte kept us cloaked and shielded until we were out of the Atlanta suburbs and on country roads, then she removed the cloak so I wouldn't have to focus so much on keeping a link between all of our minds. The connection allowed us to "see" each other, but when I didn't have to worry about maintaining it, I could let a bigger part of my mind roam, searching for familiar mind signatures.

While in Tennessee, we stopped at the faeries' cottage in the mountains to see if the sisters knew or had heard anything about Dorian or the Daemoni's plans—if they even wanted to be helpful—but Lisa and Jessica weren't home. Part of me was glad, because I had no idea what they might do if I didn't have Kali's soul in a jar the next time I saw them. The task they'd given me was daunting, but it no longer scared me. Kali's soul could never be saved—she'd never allow it—so I had no qualms about handing her spirit over to the faeries and the Otherworld. That would be one less Daemoni roaming this earth, which was my goal. Especially since she might have had something to do with Dorian's kidnapping.

On the other hand, if they'd been home and willing to help, they might have given us insight from the Otherworld. We hadn't seen Bree since the day she'd helped Tristan, Blossom, and Jax.

The faeries' cottage took us more west than Blossom and I felt we should be going, so we headed straight east from there, sticking to back roads surrounded by forest, trying to avoid checkpoints. We rode what Tristan said was the Tail of the Dragon—a curvy mountain road full of switchbacks and a popular drive among bikers and sports car enthusiasts. As we sped along the road that crossed into North Carolina, our foot pegs often scraping the ground as we leaned into tight curves, I could understand the draw. The ride provided quite the thrill.

At least, until we completed an S-curve and found ourselves at a checkpoint.

Normans ahead, I had warned everyone not two minutes before. I'd picked up on the six mind signatures and listened in on their thoughts. They hadn't spoken to each other at all, their minds focused on their hunt. With the way the road curved, I thought they traversed the woods. I didn't realize until the last second they were cops standing in the road, and they hunted supernaturals. We'd already rounded the corner, too late for Charlotte to cloak us.

Maybe things weren't looking up after all.

15

"*JUST ACT NORMAN.*" Tristan spoke to all of us through my telepathy as we slowed in front of the roadblock. "*If they don't suspect anything, they'll let us move on.*"

I didn't think it would work that way. Based on the experiences Vanessa and I had had so far, these officers would know exactly what to do to test us. Only Blossom and Charlotte could pass their tests of silver weapons—they wouldn't react to the silver, they *would* react to the pain, and they'd bleed. Jax and Sheree would bleed, too, but they'd be more difficult to injure, and depending on how much pain the officers chose to inflict, they could lose control and change. Vanessa, Tristan, and me? We'd never stand a chance.

Jax, with Blossom clinging to his back, and Charlotte moved to the head of our pack, already knowing our mages were our only hope for not being detained. But the thought of them suffering on our behalf made my stomach sick. Even knowing Tristan could heal them didn't help. My body tensed, and my muscles coiled, ready to act if the Normans did anything to my friends.

"Is there a problem, officers?" Tristan asked after we finally stopped and cut the loud engines. A deafening silence filled the air for a long moment. Not even birds, squirrels, or other wildlife in the woods lining both sides of the road could be heard. Tristan had made his voice appropriate for the situation: friendly enough, yet with the hard edge of a hardcore biker.

Four of the officers crouched behind the three marked cars, shotguns pointed at us. Two of them, wearing khaki pants and brown leather jackets to ward off the cool mountain air, held their handguns in front of them as they slowly approached us. Neither answered Tristan.

"What's your business here?" the closer one asked, his eyes—and gun—trained on Jax.

"My mates here were taking me on this Dragon ride," Jax said casually. He gave a nonchalant shrug. "It's all right."

The officer narrowed his eyes, as though he didn't buy Jax's answer. He appraised Jax and Blossom for a moment as he walked by them, while the other officer stayed at the front of our group, his feet planted shoulder-width apart and his gun held in position, ready to fire on any of us.

"Is there something wrong?" Tristan tried again as the first guy passed us, his gray eyes scrutinizing us. "Because we're just out for a good time."

The cop only grunted, so I jumped into his mind.

"I don't buy this group for one minute," he thought as he kept walking. *"On a casual ride my ass. Only thing is—"*

"Hey!" he barked aloud as he stopped at the end of our group, right next to Vanessa. "I saw that."

Oh, shit. What did she do now?

"Nothing, Alexis," she said. *"I did nothing."*

The cop suddenly grabbed Vanessa in a chokehold and dragged her off her bike. Good thing she'd already put her kickstand down.

Go along with him, I said when he held the gun to her temple.

She sighed in my mind. "*I know the drill. I'll wait for your order.*"

Tristan swung his leg over the bike and stood to his full height.

"What'd she do?" he demanded, his voice rougher now. He took a step in Vanessa and the officer's direction.

The other cop's gun clicked. "Don't you move!"

The sound of the officers behind the cars pumping shells into the chambers echoed in the otherwise still air. Tristan stopped and raised his hands to chest level, palms out, in the universal "don't shoot" position. Of course, they didn't know he practically stood in a fighting stance, his palms ready to fire.

"It's not what she did," the first cop snarled as he dragged Vanessa up to the front of the group. "It's what she *is*."

His gun-hand dropped the pistol into the holster, but came back with a silver-bladed knife. He slid the edge against the curve of Vanessa's cheek. Her jaw clenched—the silver hurting, but not badly—and I stiffened, already knowing he'd have to cut her up bad to make her bleed, and then they'd know for sure we weren't Norman. Except . . . what the hell? A small trail of red trickled down the side of her face. Among all the many thoughts I monitored in my head, Blossom chanted a silent spell.

The cop sprang back, letting Vanessa go. "I, uh—"

"You what?" Tristan demanded as he took another step forward despite all the guns aimed at us. "You thought you'd cut up some innocent chick just because you don't like the looks of us?"

The cop's head shook violently. "I could have sworn . . . look at you! No flaws on any of you." He eyed Jax's scar. "Except you. But all these gorgeous women with two men? Not your typical biker gang."

"I don't buy it," the other cop said. He swung his arm so his pistol aimed at Blossom. His trigger finger twitched.

But I moved faster.

"No!" I screamed as I jumped from the motorcycle and landed on the cop, tackling him to the ground. The gun fired into the air, the explosion right in my ear.

The other four guns immediately aimed at me as I lay on top of the cop. The officer closest to us dropped his knife and drew his own pistol. I sprang to my feet, my hands up. We were never getting out of this now. I'd crossed twenty feet, including hurdling Charlotte, in a blur. The thought of sitting in another jail cell that smelled like piss made my stomach sink.

"Now, now," came a lustrous voice from behind me. "Do we really need to do this, sweethearts?"

I didn't think I'd ever be so happy to see a faerie.

Bree, appearing in all of her golden glory, sauntered past me, her movements and her voice reminding me of Marilyn Monroe. The effect she had would have made Marilyn look like an amateur, though, and it was immediate. The guns of the two cops right in front of us clattered on the ground, and the men stared at her with their mouths gaping. She turned her full faerie glamour on them, her hair blazing in the sun and her eyes a sultry gold.

She looped an arm around each of theirs, then continued her strut toward the police cars, the two officers gladly moving along with her. I couldn't read her thoughts, and all the cops' minds had pretty much turned to mush.

"We really don't want to hurt you," she said. "That's not who we are."

"So you're . . . you're," the first officer who had cut Vanessa stammered. "Shit. What're they called? The Amadeaus?"

So they knew about us? Who were these county cops in the middle of nowhere?

Bree's eyes settled on him, full of warmth. "The Amadis."

"And you're them?" he asked as his tongue slipped over his lips.

"Oh, I'm not," Bree said with a mischievous grin.

"Oh, fuck," whispered a cop from behind one of the cars. "We're all gonna die."

The second one's pants darkened in his crotch area.

They misunderstood Bree, not knowing she could be neither, although she did favor the Amadis greatly. After all, she'd sacrificed herself to serve the Angels.

Were they scared because they knew we weren't normal humans? Or because they thought we were Daemoni? I couldn't get anything from their addled brains.

"Please don't hurt us," the first cop said. "We'll do anything. If I could only have a—" Looking as though he had no control over himself, he leaned closer to Bree, his gaze dropped to her lips, and his voice lowered to a whisper. "—a taste."

Bree let go of the other cop, who sank to his knees at her feet, apparently oblivious to his wet pants. She swiped a finger down the first officer's cheek as she gazed into his eyes. His expression slackened as he became completely helpless.

"Who put you here?" she cooed.

"I . . . I don't understand," he said, his expression pleading for her mercy. A check into his mind told me he wanted more than her mercy—he wanted everything she could give him, and he'd willingly do anything to get it.

"Who told you to put up this roadblock?"

"We heard . . . we heard they move in packs, like gangs. They like danger and often travel by motorcycle." He swallowed, then licked his lips again, his body leaning ever closer to Bree's golden form. "The Tail of the Dragon's always been a good time for their type."

I focused in on his thoughts more, picking up vague images of Norman biker gangs they'd stopped. Then a stray thought popped into his mind. "*Be careful how you handle them. They're evil and will gladly eat you for breakfast. Or make you one of them.*"

The voice belonged to Pastor Rick McCorkle.

They're okay, I thought for everyone to hear. Of course, Bree couldn't hear me, though. *They're working for us!*

"We're Amadis," Tristan said aloud for Bree's benefit. "We're the good guys. The ones you work for."

He returned to his motorcycle and nodded at me to join him. We both mounted, as did the rest of our group.

"See?" Bree said. "We're all working for the same thing. So you can move your cars and let us go on our way."

The cop nodded helplessly. Bree let him go, and as she strolled toward us, she gave me a wink. Three of the cops jumped into the driver's seats of their cars but didn't have a chance to move them.

Daemoni! I screamed into everyone's heads as soon as I picked up the mind signatures that popped into my range.

The air swooshed over us as Charlotte threw up a shield and a cloak over everyone in our group. But she'd only been able to protect us. Metal smashed into metal as a white van slammed into the cop cars. Flames erupted from the van's windows and quickly spread to the cars nearby. Several Daemoni vamps and Weres jumped out of the van, patting out the flames that burned on their clothes. A moment later, the van exploded, shaking the ground under our feet. Shrapnel flew in the air and rained back down. Black smoke rose and spread on the spring breeze, bringing the acrid smell of burning chemicals with it.

They'd used a homemade bomb to decimate the checkpoint.

"That was kick-ass!" one of the Daemoni exclaimed before he blurred over to the car farthest away. "This one's good. Still alive."

"This one, too, but barely," said a female.

"Oh, dear God," Sheree whispered. "They're going to turn them."

"We need to stop them." Charlotte dismounted her bike. She dropped the shields and cloaks, then crouched into fighting position, her palms out, ready to cast spells.

"I *knew* I'd smelled stinkin' Amadis," one of the Daemoni vampires sneered as she glared at us. "Wondered where you'd gone. Figured you'd cowered out."

"Leave the innocents alone," Tristan called out to them as he, Vanessa, and I slowly approached the burning rubble, while the rest of our group stayed back. Well, I thought they all had. A white crocodile meandered up next to me, and a tiger strode next to Tristan, her fangs bared.

The Daemoni blurred at us, as though wanting nothing more than a fight. Maybe that was the real reason they'd shown up, knowing these policemen served the Amadis, so surely there were some around. As far as my mind could find, we were the only ones.

I blasted electricity at a vamp at the same time Tristan hit him with debilitating power. The bloodsucker fell to the ground instantly, and Jax scooped him into his large jaws and shook him like a ragdoll. The female who'd been taunting us swung a punch at me, but I parried it, taking the brunt of the pain in my forearm rather than my head. I flicked my other hand, and my dagger slid out of its sheath at my hip and landed in my palm as I clenched my fist. With a quick swipe of my thumb, the blade appeared right before I sliced it across the vamp's shoulder. Her scream could make a person's toes curl, but I didn't let up. I gripped her arm with my left hand and shot Amadis power into her until she fell to her knees and shrieked for mercy.

But something came over me, and all I could see was Dorian's face. All I could feel was outrage exploding within me, not unlike their homemade bomb.

I grabbed the vampire with my other hand, and electricity poured out of my palm directly into her body. Her form lit up with a bluish glow. Then smoke began to rise. Her skin started turning purple, and a saccharine stench filled the air. The sweet smell of Daemoni death.

"Alexis!" Tristan's arms came from behind me, and his hands wrapped around my wrists and tightened until I could no longer push my powers out. "We don't kill."

"They have our son," I snarled, glaring at the vamp whose hair had fried off as her crispy body twitched at my feet. "Where is he?"

She gave a minute shake of her head.

"WHERE. IS. HE?" I screamed.

"I . . . I don't know," she stammered.

"Where are the Summoned?"

She replied with only a whimper. Her mind showed only fear.

"Let her go," Tristan murmured in my ear.

I glowered at the vampire as she stared at me with a tinge of hope in her eyes. I felt something else from her that I really didn't want to feel, but I couldn't deny it. Her soul still had hope. My own soul dared to hold *love* for this evil bitch.

With a groan of frustration, I pulled my powers completely within me. The vamp scurried away on her hands and knees.

"That's your problem," a male vamp called out from the edge of the woods. "You Amadis don't have it in you to do what you need to. You'll never win like this!"

He cackled along with a few others before they ran into the woods. I scowled at them until they disappeared from sight, my jaw clenched and my fists on my hips.

"He's right," I muttered. "We're too *good* to win."

The Daemoni had taken off, but we hadn't been able to save any of the cops. At least their souls had still been Norman before they'd died. We had to get out of here before more authorities came looking for them. Although we now knew their precinct supported our side, we didn't need the delay caused by their questions and reports.

"Thank you so much," I breathed as I hugged Bree goodbye.

"Try to keep yourself out of trouble," she said. "I don't know how many times they'll let me keep doing this without demanding something in return. And you better capture that sorceress's soul soon to repay the favor already owed, or there will come a time when none of us will be allowed to help you."

I swallowed and nodded. Damn. For as long as they lived—forever, as far as I knew—the faeries had no patience.

That night we camped by a stream in the woods, staying out of sight of the Normans and the Daemoni. Blossom and Charlotte created tents for us as shelter, and Blossom and I sat inside one, searching again. She chanted her spell under her breath, and I opened my mind. Once again we were nudged north.

As we pulled our minds back in to our own location, I sensed new mind signatures that were alarmingly close. And alarmingly Daemoni. Had they followed us? They couldn't see us . . . unless they had a Norman with them who had some kind of new trap that messed up Char's cloak. But they weren't attacking. I focused in on their minds and recognized them—Alys and Lesley, the vampires who'd been with Sonya and Heather when we found them.

Blossom and I exchanged a look, and then both of us crept downstream, Sasha at our heels, until we came close enough to hear their conversation.

"I can't believe you're doing this," Lesley's voice hissed.

"I can't believe you aren't," Alys replied. "You're better than this.. . this so-called life."

"I *like* this life. We have no rules. We do what we want. And soon—have you heard what they're giving us? The world! And you want to give that up for what? A soul you only think you have but you lost when you were turned?"

"My soul is not lost," Alys snapped. "Neither is yours. You heard Sonya—we still have hope. Isn't it worth it?"

Seeing the perfect opportunity in front of us, I crept in closer to analyze the situation. The two blond vamps sat on opposite sides of the stream. Alys's long legs were pulled up to her chin, her butt balanced on a rock on the side nearest to us. Lesley straddled a boulder on the other bank, one leg swinging impatiently back and forth.

"I think you're crazy," Lesley said, and she hopped to her feet. "But if that's what you want to do, if you're willing to leave me all alone, then I won't stop you."

"You don't have to be alone—"

"But you can't stop *me* from living the life I want. Good luck and goodbye." And with that unceremonious farewell, the shorter vampire blurred away.

Alys sprang to her feet, staring into the direction Lesley had gone, but not following. No time like the present.

"Alys?" I called out so I wouldn't frighten her. A surprised vamp could be a deadly thing.

She spun on me. "What are you doing here?"

I moved closer to her, Blossom right on my heels. "I could ask you the same thing."

Her tongue slid over her lips, and she pulled her bottom one between her teeth to gnaw on it for a moment.

"I want to convert," she suddenly blurted. Her face paled, if possible, and she wrung her hands as she continued. "I've wanted to for a long time, and I know I should have said something before, but I was scared. Now we have no home because Lesley and I got kicked out of our nest at FSU for not turning any students. We've been living in the wild ever since. She always wants to stalk campers, says it's a cheap thrill, and we don't drink them dry, but I can't do it anymore. I'm starving, but I'm so done with this life. Please ... please help me!"

If only they were all so easy. Since they weren't, I *had* to do what I did next. Without giving her warning, I jumped at her and dug my dagger into her chest, twisting and maneuvering it around, looking for a foreign object. Alys tried to hit and swat at me, but Blossom held a spell on her that made the vamp's appendages uncooperative, and Sasha grew into the size of a St. Bernard and bared her teeth in a growl. The vampire fell still. When I didn't find a faerie stone buried in her chest, I launched myself several yards away, putting a safe distance between us. But the vampire didn't come after me; she only stared at me with her fangs extended and disbelief in her eyes.

"Sorry," I said, "but I had to be sure before we went any further. You can thank your friend Sonya for it next time you see her."

Alys glared at me for one long moment, and I checked her mind to see if she'd changed it. She probably hadn't expected an Amadis daughter to be so brutal. Regardless, she retracted her fangs, and her body relaxed.

"Do you think I'll get to see Sonya soon?" she asked. "She was a pretty cool friend."

16

"THERE'S A SAFE house in North Carolina, right?" I asked when we returned to the campsite.

Everyone jumped to their feet, sensing the Daemoni vampire who followed behind Blossom and me. Sasha trotted alongside us, back in her everyday form.

"What's going on?" Charlotte asked as she eyed Alys.

"Easiest conversion we've had yet," I said. "She's Sonya's friend, and she's ready."

"Um . . . more than ready," Alys said from behind me.

"Sure she doesn't have a stone?" Tristan's mind had gone right to where mine had.

I threw my shoulders back with pride. "Already checked."

Then I grimaced, disgusted with myself for being proud of thinking like a Daemoni. Sure, we had to be preemptive, which required anticipating their moves and schemes, but I shouldn't have been so happy with myself. What did that say about me? I didn't want to know because guilt would lead to inaction, which would lead to never finding our son.

"I think there's a small safe house in Charlotte?" Sheree mused.

"A city after my own heart." Char snickered. "Yeah, there is. I'll give the caretaker a call to let her know we're coming. You'll love Terry."

The drive to Charlotte took almost a full day because we once again had to take the back roads. I rode my own bike so Alys could ride with Tristan and he could keep his power on her. Sheree rode with Char this time. I tried to suppress my annoyance that we had to do a little jog south, rather than head north, but I didn't want to drag Alys all over the eastern seaboard while she was still Daemoni and, therefore, a potential danger.

We arrived in Charlotte in time for dinner.

"Something smells delicious," I couldn't help saying as soon as we walked into the two-story home and got over the whole bowing thing with Terry, the witch who managed the safe house. The scrumptious fragrance of garlic, basil, and other herbs had me literally drooling for real food, and I had to wipe my hand over my mouth.

"Pasta with Italian sausage. My specialty," Terry said. The witch was a pixie of a thing, shorter even than me, with short-cropped gray hair and crinkles around her hazel eyes. "We'll get you settled and then you can eat before getting started."

"Good idea." I knew I'd need the energy.

Although the darkness of night would be falling soon—meaning Alys would be at her strongest—Char agreed we'd start after dinner. She said Alys was weakened already and obviously committed enough to doing this that she didn't expect a big fight.

Terry first took us to a conversion room where we left Alys under Sheree's watch, and then she showed us the rest of the house. Although not a mansion, the safe house was still large, with five bedrooms, including one for Terry. She only had one other resident: a Were who'd been badly hurt in a fight a few days ago and needed a safe place to fully recuperate. Fortunately for us, three others had recently departed, headed to an Amadis colony in the Outer Banks.

The caretaker tried to give up her master bedroom for Tristan and me, not because there weren't enough rooms for all of us, but because of the whole royalty thing. We wouldn't have it, though, and since I'd be spending most of my time with Alys anyway and Tristan always stayed near me during conversions, we didn't allow an argument.

Terry entertained everyone during dinner with stories and jokes that she laughed at herself, and her laugh was so contagious, you couldn't help but laugh along with her. But part of me had checked out of the conversation, wanting to take care of Alys, make sure we'd be leaving her in good hands, and then get back on the road. Dorian still needed us.

Dread weighed down my heart when we returned to Alys's room, knowing what we had to put her through when she'd been so nice and forgiving already. Besides Sonya, she was the most docile convert I'd ever had, and I was glad we didn't have to chain her to the bed.

ALTHOUGH ALYS COMPLIED with everything we asked of her, the Daemoni in her wasn't quite as willing to acquiesce. Char and I sat with her for forty-eight hours straight, removing the evil from Alys's soul. Because Terry's small safe house was really meant to be a haven for injured or battle-weary Amadis, not a center for conversions, she didn't have a full conversion team on staff. So we had no choice but to stay for several weeks while Sheree helped the vampire through her faith healing.

In the meantime, the rest of us rode out on short trips, searching the area for more potential converts, as well as for Dorian and his probable captors. While we were out, Blossom and I would do our thing in various locations. The nudge to go north had disappeared, though, and nothing replaced it. Unfortunately, Blossom didn't know if the lack of direction meant Dorian's presence on the scrap piece of blanket I still carried had weakened too much, or if we had moved within proximity to him and his captors. When she consulted with Terry and Char, the mages didn't have an answer—neither were experts with this spell, but they believed both options were possible— but if we were close, the cloak over our son remained powerful. We ran into an Amadis intelligence team, but they had no news to share. Mom also gave us updates, although nothing useful for our mission.

A couple of weeks in, we received a call about a Daemoni attack. We all went out, and although we could have had six new converts, we only managed to bring in two. As in two more Char, Sheree, and I needed to stay for, which kept us in Charlotte even longer.

At least Blossom had the opportunity to learn all about conversions, and not surprisingly, she was better at the first part— the transformation—than the faith-healing phase. She could keep talking to them and giving Amadis power through their internal fight, but she'd go off on too many tangents when it came to discussing faith and what it meant to be an Amadis.

The house quickly became too cramped, so everyone on my team, except Tristan and me, checked in to a hotel a block away, though they spent the majority of their time at the house. Especially meal times, because we ate quite well. Terry loved to cook, and with Tristan and me in the kitchen, too, when we had the chance, we could whip up some truly gourmet meals. When the time finally came to leave, I would miss her. But I couldn't wait to get back on the road.

Memorial Day weekend passed and the heat of a southern summer set in when we finally thought we were ready to leave, but then Terry received a strange phone call.

"That was one of ours, a were-lynx who's a detective on the local force," Terry said, her eyes lit with excitement as her gaze traveled over Tristan, Charlotte, and me while we sat at the large farm-style kitchen table after lunch on an early June day. "Lucky for us, she was called in on a bizarre case. They demolished an old bank downtown and found two bodies buried in the foundation."

"Really?" I asked, my curiosity piqued, although I wasn't sure why this news made us lucky.

"They both had silver stakes still jammed in their hearts," she continued.

Tristan raised a brow. "Sounds like Daemoni vamps who were put down."

"Exactly!" Terry said enthusiastically. "That's why she called me. And what's really crazy is they've been there since 1913. Everyone threw a fit about tearing the building down because it's a historical landmark, but a sinkhole formed behind it, and they were afraid the building would collapse. But who knew there'd be bodies in there?"

"So what does this mean?" I asked. "If we pull the stakes, they'll revive?"

"You know the only way to permanently kill vampires," Tristan said, which I took as a *yes*.

"They'll need lots of blood." Vanessa came into the kitchen and leaned against the counter. "*Lots* of it. They've been dry for a century."

Her whole body shuddered as she imagined going without blood for so long.

"How do we know they're Daemoni?" I asked.

"It's an educated guess because the stakes are silver, which probably knocked them out so the attacker could get them into the foundation," Tristan said.

My own body mimicked Vanessa's, shuddering at the thought of being buried alive.

"So if they've been down this long, we could convert them, couldn't we?" I asked. "Wouldn't the Daemoni energy be weak?"

"Bingo!" Terry said, tapping her nose with her index finger. "Perfect timing with you still here."

"Actually, it depends," Vanessa cut in. "When I was full-on Daemoni, if somebody put me down for that long, I'd be pissed off, and I'd want some serious revenge. I'd be killing every mofo who got in my way. Screw converting."

Tristan analyzed the situation. "If whoever put them there is still alive, they'd have to be Daemoni or Amadis. It's possible for an informed Norman to have done it, but it's been a hundred years. They're long dead by now."

"And no Amadis would have done such a horrible thing," Charlotte said.

"So our biggest risk is the attacker was Daemoni when they did it, but have converted to Amadis since then. That would mean these vamps could go after one of our people in revenge," I concluded. "Otherwise, they'd be going after Daemoni, and I, personally, don't have a problem with that. Or, maybe they could be happy we revived them and will convert, especially if the Daemoni put them in there."

Charlotte drummed her fingers on the table. "There's only one way to find out."

"Pull the stakes and give them blood," Vanessa replied. "And if they try to go bat-shit crazy on us, we can just stab them again and find another freshly poured foundation."

Charlotte gave her the stink eye. "Or handle them the way we do all Daemoni, and if one of our own is in danger, we make sure they're protected."

Terry gave us the address and her van, and Tristan, Charlotte, and I drove downtown to retrieve the bodies. This was one mission nobody else on my team really wanted to be a part of, which I didn't understand. My curiosity had me nearly bouncing in my seat with a perverse excitement. The Daemoni must have heard the news, too, because several of them swarmed around the area. Charlotte cloaked our van once we pulled into the parking garage next door, then kept us cloaked as we made our way to the lanky woman cop standing in the pile of rubble.

We're here, I told her silently, making her jump. *Sorry. I thought you knew about me.*

"*Of course.*" She gave only the briefest of bows, thank God, otherwise a full-blown knee-drop would have given us away. "*There's only one left. The Daemoni already got the other before I could stop them.*"

She pointed to a large wooden box, surprising me. I guess I hadn't expected them to be in coffins, but to be more like concrete statues.

Thanks. We'll take it from here.

"*No, thank you. They've been creepin' me out since the minute they called me in. My skin won't stop crawlin'.*" She shivered as though to emphasize her point.

Do you need a mage to alter anyone's memories? Char fed me the question so we wouldn't weird the lynx out any more than she already had been with the mind-speak.

"*No, ma'am. We have a wizard who oversaw the demo. We're good.*"

Charlotte set a cloak over the box, and Tristan used his power to raise the makeshift coffin and direct it to the van. We were in and out without the Daemoni knowing. Now we only had to hope the guy didn't go psycho on us when we revived him.

"I've made room in the basement," Terry said when we returned to the house, and she led us downstairs.

The basement was divided into two rooms, both of them looking a lot like what I called the dungeons at our own safe house, although the dark, windowless basement made it feel more like a real dungeon down here. It even smelled dank and musty, like I imagined the bowels of an ancient castle would. Silver chains with cuffs hung from the support beams overhead, and the concrete floor angled toward a large drain in the center of each room. Terry moved the bed out of the east room and replaced it with a worktable on wheels, and Tristan set the wooden box on top of it. Tristan and Char grasped the lid, and my excitement about seeing the nearly dead vamp suddenly waned. I stepped back to join Terry by the wall. With no pomp or circumstance, they lifted the top.

And the smell. Oh God, the *smell*.

My stomach lurched, and we all automatically pulled back as a sickening sweet odor of mold, dust, and rotting flesh plumed from the box and hung in the air. I clamped my hand over my mouth and nose to keep from gagging. Once they recovered from the assault to their noses, Tristan and Char walked around the casket, and then stood next to each other on the far side as they studied the body. When they both made funny faces, morbid curiosity got the best of me, as it did Terry, and we both crept closer. My heart stuttered in my chest as I took in the sight. The vampire looked marginally better than my overactive imagination had envisioned, especially with that god-awful smell.

A full head of dull brown hair crowned his head when, for some reason, I'd expected only a few gray and brittle strands dangling from a skull. His sunken eyes were open and blue, staring lifelessly at the ceiling, when I'd admittedly imagined him as not having any eyeballs at all. I didn't know why I expected such ridiculousness—maybe the writer in me had thought they'd been eaten away by worms or bugs. In fact, I'd actually thought creepy-crawly things would be skittering all over him, although I knew logically this vision made no sense since he'd been buried in concrete, not in dirt. A suit, which had probably looked smart and classy in 1913 but was now dusty and covered in century-old mildew, clothed his bony body. The jacket, vest, and button-down shirt underneath had been torn open, revealing a portion of his torso. His skin, muscles, and apparently all of his organs were dried up and clung to his bones, as though every drop of moisture in them had been sucked out by a vacuum, making him look like a skeleton covered with a grayish colored shrink wrap.

"Blood's ready?" Charlotte asked as she leaned over him, studying the stake in his chest—a dull silver object about the size of a conductor's wand.

"Right here." Terry brought over an armful of donor bottles, set them on a steel table, and opened one as she stood at the head of the coffin.

"Alexis, this could be dangerous," Char said. "I'd prefer you go upstairs."

"Yeah, right." I snorted. "Not a chance."

"Ugh. You're too much like your mother," she muttered as she wrapped her hands around the stake. "Terry, have a bottle ready and at his lips when I pull this out. Tristan, be ready to paralyze him. Alexis, stay the hell back until we know if we have a monster on our hands. You're not getting hurt on my watch."

I rolled my eyes, but returned to my position by the wall. Charlotte swallowed once, and then counted to three. She pulled the stake, and my breath caught as the rod unceremoniously slipped free as though it'd been stuck in nothing more than sand. My lungs kept the air trapped as Terry separated the vamp's lips and poured bottle after bottle into his mouth. Slowly his skin started pushing away from the bones and plumping up. His face gradually took on the appearance of a live human rather than a skeleton. By the time Terry opened the fourth bottle, the splotchy skin we could see on his face, hands, and torso became a smooth porcelain color, and his hair brightened from a dull dark brown to a shinier caramel color. Life sparked in his blue eyes, and he blinked.

His hand twitched.

His fangs slipped out.

His eyes moved slowly around the room as he took in his surroundings from his prone position.

His gaze landed on me and held, something flickering in those sky-blue orbs.

"Sophia?" he croaked.

My eyes widened, and the air finally whooshed out of my lungs. *Oh, crap. Did Mom do this to him?* Everyone else's focus flew to me then back to him.

"Sophia," he said again. This time it wasn't a question, but I shook my head.

He struggled to sit up, but he hadn't regained his full strength yet. He settled on an elbow, still not taking his eyes off me.

"Yes," he insisted. "You're Sophia. But why are you clothed so oddly?"

He spoke with a heavy British accent, and his tone was not accusing or frightening, but merely perplexed.

I cleared my throat. "I'm not Sophia."

He blinked. His jaw muscle popped. A harder edge entered his voice. "Why do you deny me?"

I looked at Tristan, but he only offered a small shrug.

"Because I'm *not* Sophia. I'm Alexis, her daughter."

His brows pushed together as confusion filled his face. Then his features contorted with indignation.

"Why do you attempt to deceive me?" he demanded. "Why do you tell lies? This is not proper behavior."

"Hey, man," Tristan said, "be careful what you say to her. That's my wife you're talking to."

The vamp's face grew red as he twisted in his coffin to face Tristan, and his petulance turned to outrage. "*Your* wife? How dare you!"

Tristan raised a brow, which I knew meant his patience was wearing thin.

"Wait a minute," I said, taking a step closer, and the vampire's attention swung to me again. "Who are you? How do you know my mom?"

"Who am *I*?" he nearly yelled. "I am *Winston*!"

Charlotte gasped. "Oh, dear God. Get your mother on the phone."

Did she know him? But how? Nineteen-thirteen was before Mom's *Ang'dora*, which meant before she knew anything about the Amadis or Daemoni, including knowing Char.

"Now!" the warlock barked.

I cocked my head as I pulled my phone out of my pocket and pressed the icon to FaceTime Mom, thinking Charlotte wanted this guy to see that Mom and I were two different people. The vampire shrunk away when he saw the gadget and eyed it with a mix of suspicion and curiosity in his expression. He'd come from a different time and had no idea *when* he was, let alone where. But at least the interesting object had calmed his irritation with me.

"Is everything okay, honey?" Mom asked as soon as she answered. A common greeting these days. She sat at her desk, and the angle of her image made me think she'd answered on her iPad.

"Um . . . I don't know. Do you know this guy?" I switched the phone's camera to the back lens to show the recently revived vampire. "He says his name is Winston."

Mom's face blanched.

"For the love of God," she whispered, and she grabbed the outside of the screen, her face coming closer to the camera. Followed by a crash and the screen showing the ceiling of her office.

"Mom?" I asked. "Is that a yes?" No answer. "*Mom?*"

"Alexis? Are you still there?" came her voice.

"Sophia?" Winston said, his eyes darting around the room to identify the source of her voice. "Sophia! Is that you?"

"Call me back on my phone," Mom whispered, and then I saw her hand reach across the screen and disconnect our call.

I slipped out of the room and called her on the phone, figuring she wanted more privacy than FaceTime gave us.

"Where in the hell did you find this guy, and who does he think he is?" Mom demanded with a rancor I rarely heard from her.

"Um . . . well, we found him buried in a foundation of an old bank," I said, and I told her the story. She remained so silent when I finished, I thought I'd lost the connection. "Mom?"

"Nineteen-thirteen, you said?"

"Yes, that's what Terry told us. The foundation was poured in 1913 and the building finished in 1915."

"Impossible," Mom gasped. "He died in December 1911."

"I did *not* die," the vampire yelled, apparently hearing her. So much for her plan of privacy. "I was turned!"

"What are you talking about, Mom?" I asked as I walked toward the basement steps, as far from the vampire as possible. "Who is this guy?"

Again she didn't answer for a long moment.

"I'm on my way," she finally said instead of answering me.

"*What?* You're coming *here?*"

"I'll be there as soon as I can. I believe the new jet is here and available, and if it's not, I'll make it that way."

"Mom, you're talking crazy. You don't need to come all the way over here."

"Yes, I do. I'll be there soon. Just . . . try to keep him calm in the meantime. Don't let him leave!"

"Who is he?" I asked again. "What does he mean to *you?*"

She blew out a breath, and her voice came out shaky, as though she wasn't quite sure she believed her own words. I nearly dropped the phone when she said them.

"If he's really who he says he is . . . Winston was my husband."

17

WHAT?

"Your *husband?* You never said anything—"

"I'll explain when I get there," she said, and the call fell silent. I looked at the phone screen: she'd hung up.

I tapped the phone against my chin, wracking my brain for any mention of a Winston or a husband. The only marriage I knew about was with her true love, a story she'd disclosed only a few years ago. What was his name? Otto? Orville? Something like that. Not even close to Winston.

"Sophia!" The vampire's voice grew louder and more demanding.

I crossed over to the door and had barely entered the room and opened my mouth when his blue eyes darted to me and turned bright red as they filled with rage.

"Who are you? What did you do to my Sophia?" he demanded. Without a thought to warn me, he sprang from his wooden box and suddenly stood in front of me, the blood already building his strength. He was nearly as tall and as broad as Tristan. His large hands clamped on my shoulders, and he lifted me off the ground. His nostrils flared, and he dipped forward, his nose at my throat, where my pulse thumped excitedly. He inhaled deeply, and then hissed, "Amadis."

He pulled back enough to look at my face, studying it as though trying to determine if I were really my mother. His fangs slipped out from under his upper lip, which curled up in a snarl. Hunger and desire filled his eyes. The need to drink consumed his mind. His mouth opened wide with the thought of diving for my throat, so I shot electricity at him.

Tristan or Charlotte—or both, and maybe Terry, too—must have acted at the same time. I suddenly stood on my feet again, and the vampire was in the center of the room, his arms stretched over his head and his wrists and ankles in shackles. His eyes widened as they scanned the room.

"You Amadis whores," he bellowed. "I should have known!" His gaze fell on Tristan. "Not you. I *know* you. Seth. Evil reincarnate himself. Why do you stand there, man? Help me out of this bloody mess!"

When Tristan refused, the vampire became more irate. His eyes remained a frightening red. He threw his body back and forth and side to side, trying to free himself from the silver chains. When we attempted to ask him questions or to explain what had happened to him, he yelled and hollered more profanities at us. I opened my mind to discover the same anger and blasphemies running through his head.

"That's enough," Tristan growled, paralyzing him so we wouldn't have to listen to the clank and rattle of the chains any longer. "Charlotte, muffle the room. I'm done listening to this."

He grabbed my hand and left the room, pulling me all the way up the stairs with him. His jaw muscle twitched as he sat at the kitchen table with his fists in front of him. I found a bottle of beer in the refrigerator, cracked it open, and pulled a few swigs before giving him the rest. He downed it in one gulp.

"If Sophia hadn't said what she did, I'd have hurt him a lot worse for his rude behavior toward you, and for how he treated Char and Terry, too," Tristan finally said.

I placed my hands on his shoulders and squeezed, then rubbed his back. "For a British man of his time, you would have thought he'd be more of a gentleman."

Tristan let out a harrumph. "He's Daemoni. What do you expect? He's lucky I didn't kill him, because killing a Daemoni is all I've wanted to do since Dorian disappeared. He just needs to give me an excuse."

I leaned over, wrapped my arms around him, and rested my chin on his shoulder. "As much as I've wanted to murder them, too, you know this vamp has nothing to do with Dorian's kidnapping."

He didn't reply for a long moment. I hugged him tighter and pressed my lips against his neck until he finally relaxed under my hold. He lifted his hand to my wrists under his chin and gave them a squeeze.

"Look at you, talking me down," he said. "That's a switch."

"We're a team," I murmured in his ear. "If we don't have each other's backs, then who will?"

He reached around and pulled me into his lap, but as soon as I was comfortable against his chest, Charlotte and Terry entered the kitchen. Worry lines creased Char's forehead.

"How am I not surprised this is the kind of man your mother would fall for?" she said after she grabbed a beer for herself and sat across the table from us.

Terry poured herself a glass of wine and brought a beer each for Tristan and me before joining us at the table.

"I didn't even know about him," I admitted, and I asked Char, "Do you think he's the real deal?"

"I don't know," she said. "I wasn't assigned to protect your mother when she'd been with Winston, so I only know what she's told me about him. Like the fact that he died from cancer. So I can't say if this bloke is him or not. All I *can* say is he better not hurt her. For his own sake. If he does . . ."

"Vanessa's idea of finding a fresh foundation is sounding better and better, isn't it?" I finished.

Charlotte and Tristan both lifted their beers to clink with mine.

∞

"WHERE IS HE?" Mom demanded as soon as she entered the safe house a few hours later, Charlotte right behind her. Char had picked her up at the airport since she couldn't flash, and she'd needed a protector's escort.

I looked over Mom's shoulder at Char.

"I told her everything," the warlock said. "At least, what little we know."

I couldn't imagine what had been going through Mom's head for the entire trip. I knew how I'd felt when Tristan had returned after seven years, but that was nothing in comparison, and she still didn't know if this vampire had really been her husband. She'd had to wonder for the whole plane ride over, making it excruciatingly long even at warlock speed. Of course, for all I knew, maybe he'd meant nothing to her. Maybe it had been a marriage of convenience. She'd never bothered telling me about him, after all. On the other hand, she'd been shocked to see him on the screen. She hadn't expected him to be alive in any kind of condition. So she certainly had to have questions galore, but Charlotte didn't have many answers to offer. All we really knew was that he was one pissed off vampire.

"Take me to him," Mom ordered Char. "*Now.*"

Tristan and I followed Mom and Charlotte down the stairs, and Vanessa followed us. She hadn't wanted anything to do with reviving the vampire—as tough as she was, she had a weak stomach when it came to those kinds of things—but she'd promised to be there when Mom arrived. As the only other vampire in the house, she could be a big help if things went wrong. The rest of the team stayed in position at the top of the stairs, ready to act as well.

We all stopped in front of the door. The room remained muffled, so we heard nothing coming from inside. A check into the vamp's mind told me he continued to throw a grade-A vampire fit. Charlotte grasped the doorknob, but paused and looked at Mom with her brows high.

"One more time—" she started.

"I know," Mom nearly growled, her impatience obvious. "He's dangerous. If he's who he says he is, he's always had a bit of a temper."

"Well, now he's got that temper as a vampire," Char said. "Be prepared for anything."

Mom gave her a single, sharp nod, and after another moment of hesitation, Charlotte twirled her free hand in the air while twisting the knob and throwing the door open. Winston was in the middle of another round of cursing, but fell silent when his gaze found Mom in the doorway.

"Sophia?" he nearly whispered. "Is it really you?"

Mom simply stood there, her mouth hanging open. We all stood back a few paces, carefully watching both of them, prepared to act if necessary, but they only stared at each other in silence. Eventually Mom's hands moved up to cover her mouth. She took one step into the room and to the side. Another step farther in and to the other side. Winston remained perfectly still as she studied him, only his eyes moving as he drank in the sight of her.

His whole demeanor changed. Anger no longer pulsed off of him in hot waves. The profanities and threats cleared out of his mind, revealing something else. Wonder. Confusion. Disbelief.

"Sophia?" he said again, his voice lower than a whisper.

Mom let out a little noise like a hiccup. She took a step closer. "Oliver? My Oliver?"

The vampire's face lit up in a grin, his eyes melting into a sparkling blue, dimples punctuating his lifted cheeks.

"Sophia," he said, and this time it wasn't a question.

"Oliver!" She crossed the last few steps to him in a blur and threw her arms around him. Her body shook in what I assumed to be sobs.

Oliver. That had been the name of her true love. Tears dared to prick my eyes. But wait . . .

I looked at Charlotte with wide, inquiring eyes. She only shrugged. I didn't particularly want to piss the vampire off again, especially with Mom in the danger zone, but someone somewhere was missing something.

"Um . . . Mom?" I hesitated. "This isn't—"

She turned her head away from his chest and toward me, with tears streaming down her cheeks and a smile on her face.

"It is, honey," she said as she tightened her arms around the vampire. "This is Oliver Winston Chambers. He prefers Winston, but he's always been my Oliver to me."

"And he's—"

She reached a hand up and pressed it against his face. The vamp who had been threatening to eat us all alive only a few minutes ago leaned into her hand, and if a vampire could have googly eyes, he did.

"He's my soul mate."

Memories of them together before he'd been turned and before she'd gone through the *Ang'dora* played in Winston-Oliver-whatever-his-name-was' mind as though they were yesterday. To him, they practically felt that way. He *was* the real deal. And the way Mom pressed herself against him, I couldn't deny it. Only true love could overcome the stench of his clothes so she could stand to be near him.

"Unchain him," Mom ordered, and she looked up at him. "I can trust you." She didn't make it a question.

"We have much to discuss," he said as he lowered his head. She stretched up on her toes to kiss his lips.

Wow. This is beyond weird. I hadn't seen Mom with a man since I was in my teens, and she'd never been outwardly affectionate with any of them. Now, however, she looked as though she couldn't help it.

"First thing is your conversion," she said to him.

Thank goodness no one had removed the shackles yet. Oliver Winston's body stiffened, and his eyes hardened. But for only a brief moment.

"If that's what it takes," he said, his eyes softening as they continued to stare at Mom. "Anything for you, love."

Nobody moved to release him from the chains until Mom insisted, and even then she had to give a direct order. I held my breath when Charlotte and Tristan freed the vampire. His arms came down and looped around Mom's waist. He lifted her so her face came level to his. So her throat was in reach. His eyes darted down to the pulse he could see and smell in her neck, and palpable tension returned to the room. My own heart raced as I worried about my mother.

"Oliver," she whispered, and his gaze returned to her face. "I have never stopped loving you."

"Nor I you," he replied before bringing her in for a real kiss.

If this weren't my mom and a Daemoni vampire who'd been down for a hundred years, I'd have probably been in tears. This was better than any romance book or movie ever. Definitely better than any I'd written, and my books had been called the best paranormal romances of all time. But it *was* my mom, and he *was* a Daemoni vamp. A thirsty one.

"Sophia," Char said, thankfully being the first to speak up and interrupt them. "The conversion?"

Mom pulled away from the kiss and looked over her shoulder at us. "We need to talk first. Doing it now would be a form of coercion. He deserves to know everything beforehand."

"Agreed," Char said, "so how do you want to do this?"

"I want you to leave us alone," Mom answered easily. "All of you out."

Char, Tristan, and I exchanged a look. We weren't budging.

"*Out*," Mom repeated.

"Sophia—" Char and Tristan both began.

"That's an order."

"Mom," I started.

"I will be fine. He won't hurt me. Will you, Oliver?"

He cocked his head, but his nostrils flared, and he surely inhaled the Amadis scent all over us. "I'm confused, but I will never hurt you, Sophia. Never again."

We still didn't move, but eventually Mom forced us out. Tristan, Charlotte, and Vanessa took turns guarding the door, and I stayed at the top of the stairs, trying to listen to their minds. Mom yelled at me every time I entered hers. Then she mentally yelled at me some more when I *wasn't* in her head, because she knew it meant I'd moved to Winston's. Eventually I gave up the fight, pulled out of their minds, and waited.

Hours passed. Charlotte released the muffle on the room every so often, long enough so we could be sure Mom hadn't started screaming for help or anything, and then she'd replace it to give them privacy. Finally, after the sun had risen the next morning, Mom came out of the room, pulling Winston with her by the hand.

"He needs faith healing," she said, "but the Daemoni energy has been eliminated."

Char and I rose from our seats on the stairs in surprise.

Mom shrugged. "Love can conquer anything. It was fairly easy, even on my own. In fact, we talked through much of it. Right now, though, he could use a shower and some clothes."

While Winston cleaned up, Mom told us his story. When she'd thought he had died, he'd actually been turned, and his master had taken him away. His master hadn't told him about Mom being an Amadis daughter, but had instead convinced him that he could never be with her. But he couldn't stand to be away from her. He followed her to the States, but always talked himself out of approaching her, afraid he wouldn't be able to overcome the desire to drink her dry. He'd decided to convert to Amadis, knowing he could never live like a Daemoni, and hoping he might be able to be around Mom then. But before he could take the necessary steps, the Daemoni staked him and buried him alive.

I'd never seen Mom so happy. So in love. For a long time when I was younger, I'd believed she wasn't capable of love, and now she practically swooned. She stayed with us as Sheree worked with Winston through his faith healing, and when they weren't doing that, Mom and Winston spent nearly all of their time in the bedroom. I didn't want to think about what exactly they did in there—she was my *mom*—but I couldn't help but feel happy for her.

"Their story is amazing," Blossom said one evening as we both cleaned up the kitchen after dinner. She stared out the window where Mom and Winston huddled together on a bench in the backyard, gazing at the stars.

"And yours?" I asked, nudging her in the ribs with my elbow.

"It's not nearly as romantic." She sighed before looking at me with a shy smile. "But I do really like Jax. I mean, more than like him. There's been this connection since the beginning, you know, and we have so many things in common, but lots more not in common, which is okay because that's what keeps things interesting. And he's really sweet, and his body . . . wow, his body . . ."

She became uncharacteristically silent, and I suppressed a chuckle. I knew exactly what Jax's body looked like. All of it. It didn't compare to Tristan's, but I could understand why Blossom would be impressed. The man-croc lacked nothing except for hair.

"So," I said, bringing her attention back to the kitchen, "is it serious?"

She gazed out at Mom and Winston again. "Not like that. But I think I want it to be. I just don't really know how to cross the line with Jax. He's not like any other man I've ever been with."

I dried the last wine glass and put it away, and a thought occurred to me.

"They say the way to a man's heart is through his stomach, right?" I said. "How about Tristan and I make you and Jax a romantic dinner? And *you* bake him a cake for dessert. We'll warm him up with a gourmet meal, but once he tastes your cake, he'll be putty in your hands."

Blossom grinned excitedly. "You think?"

"He'll be a goner," I promised. Not that I knew a lot about seducing a man, but I did know Blossom's cakes. They were practically orgasmic. If Jax didn't get the message after the meal and dessert we planned for him, then he didn't deserve to have her.

Fortunately, the meal went off without a hitch, and the two of them disappeared for their hotel right after, taking the cake with them. Mom and Winston were constantly alone, and she began to talk about bringing him to Amadis Island. Char was happy for Mom, knowing how long she had been alone and what she had sacrificed in the area of love. But now I felt bad for the warlock, whose husband had been a farce for most of their marriage. Sheree remained single, too, and, of course, Vanessa, whose hope for eternal love had once again been placed in the wrong person.

That reminder came to me every day. Not an hour went by that I didn't think about Owen, Kali, Lucas, or Dorian. Mostly Dorian, of course. We needed to get back on the road. We'd been ready to leave before the discovery of Winston, and Sheree had made great progress with his faith healing. Someone on Amadis Island could provide what he needed now. We had to return our focus to our missions.

"The D.C. area," Mom said one day in late June as we discussed our plans. "I feel something strong there. I sense that's where you should go."

Blossom's spell had begun to work again, at least enough to give us a small prod north, which confirmed Mom's hunch. So we finally packed up, said our goodbyes, and gave our well wishes to Mom and Winston before we headed north as they headed for the airport. The smile on Mom's face and the love I felt radiating between the two of them would forever be imprinted on my soul. I hoped this was the beginning of better times to come.

After we crossed the Virginia state line, we stopped in the Shenandoah Mountains and spent the night in the woods, where Blossom and I could let our minds roam freely. We felt a bump to the northeast, rather than straight north. And it came stronger than usual.

"We must be getting close," she said quietly, but I tried not to become too excited that Mom had been right about Washington, D.C. After all, it was a big metropolitan area.

The next day, we drove to my old stomping grounds of Northern Virginia and took up residence at the Fairfax safe house—the same one where Tristan had left me years ago. After the fight, we'd been the only ones in residence there for nearly a year, besides a few caretakers, but I'd never really explored the two-story brick structure that sprawled over an acre of land and was surrounded by nineteen more of meadow and woods. As soon as we walked in the door, I was drawn to the one room where I had spent all my time—the place where I'd given birth to Dorian.

Perhaps because of the history, his presence was heavy enough for Blossom to finally zero in, and I found it.

I.

Found.

It!

His mind signature floating in a sea of others, but definitely his.

Dorian! I silently screamed.

"*Mom?*"

18

OH MY GOD, oh my God, oh my God.

Dorian!

My heart had jumped into my throat at his mental response, and now it throbbed there. I couldn't believe after all these months I'd finally heard him. We'd found him! But then—

The pick jabbed into my brain.

My vision went completely white. Then black.

I came to screaming Dorian's name.

"No," I yelled when I realized we'd lost him. I pushed myself out of Tristan's lap and pawed at the tickle by my ear but ignored the blood on my fingers as I turned on Blossom. "Did we get his location?"

The witch frowned as she blinked eyes full of tears.

"I'm sorry," she whispered. "I was just about to, but we went blank at the last second. It was like someone shut us out."

"That fucking bitch!" I screamed as I slammed my fists against my thighs.

Tristan and Blossom both looked at me with questions in their eyes.

"I'm almost positive it was Kali pushing me out," I explained through clenched teeth. "She must have Dorian and knew I'd reached him. I had probably been close those other times, too."

Some part of me must have known it had been her all along jabbing into my brain, not Lucas, but another part had been trying to deny the theory because it meant admitting to Owen's involvement as well. But the evidence had always been there, and my soul had always known. Because every day my hatred for the sorceress had grown. Every day I wanted to kill her more than I did the day before. Every night I dreamt of when the time would come. Probably not very Amadis of me, but the bitch's soul had no hope. I fantasized about what the Otherworld would do with it.

When I didn't dream of killing Kali, I had nightmares of the only real kill I'd ever had. The Were in Hades, whom I'd stabbed in the gut and left dead in a pool of his own blood. It was self defense— either him or me—but I'd never know if his soul had any hope. If it could have ever been saved. If I had damned him to Hell without giving him the chance he might have deserved. And when I woke up from those nightmares, I couldn't help but wonder if God's wrath had taken Dorian away from me.

Maybe His sacred wrath would prevent us from ever finding him.

And maybe I deserved that.

But I hoped not. I had to believe that although God had His reason for this to happen, He didn't intend to keep Dorian away from us permanently. I had to believe He didn't want Dorian to become Daemoni. I had to have faith He was a forgiving God and would show us mercy.

Otherwise, what was the point to any of this? To us, the Amadis? Why fight for these souls if they wouldn't be given mercy and forgiveness? There had to be a point to it all.

So I would hold on to my faith and beliefs. I would hold on to the hope that we would find Dorian. I would keep fighting for my son, until the end.

"We'll keep trying," Blossom said.

"Damn straight," I said through clenched teeth before stomping off for the bathroom to clean the blood off my face and neck.

We did keep trying, but the trail had grown cold. We tried for days, then weeks. We knew we were close—the prods were so minutely to the east of us, we knew he had to be in the D.C. area, as Mom had sensed, probably here in Northern Virginia. We rode out under cloaks so I could mentally search, and every time we went after potential converts, I reached out with my mind, probing for the familiar mind signatures we sought. They continued to elude me, though, and the potential converts kept slipping through our fingers. The hope of Mom and Winston's reunion and Jax and Blossom's budding relationship had lifted all of our spirits, but our moods quickly spiraled downward.

"Here's something to cheer you up," Blossom said one afternoon as she placed a mug on the patio table in front of me, steam rising from its contents. My stomach lurched at the smell. "I've finally been able to gather all the herbs we'd lost in the plane crash."

"This is supposed to cheer me up?" I asked, making a face at the atrocious smell of the fertility tea. It was a hot summer day, and sweat already trickled down my back in the humidity. The last thing I wanted was a steaming cup of gasoline-flavored nastiness.

"A baby would lift the spirits of the entire Amadis. Can you imagine what such good news would do for everyone?"

Yeah, actually, I could imagine it. Such news would incite the council to insist on my return to the safety of Amadis Island, which I wouldn't do until we found Dorian. Well, I didn't know how long I could do it even then, although I'd have to put up with the confinement for at least a while. And that put me in a bit of a conundrum. I wanted a baby girl as much as everyone else, although maybe not for the same reasons. Drinking the tea and doing everything we could to become pregnant was the right thing to do. But what if I did conceive this very night? What if I became pregnant before we found Dorian?

Blossom noticed something was wrong—more than my problem with the taste. She sat down beside me and stroked a hand over my hair.

"What is it?" she asked.

Tears stung my eyes. I tapped my finger on my temple to give her warning then spoke via mind-talk.

If I get pregnant now, they'll make me abandon the search.

"*Ah.*" She considered this for a moment. "*We don't know how long it'll take. I don't think the potion is a one-hit wonder. It takes several doses to prepare your body. Maybe by then, we'll have found him. We are getting close. I can feel it.*"

But what if we don't? We have Tristan's stone, so this could be the one last thing we need for me to conceive. It would be my luck to get pregnant right away, before we find Dorian.

"*Well,*" she said as she gave me a squeeze, "*it's not like you'll show right away. Nobody will have to know. I can keep a secret. Can you?*"

I sighed. *Mom will know.*

"*Not if you're not around her, and I think she's pretty tied up with other things right now. She doesn't even have to know I've found all the herbs. Nobody has to know you're drinking the tea yet.*"

I knew the ploy wouldn't last for long. At some point, Tristan, Vanessa, and eventually the Weres would be able to hear a heartbeat. But my conscience wouldn't allow me to *not* drink the tea and do what I needed to do for the next daughter. If I became pregnant and the news spread to the council before we found Dorian, I'd have to make one of the hardest decisions of my life. But for now, that remained a fear unrealized.

I lifted the mug to my lips, grimaced as the gasoline smell engulfed me, and then chugged the entire contents. I clamped my mouth shut tight until I knew it would stay in my stomach.

"Let's hope it works," I muttered halfheartedly.

"Yes. But maybe not right away," Blossom said with a small smile as she picked up the mug and went back inside.

I sat on the deck of the safe house, surveying the beautifully landscaped lawn and the woods beyond. If I hadn't witnessed the battle myself, I would have never known this scene hadn't always been so peaceful. This was the exact lawn where Tristan had gone out to fight, leaving me behind, not to return for seven years.

My mood deteriorated more.

And the sudden urge to go for a run hit me like a freight train. I didn't know if the tea had begun to do anything to prime my ovaries, but it certainly gave me a big burst of energy. A workout would help expend some of the built-up tension, too, which I desperately needed. I hurried inside and found a sports bra, running shorts, and shoes in the wardrobe of our suite. I loved having mages on staff who could anticipate our every need.

"I was just coming to find you," Tristan said when I ran into him in the foyer. His gaze traveled up and down my body, and he gave me a sexy smile. "You want to work out?"

"Yeah, but not Aikido. I'm going for a run."

He nodded. "I'll go with you."

"Um, actually, I'd rather go alone." I needed some time by myself. We were always together, and usually not only the two of us, except in bed, which hadn't been the most pleasant of places between the nightmares and the lack of mental privacy. Tristan grimaced. "I won't leave the safe house property, so I'll stay in the shield."

His eyes narrowed, but he gave me a small nod. "Take Sasha, at least."

"Good idea," I said, and I popped up on my toes to give him a kiss. His lack of enthusiasm in returning it made me feel bad. Did he feel rejected? I quickly explained. "Her mind is silent to me. I need to get away from all the buzzing in everyone's heads for once."

"Just don't do anything stupid," he said, and it sounded like a grumble more than a warning. Then he walked off without a word or another kiss or the smallest of touches.

I began to second-guess myself, but once Sasha and I were outside and far enough from the safe house, I was glad I hadn't given in to my doubts. Of course, I couldn't go far enough to eliminate everyone completely from my mental range—I'd have to leave the protection of the shield to do so—but I could go far enough that I didn't hear the hum of nearby thoughts. If I wanted to, I could pick out mind signatures and listen, but I didn't want to. I relished the silence.

Sasha and I made a lap near the perimeter of the twenty-acre property, but it hadn't been enough to expend the energy I felt. She'd grown to the size of a German shepherd to easily keep up with me, and we made another round. When we reached the back of the property, a few yards in the woods, movement farther in the trees caught my eye. A blur too fast for me to see, but my mind caught the familiar signature.

Sasha sensed the danger, too, and became the size of a horse next to me. Her pearly white wings spread above her nearly two stories high. Her white snout wrinkled, and she let out a ferocious growl. Leaves stirred up from the ground, and my hair whipped against my face in a near tornadic wind as her wings beat a violent rhythm against the air. I'd never seen her so angry. So frightening. She roared like a tiger, and then she flew into the woods.

"Sasha!" I ran after her while mentally calling for Tristan and the others. *Victor's nearby, and Sasha chased after him.*

"*Let her go, Lex,*" Tristan said a moment before appearing next to me.

But the loud crack of branches breaking and other sounds of fighting wouldn't allow me to let it go. Vanessa appeared at the same moment I blurred toward the sounds. I didn't get there quick enough, though. Broken tree limbs and gouges in the dirt showed there had been a struggle, but Victor and Sasha had taken their fight farther into the woods.

"Sasha," I called, and I thought I heard something so I ran again. I'd moved way beyond the shield now, but Victor seemed to be alone. I didn't sense any other mind signatures nearby, Daemoni or otherwise.

"She'll be fine," Tristan said when he caught up with me.

"We don't know that!"

"Let her go," he repeated, this time his voice lower and more demanding. "She'll run him off and probably beat us back."

"Unless she gets hurt again," I protested. My muscles tensed in preparation for another sprint, but Tristan's hand wrapped tightly around my upper arm, stopping me.

"Don't be stupid," he said, and he definitely growled now.

I jerked my arm out of his grip. "Don't be an ass. I can't let her get hurt again."

"She can take care of herself."

"And lose another wing?" I glared at Tristan as my chest heaved. "She's not invincible."

"Neither are you!"

"Um, I'll go look for her," Vanessa said, her eyes bouncing between Tristan and me. "You need to get back in the shield."

I opened my mouth to protest.

"He's my idiot brother. My twin. I might be able to find out why he's here while I'm at it."

"Or I could," I countered as I tapped my forehead with an index finger.

"Alexis," Tristan warned. "You can do that from the safe house."

"Let me do this," Vanessa said. "Go! Get your unprotected ass out of here."

She left in a blur. Tristan grabbed my arm again, but I shook him off once more, still deciding whether or not to find Sasha myself. Electricity crackled over my fingertips, a reminder that my ass wasn't exactly unprotected. With a rumble in his chest, he snaked an arm around me and flashed us to right outside the safe house property. The air hummed as he carried me through the shield, and then he set me on my feet.

"That flash could have been really stupid," I snapped. "We could have been trapped."

"We were too close to the safe house. And don't talk to *me* about being stupid." His voice held that dangerous steel edge to it. I wasn't used to it being directed at me.

"You need to back off," I said. "You're way overreacting. It was only Victor. I can handle him easily. And like you said, we were close enough to the safe house."

"It was still stupid. Damn it, Alexis, don't you think about what it would do to me if something happened to you?" He shook his head, his sandy brown hair falling across his forehead. "Of course not. All you think about is yourself."

My breath caught. I felt as though he'd slapped me. "How can you say that? I'm trying to think of everyone. Trying to take care of everyone and ensure they're safe. Including Sasha!"

"Everyone except me," he muttered, then his voice raised with each word spewing from his mouth. "You don't give a damn what I feel every time you do something like this."

"*What?*" I asked, at a loss for any other words. I didn't know where this was suddenly coming from. I'd been good about controlling my impulses. Hadn't I?

He stepped in front of me, towering over me, his muscles straining with control. He looked down at me with eyes sparking.

"You're so damned focused on Dorian and everyone else, did you ever stop to think that I'm going through the same thing? That I'm *this* close to going on a killing spree as it is? I'm on the fucking edge, and it'll be *you* who pushes me over."

Exasperation ballooned within me, and my heart hammered against my chest.

"You need to chill out," I said through clenched teeth as I pushed a finger into his chest. "I don't know what's wrong with you—"

"*You don't know what's wrong with me?*" he roared, making me jump. "My son is missing, and there's nothing I can do about it! My wife seems to think it's okay to go off and get herself killed, too! Do you realize the darkness that would throw me into? I'm about to explode as it is, Alexis. And you don't know what's *wrong* with me? Maybe if you opened your fucking eyes and looked at me for once, you'd know."

I took a step back, blinking away traitor tears. My mouth opened and closed as words failed me. Had I really been so oblivious to him? I'd been relying on him as my rock, the foundation to hold me up because my world was so close to crumbling around me. And he'd been that for me. He'd been my strength this whole time. But ... I'd been trying my best to be the same for him.

"Are you fucking kidding me?" I demanded. "Don't *you* get it? I know *exactly* how you're feeling. And all I want to do is take that away for you. All I think about is how to get us through this! I do everything for us! For you! So I don't have to see that look in your eyes, feel the pain in your heart. I *do* see you, Tristan. And I hear you in my head and feel you in my soul. Don't you see? I feel it *twice* as hard!" The last words came out as a shout, and he pulled back with a new look in his eyes. I sighed. "If feeling both of our pain meant you didn't have to feel it at all, I would be fine with that. But you do have to feel it, and I'm sorry. I wish I could do more. I'm trying . . ."

He pushed his hands through his hair, and his ferocity deflated. "I know, *ma lykita.* The stone does it to me, too. We're both feeling each other, and unfortunately, we're both feeling nothing but negativity." He reached out for me, but I stepped away. "Look, I'm sorry. I just . . . I guess I kept that pent up for too long."

I shook my head. "That's not all of it, though. You need to stop giving me that bullshit line about being reckless. I *knew* the situation. You and Vanessa would have followed me anyway, but I could have taken Victor on by myself, and you know it. You're the one who says I'm just as powerful as you."

"But not as knowledgeable," he countered. "You've been a part of this world for two years. It takes decades to learn everything, especially about the magic. Why do you think Owen was in school for so many years? And he was raised in this world. Not to mention the politics or understanding why evil behaves the way it does. You still have way too much to learn. I can't help but feel overprotective of you. Especially right now . . . with Dorian . . . I just can't stand the thought of losing you, Lex."

"Then protect me. But from my side. I can't let everyone else do things that I wouldn't do myself, Tristan. I can't be that kind of leader. So please stop asking me to do that."

We stared at each other for several long moments, but when he didn't respond, I huffed out another sigh and stomped toward the house and up the stairs of the back deck. I leaned against the railing, my emotions stewing. Everyone was on edge lately. Well, actually, we'd all been moody for several months. We couldn't help it. When you meet disappointment followed by more disappointment, you're bound to get cranky.

As much as I hated how I felt now, though, Tristan and I had both needed to get that off our chests. He hadn't been the only one keeping things pent up for too long. And we were both right in our own ways. I needed to show him more that I knew his pain and suffering. I needed to be there for him as much as he'd been there for me. And he needed to accept that I'd always be in danger, but that I couldn't just sit in the house and let everyone else do the dirty work. That worked for Rina, but it wouldn't for me. He needed to learn to protect me without holding me back, although I could, admittedly, be a little more cautious with my actions.

"I lost them." Vanessa's voice rang across the lawn as she emerged from the woods, her tone filled with defeat.

I frowned, said a prayer for Sasha, and turned to go inside, needing to address my issues with Tristan before focusing on the ones I had with Vanessa. I found him up in our suite. When I entered, he immediately swept me into his arms.

"I'm sorry," he said, "so, so sorry, *ma lykita*. I shouldn't have lost it with you. Not you. You're my everything. You're the last one I ever want to hurt."

"Stop," I said, the word muffled as I spoke against his chest. He held me so tightly I could barely breathe. "We both said things, and we both made valid points. You had every right to be angry with me. I'm sorry for not being there for you. You've been so perfect for me, and I didn't return the favor. I didn't give you what you need, what you deserve from your wife." I pulled back to look up at him and squirmed an arm free to reach up and place my hand against his cheek. "I'm sorry, Tristan. I love you more than anything. I'm sorry I hurt you."

His thumb brushed over my cheekbone. "I'm sorry, too. You're right. I can be too overbearing when it comes to keeping you out of harm's way."

"You know that's impossible, right? You of all people should know that about the world we live in."

"I do. That's probably why I try so hard. I wish I could just put you in my pocket, or better yet, lock you up in a security vault where no one can get to you and you can't get to them. But I know that's wrong."

"I don't think I can lead the way Rina does."

The corners of his mouth turned down. "I don't think you can, either, *ma lykita*. And that's something I'll have to figure out how to accept and how to handle."

"Thankfully, we have plenty of time to figure it all out."

His eyes glinted. "Maybe by then, you'll have all this craziness worked out of your system, and you'll be happy to be locked up in the tower, telling everyone what to do with your mind."

I let out a harrumph. "Don't count on it."

He smiled. "I know. That will never be you, will it? And if I'm honest with myself, that's part of what I love about you." He leaned his forehead against mine. "Are we good?"

"I think so," I whispered. "As good as we can get."

Before anything else could be said, he tilted his head down and covered his mouth with mine. Tristan always had his ways, especially after an argument, and my body always responded, as it did now. He pulled me into our suite and closed the door behind us with his foot while he continued to kiss me, his tongue exploring every bit of my mouth. I pressed into him, my nipples poking through my sports bra and his t-shirt to brush against his chest. His hands slid up my sides and grasped my rib cage, his thumbs sliding under the bra and rubbing against the bottom bulge of my breasts. He continued kissing me as he began to push up the bra.

But I stopped him. "Not here."

19

TRISTAN'S MOUTH MOVED to my neck as his hand slid under the waistband of my shorts. "How about here?"

I giggled. "No, I mean not here at the safe house. I want to *enjoy* it."

"Ah." He groaned, his breath hot against my skin, but when he pulled back, he wore a huge grin. "As much as I hate to say it, sexy Lexi, you need to put more clothes on. We're going for a ride."

After all that talk about being unprotected and stupid, we snuck off on a motorcycle ride by ourselves. No warlock to shield or cloak us. No vampires or Weres to guard us. Just the two of us, risking our lives so we could be together the way we needed to be. Which basically proved my point that he and I could hold our own, and he knew it. Maybe doing so wasn't ideal, but when was life ever ideal?

I wrapped my arms around him and pressed myself against his back, part of me anxious to get there already, wherever *there* was, and part of me simply enjoying the ride, as if we'd gone back in time to our early days when we didn't have a care in the world. Well, at least nothing compared to this. We rode for more than an hour until we reached the Shenandoah National Park.

"It's a full moon and you brought me to the woods?" I asked once we dismounted the bike. "Do you think this is a good idea?"

He gave me a wicked smirk as he swaggered toward me. His hands grasped my waist and pulled me to him, closing the remaining distance between us.

He leaned over and nibbled on my earlobe before whispering, "I thought danger was your thing."

I smiled, unable to help it. "Well . . ."

"Besides, a little risk could add to the fun, don't you think?"

His hot mouth closed over my throat. I must have needed him badly—worse than I realized—because my body immediately throbbed with an intense ache for him.

He pulled back, though, and began undressing himself, his beautiful hazel eyes never leaving my face. He pulled off his boots and then his pants and stood in front of me in all of his glorious nakedness. *Holy fuck.* How was I so lucky? After giving me a nice eyeful, he turned and strode toward the stream, the muscles of his round, too-perfect-to-be-real butt moving in a way that made my throat dry. I couldn't help but imagine biting it.

"Are you coming?" he asked me as he stepped into the water.

Sheesh. One touch from him and I would be.

My fingers trembled as I undid the ribbon and hooks to loosen the leather corset I'd changed into, my breasts aching against the confinement. Finally they sprang free, my skin tight with their fullness and my nipples hard.

"Mmm . . . that's what I'm talkin' about," Tristan said quietly from the middle of the stream, his eyes filled with a greedy hunger. "Come on, *ma lykita*, the water's perfect."

My legs shook as I pulled off my leathers and practically ran for the stream. The water was far from perfect for a Norman—freezing cold against my hot skin—but I quickly adjusted. Or maybe the heat radiating from my body warmed it. When I'd almost reached him, Tristan swam downstream several yards, to a deeper swimming hole fed by a small waterfall. He took my hand and pulled me through the curtain of water, to a crescent-shaped area carved out of the hillside by the stream—a shallow cave hidden behind the waterfall. The ledge forming the floor ended right at the waterfall, and the water over it was only knee-deep. The ceiling of the half-cave hung low—too low for Tristan to stand. He pulled himself to sit on the ledge, and I climbed onto him. And finally he held me in his arms again, and his mouth pressed down on mine.

His full lips moved gently at first, but I was too hungry for him. I thrust my tongue into his mouth and devoured his tangy-sweet taste. The kiss deepened and became more urgent. His hands slid over my back, up into my hair where his fingers tangled into the locks, and down to the small of my back. I grasped onto his neck, grinding myself against his erection beneath me as we moaned into each other's mouths. I finally broke away, wanting to taste more of him. I moved my lips and tongue over his angular jaw, slowly making my way to the tender skin where his jaw met his neck. I sucked as though trying to eat him, my tongue swirling over his tasty skin.

He tugged on my hair, pulling me back, and his head dove for my breasts. I leaned against his hands supporting my back as he kissed the soft flesh, then his lips closed over my breast, and he sucked it into his mouth. I bucked against him as his tongue flicked and rolled my nipple and then his teeth grazed over it. My fingers dug into his shoulders when he moved to the other side. After spending some time there, I could tell he wanted to go further down. I leaned away, my head falling back, and the water poured over my hair as Tristan kissed down my stomach, his tongue making circles around my belly button.

Both of his hands slid to my butt, raising my pelvis to the surface of the water, causing me to fall backwards through the waterfall so I floated halfway out and halfway in. He lifted me higher and, understanding, I moved my legs to curl over his shoulders. My back arched to give him better access. My body throbbed with aching need. Then his hot mouth closed down on me and with the cold water flowing over my breasts, I'd never felt anything so erotic. My body bucked and writhed as his tongue moved expertly, taking me to a bliss I hadn't experienced in way too long.

When the tremors subsided, I slid my legs down Tristan's body, grabbed his shoulders, and pulled him out of the waterfall to join me. We locked in a kiss, and my legs wrapped around his waist. His erection pressed against me but didn't enter as he moved us closer to the shore. We came almost all the way out of the water, and he walked us to a big, smooth boulder. His mouth still clamped on mine, he grasped my calves and gently broke their grip on him, making me stand on my own feet.

"Turn around," he said. I turned around. "Bend over."

He positioned me perfectly with one arm underneath my breasts so none of my skin scraped against the rock. His free hand massaged my butt and stroked downward until his fingers brought me to another climax. Then he finally pushed inside me. My mind had already been wide open, but I lost any and all control as he thrust into me, slid out, thrust in again. He knew when I was about to scream his name because he clamped his free hand over my mouth. I bit down on it hard enough to draw blood when he plunged in deep and hard and sent me over the edge again. He must have liked it because he gave me several more hard pumps before exploding inside me.

He collapsed against me, his hard chest thumping against my back as we both panted. His lips trailed light kisses over my neck and shoulder until the aftershocks subsided. Then he pulled back and kneeled in the water.

"I really needed that," I said as I turned over, lay on my back on the boulder, and stared at the starry sky.

"I know," Tristan said as he scooped water into his hands and poured it over my breasts and stomach. "It's the least I could do for our anniversary."

Shit. I'd remembered this morning, but had become distracted. "I'm sorry we fought on our anniversary."

"Me, too. But it made the celebration all the much better."

"Maybe this is the time we'll get pregnant," I said as my finger caressed the stone in my chest, although I didn't tell him about the tea. For now, that would be Blossom's and my secret. "An anniversary present to us."

Tristan moved closer to me, bent over, and pressed his lips to the stone. "Maybe," he murmured. "When the time is right, she'll come."

"Mmm . . ." came my only answer. Because who knew if she would ever come? The chances were so slim, even with the stone and the tea. Although I wanted a daughter badly, I would be okay. Unlike the rest of the Amadis, I could accept it if we never had one. Because I still believed Dorian came to us alone for a reason—that, like Tristan, the Angels had created him for us. Not for the Daemoni. Regardless of some stupid curse.

So why were they making it so hard to find him?

Why did they have to make *everything* so hard? My mood slid from absolute contentedness to sour quickly. Too quickly. The moment here had been nice, but it was time to get back to business.

Tristan wanted to stay longer, but I was already out of the stream and pulling my clothes back on.

"I wonder if Sasha ever came back," I said as I laced up my bustier.

"I'm sure she ran Victor off, and she's waiting for us at home." He made his way out of the water and began to dress. "But if not, I'm sure she's romping around the woods or hunting for Dorian."

"Hmm . . . I don't like it when she takes off like that. And I *hate* that Victor's still out there." I placed my hands on my hips and scowled. "We really need a break. Some glimpse of victory for once. I mean, is that too much to ask for?"

"We do our part, *ma lykita*, and the rest will happen when it's supposed to—"

A long howl cut off Tristan's words. A wolfish sound. I held my finger in the air to keep him on pause while I reached out with my mind.

"Weres," I confirmed in a whisper. "Lots of them." I counted the mind signatures I was picking up. "Fifteen, I think."

"Daemoni."

"Yeah, but . . . they're weird." I skipped from mind to mind, and my brow furrowed as I picked up their random thoughts. "They're kind of freaking out. Really confused. I think . . . this is their first time changing."

The words were barely out of my mouth when their meaning hit me. I'd just been asking for a break, and maybe this was it, but I tried not to let my hopes rise too much.

Tristan texted Charlotte with our location, and I thought it would take them at least an hour to drive here, but apparently my team hadn't quite left us alone like we'd thought they had. Charlotte and Vanessa had stayed out of my mind's reach, but they'd followed us closely enough to be there if we needed them.

"The others are on their way with the safe house's vans," Char said when they arrived. "Let's try to make their trip worth it."

I didn't have to lead the way by following the wolves' mind signatures. Their howls and whines could be heard by all of us. We came upon a pack of fifteen scraggly looking wolves, some fighting, snarling, and biting at each other, some jumping around in circles because they didn't know how the hell they suddenly had four legs and fur, and others howling about their new freakdoms.

Trevor had told me a few things about alpha status and how to achieve and maintain control over a pack of wolves. Using this knowledge, I barked into their heads to be still and shut up while positioning my body to show domination. Their minds were very human, yet still controlled by the animal side of them. So they understood what I said perfectly and obeyed me as though I was their alpha. In no time, I had them sitting on their haunches in a line in front of us.

Through mind-speak with them, we learned how they'd all been at the same party a few weeks ago—a rough biker party that had been loud and a lot of fun, until they woke up the next morning after blacking out with the worst hangovers ever. Except the after-effects didn't go away for a few days, and they assumed they'd been ruffied. When the symptoms finally resided, they all forgot about it. Until the period of the full moon approached and their bodies ached and their skin crawled. They'd each received a text to meet at this park tonight, although it didn't explain why or even say who sent it. They'd hoped to find answers to what ailed their bodies, but they only found each other. As soon as the sun had set and the full moon showed itself, they all exploded out of their skins—and found themselves in the bodies of wolves.

By the time we reached the point of explaining what had been done to them, the rest of my team had arrived. Jax and Sheree had to transform to prove we weren't full of crap. Then we had to convince them that we hadn't been the ones who'd infected them, but we could help if they wanted it. Once they understood better, two—a male and a female with darker, edgier minds than the rest of them—thought their new forms were badass, and they took off to hunt. The others, however, agreed they wanted nothing more than to remove the disgusting desire for human flesh out of their minds forever. The wolves followed me to the vans in formation and piled in.

"Finally!" I exclaimed with a small sense of joy when Tristan and I returned to the safe house. "It would have been perfect to get them all, but *thirteen*! Thirteen souls saved. Thirteen new recruits for us. Thirteen fewer for the Daemoni."

A small victory, but a victory nonetheless.

We couldn't celebrate yet—once the moon set and the wolves returned to their human forms, we had to begin our work on them. But as soon as we could a few days later, we all sat down with the rest of the safe house staff and enjoyed a luxurious meal together. We needed the camaraderie—and the win—so badly.

Since Vanessa hadn't found Victor the other day, we assumed Sasha had chased him off, but the lykora still hadn't returned. I couldn't help but worry about her, but Vanessa said she'd seen no silver blood when she inspected every inch of the woods on a daily basis. Tristan figured Sasha would chase Victor around the globe if he'd been the one to hurt her or to take Dorian, and the thought of the vamp constantly on the run from her made me smile.

My mind couldn't stop harping on Vanessa, though . . . and Victor. And Sasha's reaction to Victor. *Was* it because he had been the one to sever her wing in the safe house suite? The one to take Dorian? If so, did that mean Lucas had been behind the kidnapping all along? Had we been too focused on Kali and Owen when we should have been looking for Victor and Lucas? And had Vanessa told the truth about not finding her brother, or was there something more? Was there a reason she volunteered to go after him and shooed me home? I still didn't know if I could trust her.

For now, however, I'd focus on our big win and celebrate with my team. My phone rang in the middle of our meal, and since it was Mom, I had to answer it.

"Hi, honey," she said, her voice still full of happiness. "I thought I'd give you some much-needed good news. Your safe house on Captiva pulled in a whole nest of vampires in Tampa. Sixteen of them converting!"

My whole team cheered loudly.

"To hope, faith, and a little perseverance," Charlotte said as she raised her wine glass after I hung up with Mom.

"A *lot* of perseverance," I said as I lifted my own glass.

"To love conquering all," Tristan said with a wink in my direction. I dazed out for a second, missing Jax and Blossom's toast.

"To good always wins," Vanessa said as her ice-blue eyes locked on mine and a small smile played on her lips. She tipped her glass of blood up and didn't break our gaze as she drank.

The pit of my stomach tightened. Her thoughts were innocent, but I couldn't help but wonder what she was trying to say with that little statement.

I WOKE UP the next morning in the closest thing I had to a good mood since the day Tristan lost his mind to Kali nearly six months ago. Happy didn't quite describe my feelings—I wouldn't be happy until my son was home where he belonged. But definitely more hopeful than I'd been in some time. I could sense a difference in Tristan, too, as we lay in bed for a few minutes longer than usual, cuddling and kissing and simply enjoying a bit of peace.

"One of these days, we'll be able to do this every morning," he mused as his forefinger stroked loops over my arm.

"If only," I said, my fingers copying his but over the ridges of his hard abs. He flexed them in response to the tickle, making me smile. "Somehow, though, I don't think our lives will ever allow such laziness every morning."

"Laziness? This isn't laziness." In one swift motion, he turned us over so I lay on my back, and he hovered on his elbows over me. "This can be our morning workout."

I giggled as he lowered himself down enough to plant a kiss on my stomach, and then my giggles turned to moans as his mouth moved lower. Although all the nearby mind signatures prevented me from enjoying the moment as much as I had by the waterfall, it was still the best wakeup call we'd had in a long time.

And we weren't the only ones in a good mood. The victory with the wolves had meant a lot more to all of us than I realized. A lighter, more playful atmosphere enveloped the whole team.

"Blossom, I think today is the day," I said to her after lunch. "I feel it. We'll break through today."

"Let's do it then," she said, and we headed for the room where I'd given birth to Dorian. She said his presence lingered more strongly there than in the room that had been his nursery. "Can I tell you something first?"

My heart skipped. I could tell by her tone we were moving into girl talk and all I could think was what a crappy friend I'd been to her. Again.

"Of course," I said with a little too much enthusiasm.

"Jax and I . . . well, your cake idea worked, if you hadn't noticed, and I, uh, well, I think he might be the one," she finally blurted as we entered the bedroom.

I stopped in my tracks and spun on her. "Blossom! Are you serious?"

She smiled shyly and gave a little shrug. "I don't know . . . we seemed to click right away, you know? And he's so kind but determined to protect you and me both, and well, he's nice to look at. Even with the scar. It's kind of sexy."

I chuckled. "Do you know how that scar got there?"

She giggled. "Yeah. He told me Tristan gave it to him. But it sounded like he deserved it. Jax can be . . . well, he's Jax. But I think I love him."

"I'm sure the accent has nothing to do with it." She seemed to have a thing for those.

"Oh my God. You should hear him talk dirty with that accent of his!"

I clapped my hand over my mouth to cover a laugh. "I don't want to know that!"

"Yes, you do. Doesn't Tristan ever talk dirty to you in all those different languages he knows?"

Hmm . . . funny how I'd never thought about it. He was holding out on me! That would have to change. Next time, I swore I'd make him do it. Although, I'd probably forget because his lips on my skin pretty much made me forget everything.

I wrapped my arms around Blossom's shoulders. "I'm happy for you. Jax is a great guy."

"You don't think a were-croc and a witch is, I don't know, kind of weird?"

I leveled my gaze at her. "Blossom. Of course it's weird. Every word you just said is weird if you don't live in our world. But this *is* our world, and weird is normal. Besides, with the way things are right now, any kind of love is good. The world needs it."

I was happy to know it was love, too, and not a passing infatuation or flat-out lust. They made a great couple, even if it was weird.

She took my hand in hers and squeezed. "Thanks, Alexis. Your blessing's important to me."

I blew it off by pulling us to the floor in the center of the room, right in front of the queen-sized bed I'd spent a straight eight months in. Mom and Rina had knelt in this very spot, helping to ease Dorian out of my body when I passed out during his delivery.

"Suburbs today, right?" Blossom asked as she crossed her legs and made herself comfortable.

We'd ridden all over the east side of the metro area and downtown right before our big win, and I'd scoured the area for mind signatures then.

"Yeah. This side of D.C., though," I answered. "But not too far west. I just did a scan the other night when we got the wolves."

"Okay, so Maryland?"

"Sure. Why not?" Of course, we'd already searched Maryland and Northern Virginia—the entire D.C. area and beyond—more times than I could count, but the chance of discovering something new always remained. Even if we didn't find Dorian, the Daemoni mind signatures in the area numbered in the thousands—it was a politicians' city, after all—and we never knew when we might stumble upon something useful.

We grasped each other's hands and closed our eyes, and Blossom began her spell. My good mood faltered, though, as we mentally traversed over the Maryland suburbs and nothing new caught our attention. We skimmed over the tens of thousands of mind signatures, looking only for the familiar ones we sought or the pricks of those belonging to Daemoni, but I should have known the afternoon made the timing bad. Too many awake Norman signatures and too many sleeping Daemoni ones. My optimism waned, and Blossom must have felt it because she began pulling back with me.

When the situation allowed, we tended to bring our minds back in a slow fashion, meandering our way to our physical selves so when we opened our eyes, we weren't completely disoriented. So we floated lazily over the state line and into Fairfax County, and we'd almost reached home when something piqued my interest. My breath caught. *Could it be?* I almost dismissed it—the mind signature was way too close, in an area we'd scoured time and again. I mentally went back to where I'd caught the proverbial scent and searched more closely. Focused in on the specific twang that had grabbed me. And . . . there.

My son.

20

DORIAN! I EXCLAIMED.

"*Mom? Is it really you? In my head?*"

I choked back a sob at the sound of his voice. *Yes, little man, it's me.*

"*Really? Because I thought I heard you before, but you never answered me.*"

I'm sorry. I . . . I lost you. Are you okay?

"*How are you in my head, Mom? How are you talking to me?*"

You know how you can fly? It's kind of like that, but this is something I can do.

"*Okay,*" he accepted easily. I wondered what they'd been telling him, if he knew all about the Amadis and the Daemoni. But that wasn't important at the moment.

Dorian, are you okay? I asked again.

"*I guess. But I miss you and Dad lots. Uncle Owen said I can't see you.*"

My jaw clenched. *Are you with Owen right now?*

"*Not right this minute. But he's usually around. He's acting all weird, and I want to go home, but he won't let me. Are you coming to get me?*"

Oh, baby, we are! But we don't know where to find you. Do you know where you are?

"*Not really. A stupid, boring room where I always am.*" He glanced around, and I peered through his eyes to see a small room with gray commercial-grade carpet, a twin-size bed, and a TV with a game console hooked up to it, probably to keep Dorian quietly entertained.

Have you been there the whole time? I asked.

"*Not always. Sometimes we go places. There's a big lake outside the building and sometimes Uncle Owen will take me out there. But not for long. And never when Kali's around.*"

A growl rumbled in my throat. *Can you picture in your mind what it looks like outside? The building and the lake?*

He fed me a picture, but nothing was familiar. After all of the miles we'd put on the bikes, we'd never been past that place before. How would we—

"Got him," Blossom murmured under her breath.

Unable to control myself, I jumped to my feet and let out a squeal.

As always when we tried to locate Dorian, Tristan had been nearby, and he must have heard us, because he appeared in the room in a flash. I kept my mind linked to Dorian's as they looked up the location—only eight miles away. Eight freaking miles. How long had he been so damn close? The desire to kill Kali and do some serious harm to Owen became a fervent ache.

We're coming, Dorian, I promised him.

The seven of us jumped on the motorcycles and peeled away from the safe house. Charlotte muffled the loud engines so we could get as close in as possible. We turned down a street nearly hidden by heavy lines of trees—no wonder we'd missed it in all of our searches—and approached a parking lot at the end. I recognized the three black-brick office buildings set in a horseshoe shape around a lake as the same scene Dorian had shown me.

"What the hell?" Tristan muttered.

A small sign stood at the entrance to the parking lot:

UNITED STATES OF AMERICA
DEPARTMENT OF DEFENSE

He pulled the motorcycle off the road and parked it in the trees, and the rest of our group followed.

"What's Dorian doing here?" Blossom whispered.

"We might not want to know," Char answered, her voice dark and heavy.

I could only imagine one reason the DoD would want Dorian—they'd consider him no different than an alien life-form—but why would Kali do such a thing? What was in it for her?

"It could be a front," Tristan suggested.

My mind had already been open to new signatures, but none had been threatening or close, so I hadn't paid them much attention. I now zeroed in on the only ones nearby. All of them were Norman and in the same building, the one directly in front of us and farthest away from the entrance, and they were all on the same floor—where Dorian was. Then I found several others—all Daemoni but similar in quality to Dorian's, although much older. And then . . .

"Owen," I whispered as I opened my mind to the others.

"*Mom?*" Dorian spoke to us. "*Are you still there?*"

Yes, little man. We're coming.

"*Mom! Don't leave me again!*"

I'm still here, Dorian. Almost there.

"*Mom! Please!*" Anguish and tears filled his mental voice, and all I wanted to do was reach out and grab him. "*No. Please. I don't want to go!*"

He actually shouted aloud now, meaning he pled with someone else. It had to have been Owen. Tristan and I traded the same look of horror, he nodded, and we both took off in a blurred sprint for the front of the building.

We're coming, baby. We're coming, Dorian!

"*Shield!*" Charlotte and Blossom both yelled in my mind, sensing the magic before we had.

Tristan suddenly stopped, and I slammed into his back, bouncing off of him like a rubber ball off a wall. I thought I heard Vanessa snicker. We must have looked like a cartoon. *Boom! Pow!*

"Holy super-brakes, Tristan," I muttered as he reached back to catch me with one hand while lifting his other to press against the invisible wall that kept us from our son.

White-hot pain knifed through my brain, though, making me stumble backwards and out of his reach. Then the force of it, the screaming agony, brought me to my knees. *Kali.* She was here, too. I clasped my hands over my ears and doubled over my thighs as I tried to push her out of my head, but my mind began to gray out. Then went blank. As did my vision.

I didn't think I'd actually passed out this time, but the next thing I knew, the others had caught up to us, standing next to Tristan and me. Vanessa sprinted away, toward the far end of the parking lot, but after what I didn't know. Pressing the heel of my palms to my temples, I squeezed my eyes shut and forced my mind to focus inside the building. But Dorian's mind signature was gone. Kali and Owen seemed to have disappeared, too . . . as well as one of the others, one of the Daemoni who had been there.

"Shit!" I screamed. "We were so close!"

"*Amadis royalty,*" I heard in my head, coming from someone in the building. "*I feel it in my blood.*"

"*I feel it, too. They're close. But they can't help us. We're locked up like fucking lab animals.*"

They weren't only thinking, but spoke to each other. Daemoni being held prisoner. At a building that may or may not have belonged to the DoD. Why? And what did Kali have to do with it?

We can *help you*, I dared to tell them. *Just tell me what's going on.*

An evil laugh cackled in my mind. "*You can't help us, princess! Even if we wanted you to, we can't ever go with you.*"

"*Not that we want to,*" another added, his voice vaguely familiar from a distant memory, but I couldn't grasp it.

They growled more words at each other, but they were incoherent in my mind.

"I don't know what they're doing in there, but I don't think locked up Daemoni is a bad thing," I said as I tried to push myself to my feet, but Tristan's hands were heavy on my shoulders.

"Are you okay?" he asked with a raised brow. "You slammed into me pretty hard."

"It wasn't that. Kali was in there, too, and she shoved me out of her head by sticking a knife in my brain. I'll be fine." I lifted my brows until he finally let me up. "We just need to figure out where they went."

"I tried to catch them," Vanessa said as she ran up to our group, "but Kali or Owen put up a cloak. They disappeared from sight."

I swallowed down the sob threatening to explode. We'd been so damn close. So close to holding our son again. So close to killing the bitch sorceress and her traitor son. My eyes cut guiltily over to Char, glad she hadn't heard my stray thought. She paid no attention to the rest of us, but glared at the black DoD building with hard sapphire eyes, her jaw muscle popping in and out as she seemed to grind some kind of thought between her teeth. I thought about peeking to see what she was thinking, but decided to give her privacy. I didn't really have to wonder too hard about it—she wanted to kill Kali as much as I did.

We pulled back into the woods and kept surveillance on the building throughout the night, in case they all came back, including Dorian. When it started to look like they might not return at all, we took shifts watching while the remainder of us rested at the safe house. At some point between my first and second shift, an unknown Daemoni warlock had come in and strengthened the shield, blocking the mind signatures inside from me. The stronger shield also meant no one could flash in or out without us knowing. The only people who came and went, however, were Normans dressed in either security coats or civilian clothes. What were they doing in there? And had they already done it to Dorian?

I held on to his word that he was okay. I hoped he would have told me if they had been running some kind of tests on him or experiments. Surely in the short time we were connected he would have brought that up. But maybe that had been Kali's plan—to deliver Dorian to the Normans who were so interested in learning more about us. But what would be her motivation? Why would she hang around? Why would she take him out now when we'd found him?

Tristan suggested the Daemoni had taken the building over from the DoD, who may have had nothing to do with any of it. This theory seemed like another good possibility, given the evidence, but still— why would Kali and Owen keep Dorian there? Was it like Lilith and Bree, when Kali had kept them in the Everglades, right under our noses simply because she could? Or was there more to it?

The only way to get answers was to find them all.

Every time Blossom and I were at the safe house together and both of us well rested, we did our search, but Kali had caught on. Whatever had caused her to lift the cloak long enough for us to come as close as we did must have been a mistake she wouldn't make again. But we also weren't feeling any kind of nudge to move out of the area. We were essentially stuck in limbo until something broke again.

Without a clue or a prod or anything, we began debating among the team whether to make a charge on the building. If we couldn't find Dorian, then we could at least find out who the others in the building were and what was going on in there.

"From what Alexis could tell before they put the shield up, they were all Daemoni," Tristan said. He leaned against the railing of the wooden deck outside, where we'd all gathered for a drink to go with our afternoon debate. I leaned against him, his arms wrapped loosely around my shoulders, a beer in his hands in front of me. "The most obvious and best option is they're the Summoned brothers and their offspring. The ones Rina told us about."

"Unless they're fools who were caught by the Normans in their traps and checkpoints," Vanessa countered. She hopped up onto the railing, and gracefully swung down to sit on it, giving no regard to the fact that we were twenty feet above ground. "And they're probably being tortured and prodded like freak aliens."

"Which means they could have Amadis in there, too," Sheree said. She sat on a cushioned lounge chair, gnawing on her fingernails.

I shook my head. "I'm positive they were all Daemoni. Besides Dorian, of course. And the Normans who have been coming and going since."

"They could be keepin' the Amadis someplace else," Jax suggested before taking a swig of his beer. He, too, sat on the railing, his legs swinging in front of him.

"And torturing and prodding *them*," Blossom added as she moved to stand between Jax's legs. "We have to find out. We can't leave them there."

"Unless they *are* all Daemoni," Char said. She sat under the umbrella's shade over the outdoor table, an elbow on the glass top and her head resting on her hand. "Then I'm with Alexis—let's leave them there. Better than on the streets, especially if we can't convert them."

"They said we couldn't save them," I reminded them all.

"Because they're probably the Summoned brothers," Tristan said again, bringing us full circle.

I rocked forward on my feet and placed my hands on my hips. "Well, in that case, we need to find Dorian first anyway. Rina said he's probably the key to finding the brothers. Maybe even saving them."

Everyone's eyes darted around as they thought about what our next step should be.

"You two keep trying," Tristan finally said, "and the rest of us will create a plan. In the very off chance that I'm wrong."

I jabbed him with my elbow.

"What? I'm rarely wrong. If ever."

"I know," I said with a small smile. "I agree with you. But . . ."

"If you *are* wrong . . ." Blossom continued.

"We can't take the chance there are Amadis locked up somewhere, too," Char finished, "being treated like animals."

So Blossom and I tried her spell one more time while they created a strategy to make our move on the DoD building.

And the break we needed came. We locked on to Dorian again.

He was with Owen, and they were on the move. Once again, we all rushed for the motorcycles. My heart stuttered for a moment when I sensed them quickly approaching our direction. Could Owen actually be bringing him to us?

No. They went right on by us. But now we knew where they were, and we sped after them. Owen drove a white two-seater Mercedes-Benz, practically flying down the country roads. We closed in on him, but he sped up. Right when Tristan said to make our move, another sports car flew out in front of us. A black BMW, right on Owen's tail. Kali and someone else—another Daemoni—were inside. Tristan eased off the gas, and everyone else eased back, too.

"What the hell, Tristan?" I demanded. "Let's get him!"

"Give me a minute," he said as the cars pulled farther away from us. "We don't know who's with Kali, and she and Owen are pretty formidable by themselves. We don't want Dorian involved in the crossfire."

I groaned with frustration, but when the two cars rounded a corner and we could no longer see them, I couldn't hold back a minute longer. If only I were driving. "Come on, let's go before they get away!"

Tristan must have agreed because he gripped the accelerator and twisted, pushing the motorcycle to its top speed. Our knees practically slid over the ground when we made the tight turn. The two cars were about two hundred yards ahead, and then . . . they disappeared. But not like they were suddenly cloaked. The cars disappeared front to back, as though they drove into or through something. But nothing was there.

We all came to an abrupt stop in the middle of the road.

"Why are we stopping?" I demanded.

"Yeah, what the hell?" Vanessa asked. "They're getting away!"

"We don't know what that is," Tristan said through his teeth. He dismounted the bike and strode up to the place where the cars had disappeared, studying it with deep concentration.

Charlotte appeared by his side. She moved her hands in front of her, creating a ball of yellow light, then grew it larger before throwing it up in the air. An outline of what almost looked like a large door briefly appeared, a different landscape beyond it than the actual landscape in front of us. Tristan stuck his hand through it and left it there while the outline and the image beyond disappeared.

"It's cold and wet," he said, his brows pushing together as he held his damp hand up as proof. Here was a hot, humid day with not a single cloud in the sky.

"Huh," Charlotte muttered. We all looked at her. "I've never seen a real one."

"What?" I just needed for her to deem it safe so we could go.

"It's a portal," Vanessa said as she walked up to it, and for some reason, the fact that she knew this made my hackles rise.

"Of course," Tristan said, his voice low as he tried to study what could not be seen.

Charlotte turned to Vanessa and eyed her with the same suspicion I felt. "How do you know? These are very rare. Only used by the occasional—"

"Sorcerer. Or, in this case, a sorceress. I've heard they could create them, then I saw one used. By Owen." She peered at all of us as though surprised by our ignorance. "That's how Kali got off Amadis Island. He never told you? She'd created a portal in case she ever needed it, and when she did, Owen followed her. I didn't see Kali's spirit come through—I don't know if I *could* have seen it. But I was standing on the hillside in a Himalayan village when Owen seemed to fall out of a hole in the air."

"A portal. But where does it go?" Tristan asked.

"Does it matter?" I said. "Our son is there, wherever it is."

"Right," Vanessa agreed. "Who the hell cares? Owen *and* Dorian are through there. We need to go."

And that's what bothered me. Was she here to help us find Dorian? Or had this always been about Owen for her? The man who had stolen our son. Was she trying to set us up by convincing us to go through the portal? For all we knew, Kali, Owen, and possibly even Lucas and more Daemoni waited on the other side to ambush us. Of course, she blocked out such thoughts if she had them.

"How do we know to trust it?" I asked her. "How do we know it doesn't go straight into the heart of Hades? And regardless of your answer, why should we even trust you? For all we know, you have—" *Holy shit.* Why hadn't I thought of this sooner? Any of us? It would explain her behavior and my oscillating feelings about her. "Do you have a stone implanted in *you*? Is this Kali trying to get us to go through there?"

Vanessa eyed me, her face hardening as I palmed my dagger and swiped my thumb over the amethyst. I'd barely withdrawn it from its sheath when she lunged for me and snatched it out of my hand. She was instantly several yards away, gripping the hilt in both palms, the point of the blade at her heart. We all gasped as she plunged the dagger into her own chest, but we only stood there, saying or doing nothing to stop her. Her face twisted as she carved, drawing the blade in a grotesque crisscross pattern over her heart. My heart flipped and rolled at the sight, and my mouth opened and closed, but still, I did nothing but stare at her. She continued to dig until her porcelain skin became nothing but a shredded mess of flesh and blood.

And the knife never connected with a stone, nothing fell out.

She looked at me with a brow raised over one icy eye, as if asking if I was happy now. I had no response. While one of her hands held the ribbons of her skin together as they healed, she flipped the dagger in her other and walked over to us. She held the hilt out toward me while leaning closer.

"Some day, little sister, you're going to have to trust me." She straightened up and rolled her shoulder. "For now, I'm going after your little boy, regardless of what Owen does."

Then she sprinted down the road. In a heartbeat, the air seemed to swallow her whole.

Dumbfounded, I stared where her form had just been while my heart eventually settled. Had she really just done that? *Vanessa* mutilated her perfect self? She had. And because of me. In a daze, I wiped my blade over my pants a couple of times, then returned the dagger to its sheath.

"I'm sorry," I said to whoever would listen, though I stared at the ground. "It's just . . . she came . . ."

A small, warm hand landed on my shoulder and squeezed.

"She came to you about the same time as Sonya," Blossom said. "I thought of it just now, too. I can't believe none of us considered it when Sonya told us about hers."

"Because we all know Vanessa's really Amadis," Sheree said. "We know it in our hearts, including you, Alexis."

That didn't make me feel any better.

"It's not like I threw a spell to stop her just now or anything," Charlotte added. "None of us tried."

That did make me feel a little better, and I blew out the breath I'd been holding. The regret didn't expunge with the air, but it helped to know I wasn't the only one who'd suspected. I hadn't been the only one to stand there and watch expectantly rather than try to stop her. But I *was* the only one who had threatened to do it myself simply by pulling the blade out in the first place. The only bit of mollification was that the cuts didn't hurt her—too badly anyway. I finally looked up at the others. Tristan, whose opinion of me I worried most about, shook his head but lifted his arm for me to walk into.

"Trust has never come easy for you, I know," he murmured into my ear as he gave me a squeeze. "Nobody blames you. We've all wondered at one point or another, but I think we know now."

I nodded against his chest, a sense of relief washing through me for many reasons. But the feeling was short-lived.

"So, mates," Jax said, reverting our focus to the problem at hand, "are we goin' or not?"

"We have no idea what's on the other side," Blossom said. "And I'm with Alexis. I don't completely trust Vanessa."

"Except our son's on the other side," I muttered as I kicked a pebble in the road.

"The portal won't last forever," Tristan said, "from what I've heard about them."

"They *can* close on their own," Blossom affirmed, "but usually the creator closes it. I'm surprised Kali's kept it open this long."

"So she's probably waiting for us to go through it," Sheree said. "And now Vanessa's there by herself."

"Kali and Owen probably set it up so we'd chase them in," I said. "Owen knows it would work. He knows what I would do for my son."

"I could go through first, and if it's safe, come back to get you mates," Jax suggested.

"Portals don't work that way," Char ground out between clenched teeth as she paced back and forth on the pavement, her eyes on what appeared to be the road stretching in front of us, but her mind focused elsewhere. On Owen and Kali, who were on the other side of the portal. "They're created for a connection from point A to point B. It's not a two-way street."

She stopped her pacing in the middle of the road and stood with her feet shoulder-width apart. She pushed her hand through her blond hair, then spun on her boot.

"Sorry, Alexis, but I'm going with or without you," she said. She strode back to her motorcycle with purpose, mounted it, and cranked it over. "Are you coming with me, Sheree?"

The Were bit her lip, not answering right away.

"See you on the flip side then," Char called over the rumble, and she sped down the road and disappeared.

"Shit," I muttered. Charlotte was pissed. That was the only way to explain her behavior. She was going after Kali and Owen no matter what, even if it meant leaving me, the person she'd sworn to protect. "I'm going, too."

I climbed onto my bike, which Sheree had ridden here, and cranked it over.

"Alexis," Tristan said, already heading to his motorcycle. His thoughts told me he had no plans to stop me—he would stand by my side—but he used my name as a reminder.

"You know what Char's going to try, and we can't let her do it alone," I yelled over the rumble of my engine. "Besides, they have our *son.* Let's go get him!"

From the corner of my eye, I saw him nod as I kicked the clutch, put the motorcycle in gear, and twisted the accelerator. I sped down the road and through the portal, blasting into the unknown.

21

I EXPERIENCED NO whooshing of air from my lungs. No tunnel of darkness as I rode from Point A to Point B. In fact, I physically felt nothing odd as I rode through the portal and only knew I had succeeded because cold night air suddenly engulfed me and tiny raindrops sprayed my face. Well, that and because Vanessa and Char stood in the beam of my headlight when I turned it on. A rumbling behind me signaled Tristan's arrival, so I pulled forward in case the rest of our group decided to follow him. Of course they did. They were loyal through and through. I just hoped we wouldn't get them killed.

At least we seemed to be safe so far.

We shut off our engines, and I immediately searched for mind signatures, but the closest ones belonged to Normans in a town about five or so miles away. Well, besides those of animals, but they were normal beasts, too: sheep, cows, hogs, and some wild creatures. We'd been transported to a country road in the middle of nowhere, the pavement stretching north and south, and pastures spreading out in all directions. Clouds blanketed the sky, and a light rain fell on us. At least we hadn't fallen through a hole in the air. That wouldn't have been good for the motorcycles—or the cars Kali and Owen had been driving, which meant they hadn't created the portal as a quick escape to somewhere random. They'd had a plan.

"Where are we?" Sheree asked, her voice small as she sat on the motorcycle Vanessa had left with us back in Virginia.

"Definitely not Hades," I said with extreme relief.

"No. Feels like northern England," Tristan said. I glanced over at him as he pulled out his phone, and the screen lit up his face. How would he know that so easily?

Vanessa inhaled deeply. "I agree."

Following her lead, I took my own whiff, and the air definitely smelled different. I supposed they had enough years and experience in various locations around the world to be able to tell the difference by smell and feel.

"We're close to York," Tristan said while studying the phone screen. "About five miles north."

"York, England," Charlotte said, not as a question, but as a confirmation. "I guess the bitch has a thing for the United Kingdom."

"She did when she held Lilith and Bree captive," Tristan agreed. "Bree said Kali found them in Ireland and moved them to various places in the U.K. before taking them to the U.S."

Char nodded. "She left Martin as a baby in Ireland after killing his parents."

"And I think she once had a castle in Ireland," Vanessa said, then added, "Or was it Scotland? She'd never admit to exactly where. I'm surprised she didn't go there."

"Actually, it's either southern Scotland or northern England," Tristan said. "Lucas had me track her once, but I lost her near the border."

"So that's where she's going?" I asked. "That's where they're taking Dorian?"

"It's the most logical answer," Tristan said.

I toed the kickstand to make it drop and sat back on my bike with a huff. "But neither of you know *exactly* where it is. There's no sign of any of them—Kali, Owen, Dorian, or the other guy—*or* their minds. How do we know this isn't a decoy? How do we know they didn't go through another portal and are back in Virginia or went somewhere else? They could be anywhere in the world!"

"Yes, they could be," Tristan said as he rubbed his chin. "It would be a quick and easy way to throw us off their trails. Kali would know Vanessa and I would think she went to her castle, so she could have sent us on a wild goose chase."

I groaned, although I really wanted to punch something. "So what do we do?"

"We can't go back through the portal," Charlotte reminded us.

"We really only have one option," Tristan said. "We go to the nearest town and see if we can find anything out. Maybe someone saw them drive through or—"

"You know they're cloaked by now. Otherwise, I'd sense their mind signatures," I said.

"Someone might still know something," Blossom suggested.

"If her castle's nearby, maybe someone in the village has seen her around before," Jax offered. "Maybe did some work for her?"

"I could scan their minds from here," I said, not liking the idea of moving, because it could mean putting more distance between Dorian and us, even if it was only five miles.

"They won't be thinking about it unless someone's bringing up the subject," Tristan pointed out.

"Some of us have senses, too." Sheree sniffed in emphasis. "Senses we can use to help you, but not from this far away."

True. She, Jax, Vanessa, and Tristan could smell fear, desire, and even lies, and they had powerful hearing outside of people's minds. Charlotte and Blossom had their ways, as well. And Tristan was also right about standing out here in the rain not being much of an option. It wasn't like the sky was dropping answers on us. Only water.

So we headed for the nearest town, and my mind stayed open to other signatures the entire time. I was pleasantly surprised, yet suspicious, to find only a couple of Amadis mages in the area and no Daemoni.

"They're in the bigger cities," Tristan said as we rode. *"This part of the country isn't populated enough for them, but it's only a matter of time."*

I wondered how many towns like this—unaffected so far—still remained in the world. We'd already become expectant of checkpoints in the U.S. The freakin' United States of America, home of the free. Yeah, right. Thanks to the Daemoni and evil in high offices, the people weren't really free anymore. They complained about their rights being taken away, but they didn't know the half of it, what went on this very minute behind closed doors. And when they did find out? They'd have no chance in a revolution. Not when they were fighting creatures that shouldn't exist in their world.

Sudden despair hit me with the thought that my books hadn't been enough to prepare the Normans for the battle hovering on the horizon. Not even close. Such a paltry attempt, I saw now. Rina couldn't have actually believed they'd been enough to make a difference. She must have been humoring me with her explanation of why she allowed them to be written and published. She had to have been indulging me, knowing how much I needed to write those stories to stay somewhat sane during Tristan's absence.

Because the humans needed more. So much more.

They needed the Amadis. We needed our army.

We needed to find our son and get back to work.

We drove into York, and as we rode around the town, I thought about how the writer in me would have loved to spend time here. A palpable sense of deep history rose from the cobblestones and poured out of the ancient buildings, and a part of my mind couldn't help but think about all of the people who had passed through these very streets over the centuries. I envisioned burly men with long beards and dressed in fur coats and boots making trades at the local merchants, and others drinking ale from steins in a lodging house. So many stories to be told dating back millennia. But indulging in those stories—even thinking about them—was something I couldn't do now . . . or probably ever again. Real life needed my focus. There would be no more escapes into a fictional world, for me or for my readers. Real life had become exactly that: very *real*.

As we passed a huge, gorgeous, and very old cathedral, something golden darted out in front of us. Bree.

"This way," she said as she pointed down a road headed north, and she disappeared. Tristan turned, and we all followed. Bree reappeared and rounded another corner, but she was gone before we reached her. We made the turn, and she appeared down the road again. Tristan, with the rest of us behind him, continued following her until we turned into a driveway in front of a cobblestone cottage. I pulled up next to Tristan and looked at him. He lifted a shoulder in a shrug, before cutting his engine and turning to Bree.

Before she could explain, two women flew out of the house, bubbling with excitement. Bree chatted with them in a language I didn't know, but I felt pretty sure it wasn't Earthly. The sounds were too musical, too sexy, too unnatural to have been created by sensible humans. Finally, Bree turned to Tristan and me with a small smile on her face, although her golden eyes were cautious.

"I can't stay to help," she said, "but Stacey and Debbie have agreed to do so. It's the best I can do for now."

She gave us an apologetic smile, and then made introductions before disappearing again. I frowned as I glanced around the premises, but she didn't return.

Stacey and Debbie, the two faeries remaining in front of us, had similar features that made them difficult to tell apart: petite bodies, big blue eyes, and hair whiter than Vanessa's, although not *entirely* white. I wondered if they were twins, like Jessica and Lisa, and if twins were common among faeries, but at this moment, I didn't care enough to ask. Apparently Bree had only expected to find Stacey, but Debbie had been visiting, so we got a two-for-one deal. I didn't know if that was good or bad. I tried to believe it was good. After all, we'd been at a dead end before Bree popped into our realm, so anything was better than the nothing we'd had before.

"There's defo summat goin' on," the one introduced as Stacey said. Her hair blended from white at the crown of her head to cotton-candy pink at the bottom, which barely grazed her chin.

"Stacey's always naughty, but I got 'er to be'ave for a bit," said Debbie, whose hair had shades of purple in it. Their hair provided the only way to tell the two apart. That and when they spoke—Debbie's British accent sounded different than Stacey's. So much for the twin theory.

"Oh, I'm not naughty!" Stacey protested with a flirtatious giggle. "Not most of the time, anyway." She batted her eyelashes at Tristan. "And I would do anythin' for you."

"You mean because he's our fambo," Debbie reminded her with an elbow jab into the other faerie's side, although she gave Tristan a mischievous grin, too.

He grabbed my hand and squeezed, but I didn't worry. He was impervious to their effect, and not only because our love diluted their powers. He *was* one of them. Half, anyway. Enough to be their kin, as Debbie had said. At least, I assumed that was what she meant.

"So you do know something?" I asked, hoping to focus them on our problem.

"We were in the Otherworld with Bree," Stacey said, her bottom lip jutting out in a pout with my let's-get-serious attitude. "She was watching you in America, but we saw what happened here. Your lad went north."

"That loony sorceress 'as 'im and another," Debbie added.

"And Owen?" Vanessa asked.

The faeries exchanged a glance, their eyes sparkling as though they knew a secret. I sighed with annoyance because I couldn't hear faeries' thoughts.

"That sexy warlock's with them," Debbie finally said.

"Where, exactly?" Tristan asked.

Stacey giggled. "Go to the coast then north. You can't miss it."

"We can't wait to see wot 'appens," Debbie said, her voice laced with excitement.

And with that, the girls disappeared.

"Damn faeries," Tristan muttered. Vanessa and Jax both snorted. Tristan let out a growl. "I'll *never* be one of them."

"Let's go," I said, and we headed back for the bikes, our only transportation. There may have been no Daemoni around, but we still wouldn't take the chance of flashing. I swung my leg over the seat of my motorcycle, anxious to be on our way. "If they're messing with us, the sooner we find out and the sooner we can get back on the right trail."

Since the faeries hadn't been completely clear in what we were looking for, we did what Stacey said and went east to the coast and then north. Tristan led the way, ensuring we stayed on the left side of the streets—I kept drifting to the right—while his phone's GPS guided us on roads near the coast. Salty air tinged my nose and coated my lips. The light rain had let up, but a storm brewed over the sea, not far from the coast and headed our way. Lightning flashed ahead and to our right, followed by low rumbles of thunder.

An ominous feeling settled over me, causing a tingle down my spine. The hairs on my arms and the back of my neck rose. Then I sensed it. A Daemoni mind signature. Only one, but the first I'd found since arriving in England. I sped to the front of the pack and led the way. The electric feeling became stronger, and when I saw the looming structure, I had no doubt. Stacey was right—we couldn't miss it. We followed the road until it ended, then parked the bikes, climbed off, and stared.

The eerie structure stood another few hundred yards ahead, towering over a cliff that dropped to the sea below. The silhouette against the black, stormy sky was disorienting. In the dark, it appeared to be a large, ancient castle with a clock tower and turrets reaching several stories into the sky and looming over an expanse of lawn. But when lightning flashed and lit up the scene, the structure looked more like a skeleton of its former glory, ancient ruins of something that had once been majestic. Black and then bright light and then black again showed through the arched windows that were at least two stories high, none of them reflecting light because they held no glass.

The scene had me mesmerized. With one hand on the hilt of my dagger, I slowly started toward the castle that must have belonged to Kali. Tristan strode up next to me, and the others followed closely behind, nobody saying a word. The air felt thick and heavy, electricity humming through it, making the currents within me zing. Lightning flashed, lighting up a cemetery not too far ahead, with ancient looking tombstones that stood at crooked angles, the earth below them sagging from centuries of holding their weight. Thunder clapped almost directly overhead, making my heart stutter. Someone behind me gasped, and Blossom let out a small whimper.

"I'm not likin' this place, mates," Jax said, his voice barely above a whisper. "Somethin's not right about it."

But that was the thing. Where we were now, this far away—no, it didn't feel right. Evil hovered nearby, the feeling heavy in the air. The castle, however, as creepy as it looked, *did* feel right. I thought it did, anyway. The structure seemed to be pulling me to it, which didn't scare me at all. In fact, I knew I'd find relief if I could only get to it. As though it offered security. A place of refuge.

Was Dorian there? Had he found safety within its walls?

A low hum filled my ears, and at first, I expected more lightning to flash. I hurried my steps, wanting nothing more than to get to the castle. To the promises it told. But the hum didn't disappear with the next flash of lightning and only grew louder. And then I realized . . . I held out my hand in front of me. The dark of night hid the wrinkle in the air, but I felt it. A shield. Of course.

And I shook myself out of the near trance I'd been in. The structure before us was the furthest thing from a place of refuge. That was Kali's castle!

"Why would they shield a church?" Sheree asked.

"That's a church?" Blossom asked.

"An ancient abbey, actually. Whitby Abbey," Tristan clarified.

"So it's not Kali's castle?" I asked.

Tristan shook his head. "This was Bram Stoker's inspiration for Dracula's castle, but it's not a castle at all."

"I can feel its sacred ground from here," Sheree said. No wonder it had felt so *right* to me.

"So why would they shield it?" Charlotte sounded as befuddled as Sheree had.

"To keep us out of it," Tristan said easily. "They can't enter the grounds, and they're not about to let us do so."

"So they're wantin' to fight?" Jax asked.

"Possibly. They certainly don't want us to be able to hide, but I don't sense anyone around," Tristan said, and he looked at me. "Do you?"

I reached my mind out, searching for Daemoni mind signatures. A town lay beyond the hill where the abbey stood, and I only sensed more Normans there. And I couldn't find Dorian's mind signature anywhere, so he was either cloaked or not nearby at all. Had the faeries tricked us? They could have simply been getting their kicks by wreaking havoc in our lives as today's source of entertainment. Or maybe their tendencies favored the Daemoni, and they had, indeed, distracted us by sending us on a wild goose chase. Maybe even into some kind of trap. Bree had trusted them to tell us the truth, but . . . they were faeries after all. They probably couldn't even trust each other.

Then I caught it. The mind signature I'd sensed when we first approached the area. I turned to the left, and squinting through the drizzle that had once again begun to fall, I made out a tall building several hundred yards away. Inside was a single Daemoni mind, and now that I'd moved closer, I recognized the signature as the same one that had been in the car with Kali earlier, in a whole different part of the world.

Without a word of explanation, I took Tristan's hand and led him for the flash, not wanting to take the time to run. Charlotte, Blossom, and Vanessa showed up a second later. Sheree and Jax ran, morphing on their way, preparing to enter battle. This Daemoni may be alone for now, but we didn't know who lurked behind a cloak nearby. Hopefully Kali did. Hopefully a whole Daemoni army didn't.

Tristan directed the others to stay down here at ground level and keep watch, and then he and I entered the small, circular building and silently climbed the several flights of stairs winding along the wall of what seemed to be a lookout tower. My heart pounded harder with each step we took, but not from exertion. From the anticipation of the unknown we'd be facing. From the anxiety of possibly finding Dorian and hoping he was still okay. When we finally reached the top, the stairwell opened into a single, round room walled by windows. A lone figure stood in front of the wall that looked toward the abbey.

He was nearly as tall and as broad as Tristan, with dark brown hair flowing in waves past his shoulders. When he turned his muscular body toward us, my breath caught. He had a dangerous beauty, more rugged than Tristan's and not quite as otherworldly, with a strong jaw, a straight nose, and olive skin stretched over high cheekbones. His brows, one with a scar through it, arched severely over piercing eyes that appeared dark brown until lightning lit up the room, and then they looked green. And they were leveled at me as something familiar yet terrifying swirled in their depths.

"Seth," the man growled, though his eyes never left my face.

My gut clenched, and I grasped Tristan's hand.

"Noah," he replied, his voice polite, though steely. My jaw dropped. *Noah?* As in Mom's twin? "Meet Alexis."

"My niece," Noah said, his voice deep yet alluring. So that was a yes. And he hadn't asked it as a question—he also recognized me. "My sister must be so proud. And your son ... he is ... entertaining."

A growl rumbled in Tristan's chest, but I squeezed his hand. I had a number of choice words to hurl at this hulk of a man for even mentioning my son, but Noah gave me . . . an odd vibe. An unexpected one, for sure. The energy he put off reminded me of

Tristan right after I'd gone through the *Ang'dora*, when good and evil battled inside him. Was there hope for Noah?

"*You* can't save me," he snarled, as if reading my mind, although I knew my mind remained closed to his.

I swallowed the lump that had formed in my throat. "What about Dorian? Can we save him? Do you know where he is? Will you tell us?"

I didn't know why I asked like that, rather than demanding that he hand our son over or at least tell us his location. Something about this guy—my *uncle*—who was supposed to be Daemoni through-and-through and was obviously pretty badass, gave me the feeling that there might be hope. Maybe not for him, but for us. For Dorian. As though he'd long ago accepted his fate, but knew it didn't have to be Dorian's fate, too, and he would ensure it wasn't.

Or maybe I was being stupid.

Which was confirmed when another figure popped into the room.

"Don't, Noah," the newcomer ordered. "Don't even *think* about the boy. She can read minds, remember."

My stomach jumped into my throat at the sound of the familiar voice. Renewed fury shuddered down my body from the back of my neck to my feet, like a robe sliding over me. I struggled to breathe as I turned toward the newcomer. And seeing the familiar face caused rage to slam into me like a wrecking ball. The breath flew out of my lungs. Every muscle in my body coiled. And I flew at him.

"You. Fucking. TRAITOR!"

22

MY FIST CONNECTED with Owen's jaw only once before Tristan yanked me back into his arms.

"I can't believe you did this to us," I screamed at my former protector as I struggled against Tristan's unrelenting hold on me. "You are a traitor of the worst kind! I trusted you, Owen. I trusted you with my life. With my son's life! And this is what you do? Betray us like no other? Take away what's most important to us?"

His sapphire blue eyes flickered once before hardening as he glared at me. "At least you still have each other," he sneered. "I thought *Tristan* was more important to you than anything."

Tristan growled now, louder than before. "Jealousy, Scarecrow? You did this out of *jealousy*?"

Owen didn't answer, but his eyes flickered again. I didn't know if he'd softened for a brief moment at the nickname, or if the accusation flared his temper.

"It doesn't matter," he finally barked, and then he turned toward Noah. "You didn't say anything? Think it?"

Noah shook his head, but I entered his mind, searching for thoughts about Dorian, because he obviously knew something. Owen must have coached him, though, because he kept his mind nearly blank, focused only on an image of the abbey. Was Dorian in there? But how, if their evil selves couldn't step onto the grounds? Or could the abbey be a mirage? Another image created by Kali that wasn't really there? The sorceress bitch was good at making it hard to tell reality from the false alternatives she created. She'd completely messed with Tristan and me when we were in South Beach last year. She'd done it again when Vanessa and I were in Hades. Tristan hadn't been surprised to find the abbey and knew exactly what it was, though. However . . . the sorceress loved to play mind tricks on us.

"Where is he, Owen?" I demanded, spitting out the warlock's name. "Where's Dorian? You can't do this to us!"

"I can. And I did," he replied calmly.

I turned toward Noah, hoping to find that bit of something I'd seen in him earlier. "Please, Noah. Help me. Help us. You know Dorian doesn't belong with the Daemoni."

A sound rumbled in Noah's throat.

"*No*," Owen yelled, pointing a finger at Noah's chest. "Don't you do it. You remember yourself."

Wow. Owen had turned into a real ass, even with his own kind. His new own kind.

"So you do know where he is," I said to Noah, and I entered his mind again. *Tell me silently. Owen doesn't have to know. Help us, please. Rina and Sophia would want you to. They love him and miss him as much as they do you—*

A blue light flashed at me, and I soared across the room. My back slammed into the stone wall, and the wind flew out of me. I landed on my feet. My eyes narrowed as red rage filled my vision. *Did he really just attack me?* I flew at Owen again. And this time Tristan didn't stop me.

Owen's hand shot up, and I crashed face-first into a shield he put up around himself.

"Cheater," I snarled as I wiped at my nose, expecting blood to be pouring from it.

"Back off," he growled back. "Even you aren't powerful enough against me."

Oh. And he'd become quite cocky, too.

My hand flew out in a karate chop and connected with an invisible wall. Owen shot across the room, but his stupid shield protected him like a bubble, and the impact against the hard wall barely affected him. I fired electricity at him and blue-white light zapped over his shield, illuminating what really did look like a bubble. I pushed more current until cracks began to fissure into it. One grew wide enough to create a hole. Tristan blasted a ball of flame directly into it, but Owen put the fire out before it hit his body, then shot a spell at his former best friend. Tristan ducked, and a stone in the back wall cracked and crumbled.

Out of the corner of my eye, I noticed Noah simply watching us, doing nothing to help his comrade. Why didn't he fight? His eyes bounced back and forth, as though he didn't know who to fight for. His mind indicated the same hesitation, although he kept his actual thoughts masked with nonsense. Then his eyes and his mind completely glazed over as if his brain had shut down. His head gave one twitch then fell still.

Owen must have noticed, too, because he let out a feral growl. He twirled his hand in midair as if to shoot another spell at Tristan or me, but Tristan's paralyzing power made its way through the hole in

Owen's shield. The warlock appeared to be frozen in space. Except his eyes. He narrowed them at us, blue orbs hard as marbles.

"All's fair in love and war," Tristan said with a dangerous smirk.

"Exactly," Owen retorted, his voice nearly as treacherous as Tristan's. *I'll kill—*

Two people popped onto the stairs half a story below, cutting off any thought I'd been sharing with Tristan.

"What is going on here?" exclaimed a familiar, accented voice, formal like the gowns its owner wore.

"*Noah?*" Mom gasped.

She and Rina stepped onto the top of the stairs and into the room, their brown eyes wide as they surveyed their surroundings. Owen's eyes sprang wide open, too, and my mouth gaped. Noah's eyes, however, instead of being full of recognition or regret or even hatred, remained glassy. Empty as could be.

"What are you doing here?" I practically yelled at the matriarch and her second—at my grandmother and mother. They couldn't be here. Especially Rina. It was too dangerous. She was too weak. What. The. HELL!

"A mother always holds on to a little hope," said another familiar voice. The redheaded witch whose body Kali had taken over cleared the landing of the stairs right behind them, her fist clamped around Charlotte's neck as the sorceress dragged the warlock over the last step, then shoved her toward us. Charlotte stumbled once then caught and steadied herself. Kali's bright green eyes lasered in on Mom, then Charlotte, then me, and then came to rest on Rina. "Doesn't she? Even when she knows any hope is futile?"

You let her risk her life to see Noah? I asked Mom, disbelief coloring my mental voice.

"*He reached out to her for the first time in over a century,*" Mom replied. "*Nobody could stop her, even if they tried.*"

Kali's green eyes flew to Mom then me and back to Mom, as though she'd "heard" us mind-talking.

"Oh, yes, I heard you. And of course I was right. A mother can't stay away. I've been *counting* on that." Kali's green eyes swung to Charlotte for a moment, and then pierced into me. "Still . . . I hadn't expected *you.*"

What? What did that mean? She drew us here. She left the portal open so we would come. Wasn't it a battle that she wanted? Obviously—she'd gone so far as to bring the head of the Amadis into it. She had to know more Amadis would follow. And sure enough, several pops came from outside on the ground below. I dared to let out a breath as I sensed the Amadis mind signatures.

"I knew you wouldn't come alone," Kali said, and she snorted. "As the silly Normans say, the more the merrier. This will be so much *fun.*"

Do you have a plan? I asked Mom. She gave a slight shake of her head without looking at me. Her and Rina's full attention remained on Noah. He still stared at . . . nothing. His head twitched again. I glanced at Tristan. *Do you?*

His eyes tightened infinitesimally. "*Not until I figure hers out. Rina and Sophia aren't here by accident, but I don't know what she wants from them.*"

A smile formed on Kali's bright red lips. She, obviously, did have a plan. And she had a way of protecting her mind from me.

"Drop the shield, Owen," Kali ordered. When he didn't respond, her head cocked, and anger flashed in her eyes. She turned that full force on the man she called her son. "I said to drop the shield and cloak. Your little game is over."

My eyes flicked between Owen and Kali. What did she mean? I pushed my mind, trying to break through the protection she had on her thoughts and on Owen's, too. I'd broken through her magic before, and I'd grown stronger since, but so had her spell.

A moment passed before Kali figured out that Owen couldn't do anything because Tristan held him paralyzed. She flicked her wrist. Her staff, with its glowing blue ball at the top of it, appeared in her hand. She curled her fingers around the gnarly wood, lifted it in the air, and slammed it back down on the floor, making the entire structure shake. The roof of the building flew off as if whipped away in a tornado. The walls shattered and the glass disintegrated into dust, leaving us three stories above ground on nothing but a platform. Straight below us, Solomon, Julia, Winston, and several other Amadis vampires and Weres stood with my team, everyone in fighting stances.

Lightning shot across the sky and down to Kali's staff. A gale of wind blasted at us, whipping my hair against my cheeks. She pointed the staff toward the abbey and thrust it out. Another whoosh of air blasted past us.

"Don't worry, *Owen*," she sneered before turning to face the abbey, "I took care of it myself, like I always have to do. You think you're so smart, what you did. As if sacred grounds could stop *me*." The sorceress flipped her red hair back and looked over her shoulder at us. "But once again, you're wrong. The boy is mine. And if any of you try to stop me, those soldiers down there will shoot your precious Dorian. Nice of Her Majesty to let me borrow them, don't you think? Of course, she doesn't know, but that matters not."

My gaze followed Kali's lead. They hadn't been there before, but now an army of human soldiers—a few *hundred* Norman mind signatures—encircled the abbey grounds, armed with automatic, military issued guns and plenty of ammo hanging across their chests and backs. How had they suddenly appeared out there? As if on cue and moving as one, they all gripped their guns, stepped their right feet out, and aimed at the center of the dark structure. I felt out for Dorian's mind signature, and suppressed a gasp when I found it inside the abbey.

Dorian, are you okay?

"*Mom? Is that you again?*"

Yes, little man. Dad and I are here. But don't come out, okay? It's too dangerous right now.

"*Okay. I'm fine. I'm not even scared, Mom.*"

Hmm . . . his lack of fear wasn't necessarily a good thing. I appreciated his bravery, but at least a little fear was healthy in this situation. It kept you alert and ready to act. Such fear of Kali and her unpredictable behavior brought my focus away from the abbey and back to the scene directly in front of me.

"You come with me," Kali said, although she didn't specify whom. She didn't have to. She waved her staff, and Noah followed her like a robot as she stepped off the edge of the floor and floated over the heads of the Amadis and to the ground. Noah landed on his feet next to her without so much as a grunt. "You, too, *darling.*"

She waved her staff again. With a surprised cry, Rina flew off the edge of the building, her back arching and her white ball gown whipping behind her as she plummeted toward the ground.

"Rina!" I screamed as I jumped off the edge, hoping to beat her to the ground and catch her. But when I landed on my feet, Kali caught my grandmother in one arm.

Mom landed next to me and ran to Kali's side. She wrapped her hand around the sorceress's arm and gripped tightly. "You don't need to do this, Kali. Whatever it is you have planned, it's not the right strategy. It will fail. You need to stop and think for a moment. You can do better."

She nodded her head, tried to pierce Kali with her gaze. She was using her power of persuasion.

"Save your breath," Kali gnarled. She jerked her arm out and slammed her elbow into Mom's gut. Mom landed several feet away, doubled over on her knees.

"Sophia!" Charlotte appeared by Mom's side.

Kali let out a small chuckle. "You're next, sweet one."

"Come and get me," Charlotte growled.

"Oh, I will. But not yet."

"No!" Winston bellowed, and he blurred for the sorceress. She waved her staff. The vampire flew backwards, as though punched in the gut, and landed next to Mom and Char.

Dragging Noah and Rina with her, the sorceress turned toward all of us. My team stood behind me, except Char, who was off to my right with Mom and Winston, and Tristan, who remained on the platform above, holding Owen. Her eyes lifted to them, and then she banged her staff against the ground. More lightning shot down to it, but at the same time, electricity pulled out of me. She was draining me of my power, exactly as she'd done nearly two years ago in the courtroom on the Amadis Island. With the cries and whimpers around me, I knew she was doing it to all of us.

Her spell must have broken Tristan's hold on Owen, because the warlock appeared next to Kali, but with a glare from her, he crumpled to his knees. "You're a worthless liar. I should have known."

I tried to delve into their minds, to find out what that meant, but her mind-shield remained strong against my sapping power. I had no energy to do anything but sink to my knees on the ground. Tristan landed on his feet next to me, his hand palm out toward the sorceress, but even paralyzed, she was able to continue drawing power from her surroundings. She was gaining too much strength from me and everyone else, while we grew too weak to fight her. I shot what Amadis power I had left, and she shrieked with the pain, but the effort to push it at her quickly became too much for me.

"Now, here's what's going to happen," she said as she continued bringing all of us to our knees. Everyone except Tristan. I struggled against the pull of power, trying to keep some energy for myself to at least pull out my dagger. "You lot are going to stay here and behave, while I retrieve the boy. And if you don't—"

Tristan grabbed the dagger out of my hand and blurred for the sorceress.

"Don't kill the host," Mom screamed as he arced the blade down.

At the last second, Tristan's hand dipped and instead of sinking the blade into the top of the witch's head, he buried it in her shoulder. Blood streamed over her chest and arm, and blue smoke rose from the silver's contact. Her green eyes filled with pain as her red lips formed a surprised O before her body slumped to the ground. The power drain stopped. Kali's hold on us released. Summoning every bit of energy I possibly had left, I yanked my backpack off and retrieved the jar still hidden inside. The soul. I needed the soul. I needed to capture the soul and be done with this bitch. Then we could retrieve Dorian and take him home. Then maybe I could breathe again.

My hand paused in midair, though, when Rina's body jerked, convulsed, and then became still as she stood next to the Daemoni witch's body, an awkward angle to the matriarch's normally straight posture.

Rina jerked once more, straightening herself.

"Dorian?" she called out, her voice carrying over the lawn. "You can come out now."

I knew I should have been trying to capture Kali's soul, but I stood there with baited breath, anxious to see my boy. A long moment passed. Then . . .

"Rina?" Dorian's voice—familiar, yet deeper—rang out from the dark shadows of the abbey, although I couldn't see him.

Rina turned back to us. Her lips pulled up into a smile. But her eyes . . . they weren't right.

"If you don't behave," Kali's voice continued, but coming out of Rina's mouth, "both Katerina and the boy will die."

Every other soldier on this side of the circle spun, as though on command, and aimed at Rina's body. Fifty or more barrels pointing at our matriarch. At my grandmother.

"Noah here," Kali said as Rina's lips moved and her arm flipped out toward her son, "has a special stone. Lucas gave me a grand idea when he had me implant the faerie stone in your little friend Sonya. Why couldn't I create my own loyalty stones? I only needed some rocks and a spell. And I didn't make only one, but several."

Several loyalty stones? She had control over that many people?

"Oh, it's worse than that," she said, as though hearing my thoughts. "You see, Noah had a much bigger stone at one time, and I had all kinds of fun with him, but then we *broke* it. We divided it. And now all those soldiers out there have a piece of Noah's stone. So I control Noah, and he controls them. Brilliant, aren't I? Especially because I know you Amadis won't harm those Norman soldiers out there. And how convenient that they can enter sacred grounds. Oh, as can Katerina."

Rina's body disappeared in a flash and reappeared in the circle of soldiers. All of those that had been aiming at her turned in unison, once again directing their barrels at Rina.

I yanked my dagger out of the witch's limp body, and we all blurred for the soldiers. We stopped right behind them, though, when Rina's power allowed Kali's voice to sound in our heads.

"*You try to stop me or come after me, I order them to shoot,*" she said. "*There are many bodies here for me to take, but Katerina and the boy . . . they only have their one.*"

"*Alexis,*" Owen's voice shouted in my mind as he appeared next to me. "*She's weakest now. She's weakest right after taking a new body. This is our chance!*"

What the hell was he talking about?

"*Tsk, tsk, Owen,*" Kali said. "*I've told you which body I'll take next.*"

Owen blanched as his eyes darted to Charlotte. "*No.*"

"*Maybe not,*" Kali offered. "*There's always yours.*"

"You take me, you cowardly bitch," Char yelled aloud.

"What the hell is going on?" Tristan whispered, his voice so low Rina's ears shouldn't have been able to hear it.

"This is what I've been waiting for," Owen replied, and his sapphire eyes landed on me. "This is our chance, Alexis. But it has to be you."

I cocked my head and narrowed my eyes.

"And what exactly have you been waiting for?" I said, not sure whether to believe what I thought I heard. God, did I want to. I wanted to know my protector and friend had been working on our side all along. But . . . "You *stole* our son."

"I'll explain it all later, but I've been planning this all along and now she knows!" His voice, though still hushed, became more distressed. "She's weakest now, when she's new in a body. But if we don't hurry, she'll have Dorian, and she'll disappear with him. I've blown my cover and won't be able to track her anymore."

"What do you want Alexis to do?" Tristan demanded.

"Kill her!"

23

OWEN'S VOICE HAD risen with urgency, and he lowered it again. "I haven't been able to tell you, to warn you or anything because she's been in your head for months, Alexis. She's been needling her way in every time you got close. But this has been my plan. And it has to be *you.* You have to get her soul."

A storm of emotions battered at me—relief about Owen, confusion with all of the unanswered questions, anger at his means to reach this end, and so much more, but . . .

"Owen," I said as I looked back at the lawn in front of the abbey, where Kali stood as though waiting for her betrayer to finish, as if indulging Owen. Her soldiers also stood perfectly still but on high alert. "She's in *Rina's* body now. We can't . . ."

"Martin didn't die. He's back at that building in Virginia," he said with renewed urgency. He flipped his hand to the redheaded witch behind us. "Neither did she. Rina won't die. She'll—"

"You want us to attack the matriarch?" Tristan asked. "*Hurt* her?"

"Just enough—"

"Owen," Vanessa said as she closed her hand around his arm. "I've been defending you from the beginning, but this doesn't help your case, dumbass."

"Do you have any better ideas?" he demanded. His blue eyes flitted over all of us, but nobody could answer.

What were we to do? Could we trust him, or was this another of his tricks while he still worked with Kali?

"We can't let her stay in Rina's body," I murmured.

"She's already so weak," Mom said, her voice full of worry.

As though she'd been listening and had grown bored of indulging us and our debates on how to kill her, Kali called out in Rina's voice, "Come out, Dorian. You are safe now, darling. Your mother and father are here. So is your grandmother. You can come out."

A creaking sound, like an old metal or iron door swinging on rusty hinges, came from the abbey's darkest shadows. Lightning flashed and thunder boomed simultaneously, lighting up Dorian's figure as he stepped forward.

Dorian, no! I yelled into his mind. *That's not Rina. It's a trick. Stay away from her!*

And without further thought, I flashed to him.

"*I warned you,*" Kali said over another loud clap of thunder.

One moment of utter peace passed.

Followed by chaos as rapid gunfire shattered the night.

All aimed at Dorian and me.

I shoved my son's unexpectedly large body back through the door he'd come through and followed him into the tiny, nearly pitch-black room as bullets ricocheted off the old stone walls of the abbey. Screams came from outside. I looked around us, and then up, where I found the only other way out of this room.

"It's a tower, but no stairs," Dorian murmured, then he wrapped an arm that was too big to belong to my little boy around me and flew us to a window ledge at the top. Tristan must have seen us, because he appeared in front of us, stopping the bullets in midair and flicking them to the ground.

I peeked around him to see Mom in the center of the abbey's lawn now, her hands on Rina's shoulders, shaking her. "Stop! You're letting her win. You're letting her hurt your family. *Please, Mother!*"

Kali gave a quick nod of her head to Noah. He lunged at Mom and wrapped his huge hands around her neck. Winston yelled and blurred toward them, but Kali twitched her hand, and he flew back once again. Mom swung her fists at Noah but she was too small, her arms too short to reach him. She kicked her legs out and struck Noah in the groin, but the kick didn't faze him. His face contorted with pain as she pushed her Amadis power into him, but she became too weak. Tristan's hand flew up, and Noah froze. But it was too late. Mom's body hung limply in his hands, which still held tightly around her neck.

"*No!*" Rina's voice screamed in my mind. Probably all of our minds. "*Sophia! Noah! Noooo!*"

The soldiers stopped firing. Silence filled the air.

"Stay here," I told Dorian before I flashed to Mom's side.

Tristan appeared next to me and plowed his fist into the side of Noah's head, then released his power. Noah dropped Mom as he slumped to the ground. Tristan caught her, and then flashed with her to where Owen still stood with the rest of my team and the Amadis. They'd barely moved by the time I rejoined them. Everything had happened so lightning fast.

"*Leave my body,*" Rina snarled in our minds. I'd never heard her so angry.

"*Not until I kill you once and for all,*" Kali's voice replied. "*Soldiers, aim!*"

Nothing happened.

Rina's eyes fell on Noah's body that lay in a heap on the ground. Her foot swung out from beneath her ball gown and connected with Noah's stomach.

"*No!*" Rina cried out.

Noah grunted.

"*Soldiers, aim,*" Kali ordered again. Noah's head twitched. All of the soldiers swung around. All of the guns pointed at Rina's body.

Pain jolted through my head. The same icepick agony of before, and now I knew for certain it came from Kali. Had Rina tried to shove her out? The sorceress was becoming aggravated.

"Leave her alone and come get me," Charlotte taunted. "It's me you really want, isn't it?"

"It was tempting before," Kali sneered, "but I think I'll have more fun with Owen. You obviously won't kill me in this body. You'll never be able to once I'm in his. But first . . . *soldiers, fire!*"

The tat-tat-tat of automatic gunfire rattled through the night. Again.

Owen thrust his hands toward Rina. I jumped onto Mom's body, and Charlotte threw a shield over the both of us. I lifted my head to see several bullets stop in midair all around my grandmother and then fall to the grass below. More bullets missed Rina and her shield, flying across the abbey's grounds. Rina's hand jerked, and Kali's staff shook. A bullet whizzed by Rina's ear. Owen shoved his hands out harder, but Kali fought against his shield.

"Mum, I need help," Owen yelled.

"Blossom," Charlotte called out to the witch. "Hold my shield over here."

Blossom thrust her hands at Mom and me, her face straining with the power she gave it.

"Disarm them!" Tristan shouted as he blurred in one direction of the circle of soldiers. Vanessa took off in the other direction. A crocodile, a tiger, Solomon, Julia, and the rest of the Amadis followed them, while I remained plastered to Mom.

Winston blurred straight to the sorceress herself, although I didn't know what he planned to do since she occupied the matriarch's body. Before he reached them, though, Kali's staff pointed at him and flames flew out of the blue orb. Fire engulfed him. I clapped my hand over my mouth as he screamed, and the fire brought him to his knees. His body writhed on the ground as he tried to smother the flames, but the sorceress continued shooting more at him.

Mom shifted underneath me, and her eyes flew open. Winston's shouts immediately drew her attention. She pushed me off of her and raised her hand. Water shot out of her palm and across the lawn to her lover's body, dousing the flames. But Kali wouldn't relent, and it became a battle between her and Mom. With blood diluted by generation of Norman fathers, Mom wasn't strong enough and would quickly lose.

"Alexis, now! While she's distracted," Owen yelled at me.

Not knowing what else to do, I pulled my dagger out and charged for my grandmother. If Owen was right about Kali being at her weakest now, maybe I could slash through her shield and push enough Amadis power into Rina's body to force Kali's soul out.

I'd almost reached her when the sorceress banged her staff against the ground. The breath slammed out of me, and all of my power and energy went with it. I crashed to my hands and knees. Kali drew on my power again, and this time she was quickly draining me. Charlotte, Owen, and Blossom slid to their knees, too, while still trying to shield Rina, Mom, and me.

"She'll grow too strong," Owen said, his voice croaking as he strained against the sorceress. "You have to hurry!"

He'd barely said the words before he collapsed. His shield over Rina fell. Kali cackled and threw her arms in the air, and all of the gunfire ceased. Her gaze fell on Owen with a gleam in her eye. She moved her staff to point it at him.

"No!" Charlotte yelled, throwing herself in front of her son. "You take me, you bitch!"

"Gladly," Kali said through Rina's smile. Lightning shot out of the staff and hit Charlotte. The warlock's body fell next to Owen's. "Time to finish this night once and for all."

"I don't think so," Tristan growled, and he paralyzed Rina's body.

Her form trembled against his power, but not because Kali fought Tristan. Rina fought Kali, trying to push the evil soul out. A ghostly image began to emerge from Rina's body.

"*Alexis, I need your help, darling.*" Rina's voice grew weaker in my mind with each word.

"No!" the sorceress shrieked.

"*One . . . chance,*" Rina said. "*Now!*"

The muscles in Rina's neck strained, and her eyes popped wide open. A combination of pain and effort mixed in the scream that emitted from deep within her. With every ounce of energy I had left, my hands and feet scrambled at the ground until I could push myself to my feet. I staggered and lurched toward my grandmother. The gauzy image of the sorceress grew larger and more whole as Rina pushed the soul out of her body. My arm felt dragged down as though a magnet in the earth pulled my dagger toward its center, but I forced it up. I lifted the blade to waist height and then straight out in front of me. Rina's hands reached out for me, for my arm, and she helped me lift the dagger higher. Over my head.

The soul released, but Kali's yells of frustration turned into a shriek of victory as she streaked toward Owen and Charlotte.

"No!" Vanessa threw herself in front of the gray light of the ghostly image.

Blossom's hands shot out and created some kind of block. The soul's light slammed into an invisible wall and plopped to the ground with a sickening splat like an egg hitting a rock.

I plunged my dagger downward at it.

Into the swirling light.

An ear-piercing siren screamed through the night, making my toes curl. I slashed and twisted the blade in the gauzy substance until the soul became nothing but a stringy clump wrapped around the tip, and I could barely hold my grip on the dagger. The icepick in my brain dug deeper as Kali continued screaming. I began to sink to my knees, my trembling legs unable to hold me any longer and my head close to exploding. Tristan caught me and held me upright as my shaking hand fumbled inside my jacket pocket for the soul jar. As soon as I freed it, he grabbed the small container and twisted the lid off. I lifted my dagger with Kali's soul on the end of it and wiped it into the jar as if it were nothing more than extra mayonnaise on a butter knife. Tristan clamped the vessel shut, and it sealed with a hiss.

The world fell silent.

No more sorceress screaming her last moments. No more gunfire tearing apart the night. Even the thunderstorm quieted, as though the sorceress herself had brewed it. Perhaps she had.

Dorian landed next to me and whispered, "Hey, Mom and Dad."

I tackled him in a hug and peppered kisses all over his face, not quite believing I actually held my son—my *baby*—again after so long. Without pulling away long enough to study him, I could tell he'd grown quite a bit in the six months since he'd been taken. I wouldn't worry about that right now, though. I would push away all the negative thoughts for the moment and focus on the boy finally swathed in my arms once again. My Dorian. We had him back. Tristan wrapped his arms around both of us, and my heart swelled at our reunion.

But something about the moment gnawed at me.

Tears and anguish and heartbreak in the distance.

Sobs. Loud, ugly sobs. And not mine.

Mom's.

But Mom never cried, let alone sobbed.

With a surreal sense of this-is-not-happening, I turned my head toward the ruins of the abbey, toward the sounds of loss and desperation. My head tilted at the sight of one body huddled between two others, as my brain slogged through the last few minutes as though my heart tried to prevent it from remembering. From remembering Mom trying with all her might to put out the fire consuming her soul mate. From remembering Rina's small body crumpling to the ground once Kali's soul had been exorcised.

One moment I held my son in my arms, and in a flash, I fell to my knees next to Mom.

"No, Winston," Mom cried, tears and snot flowing down her face as she held the vampire's burnt body in her arms. "You can't leave me again, my love."

I rubbed my hand down her back, but it was Rina's small body, so tiny and frail looking, that caught my attention. She lay so still on the ground. *Too* still. But her eyes, warm and brown and full of wisdom and love like they always were, rolled toward me.

"Rina?" I said as I crawled over to her. "Are you healing?"

She blinked slowly. Very slowly. So slowly I thought she might not open her eyes again.

"Rina," I said more urgently as I placed a hand on her shoulder. I wanted to shake her, to wake her up, but I feared I'd break her even more.

"No, darling," she finally said.

"Tristan!" I yelled, jumping to my feet and searching him out. "Hurry! Rina needs you."

"No," my grandmother gasped. Mom's body heaved as she looked over at us, at her mother. She choked back another sob and joined me at Rina's side. My eyes jumped to Rina's hand, which twitched as though reaching for mine. I sprang to her other side and fell back to my knees before taking her hand into mine. Julia appeared next to Mom, and Solomon at Rina's head. He lifted her shoulders and pulled her halfway into his lap. Rina whispered, "It . . . is time."

Solomon stroked Rina's hair, and Mom pressed her palm against her mother's cheek.

"I know, Mother," she said while tears continued to stream down her face. "You have been so strong. But you can rest now."

"What?" I demanded.

"She knew it was coming," Julia said quietly.

Tristan appeared next to me. "Are you sure?"

"Yes," Rina said, her voice weak. "They . . . are waiting."

"She insisted on seeing Noah first," Solomon said. "I told her it was a bad idea."

Rina's eyes rolled upward to look at Solomon, and her mouth jerked in a sad smile. "No, darling. I needed it." She looked at Mom. "Tell Noah I love him." She struggled to pull in a breath as her gaze traveled to the faces hovering over her. "I love . . . all of you. I am . . . grateful for . . . my life . . . with you. But . . . I must . . . go."

"No, Rina," I cried, not wanting to believe any of them. "You can fight this. You can't give up!"

Her hand gently and oh so lightly squeezed mine. "I don't . . . give up. I . . . ascend."

Her eyes closed. Her head lolled to the side. A peaceful smile donned on her lips.

Julia cried out and threw herself on top of Rina's body. Solomon stroked Rina's head, and Mom scooted away, toward Winston again. She pushed herself to her knees and then folded herself over them, crying into her thighs, both hands reaching out to the side of her. One still held Rina's hand and the other rested on Winston's charred body. Pieces of his skin flaked off and disintegrated into ash.

Without thinking about it, I somehow managed to push myself to my feet. Tristan sprang up and wrapped his arms around me. I hugged him tightly, my cheek pressed against his chest as I inhaled his tangy-sweet scent and let it wash over me, calm me, bring the relief we deserved. Relief that we had our son, and we'd rid the world of an evil sorceress. Relief that although we'd lost Rina, she'd no longer be sick and weak. Relief that the fighting had ceased, and we would lose no more. At least not tonight. For the moment, anyway, we could live with a little peace.

But hot tears streamed down my cheeks as I took in the scene surrounding us.

Blood soaked into what once had been sacred grounds. Several Norman soldiers lay bloodied and dead after taking hits from their own men. Others stood like statues, no life in their eyes. Noah lay on the ground, though not dead. Blossom tended to Jax's injuries off to the side of the circle of men, while Vanessa and Sheree helped other hurt Amadis. Charlotte and Owen remained unconscious, but their chests rose and fell, so I knew they weren't dead.

But Winston appeared to be.

And Rina definitely was. My grandmother was . . . gone.

A familiar, icy voice resonated from the dark on the other side of the abbey: "Such a shame, all of this destruction because of a mother's wrath."

24

TRISTAN AND I both stiffened.

Dorian, get back to the abbey, I mentally yelled at my son. He flew overhead, his form disappearing into the dark ruins right before another emerged from the shadows.

Lucas walked out to where we could see him, and he stood with the toes of his black boots inches away from the far side of the abbey proper, inches from the line of the sacred grounds. His white-blond hair was pulled into a ponytail that draped over his shoulder. His brow was scrunched together over his eyes that looked dark now, but I knew were ice blue like Vanessa's. And he held Sasha in his arm, his other hand slowly petting her.

He had been behind Dorian's kidnapping all along. Behind the mages' deaths and Sasha's injuries. And her disappearance, too, apparently. He'd orchestrated it all. And he was ultimately responsible for the destruction around us. Including my grandmother's death.

My eyes cut to Tristan.

His cut to me.

We both lifted our chins in a slight nod.

And we charged the fucker.

My hand held my dagger as I streaked toward my sperm donor.

In the two seconds it took to cross the lawn, however, Noah and several of the Norman soldiers gathered around Lucas. And they were *huge*. Their muscles bulged out of their clothes, ripping them into shreds, and they grew two feet as we watched. Fire filled their eyes, and as one, they all let out a terrifying growl.

Tristan suddenly stopped in front of me and threw his arm out. I slammed into it as though it were an iron bar.

Lucas snickered from behind the wall of men. "Too bad you can't hurt them, eh? They're only *human*, after all. There's nothing you can do." He lifted his lip in disgust as he surveyed Tristan. "All that power we gave you gone to waste because of your *beliefs*. Sure, you could probably kill me—I guarantee there's no hope for my soul— but who are you willing to lose in the process? Alexis?" The guns all pointed at me. "Dorian?" Some of the soldiers aimed toward the abbey. "I won't need them anymore, so why would I let them live?"

Tristan let out a growl.

"That's what I thought. Your Amadis vows won't let you do anything. Not with human lives at stake."

"Those things don't *look* human," Tristan snarled, although we both knew they were definitely Normans.

"Ah, yes. They do have some of Noah's blood. Oh, and some of your lykora's." Lucas's icy blue eyes glanced behind me to where Owen's and Charlotte's bodies lay, and then came back and pierced into me. "Thank you for that, by the way. I'd smelled lykora on you when you came to visit me and sent Victor to get her. But Kali took the opportunity to send warlock-boy in to snatch your son and make *me* look like the bad guy. Imagine that." He rolled his eyes and let out a mocking laugh. "Because of that damn warlock, Victor didn't get the lykora, but he was able to collect some of her potent blood. A whole wing, actually. Enough to see that it worked. And now I have the dog herself."

My nostrils flared, my mind seething.

"Oh, yes, indeed," Lucas said. "These soldiers here—*all* of them—have some of Noah's inhuman speed and strength, but his blood was too diluted to give them much else. The stones were a nice touch, too, I'll give Kali that. But the *lykora* . . ." He said the word with a glee that sounded odd in his voice. And evil. Very evil. Sasha growled under his hand. "Her blood gave them the ability to grow, to fight ferociously, and to be extremely loyal. Kali's little stones were nothing compared to this. They're almost as loyal and protective as a mother. But not quite. What, exactly, would you do to keep your son, Alexis?"

"I already have my son," I said through clenched teeth.

"Only because I allow it. I have no use for him until he comes to me on his own. Do you know why I let you go when I had you in Hades?"

I glared at him, refusing to indulge him with a guess because I still didn't know. Yet, I remained quite curious.

"For the same reason. I have to admit, I still have hope for your potential. And I know one of these days, you'll come around and see things my way when Katerina and Sophia never would. They live in a sugarcoated, lovey-dovey world whereas you, Alexis, my daughter, you know differently. You've had your own dark thoughts. You know that some people do deserve to die."

His words were like a knife in my heart. The *truth* of his words cut deep to the bone. I couldn't deny them. Because at this very moment I was thinking he certainly deserved to die.

"I have no qualms about killing my own when they betray me. In fact, I thank you for taking care of Kali for me. She'd become quite the hindrance. You shouldn't have such qualms about killing, either.

You *should* be able to kill your enemy. You should be able to fight this war that's brewing without having to hold back. You, my daughter, might still have that in you. You better—that's the only way you'll win." His tongue slid over his lips as he considered me. He must have seen the hatred in my eyes. The willingness to fight. He nodded. "This world is about to change, and I want to see you and Seth ruling it. You deserve it. So does Dorian. And when that happens—when you are in power—I will happily descend."

"I'll never fight for you," I said, my voice quiet but full of determination.

"We'll see about that. You are your father's daughter, I do believe."

"Never!" I screamed as I lunged for him, my dagger out.

One of his soldiers snarled and snapped, and when I didn't back off, he threw himself at me. My hands flew up. I stopped him in midair, and his face filled with surprise. I hadn't even set him on the ground, though, when his body soared at me. Lucas laughed as his soldier landed on top of me, my dagger piercing straight through the man's body. He immediately became dead weight.

No! Oh, no! By the time I pushed him off and scrambled to my knees to inspect him, he was already dead. And *I'd* killed him. I sprang to my feet, my heart pounding, my stomach a small pit.

"So what will you do for your son?" Lucas asked. "How far will you go for those you love? What will you do to keep him *alive*?" His eyes darted around the scene before they came back to me. "Does Dorian understand all that's been lost for him? And when he doesn't deserve such protection from these people he'll only abandon?"

"Leave him out of this," Tristan seethed.

Lucas ignored him, and called out, "Dorian? Come here my boy."

No! I yelled at him.

"Come on out, Dorian," Lucas yelled louder. Everyone behind us stilled; their sobs and whispers fell silent. Out of the corner of my eye, I saw Mom rise to her knees, staring at Lucas with confusion. Sasha wriggled in Lucas's arm, but he held her tightly. "Come see what has happened on your behalf. Come look at all the death and lives ruined because of you. But truthfully, it's only your mother and father who love you, son. Everyone else blames you. And even your mom and dad will come to despise you one day."

Don't listen to him, Dorian, I told him. *He lies!*

"They're going to tell you that I say nothing but lies," Lucas said, his voice still carrying across the grounds. "But it's they who lie! I want to take care of you. I can make you a king. I can give you everything you've always wanted and more! But they . . . your mother and father and everyone else you know will blame you for everything. For Katerina's death! See your great-grandmother's body lying on the ground? She's dead, Dorian, and they blame you. But I don't."

"Mom?" Dorian's voice called out from the shadows. "Rina's really dead?"

At the sound of her master's voice, Sasha squirmed harder in Lucas's arms.

"Come with me, son. Let us go before they take their revenge out on you." Lucas's voice had grown more and more agitated the harder Sasha struggled. He became more demanding of Dorian even after telling us he had little need for our son right now. But he lied. He needed Dorian to be able to keep Sasha. And he needed her blood. Lucas yelled, his voice booming in the night: "Come on, Dorian! I've had enough of this!"

"Who *are* you?" Dorian demanded as he stepped out of the abbey. At the sight of him, Sasha sprang out of Lucas's arms, and by the time she landed on her feet, she'd grown to her size large lykora protective form, wings flapping and lips lifted in a growl, baring long fangs.

Lucas's thought hit me at the same time his hand twitched: He was about to force Dorian to him.

"Sasha, protect," I yelled.

The lykora attacked Lucas.

Her jaw snapped at his face as her huge paw swiped at his chest. Her claws drew fat lines of blood in his shirt and skin.

"Soldiers, protect," Lucas ordered. The Norman soldiers all lifted their guns again and aimed them at us. "No! Get this mutt off of me!"

But the huge soldiers refused to obey. Would they not attack Sasha whose blood flowed through their veins?

Lucas growled, the sound not quite as ferocious as Sasha's, but pretty near Tristan's. His icy eyes found me.

"Fine," he said as his arm swung out and smacked Sasha hard in the side. She tumbled away from him. "Let's see how you feel, Alexis, when they're *all* your children."

What? I didn't understand what he meant.

"Soldiers, aim," Lucas ordered, and all of the barrels in front of him as well as those belonging to the eighty or so soldiers in the circle who hadn't been killed or injured aimed toward the center of the grounds. Toward Julia and Solomon who still hovered over Rina's body. Toward Vanessa who now stood protectively in front of Dorian. Toward Charlotte and Owen, who were just now beginning to stir. Toward Mom, who rose to her feet between her dead husband and her dead mother, her eyes wide and her head tilted as she looked questioningly at Lucas.

"I see you enjoyed my gift to you," he said to her as his eyes flitted to Winston's black body before returning to her face. He laughed at her expression, but only once. Sasha flew toward him again. He gave one final order before he disappeared from sight:

"Soldiers, *fire!*"

For the third time in ten minutes, gunfire tore through the night. I spun around as each soldier let off a single round this time. Only one. That was all. That was all that was necessary.

I hadn't realized it, but Lucas had aimed all of the guns only at Mom. Her brown eyes filled with fear as she swung her gaze toward me. Her arms lifted, and she reached out for me. Her mouth moved, and she called out my name. As though she thought *I* was the one being shot, even as her own body jerked in all different directions with each hit she took. She tried to run for me and stumbled a few times, but she kept moving. Kept going. Kept yelling my name.

"ALEXIS!"

And then she fell one last time.

"*MOM!*" I screamed.

"Mimi!" Dorian yelled, and Vanessa threw her arms around him and held tightly before he could fly into any more danger.

Rage filled me. The urge to kill every single one of those soldiers surged through my body, and I trembled as the pressure built inside me. I no longer cared that they were Normans. That they were merely humans under someone else's control. That they were the souls I was supposed to protect. The murderous rage I felt the first night Dorian disappeared burned like fire through me, consuming any rational thought.

"*How far will you go?*" Lucas whispered in my mind.

And I knew that's what he wanted. He wanted to see me unleash the wrath I'd kept so tightly balled inside me. He wanted me to lose control. To cross the line. To ignore my values and beliefs—to trade them for his. He wanted me to prove to myself and to everyone else that I was his daughter.

But I wasn't.

I never would be.

I was my mother's daughter. And I ran for her now.

"Mom," I cried as I skidded on my knees next to her. I scooped my arms under her shoulders and pulled her into my lap. "Stay with me, Mom. *Please.*"

I could barely see through the tears in my eyes. I swiped at them angrily.

"Mom, please," I begged. "Heal. You're healing, right?"

Mom's head moved slightly in my now blood-streaked arms. "I can't, honey. It's too much. I'm not as strong as you."

"Of course you are! You're the strongest woman I know. Tristan!" I yelled again. Could this really be happening for the second time tonight? No. No, no, no. It couldn't be. "Tristan, Mom needs you. Help her heal. Please, hurry!"

He came around to Mom's other side, and his mouth turned down as his eyes took in all of the bullet holes riddling her little body. Charlotte crawled over to us, with Owen right behind her.

"Honey," Mom whispered, "it's time for me to go, too."

"No. It's. *Not,*" I growled. "You can't *leave* me!"

"Don't you do this, Sophia," Charlotte ordered as she gripped Mom's hand.

"It's your time, Alexis," Mom said, her voice growing fainter. "Your time to lead."

"No." I shook my head vehemently. "I'm not ready. You're not supposed to go yet! Mom, *please.* Don't do this to me. You both can't leave me!"

Mom's eyes glassed over, and then they closed. The corners of her mouth turned slightly up.

"They're ... calling ... for me," she gasped.

"No, Mom. *Sophia.* I can't do this without you." I crouched further over her, sandwiching her between my thighs and upper body, trying to hold on as tight as I could because they couldn't have her, not yet, it was too soon. I needed her here, the Amadis needed her, they already had Rina, why my mom, too, why, why, *why*?

"You . . . can. You are . . . so . . . strong."

Tears flowed down my cheeks as I pulled back. "Mom, you must fight this. You can make it through this. Please don't give up. *Please.*"

Rain began to fall again, leaving streaks in the dirt and blood on Mom's face. Tristan brushed his hand over her forehead and wrapped his other arm around my shoulders.

"Mimi," Dorian cried as he fell to her other side. "Don't die, Mimi."

"Help her, Tristan. Please help her," I begged.

"I'm sorry, *ma lykita*," he murmured as he huddled over us, pulling me closer to him. "*She's too injured. She won't recover.*"

"He's . . . right," Mom said.

"No. Mom, please. Don't give up."

"Take care of her . . . Tristan. Be . . . what . . . she needs," Mom said, air whistling in her lungs.

"I promise," Tristan vowed.

"Be . . . strong . . . Alexis. You. . . must . . . lead." She paused, and her chest rose as though in slow motion as she inhaled a wheezy breath. The last one she would ever take. Her eyes rolled to Tristan and up to Dorian, then back to me. "I . . . love . . . you. All of you."

I watched as her mind replayed her memories of us, starting with the first time she saw me and cradled my tiny body in her arms on the day I was born. She remembered our days of my childhood, our friendship even through my teen years. She recalled Tristan's and my wedding day and then bringing Dorian into the world, and the pride she'd felt then. Her mind played out all of our hugs, all of our laughs, all of the joys we experienced together. It slowed as she remembered the last few months with Winston, and I realized then just how lonely she had been when Tristan and I had married, and how happy she'd been to find her Oliver again.

And then her mind blanked out. The light in her beautiful mahogany eyes extinguished.

My mother left us.

"NOOOOO!" I sobbed as I held her body against my chest. "Oh God, *NO!*"

I clung to Mom's small body, refusing to let her go. Tristan tried to pull me tighter to him, but I shrugged him off and began rocking her back and forth. Dorian scooted closer to me, but I couldn't acknowledge him. I couldn't do anything but try to hold onto my mother, my confidante, my best friend, the woman who had given me life and then gave hers to save mine and my son's.

And then I reached out and pulled Rina's body to me, as well, holding them both as tears streamed down my face faster than the rain fell.

"I can't do this without you two," I cried. "We're supposed to conquer everything together. And now you've left me. You've both left me to do this on my own. How can I fight without you by my side? I'm not ready to lead alone!"

"*You are not alone, dear Alexis.*" Though the words came as only a whisper, I recognized the voice. Cassandra's. "*We are always with you.*"

The air around us suddenly changed.

The thick weight of evil I'd felt earlier disappeared. The rain stopped as though turned off at a faucet. The clouds above us parted in a circle, exposing a nearly full moon that shone down on my mother's pale, still face. On my grandmother's lifeless body.

And I saw them.

A hundred or so women, *here* but not quite, surrounding us, and although I couldn't *really* see them as physical beings, I knew they had dark hair and dark eyes and looked like Rina and Mom and me. I also knew they remained on the other side of the veil, in the Otherworld, but their presence felt so close, pushing warmth and love into our world, enveloping us with it. And I knew why they were here: to escort my mom's and grandmother's souls home, to the Otherworld, ensuring their safety while reminding me that I would not be alone. I was never alone.

But, God, did I feel like I was.

25

OWEN EVENTUALLY REGAINED his energy, and Charlotte recovered from the blast Kali had given her. Along with Julia and Solomon, we all crowded around Mom's and Rina's bodies, saying our final goodbyes. None of us seemed able to move for a long time, as though we believed if we waited long enough, their spirits would return, and they'd rejoin us. But of course that didn't happen. There would be no reunion until each of us joined them in Heaven. In the Otherworld.

The rain returned and drizzled over our misery for a while, but by the time the sky began to lighten, the clouds had scattered. The sun rose and shone over us from its perch in a perfectly clear blue sky. And I couldn't decide if it was all wrong for the day to be so beautiful and warm when my mom and grandmother were no longer here to enjoy it—when their bodies lay dead and cold—or if it was right because it meant they were happy where they were. That they'd finally found peace and joy for the first time in decades, and they wanted us to know it.

At some point before we left the U.K., Lisa and Jessica popped in to take the vessel that held Kali's soul. My mind remained in a fog for a long time, but although I couldn't pinpoint the exact place and time, I clearly remembered handing over that jar, never so happy to be rid of something in my life. And I remembered the faeries letting out a squeal of joy when they took possession. Debbie and Stacey joined them, and they all left for the Otherworld, taking the sorceress's soul with them. Removing it from this realm once and for all.

Noah and all of the soldiers had also left the abbey grounds, though my foggy mind didn't notice when or how.

I barely noticed as someone escorted us to the Amadis jet in nearby Whitby. The journey to Amadis Island was hazy as grief consumed me, but I remembered the underlying happiness of having Dorian back at my side. And of Charlotte's delight of having her son where he belonged, too. I knew Owen told his side of the story on the plane ride to the island, but I barely listened, my heart dulling my brain so it wouldn't think about the bodies in the boxes below us in the cargo area.

The triple funeral was a formality. I already knew Mom's and Rina's souls were gone, probably already at work in the Otherworld, and Winston had surely joined Mom. But of course we gave them an Amadis send-off with all of the pomp and circumstance worthy of them. Amadis from all over the world crowded onto the island for the service, and we all watched from the cliff side as flames licked the sides of the pyre they shared before the whole thing disappeared, taken by the Angels.

The council swore me in as matriarch—the first coronation ceremony I'd actually had. It wasn't as bad as I'd expected all these years, although my numb mind might have had something to do with the fact that I didn't notice all the attention on me, even when everyone took to their knees, their heads bowed. In fact, the numbness still hadn't allowed me to think about how on earth I was going to lead the Amadis. The reality of being matriarch hadn't quite set in.

But I did understand Lucas's statement now. He hadn't returned that night at the abbey. He hadn't been able to walk away with my son or the lykora. But he *had* made his point. He'd taken away those who were precious to me. And he'd taken away my security. He'd put me into a position he knew I wasn't ready for. He wanted to see exactly how far I would go, and not only for Dorian. Because he'd ensured that *all* of the Amadis were now my children. Not Rina's, not Mom's. *Mine*. He wanted to see my real wrath.

Lucas had declared war against his own daughter.

And war he would get.

But he had no idea the true wrath I could unleash. I didn't know myself how far I would go. But we would all soon find out.

For now, however, as Tristan and I sat in our suite in the Amadis mansion, I needed a moment. A moment to be me, Alexis: a mother, a wife, a daughter, and a granddaughter. A friend and a lover. Not a matriarch. Not a warrior. Just a person with hopes and dreams that had been shattered. A person who had experienced tremendous loss. A person who needed to mourn so she could recover and become even stronger.

I'd cried when Mom and Rina first died, unable to control my emotions at the time, but I'd maintained control ever since. And it had been the only time I'd cried since the day Dorian disappeared. But now that it was all over, I could no longer hold up the dam. I curled up on the antique loveseat against my husband, and he wrapped his arms around me.

"It's okay, my love," he murmured against my ear. "Let it go."

And finally I did. I sobbed.

I sobbed for the friend and protector I thought I'd lost and had regained. I sobbed for Sasha who had fought so hard for us and would protect us until her last day, which was hopefully a long ways away. I sobbed for my son and all that he had been through and that he was back home where he belonged. Where he would always belong. I sobbed for how much he had already changed, how he brooded even now as he sat in his bedroom with Sasha, rather than playing outside.

I sobbed for my grandmother, my leader, my role model, my idol, the woman I thought I could never understand, but I understood more than I knew, for realizing too late how much she loved me and everyone else. I sobbed for my mother, who had raised me on her own as a Norman for my safety, who had always protected me, who had taken care of my son so I wouldn't have to be a single mother, who had taught me to be strong and noble and loyal. I sobbed for the life we shared and for the future I now had to live without her. I sobbed for the baby girl we still hadn't conceived and maybe never would. I sobbed for the Amadis, the ones we had already lost, the ones we would still lose, and the ones we would gain. I sobbed for all of humanity and the dark future ahead.

When I finally finished, my gut aching from crying so hard, I wiped away my tears and looked up into the most caring, understanding, loving, and beautiful pair of eyes I would ever know. My husband's. He gave me the strength I needed. He was my rock, my pillar, my Second. I didn't have my mother or grandmother in this world with me, and I didn't have a daughter. I was the only one of my kind left. The only Amadis daughter.

But I had my son and my Tristan.

He brushed his lips across my forehead and pulled me tighter against him in confirmation.

And for the first time in weeks, I smiled.

EPILOGUE

"**EXPLAIN TO ME** again how your taking Dorian was in everyone's best interest." I leaned over Owen, who actually looked kind of small as the chair seemed to swallow him. I sat on the edge of my desk in Rina's office, which I'd reluctantly taken over, with my arms crossed and my fingers tapping against my bicep, as he slid lower in his seat. "I'm still not sure I understand."

Weeks had passed, and by now I'd heard his story several times, but I didn't miss an opportunity to torture him. Whatever I could dish out would never compare to what Tristan and I had gone through when our son had been taken.

"You'd barely left Hades before Kali told me what Lucas had planned, and she divulged her own plan to me," the warlock explained once again. "She thought she had everything figured out with the stones she created. *Lucas* had asked her to create them—they weren't her own idea, although she took credit for them. He's been working with governments around the world, promising them super-soldiers, but his real goal was to be able to take control of the Normans and use them."

"But why?" I asked. I hadn't yet tried to make sense of this part of the story, but I needed to understand now. As matriarch. My stomach knotted as it always did when I was reminded of my new title. "He has his own army already."

"Because Normans are expendable," Owen said, and he cleared his throat when I gasped. "In Lucas's eyes, that is. He wants an army to fight the worst battles so he doesn't lose too many of his own. But when he asked her to create the stones, Kali saw them as *her* opportunity to take control. Her goal for centuries had been to oust Lucas and take over as leader of the Daemoni. So instead of making the brothers and their offspring—which also meant the soldiers who shared their stones—respond to Lucas, she ensured the spell made them respond to her. But Lucas had already come up with the idea of the lykora blood." He let out a dark chuckle. "Kali threw a fit when Lucas was about to one-up her like that. Since both you and Tristan were away from the safe house, Lucas acted, and Kali knew she had to act, too. Lucas wanted Sasha, but Kali wanted Dorian."

"Why?"

"To use him, of course. She had all kinds of plans to use him against Lucas. Starting with pissing you off so you'd go after him. She thought you and Tristan had the best chance of killing him, and then she could lead. But even if you didn't, she had possession of what the Daemoni wanted most. She wanted the Ancients to see she wasn't afraid to take Dorian. She wanted to hold him as a pawn over them *and* the Amadis. Along with her Norman army, Dorian would be her key to the throne." He shifted in his seat, sitting up higher as he explained his actions. "I instantly saw that the fastest way to hammer down her trust in me was to volunteer for the job and follow through on the one thing that would hurt you the most. Plus, it meant *I* had

Dorian and nobody else did. I could make sure he stayed safe. I was *protecting* him."

"Which you could have done by not abandoning us in the first place," I pointed out. Once again.

"Right. But you needed Kali's soul, and I wanted her gone, out of this world forever. And I needed you to do it. We had to work together. I discovered her weakness. You had the jar, and I knew you'd do it right."

"And why couldn't you let us know you were behind it all but still on our side?"

His Adam's apple bobbed as he swallowed. "You know that first time you reached Kali's mind—when you ticked her off so bad? She said you felt her." I nodded at the memory of the scream in my head. I hadn't recognized it as Kali at the time, but knew that's what he referred to. "She implanted a mind-trigger in you. Every time you got close, she hit it, and it gave her access to your mind. It's kind of along the same lines of what she did with some of the council members a couple of years ago. So if you knew, you could give me away without knowing it. Then Dorian and I both would have been dead."

I exhaled sharply. "Okay, but six months, Owen? Really? Do you have any idea what we went through?"

Six months had felt like a lifetime. When I noticed how much Dorian had changed, it still felt as though years had passed. I swore Kali put some kind of age-progression spell on him. He'd grown half-a-foot, standing three inches taller than me, and looked more like his father than ever. His hair had darkened to a dirty blond, and he appeared to be twelve or thirteen rather than nine. He had the attitude of a preteen, too. Owen said he wouldn't be surprised if Kali had done such a thing—the faster Dorian came into his full powers, the more valuable he became—although the magic had probably died with her. I hoped so. He was already growing up way too fast without any help.

"I'm sorry," Owen said for the thousandth time. "I am so, so sorry, Alexis. I don't know how many times I have to say it. I tried to make it happen sooner. I dropped the cloak so you could find us, and I left clues for Blossom's tracking spell to pick up on. But Kali was *psycho*. She'd get all paranoid for no reason and change her plans without telling me. *I* made the portal, instead of letting her do it, so I could keep it open for you to come through. Before that, I took us on the route by the Fairfax safe house so you would pick up our mind signatures."

"Well, you really pushed Blossom and me," I said, pouring on the guilt factor. He probably didn't need it. Rina had told him many times before that he pushed our limits—especially mine—way too far, and he needed to be careful. Sounding like her made me sad, so I could only imagine how it made him feel, being on the receiving end.

"Are you done torturing Scarecrow for the thirtieth time?" Tristan asked as he sauntered into my office. "You know that's not the real reason he's in here."

I shrugged. "We were waiting on you. What better way to pass the time?"

I glared at Owen, silently daring him to roll his eyes or make a smart aleck remark. He knew I'd forgiven him, but he also knew I wouldn't forget for a very long time. Not three days before he'd taken Dorian had he promised me he would never take my son anywhere without our permission. He'd broken that promise—and all kinds of trust on multiple levels—and I wasn't going to let him off easy. Even if he did blame himself for Rina and Mom.

Owen had never known the part of Kali's plan that brought Mom and Rina into danger. He'd thought she'd chosen to go to northern England because she had a castle near there, not because the soldiers tied to Noah were based out of Yorkshire. And apparently she'd chosen to take Noah specifically to get her revenge on Rina.

Owen had hoped we'd followed them through the portal and were on our way. When he planted Dorian on the sacred grounds, he had no idea Kali had used Noah to lure Rina and Mom to her, so it had never occurred to him that Kali would use Rina the way she did so she could enter the sacred grounds. We decided that Kali had altered her plan for revenge when Tristan and I showed up and she realized Owen had double-crossed her.

Rina's and Mom's deaths changed me, and I'd do anything to have them back, but Owen's plan could have gone even worse. We all could have died in a bloodbath. He'd been right about Kali being too arrogant to call in other Daemoni for backup, but she'd still had a lot of firepower at her fingertips. Firepower that now belonged to Lucas.

Which was the real reason we'd gathered in my office right now.

"So you were going to tell us about Noah and those soldiers," Tristan said as he sat next to me on the edge of my desk.

"Yeah, that," Owen said. He inhaled a deep breath before diving into it. "That really was a DoD building where you almost caught us, and that's a Lucas thing, not a Kali thing. Not entirely, anyway. Lucas got fed up with the so-called weakness of the Summoned brothers and their offspring. I guess he also finally used up his patience with trying to replicate Jordan's Juice. So when he made ties with the U.S. military, they came to him with the idea of creating these super-soldiers using Daemoni blood. They said they'd give him more infiltration in the higher ranks if he could give up some of his people and their blood, and not just to the U.S. Several countries are involved. He gave them the brothers and a bunch of their descendants."

"That's who's locked up in there?" I asked, my teeth on edge. I shouldn't have been surprised—this was *Lucas* we spoke about—but I still couldn't believe he'd give up those he'd worked so hard to get.

Actually, I guess he hadn't. Tristan, Dorian, and I were the only ones he really had to work for. And the only ones he'd never get.

"There and in other places around the world. And Kali wormed her way into the project with her promise of the stones. She implanted the stones in the Summoned and their offspring who were taken to the DoD, let them soak, as she put it, then took them out, broke up the stones, and implanted the pieces in all the soldiers who had previously been given Daemoni blood. Then not only would those soldiers be stronger and maybe have certain extra abilities, but they'd essentially be remote-controlled fighting machines. And the *Daemoni* would be able to control them, not the DoD."

"You mean Kali would have the control," Tristan clarified.

"Like I said, it was supposed to be Lucas—that had been *his* plan after all—but she'd tried to put one over on him."

"But . . . she's gone," I said. "Who has control now?"

"Well, obviously Lucas," Tristan answered for Owen. "As Scarecrow said, Lucas trumped Kali with the lykora blood."

"But he couldn't have taken that much of Sasha's blood," I said.

"Couldn't he have?" Owen asked. "I don't know how long he had her. I don't know how much they need to be affected."

"If his primary goal is control and loyalty, he wouldn't need to give the blood to everyone," Tristan said. "We saw it used on the Norman soldiers, but he doesn't *have* to give it to all of them. He only has to give it to the Summoned brothers and their offspring."

"Right," Owen said. "All of the Norman soldiers with stone-chips in them would feel the same thing their so-called masters do. So Lucas only needs to control the masters—the brothers and their descendants. Oh, and Martin. Kali gave him Martin, too, but I don't know if Lucas bothered using him or not."

Tristan steepled his fingers together and rested his chin on the tips. "So we could potentially have thousands, maybe tens of thousands of human soldiers under Lucas's control. Some of them, if not all of them, extremely dangerous."

Owen nodded, his face grave. "And of course, we can't kill them."

"If that's not bad enough," Char said as she walked into my office with long, purposeful strides, "you need to turn on the TV."

Vanessa followed her in and brushed her hand over Owen's arm, but she came to my side. She propped herself against my desk and draped an arm across my shoulders, and I leaned against her, into her hug. What can I say? I'd been wrong about her. She was Amadis through and through. She was also my sister. And I needed her.

We all turned our eyes toward the flat screen in the corner. I didn't want to make too many changes to the Amadis mansion so soon after Rina's passing, but Tristan and I insisted we have electricity in our offices, along with computers, Internet service, and access to the news networks. Tristan picked up the remote from my desk and turned the television on. Every channel showed the same thing:

"It's happening in several major metropolitan areas around the world," the reporter was saying as the screen displayed what at first glance looked like anarchy in a city's streets—like a riot after a big sporting event or a controversial court case. But when I watched the action more closely, I saw.

"Oh my God," I gasped, clapping my hand over my mouth. "Those are . . . *vampires*. Attacking right there. In the open."

As if to demonstrate my words, a vamp's mouth clamped over a Norman's throat, blood spilling down the woman's white blouse.

Then a naked man ran into view, and as he lunged for the camera, he exploded into a wolf, were-goo raining all over the street and onto the camera lens. The camera banged around on the ground for a minute followed by bloodcurdling screams that caused my stomach to clench, and then the camera came upright. A familiar face with pale red hair, crooked yellow teeth, and an ogre's grin came on screen—the same face that had sat across the table from me years ago and told me the man by my side didn't really love me.

"Ian," Tristan muttered.

"Guess what, mates?" Ian said into the camera, sending a chill through my veins. "Vampires, werewolves, witches, and warlocks—we're all *real*." He leaned closer to the camera, a sinister gleam in his eyes as his tongue ran over his bloodied lips. "And we're coming for your blood . . . for your flesh . . . for your *souls*."

ABOUT KRISTIE COOK

Kristie Cook is a lifelong, award-winning writer in various genres, primarily paranormal romance and contemporary fantasy in the New Adult and Adult age categories. Her internationally bestselling Soul Savers series has 13 books planned, as well as several companion novellas. Over 1 million Soul Savers books have been downloaded, hitting Amazon's, B&N.com's, and iBooks' Top 100 Paid lists.

Kristie has also written The Book of Phoenix trilogy, a New Adult paranormal romance series that includes *The Space Between*, *The Space Beyond*, and *The Space Within*. The full trilogy is available now.

Besides writing, Kristie enjoys reading, cooking, traveling around the world, RVing, and riding on the back of a motorcycle. She has lived in ten states, but currently calls Southwest Florida home with her husband, a beagle, and a puggle. On good days, you might find her hanging out with her three adult sons or sitting on the beach with a drink in hand and toes in the sand.

CONNECT WITH KRISTIE ONLINE
Email: kristie@kristiecook.com
Author's Website & Blog: http://www.KristieCook.com
Soul Saver Series Website: http://www.SoulSaversSeries.com
The Book of Phoenix Trilogy: http://www.TheBookofPhoenix.com
Facebook: http://www.facebook.com/AuthorKristieCook
Twitter: http://twitter.com/kristiecookauth

Be sure to subscribe to Kristie's newsletter at www.KristieCook.com to stay up-to-date about releases, appearances, and other news.

ACKNOWLEDGEMENTS

Glory first to God Almighty and Jesus Christ, my Savior. He has blessed me in countless ways, including giving me this book and the story of Alexis and Tristan.

Shawn, Nathan, Austin, and Zakary, once again, your patience, support, and understanding do not go unnoticed. You are my rock and my foundation. Mom, Dad, and Keena, of course I wouldn't be here without you, but I mean "here" in a variety of ways.

Chrissi, thank you for your help when I needed it. You know how difficult this book was for me. Brenda, my talented friend, I love you hard. Julie, Stacey, Debbie, Kate, Inga, Jessie, Rissa, Christina, Heather, Mindy, and Rebecca—aka, my betas who are the bomb—thank you for your valuable insight. I sincerely appreciate everything else you do, as well as the rest of Kristie's Crew: Claire, Kath, and Lisa. Thank you also to Kristie's Warriors. We might be small, but we're mighty. I look forward to all of the fun we have ahead of us. Also a thank you to Team #KnightRiders who provide immense support to Tristan (and the rest of the gang) when needed.

Jen and Kristen, because of you, this story shines like a polished gem. Regina at MaeIDesign.com, for your amazing design talent on the outside, and Nadège, for yours on the inside. Dani, thank you for making Alexis awesome.

Finally, a GINORMOUS shout-out to my readers. You have come so far with me, and with Alexis and Tristan, and I am actually pretty overwhelmed that you're still here. I would have written this story anyway, but I'm amazed at how people around the world love these characters as much as I do and are dying to know what happens next. I hope you enjoy this installment. But be prepared—you'll need tissues.

UNHOLY
TORMENT

"**THEY'VE COME OUT** to the Normans," Sheree said from the doorway, her voice full of disbelief, and her brown eyes wide and round. She lifted a long finger to her mouth and gnawed on a fingernail.

Vanessa slapped her hands on her thighs. "It was only a matter of time. Lucas has been planning it for ages."

We remained glued to our spots throughout the morning and into the afternoon as we watched the carnage unfold around the world. Blossom and Jax had come into my office and watched with us, and then Ophelia and other household staff joined us, too. Everyone's minds churned over the same question: What were we going to do now?

Then Charlotte thought and began to voice exactly what Tristan and I had been thinking. "Looks like our reprieve is over. It's time to plan for war—"

Her words were stifled by the sound of a loud explosion and the ground quaking under our feet.

I gripped the edge of the antique desk with one hand and reached out to hold onto Tristan's forearm with the other until the shaking stopped.

"That wasn't an earthquake." He barely spoke the words before another bang and subsequent tremors rocked the ground.

"*Daemoni!*" The thoughts came from all over the island, screaming into my head the moment I opened my mind to them.

"We're under attack," I announced before delving into a sentry's mind—a wizard keeping watch from the tower near the village.

Through his eyes, I shared with everyone in the room the vision he saw—Daemoni surrounding the island, uncloaked and in broad daylight. All mages hovering over the water, all shooting spell after spell at our shield.

"Owen and Char—" I started.

"Already on it," Owen said, his voice strained.

My mind left the wizard's, and my vision returned to my own, finding the two warlocks standing in the center of my office. Their hands lifted high above their heads, and their brows and lips set into hard lines as they concentrated on keeping the shield over the island as strong as possible. We took another hit, and both their faces turned various shades of red as the chords in their necks tensed and tightened.

Sweat beads popped out on Owen's forehead. "They have some powerful warlocks. Maybe a sorcerer."

"Go join the others," I ordered. "Do what you can."

Owen and Char disappeared from the room to join the mages who maintained the shield on the other end of the island. When they came together as a group, their power would multiply. Hopefully, it would be enough.

"We have to get to town," I said. "In case they make their way through."

"Change first." Vanessa pointed at Tristan and me before popping out of sight.

Right. We both still wore Norman clothes that provided no protection. We flashed to our suite and changed into our fighting leathers within a minute. After making sure Dorian was safe in his room with Sasha, we flashed to the Amadis village on the other end of the island. We appeared in front of the council hall at the top of a hill, looking down the main street of town that sloped toward the pier and the sea. Some panicked people ran amok in the streets, but many apparently hid in their homes and businesses.

The air crackled with powerful dark magic feeling thicker than it should have. The intensity of it meant our shield was failing, and if the Daemoni managed to pierce it, we'd be in deep trouble. Most of the Amadis who lived here on the island were among our weakest. My personal team contained some of our strongest fighters and other guards protected the mansion and council hall, but for the most part, everyone else lived here because they weren't warriors. This island was their place of refuge. If the Daemoni broke their way in, though, it would be far from a safe haven.

Tristan and I lifted our hands to aim our palms toward the Daemoni to return fire, but the mages were too far away. By the time our powers reached the enemy, their potency had weakened too much to penetrate the shields and were easily deflected. Blossom and two other witches joined us, but their spells also bounced off the offenders' protection.

Owen, can't you blast them with something? I called out to him.

"*Not if you want me to hold this shield up,*" he answered from his position in the tower with Char and the other mages. "*There are too many, and they're too powerful. We're losing our hold as it is.*"

Real panic started to rise from the pit of my belly, sending my heart into a gallop. I needed to protect my people.

What if we made the shield smaller? I asked Owen. *Would it be easier to hold?*

"*Yeah, but how? We've already brought it in from the sea to the edges of the island, but we have to cover the entire thing.*"

No, you don't. Hang on. I used my telepathy to call to Ophelia and ordered her to clear everyone out of the mansion and to take cover in the village. *Tell the guards to come to the council hall.* Without waiting for a response, I switched to my son's mind. *Dorian, I need you to bring Sasha and come here to town. Now!*

He ignored me, but I could feel his mind signature, locating him where we'd left him in his room at the mansion.

Dorian! Now! We're under attack!

"*Ugh! Whatever. I'm coming. Geez.*"

The sulfuric stench of dark magic filled my nose. A red flash of light flew from the sea and slammed into the island. A building near the shore exploded into shards of wood and pieces of plaster.

"*They're getting through,*" Char said to me. No kidding.

Dorian dropped from the air to my side with Sasha in his arms, apparently having flown here. I reached my mind out to the mansion and found no signatures there.

"Get inside the council hall," I told my son, but he ignored me again, his gaze locked on the Daemoni in the distance.

I wanted to shove him away and prevent him from ever setting eyes on them again, but I didn't have time for the argument. My mind scanned the entire northern half of the island from the beach to the forest to the cliffs to be sure no one remained before I gave the orders. That part of the island was clear of any mind signatures. Perfect.

Tighten the shield to only surround the village, I ordered Owen.

"*But the mansion—*" He began to argue.

There's nobody there. Just protect the people. Another flash of light hit a second building. People poured out of the pub next to it, screaming with panic and running up the hill toward the council hall. *Do it, Owen, before it's too late!*

More spells soared through, one hitting an old cypress that exploded into slivers. Another hit the blacksmith's shop not too far below us, taking out one side of it. The people running up the hill dropped to the ground or scattered between the buildings, fleeing the main street. Tristan swept Dorian and me into his arms and plastered us to the ground, making us smaller targets as another spell headed straight for us. It soared over our prone bodies and took out what sounded like a tree behind us, but I couldn't get up to look.

The odor of Daemoni and dark magic faded, and the next round of spells ricocheted seemingly in midair. Owen and his mage team must have strengthened our magical armor. Sounds of explosions from the north side of the island meant they had, indeed, contracted the shield to protect the people. That was okay, as long as they were safe. Although millennia of history filled the halls of the matriarch's mansion, ultimately it consisted of only stones and material possessions. We could always rebuild it.

The attack on the northern side of the island lasted for several more minutes. Knowing we were safe here, though, Tristan and I sprang to our feet to check on our people. I reached my mind out for everyone on my team—Owen, Char, Blossom and Jax, Vanessa, and Sheree—and found them safe and sound. Blossom, Jax, and Sheree were already helping some of the Amadis in the lower part of town who'd been hurt from debris. Vanessa stood on the roof of the council hall, her fists on her hips and her ice-blue eyes staring hard at the Daemoni on the other side of the shield.

"They're all warlocks," she said after she jumped down to stand next to Sasha, who had already grown to her extra-large size, towering over all of us. "All of their best mages."

I reached my mind out to those on the other side of the shield, bracing myself for entering the Daemoni's putrid minds that filled me with the worst kind of dread. I pushed past the evil and listened to their plans.

"They've sent their most powerful mages here while their vamps and Weres are attacking the Normans."

I skipped to a new mind signature, and as soon as I tried to latch onto the thoughts, intense pain seared through my eyeball and into my brain as though a nail had been driven into it. I clutched at my head, doubling over. I squeezed my eyes closed and concentrated on pushing the pain out.

"Lex, what's wrong?" Tristan's large hand landed on my back and tried to soothe me.

My head tilted, and my jaw clenched until finally, the agony dulled.

"They have a . . . sorcerer . . . *and* a sorceress with them." I tried to breathe through the lingering pain and finally managed to open my eyes to find Tristan and Vanessa hovering over me. "Kali must have taught them how to block me from their minds. Shit, that hurt."

Tristan reached out and wiped his thumb over my upper lip. It came away bloody.

"They haven't been involved in the attack, though. Yet," I added.

"They're just wearing us down right now," Vanessa said.

Avoiding the sorcerers, I took my injured mind to one belonging to a warlock to study her thoughts further and nodded. They'd already figured out the north end of the island had been deserted, so they gave up on their attack up there, and the explosions stopped. But they weren't giving up for good. They were only regrouping.

"They're getting ready to hit us with their heavy guns," I confirmed, and I opened my mind to those of the entire island. *Everyone take cover! It's not over!*

People shrieked and ran into the streets before flashing away, hopefully gathering together under the protection of our weaker mages, which was protocol in the event of an attack. Many of the witches and wizards of the village may only be able to shield their homes or a single room, but that was better than nothing if our main defense collapsed.

"*Sorcerers?*" Owen asked me.

A sorcerer and a sorceress, I told him and Char. *Can you hold them?*

"*We will for as long as we can,*" Char said. "*But Owen needs to get down there to protect you and Tristan.*"

Before I could argue, a succession of bright yellow and orange lights shot across the water and blasted into our shield, breaching it almost immediately. The next spell hit our watchtower right behind the council hall, blowing it into pieces. The very tower where our mages powered the shield. Owen appeared next to me at the same moment and immediately threw a bubble over Tristan, Dorian, and me.

"Come on," Tristan said, pulling Dorian back into his arms.

He flashed, and I followed his trail with Owen and Vanessa right on mine. We appeared inside the dungeons under the council hall, where they'd once jailed Tristan when he'd been accused of betraying the Amadis. I called the others to come join us, but Blossom, Jax, and Sheree refused to leave the injured behind.

"*I have a shield on them,*" Blossom assured me. "*You just stay safe, Alexis.*"

Char didn't answer me, and I couldn't locate her mind signature in the chaos, but she'd been in the tower with the other mages when the Daemoni had hit it. My heart wobbled, but I refused to believe she was dead. I couldn't handle another death so soon, especially hers. I glanced at Owen, and his face remained stoic. He refused to believe, too.

I sat against the cold, stone wall of one of the cells, closed my eyes, and used my mind to peek into others' heads until I found a vampire who peered outside from his window. Now that the main shield had collapsed, the sorcerer and sorceress seemed to have backed off. In fact, magic spells no longer rained down on the town. Only a few random shots came, as though they were double-checking that the shield had actually fallen.

I heard, "*It's a go*," from one of them before they all disappeared, only to reappear several miles away, nearly out of my mind's reach.

"What are they doing?" I asked aloud, not about to give the all clear to the island yet. Something was up. Then I heard the planes in the distance, quickly approaching—with no mind signatures inside of them. Were they drones? The answer to my question came a moment later when the bombs began dropping. On Amadis Island.

"We can stop them," Tristan said after several bombs hit the town with loud explosions, shaking the ground beneath us. Dirt fell from the ceiling and walls.

Owen's sapphire-blue eyes squinted. "It'll take a minute to power up the shield."

"I meant *we*." Tristan looked at me, and I nodded.

"Stay here," I ordered Vanessa and Dorian.

Tristan, Owen, and I flashed outside, and we all raised our palms to the sky as more planes flew overhead and more bombs fell. We used our powers to stop three from slamming into the village and turned them toward the sea. But we'd barely rerouted them when more came. It took almost every ounce of energy I had to keep them from hitting the island. Then finally, they began to ricochet in midair like the spells had done earlier.

"*We can shield against those!*" Charlotte whooped into my mind, and I let out the air I'd held trapped in my lungs at the sound of her "voice."

Owen joined his mother and the other mages who'd survived, and they strengthened the shield over the town. Unable to hit us anymore, the jets banked away and flew off. Dozens of columns of black smoke rose into the air from the main street in town and more in the residential district. My stomach sank at the thought of Amadis lives lost. I felt the grief spreading from people's minds at the heartache right before them, but we still hadn't given them the all clear to come out from their shelters.

"Take cover, Alexis," Owen said. "We don't know if they're gone for good."

Tristan took my hand and flashed us back to the dungeons.

"Is it over?" Vanessa asked.

"Can I go back to my room?" Dorian demanded.

"We don't know yet," I said, and I gave Dorian the mom-eye for his rudeness. "And you can go back when we say you can go back."

He rolled his eyes and diverted his attention to Sasha, who had shrunk some, but remained alert.

We sat in the cold, dank cell for hours. The Daemoni mind signatures hadn't slipped completely out of range—they remained close enough for me to feel them, but not close enough to hear their thoughts and plans. I wouldn't give the green light to my people until I knew we were safe.

"*Alexis,*" Charlotte mind-spoke to me from where she and the other mages continued powering the shield from the main room above us. "*Chandra just called. She's been trying to reach you. One of her villages in India has been bombed, too.*"

My stomach sank. A little while later, another, similar report came in on Char's phone, this one from Jelani in Africa. One by one, Rina's council members checked in, delivering the same news over and over. The Daemoni, using the Normans, had bombed dozens of our villages and colonies around the world.

And I couldn't do anything about it. I was stuck here in the dungeons, but even if I weren't, what could I have done? The attacks had stopped hours ago, so all I could do now was to tell them to stay undercover and keep safe.

"I feel like I'm telling everyone to just squat down like sitting ducks, when we should be fighting back. What kind of leader am I?"

"You've told them exactly what Rina would have," Tristan said, trying to assure me. But it only irked me.

I shook my head as I paced the cell. "No. We have to do more. We won't survive if we're always on the defensive. We're stronger than this. We have to fight back."

Finally, the Daemoni mind signatures retreated completely, and after having Owen return the shield to cover the entire island, I gave the all clear. We popped outside, and my heart dropped at the sight.

In contrast to the stunning sunset on the water, the destruction was heartrending.

The main street from the council hall to the pier at the other end housed the business district. Most of the village's suppliers of goods and services lined the cobblestone street, and those buildings closest to shore had been completely annihilated—the only supplier of mage reagents on the island, the Blood Bank where we donated blood for our vamps, and one of the three pubs. Other structures, like the blacksmith shop, had suffered major damage. Several homes had also, and two were destroyed altogether.

We had three fatalities on the island, and I supposed we were lucky with such a small number, but my heart shrank at more losses and more funerals. Dozens of people had been injured, several badly. Fortunately, most of them could heal themselves, and the mages who couldn't drank a healing potion made from vampire blood. It wasn't perfect and didn't completely eliminate their pain, but it helped speed the healing process.

Owen, Charlotte, and the rest of the mages did their best to put homes and businesses back together, but some parts had been completely disintegrated or burnt to ashes and others damaged beyond repair, returning none of the structures to how they'd been before the attack. We had to make the decision to destroy two more business buildings and three homes—one of them Char's—because they weren't safe for anyone to be near. She'd been able to retrieve some of her belongings, but most everything she'd owned had been destroyed by fire from the bombs.

As everyone came together to help each other, I fielded calls from around the world. The Amadis had lost hundreds of people. The Daemoni had flattened entire villages. Each casualty report felt like a punch to my stomach, leaving me breathless and my body trembling.

Not until the quiet hours between midnight and dawn were we able to return to the matriarch's mansion to assess the damage there. My stomach knotted itself once we decided our people were taken care of and we could go. I feared the extent of the destruction of the beautiful marble and stone structure that had been here for millennia. We didn't know its true age because it had already been standing when Cassandra found it over two thousand years ago, as if waiting for her discovery. If Charlotte's house hadn't just been demolished, I would have suggested we stayed there for the night so we could see the bad news in the light of morning. Not that the darkness would affect our vision. It just seemed that the sight we would see would be more dreadful in the night.

My breath caught when we appeared in front of it.

Made in the USA
Charleston, SC
13 February 2016